THE KNIGHT TEMPLAR

Also by Jan Guillou

The Road to Jerusalem

THE KNIGHT
TEMPLAR

JAN GUILLOU

Translated by Anna Paterson

ORION

First published in Great Britain in 2002 by Orion
an imprint of the Orion Publishing Group Ltd.

Copyright © Jan Guillou 1999
Original Swedish title: Tempelriddaren
Original title: The Crusades Trilogy – The Knight Templar

Translation copyright © Anna Paterson 2002.

A CIP catalogue record for this book is
available from the British Library.

ISBN 0 75284 648 5 (hardback) 0 75284 650 7 (trade paperback)

Typeset by Deltatype Ltd, Birkenhead, Merseyside

Printed in Great Britain by
Clays Ltd, St Ives plc

The Orion Publishing Group Ltd
Orion House
5 Upper St Martin's Lane
London WC2H 9EA

The Lord in all His splendour is great. In the night He led His servant from the sacred place of prayer called Kaaba to the most distant place of prayer and we praise the place in its entirety, in order to show him our portents, for He is the Lord who hears all and who sees all.

The Holy Quran, sura 176, verse 1

THE HOLY LAND

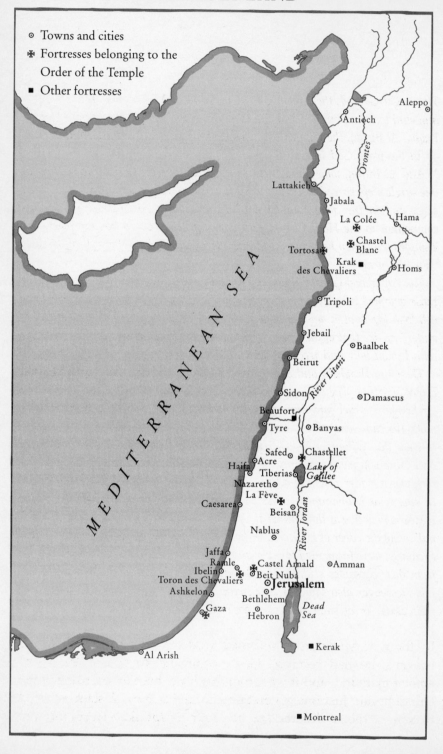

Towns and cities

Fortresses belonging to the
Order of the Temple

Other fortresses

MEDITERRANEAN SEA

Aleppo

Antioch

Orontes

Lattakieh

Jabala

La Colée
Hama

Chastel
Blanc

Tortosa

Krak
des Chevaliers

Homs

Tripoli

Jebail

Baalbek

Beirut

River Litani

Sidon

Beaufort
Damascus

Tyre

Banyas

Safed

Chastellet

Haifa

Acre

Lake of
Galilee

Tiberias

Nazareth

La Fève

Caesarea

Beisan

River Jordan

Nablus

Jaffa

Ramle

Castel Arnald

Amman

Ibelin

Beit Nuba

Toron des Chevaliers

Jerusalem

Ashkelon

Bethlehem

Dead
Sea

Gaza

Hebron

Kerak

Al Arish

Montreal

PROLOGUE

That night Gabriel, the Archangel of God, came to Muhammad, peace be upon him, and took him by the hand and took him to the sacred place of prayer called Kaaba. Al Buraq, the winged one, was waiting there in readiness to lead them on to the place God intended.

And Al Buraq, who could traverse the distance from horizon to horizon in one single step, spread his white wings and rose straight up towards the starlit space and in this way conducted Muhammad, peace be upon him, and his companion to the Holy City of Jerusalem and then on to the site where the Temple of Solomon had once stood. The most distant place of prayer at the west wall was nearby.

The Archangel Gabriel then took the messenger of God by the hand to meet those who had been his forerunners: Moses, Jesus, Yahia, who the unbelievers call John the Baptist, and Abraham, who was a tall man with curly black locks and a face like that of the Prophet, peace be upon him. Jesus was a shorter man with brown hair and freckled skin.

Then the Prophets and the Archangel Gabriel offered God's messenger a choice of drinks. The choice was between milk and wine and he chose milk. The Archangel Gabriel said that was good and that henceforth all believers would make the same choice.

Then the Archangel Gabriel conducted God's messenger to the rock where once Abraham had been prepared to sacrifice his son, and leaning against this rock was a ladder reaching all the way up through the Seven Heavens to God. In this way Muhammad, peace be upon him, ascended through the Seven Heavens to arrive at the Throne of God, and on the way he saw the angel Malik pull away the cover of Hell, where the condemned, their lips cloven like the lips of camels, were tormented for ever and forced to eat burning coals that emerged from their backsides still on fire. But during his ascent to the Realm of God, His messenger also saw Paradise, with its flowering gardens and streams of fresh water or of such wine that does not disturb the mind.

By the time Muhammad returned to Mecca after his travels in the heavens, he had received God's command to spread the Word among mankind, and it was from that time that the recording of the Quran began. Just one generation later the armies of Islam emerged from the Arabian deserts. The new faith swept like a storm through many countries. In its wake grew a huge new realm, ruled by the Umayyad Caliphs and based in Damascus.

Between 685 and 691 one ruler, known as Al Abdal Malik bin Marwan, had many mosques built. One was on the old Temple Mount in Jerusalem, the site above the rock where Abraham had planned to sacrifice his son and from which Muhammad ascended to Heaven. This mosque was called Al Aqsa, 'the most distant', and also Qubbat al Sahkra – the Dome of the Rock.

In Anno Domini 1099 a disaster hit the third most holy of the true believers' cities, which was also their third most significant place of prayer. The Christian Franks took the city and desecrated it in the most appalling way imaginable. Everybody found alive was killed with swords and spears, except for the Jews, who were herded into a synagogue and burnt alive. Blood flowed in the streets, so plentifully at times that it reached above a man's ankles. Even for a world ruled by warriors this was an uncommonly gruesome massacre.

At first the Franks adopted Al Aqsa as their own place of prayer. Less than a decade had passed when Baldwin, the Christian King of Jerusalem, decided to let the Knights Templar use the buildings on the Temple Mount as their sleeping quarters and stables. To the Muslim believers, these knights were the most terrifying of all their enemies.

I

The year was 575 after Hijra, or Anno Domini 1177 as the Christian unbelievers would have it. That year Moharram, the Shia Muslim holy month of mourning, fell at the hottest time of the summer and God intervened in a most unexpected way on behalf of the man He loved best among all His faithful.

Yussuf and his brother Fahkr were riding for their lives. Behind them, and a little off course, they were followed by the amir Moussa, the commander of their guard, there to protect them from the arrows of their enemies. Six robbers were chasing them and steadily gaining ground. Yussuf damned his own arrogance. Because of his conviction that he and his companions had stronger and faster horses than anyone else, he had believed nothing like this could ever happen. But in this arid valley of death it was dangerous to push the animals too hard. Here, immediately to the west of the Dead Sea, the bare landscape was rocky and inhospitably dry, and riding too fast meant taking grave risks. Their pursuers did not seem too worried, but a fall would have been much less dire for one of them than for one of their prey.

Yussuf suddenly decided to steer his trio sharply to their left, up into the foothills of the mountains where a safe hiding place would be easier to find. They soon came to a wadi, a dried-out riverbed, and began riding along its steep upward course, but as the wadi grew both deeper and narrower, they realised they were caught in something like an elongated bowl. God was guiding their flight in one direction only, and as the route grew steadily steeper, so it became ever harder to maintain their speed. The pursuers were coming closer all the time; soon they would be within arrow-range, and the pursued had already strapped their round, iron-clad shields to their backs.

Yussuf was not in the habit of praying for his life. But as he was

3

forced to rein in his horse to pick his way between the treacherous boulders littering the bottom of the wadi, God's holy words came to him in the form of a verse that he rattled off breathlessly between his dry lips.

'He, Who has created life and death in order to test you, allows you to show who of you are best able to act well. He is the Almighty. The One Who always forgives.'

God did indeed test His beloved Yussuf, who there and then saw the most terrible sight that any true believer could see, especially at such a difficult point in a chase. At first the sight outlined by the setting sun seemed no more than a mirage: a Templar knight, his lance lowered, riding down the wadi from the opposite direction, his sergeant riding behind him.

These two enemies of all that is alive and all that is good were travelling at such a speed that their mantles flew behind them like the great wings of a dragon. Both were rushing along like the djinns of the desert.

Yussuf instantly stopped his horse and began fumbling with his shield, which he now had to get off his back so as to protect himself from the unbeliever's lance. He felt no fear, only the cold excitement of being close to death, as he steered his horse closer to the steep wall of the wadi in order to make himself a less direct target and force the enemy to increase the striking angle of his weapon.

When he was no more than a few breaths away, the Templar knight raised his lance, but just waved at Yussuf and the other believers to stay out of the way. They did, and the next moment the two knights thundered past, releasing their mantle clasps so that the mantles fluttered down into the dust behind them.

Yussuf quickly signed a command to the others to move on and they laboriously followed the wadi's upward course, the horses' hooves slipping on the stones at every step. When they found a place with a good view, Yussuf stopped and turned to see what was happening. He wanted to understand what God intended with all this.

His two companions argued that they should use the opportunity to get away, leaving the Templar knights and the highwaymen to settle their scores as best they could. Yussuf cut them short with an irritated gesture, keen to follow the confrontation below. He had never in his life been so close to a Templar knight, evil demons that they were. He felt strongly, as if truly told to stay by the voice of God, that he had to understand the events about to take place and that no common-sense advice should be allowed to get in the way. It would have been usual and practical to continue riding on towards

Al Arish for as long as the light held and until darkness threw its protective mantle over them. But Yussuf stayed and, as a consequence, saw scenes he would never forget.

The six highwaymen had little choice when they discovered that, instead of chasing three wealthy men, they had to confront two Templar knights, lance against lance. The wadi was far too narrow to allow their retreat and escape before the Franks caught up with them. After a moment of confusion, they did as they had to and regrouped into pairs, digging their spurs into the sides of their horses in order to meet the attack on the move.

The proper Templar knight in his white tunic was riding ahead of his sergeant. He began by feigning an attack against the first robber on his right, who had raised his shield to break the terrible blow of the lance. Yussuf only had time to wonder if the robber realised what was to come, when the knight threw his horse round in a manoeuvre that should have been impossible on such difficult ground. Using the new angle, he drove his lance right through both the shield and the body of the robber to his left and, in the next instant, let go of the lance to avoid being twisted out of the saddle. At the same moment, the sergeant made contact with the confused robber on the right, who had been crouching behind his shield waiting for the strike that would never come. When he glanced over his shield, the other enemy lance homed in on him from the wrong direction and pierced his face.

The knight in the white tunic bearing that repulsive red cross was now confronting the next two enemy riders in a passage almost too narrow for three horses side by side. He had drawn his sword and seemed ready to attack straight ahead, an unwise move given that he would only have armed backing from one side. But suddenly his handsome stallion, a roan in his powerful prime, turned and kicked out with his hind legs so that one of the robbers was knocked out of his saddle.

The other highwayman clearly thought that this was a good moment to attack, for his enemy was moving almost backwards across his path, his sword held without room to swing and on the side away from him. The robber had no time to grasp that the knight let go of his shield, shifting his sword to his left hand. When the robber leaned forward in the saddle to stab with his sabre, he exposed his head and neck to a blow that fell from the wrong direction.

'If a head can hold on to a thought just at the moment of death, even if just for one breath, then it was an astonished head that just

5

fell to the ground,' Fahkr said, amazed. He too had got caught up in the spectacle and wanted to watch it all.

While the knight slowed enough to kill his second man, the two last robbers had thought better of it. They had turned their horses and escaped down the wadi at speed.

At the same time, the sergeant in his black tunic could be seen arriving at the spot where the one other surviving highwayman was lying, the godless dog kicked by the knight's horse. The sergeant dismounted, calmly taking hold of the reins of the robber's horse with one hand and, with the other, plunged his sword into the base of the neck of the bruised, confused figure on the ground. The sword entered just above the neckline of the man's leather vest, covered with steel scales.

Once the sergeant had dispatched his victim, he made no effort to follow his master who had set off in brisk pursuit of the fleeing robbers. Instead, he tied the reins round the captured horse's front legs and went about getting hold of the remaining horses by approaching them cautiously and speaking gently to them. It was as if all he cared for was the horses and not his master, whom he should have been protecting. In truth, it was the most peculiar sight.

'That one, the one you see over there, my master,' said Moussa, pointing at the white-clad knight, now far down the wadi and nearly out of sight. 'That's Al Ghouti.'

'Al Ghouti?' Yussuf said wonderingly. 'You say his name as if I ought to know it. I don't. Who is Al Ghouti?'

'You *should* know of Al Ghouti, master. God has visited him on us for our sins,' Moussa replied between clenched teeth. 'Of all those demons with their red crosses, he's the one horseman who rides with either the turcopoles or the heavy cavalry. Look at him now, riding an Arabian stallion the way a turcopole would, but still using a lance and a sword as if he were sitting on one of these fat Frankish beasts. They have made him the amir of all the Knights Templar in Gaza.'

'Al Ghouti, Al Ghouti,' Yussuf mumbled thoughtfully. 'I want to meet him. We'll wait here!' His two companions looked alarmed but did not bother to make even the most carefully considered of objections. It was obvious that Yussuf had made up his mind.

The three Saracens waited on horseback by the edge of the wadi, watching as the knight's sergeant calmly went about his business. Having tethered the four dead men's horses, he next started hauling and heaving at the corpses until each one was slung across the saddle and tied into place on his own horse. It looked like a hard

6

day's work, even though the sergeant was a powerfully built man. The Templar knight and his quarries were nowhere to be seen.

'Good move,' Fahkr muttered to himself. 'Matching the man with his horse. Blood or no blood, that'll help to calm the animal. Seems they want to take the horses with them.'

'They are very good horses, really,' Yussuf agreed. 'You know, I don't understand how these rogues can afford horses fit for kings. Why, they were keeping pace with us.'

'Worse, they were catching up,' Moussa pointed out. He was never less than straight with his master. 'Anyway, surely we've seen what we wanted? It's getting late in the day. Wouldn't it be better to be off now and get well away before Al Ghouti comes back?'

'What makes you so sure he will?' Yussuf asked, amused.

'He'll be back, no fear,' Moussa replied. 'Reckon I'm as sure as the sergeant down there. He didn't bother to follow his master, even though he might have needed help to deal with two fast-moving enemies. But didn't you notice how Al Ghouti sheathed his sword and instead got his bow ready?'

'What, a bow? A Templar knight?' Yussuf asked, raising his narrow eyebrows in surprise.

'That's it, master,' Moussa replied. 'As I said, he can ride fast and lightly armed like a turcopole and shoot from the saddle, just like one of them, though he's using a bigger bow. Already far too many true believers have died, pierced by his arrows. So, master, I would take the liberty to suggest once more . . .'

'No!' Yussuf interrupted him. 'We'll wait here. I want to meet him. At present there's a truce agreed with the Knights Templar and I've decided to thank Al Ghouti. I owe a debt of gratitude and have no intention of remaining indebted.' Moussa and Fahkr realised that arguing would get them nowhere. Their talking died down.

For a while they waited together in silence, leaning forward and supporting themselves with one hand on the raised front edge of their saddles while they watched the sergeant, who had finished organising the transport of the corpses. He went on to collect the scattered weapons and the mantles that he and his master had shed just before the attack. The cut-off head seemed to bother him: he stood there holding it, obviously pondering the problem of how to pack it. In the end he pulled the aba off one of the robbers, wrapped the head in it and tied it to the pommel of the decapitated robber's saddle.

Finally the sergeant was ready. After testing that the packing was secure and the horses tied up, he started his caravan. As he passed below the escarpment with the three watching Saracens, Yussuf waved, and greeted him politely in Frankish. The sergeant smiled hesitantly in return and said something they could not catch.

Night was approaching now. The sun had set behind the great mountains in the west and the saline sea far away in the distance was no longer a gleaming blue. The waiting horses seemed to sense the impatience of their riders and were snorting and tossing their heads from side to side, as if wanting to get away before nightfall.

Then they saw the white-clad figure of the knight down there in the wadi. He brought with him two horses, their now dead owners hanging over their backs and tied into place. The knight moved slowly, his head lowered as if in prayer, although he was probably just trying to pick his way across the rough, stony ground in front of him. He seemed not to have seen the three waiting Saracens, even though from his point of view they must have been clearly outlined against the lightest part of the night sky.

But when he reached them, he reined in his horse and looked up at them without speaking.

Yussuf was completely thrown and silenced by the man he saw. Nothing about him matched what might have been expected, given what he had just done. This Al Ghouti, this devil from hell, radiated peace of mind. His helmet was off, hanging in a short chain across his shoulder and showing that he had all the demonic features, the bright blue eyes, short blonde hair and coarse untrimmed beard. But here was someone who had just killed three or four men – in his agitation Yussuf could not quite keep count, which was very unlike him – and Yussuf had seen many men at just that moment of victory, when they had finished with killing and won their battle. This man was different. Yussuf had never seen anyone who at such a time looked as if he had just returned from a day's work, harvesting grain in the fields or sugar cane in the marshes, filled with the good conscience that only hard work well done can give a man. There was no triumph or gloating in these blue eyes.

'We waited you ... we say ... thank you ...' Yussuf said in his version of Frankish, hoping that the other would understand.

The man, whose name in the language of the true believers was Al Ghouti, looked searchingly at Yussuf. Slowly a smile lit his face, as though he had ransacked his memory and finally found what he had been looking for. This caused the amir Moussa and Fahkr, though not Yussuf himself, to reach cautiously for the sabres that hung from the side of their saddles.

The knight had no difficulty seeing their hands moving almost unconsciously towards the weapons. He raised his eyes up towards the three men above him and spoke in God's own language.

'In the name of the Merciful God, at this time we are not enemies and I do not seek to do battle with you. Recall the words from your own scriptures, uttered by the Prophet himself, may peace be with him, for he said, "Never take another man's life, which God had declared sacred, unless for a rightful purpose". You and I have no such rightful purpose, because we are party to an agreement to cease hostilities.'

The Knight Templar, having spoken, smiled even more broadly, as if he wanted to make them laugh. He was perfectly aware of the impression he had made on his three enemies by addressing them in the sacred language of the Quran. But Yussuf, who felt he must keep his wits about him and quickly take control of the situation, answered the knight after barely a moment's hesitation.

'The ways of the Almighty God are indeed inscrutable.'

At this the knight nodded, as if the words were well known to him.

Yussuf continued, 'He alone knows why an enemy was sent to aid us. Still, I owe you thanks, knight of the red cross, and I wish to let you have a share of that which these damned men chased us for. I'll leave one hundred dinars in gold here in this place and the money is for you as a reward for the acts you have completed in front of our eyes.'

Yussuf felt he had spoken like a king, a king as generous as royals should be. It annoyed him, and even more so his brother and his amir, that the knight's first response was open, genuine laughter.

'In the name of God, who is merciful, you speak with as much ignorance as goodness, because I cannot accept your gift,' the knight replied. 'I acted as you saw because I had to and would've had to, regardless of your being here. I own nothing and so cannot acquire any possessions of any kind. The one way round this promise of mine is that you donate your hundred dinars to the Templar treasurer. And I must say, my unknown enemy or friend, I suspect that gift would surely be difficult to explain to your Prophet!'

The knight gathered up his reins, checked with a glance over his shoulder that the two extra horses and their corpses were under control, and spurred on his Arabian stallion. At the same time, he raised his right fist in the greeting of the godless Order of the Temple and looked as if he found the whole situation really funny.

'Wait!' Yussuf said, so quickly the words came out without

thinking. 'Instead, please accept my invitation to share our evening meal!'

The knight held his horse back and looked thoughtfully at Yussuf. 'I accept your invitation, my unknown enemy or friend,' he answered slowly. 'My only condition is that you give your word that neither you nor your servants intend to attack me and my sergeant during the time we're together.'

'You have my word, by the true God and His Prophet, peace be with him,' Yussuf said quickly. 'But do I have yours?'

'Yes, you have my word, by the true God, His Son and the Holy Virgin,' the Templar knight replied as swiftly. 'If you ride on, aiming some two fingers south of the point where the sun is setting behind the ridge, you'll find a stream. Follow it in the north-western direction until you get to a group of trees where the stream forms a pool. It's a good place to rest overnight. We will be following the same stream, to the west of you and higher up in the hills. We promise not to foul the water. Soon it will be nightfall, you must be at prayer, and so must we. But when we approach in the night, you'll hear us – we won't come stealthily, as if with evil intent.'

The knight spurred his horse and waved his goodbye greeting again. He did not look back as his little caravan disappeared into the dusk. The three true believers stared after him for a long time, without moving or talking. Their horses were snorting impatiently, but Yussuf was deep in thought.

'You're my brother and nothing you do or say should surprise me any more,' Fahkr said. 'But just now you did it after all. Sharing a meal with a Templar knight! And to choose the man they call Al Ghouti!'

'Fahkr, dear brother,' Yussuf replied, as with an easy movement he steered his horse round to point in the direction his enemy had shown him, 'knowing one's enemy is something we often talk about, isn't that so? And of all enemies, surely the most terrible one is the most important? God has given us a golden opportunity, so let's not miss it.'

'But how can you trust the word of such a man?' Fahkr asked after a while.

'Actually, yes, you can,' Moussa told them. 'The enemy has many faces, some known to us, some not. But that man, I tell you, you can trust as much as he can trust your brother.'

Following their archenemy's instructions, they soon found a small stream with fresh clear water where they stopped to let their mounts drink. They followed its course and, just as the knight had said, the ground flattened and they could see a group of trees and shrubs. The stream had formed a pool and there was some meagre grazing for their horses. They took the saddles off and tied the animals' front legs together, so they would not take off in search of more grass where none would be found anyway. Then, as the rules ordained, they washed carefully before praying.

When the pale crescent moon first showed against the light sky of the summer's night, they were saying their prayers in sorrow for their dead and in gratitude to God for having sent one of their worst enemies to their rescue.

They spoke a little more of this matter afterwards and Yussuf explained that he thought God had almost humorously shown them that He is truly almighty. Why else send a Knight of the Order of the Temple to save the one man who would defeat all the Knights Templar?

At least, this was something Yussuf told himself as well as everyone around him. The Frankish invaders came and went in the Holy Land. Sometimes they were as numerous as locusts, at other times there were fewer. Year after year new warlords arrived and either won and plundered or lost and died. When they had won, most of them left laden with booty.

Some of the Franks never left, though. The foreigners who stayed were both the best and the worst of their kind. Best, because they took no particular pleasure in destroying the land and instead agreed to peaceful negotiations and trading contracts. Worst, because some of them were terrible to meet in combat. The very worst were the orders of warrior monks, who were damnably faithful to their beliefs. The orders were the St John's Hospitallers, the Teutonic Knights and the Templar Knights. Whoever was to recapture Al Aqsa, the Dome of the Rock, in the Holy City of God, must first be the victor in the battle against the knights of the holy orders.

These damned unbelievers seemed impossible to conquer. They fought fearlessly, convinced that if they died on the battlefield they would go straight to Paradise. They never surrendered, because their rules forbade any deals to release captive brothers from their imprisonment. The knights spiritual were useless hostages and there was no point in keeping them. The only choice was between letting them go or killing them, so they were always killed.

The saying was that if fifteen true believers encountered five of these knights on a field, either all would stay alive or none. If the fifteen true believers attacked the five unbelievers, none of those of the true faith would escape alive. To make sure, the right side had to

11

produce more than four times as many men as the opposition and still be prepared for heavy losses. This was quite different from how it was with ordinary Frankish fighters, who were easily defeated even with fewer men on the rightful side.

While Fahkr and Moussa gathered firewood, Yussuf lay on his back, his head resting on his crossed arms, and stared up at the sky where more and more stars were being lit. He pondered on his worst enemies and the events he had witnessed just before sunset. The man called Al Ghouti had been riding a horse worthy of a king, a horse that seemed to think the same way as his master and obeyed his every wish before being told.

It could not be magic. Yussuf was the kind of man who would reject that explanation for as long as possible. Simply, it must be that man and horse had practised together systematically, fighting in many battles over a long time. Among the Egyptian Mamelukes some of the men and horses learned to work together in the same way. True, Mamelukes had no choice but to practise until they became successful enough to be promoted to officers. Then they were given their freedom, some land, and a payment in return for their hard-working years of wartime service. No magic tricks or miracles needed. Human beings, rather than God alone, created that perfect horsemanship. Which was the crucial factor remained an open question.

Yussuf's answer to that question was always that the most important thing must be pure faith. A man would become an irresistible warrior if, in every respect, he held on to the words of the Prophet, peace be with him, about the meaning of Holy War, which he called Jihad. True, the Mamelukes in Egypt were far from fervent believers in Islam. These Turks were usually rather superstitious and believed in spirits and sacred stones and suchlike, while paying lip service to the pure and true faith.

But then, it was harder still to see the reason why even the unbelievers should count men like Al Ghouti among them. Was everyone free to decide what to do with his life? Would the separation of true and false believers take place first in the sacred fire? This was a depressing thought. Why had God given the true believers enemies who were impossible to defeat? Was His intention to show them that the true believers must unite in such number that they would be victorious in the end, regardless of the fighting prowess of the Franks?

Yussuf recalled the details he had memorised about Al Ghouti. There was the man himself and his calm eyes. There was that stallion and its black, well cared-for and oiled tackle. There was the rest of his equipment, all of which was fashioned for the satisfaction of the hand rather than the pleasure of the eye. This was worth considering, for all too often had men died for their vanity – say, for their inability to resist a tunic stiff with gold embroidery that restrained their movements when it mattered. All these observations must be stored away for the future, for how else to drive out the devils that occupied God's Sacred City?

The fire had taken well and the firewood was crackling. Fahkr and Moussa were busy setting out their provisions and beakers of water on a muslin cloth spread on the ground. Moussa was squatting down to grind the mocha beans for his black Bedouin beverage after the meal. When darkness fell, the cold came with it. The first sign was a cooling breeze blowing down the slopes from Al Khalil, the city of Ibrahim. Soon, the cool of the evening after a hot day would turn into the chill of night.

It was the odour carried on the west wind that first alerted Yussuf to the approach of the two Franks. It was a stench of slaves and battlefields. Clearly these barbarians were true to form and arrived unwashed to the evening meal.

When the knight stepped into the circle of light cast by the fire, they saw that he was holding up his white shield with the red cross. This was no way for a guest to present himself and Moussa took a few cautious steps towards the place where they had piled up their saddles and weapons. Yussuf caught his worried gaze and shook his head lightly.

The knight bowed to each of his hosts in turn, and the sergeant awkwardly followed his master's example. Then Al Ghouti surprised the three true believers by putting his shield with that disgusting cross as high up a branch as he could reach. He explained that, although he had no reason to believe that there were bad folk about, there was no telling for certain and the sight of a Templar shield would cool the ardour of most. Generously, he offered to let the shield stay in the tree overnight, and pick it up in the morning.

As the knight and his sergeant began unpacking their own fare – dates, mutton, bread, and some unclean objects – Yussuf could no longer hold back his laughter. Everybody stared at him, waiting for an explanation of the joke. The two Franks raised their eyebrows with annoyance at the thought that they might have provided a comic turn.

Yussuf explained that if there was anything unforeseen in this world, it was that he should be under the protection of an enemy shield bearing what was for him the worst emblem in the world. It did confirm something he'd always believed about God, he said, which was that the Almighty had a sense of humour and, at times, could not resist playing a joke on His children. They all joined him in smiling at this.

Then the knight discovered the piece of smoked meat among the provisions, barked out a short order and pointed at the meat with his long sharp knife. The sergeant reddened and took the meat away, while the knight shrugged his shoulders apologetically and said that one man's unclean objects could be another's good food.

The others realised that their meal had been contaminated by the flesh of pigs and that they should regard it all as unclean. Yussuf reminded them in a quick whisper that God's words also stated that one's own household rules don't apply in extreme situations. The fact was that they had no more food and they could therefore eat what they'd served.

Yussuf blessed the meal in the name of the Merciful and Charitable God and the Templar knight blessed it in the name of the Lord Jesus Christ and the Holy Mother of God, and none of the five men showed any distaste for the alien faith.

Each began urging the other to taste his provisions and, finally, at Yussuf's insistence, the knight used his plain but terrifyingly sharp knife to halve a piece of mutton baked inside bread. He handed one half stuck on the tip of the knife to his sergeant, who put it in his mouth with barely controlled suspicion.

They ate in silence for while. On the true believers' side of the cloth the mutton in bread was accompanied by a confection made from almonds and green pistachio nuts, spun sugar and honey. On the side of the unbelievers, now that the pig meat had gone, was only some plain dried mutton, dates and stale white bread.

Yussuf broke the silence. 'Knight of the Templar, there's something I'd like to ask you,' he said. His voice was low and intense, and those who knew him well realised he had in mind something he had thought out carefully and needed to reach a conclusion about.

'You are our host and we have accepted your invitation. Just remember that as far as we're concerned, our faith is the true one and not yours,' the knight answered, and his face suggested he actually dared make a joke about faith itself.

'I'm sure you understand what my feelings are in that matter – but now, about my question. You rescued us, but we are your enemies. Both statements are true and I've already thanked you for coming to our aid. My question is, why did you?'

'We didn't act to save our enemies,' the knight replied thought-fully. 'We'd been searching for these robbers for a long time and trailed them at a distance for almost a week, waiting for a good opportunity to get them. Our task was to kill them, not to rescue you and your companions. But, as it happened, God was holding His protective hand over you then. Neither you nor I know why.'

'You're Al Ghouti himself, though?' Yussuf went on.

'Yes I am,' the knight said. 'That is, the unbelievers who speak the language we're using now call me Al Ghouti, but my name is Arn de Gothia. My task was to free the world from these six unworthy creatures and I have completed it. That's all I can say.'

'But why you? Why is it that *you* have been given this task, which is both lowly and dangerous? Just travelling through this hostile land in order to kill robbers, what's that for someone who is not only a Knight of the Templar, but also, if I'm rightly informed, a man of rank within your order, the commander or amir of your fortress in Gaza?'

'That's to do with the origin of our order, in times long before we were born,' the knight replied. 'From the first period after our liberation of the tomb of our God, pilgrims had no protection during their pilgrimages to the River Jordan and the place where Yahia, as you call him, once baptised Lord Jesus Christ. Nowadays, the pilgrims leave their possessions with us for safekeeping, but then, they journeyed with them, and were easy prey for robbers. Our Order was created to protect them. To this day, the command to kill robbers and offer help to pilgrims is considered an honour. In this case, God was with us.'

'You're right, of course,' Yussuf answered with a sigh. 'We should all make a point of protecting pilgrims. How much easier would not life here in Palestine be if we all did? By the way, this Gothia, which Frankish land is that part of?'

'No Frankish land at all, to be precise,' the knight said, an amused glint in his eyes as if all his solemnity had been blown away by the wind. 'Gothia lies very far to the north of the Frankish countries, practically further away than any land in this world. At home in Gothia, I can walk on the water for half the year, because the cold is so fierce that it hardens the water. But where do you come from? You don't speak Arabic like those who are born in Mecca.'

'I was born in Baalbek, but all three of us are Kurds,' Yussuf said, clearly surprised. 'This is my brother Fahkr and this is my . . . friend Moussa. How and why have you learnt to speak the language of the believers so well? Such men as you do not usually end up in captivity for a long time?'

True enough,' the knight said. 'Men such as I are not kept as prisoners and you surely know why. But I've lived in Palestine for ten years. I didn't come here to steal as much as I could and leave for home after six months. Most of those who work for our Order here can speak Arabic. By the way, my sergeant's name is Armand de Gascogne; he's a fairly recent recruit and doesn't understand much of what we're saying. That's why he's silent, not because he's not allowed to speak – unlike your people who must have your permission.'

'You're very observant,' Yussuf mumbled, and blushed. 'You see, I'm the oldest – you'll have spotted the grey streaks in my beard – and I manage the money in my family. We're merchants on our way to do an important deal in Cairo and . . . I cannot think what my brother and my friend would want to ask one of our enemy's knights. We're all men of peace.'

The knight looked searchingly at Yussuf but said nothing. He munched some of the honeyed almond confection, stopping only to scrutinise a piece of the delicacy by the light of the fire, suggesting that these sweetmeats must come from Aleppo.

When he had finished eating, he pulled out his sack of wine, drank without asking permission and handed the sack on to his sergeant. Then he leaned back comfortably, wrapping himself in the thick white mantle with its frightening red cross and looked quizzically at Yussuf. He seemed to regard his host less as an enemy and more as a partner in a game of chess who requires careful evaluation.

'My unknown friend or enemy, what use is untruth to either of us, now that we're eating peacefully in each other's company and have given our word not to harm each other?' he asked finally. His manner was calm and his voice carried no challenge. 'We are both warriors. Should it be the will of God, the next time we could face each other on the battlefield. Your clothes reveal your kind, and so does everything else about you. Your swords were made by craftsmen in Damascus and none is worth less than five hundred dinars in gold. Our peaceful moment together will soon end and the truce between your side and mine will be lifted in the near future. You'll soon learn of this, if you don't know it already. So, let's enjoy this rare, strange encounter. It's not often that a man comes to know an enemy face to face. But let's stop lying to each other.'

Yussuf felt an almost irresistible impulse to tell the Templar knight who he was. But he, too, knew that hostilities would soon be resumed, even though the soldiers in both armies did not. Their decision to enjoy this meal together in peace could only have been made this very evening. They were both lions, but for once, and once only, trying to behave like lambs.

'You're right, Templar knight. *Insh'Allah* – should it be the will of God – then we'll meet again on the field of battle. But I agree with you about the value of knowing one's enemy. In fact, you seem to know more about the true believers than we know about you. I'll give my followers permission to address you now.'

Yussuf leaned back, pulled his mantle more tightly round himself against the cold and signed to his brother and his amir that they had permission to speak. Since they had both anticipated a long evening of staying silent, they hesitated, and the knight turned to his sergeant. For a while they spoke quietly together in Frankish.

'My sergeant wonders about one thing,' said the knight. 'Your weapons and your horses alone are worth more than these miserable robbers could have dreamt of. How come you decided to take this dangerous route to the west of the Dead Sea without a strong escort?'

'Because it's the fastest way to . . . because an escort would have aroused too much suspicion . . .' Yussuf replied uncertainly. He wanted to avoid the embarrassment of telling untruths again, but had to choose his words carefully. His appropriate escort would have attracted notice, to put it mildly. In order to ensure safety, he would have had to be accompanied by at least three thousand men on horseback.

'And since we trusted our horses, we felt sure no Franks, let alone any useless robbers, could catch up with us,' he added quickly.

'Wise, but also unwise,' the Templar knight said. 'These six robbers have been marauding all over this region for more than six months, knew it like the back of their hand, and felt more confident about riding fast over dangerous ground than most of us. This is how they enriched themselves – until God punished them.'

'There's something on my mind that I'd like to ask you about,' Fahkr said quickly, stumbling over the words. It was the first time he had spoken up and he had to clear his throat a couple of times before going on. 'It's said the Knights Templar who . . . are about in Al Aqsa have allowed a *minbar* there, a place where the true believers can come to pray. And then it's said that sometimes a Templar knight might punish Franks who interfered with the believers' right to pray. Is all this really true?'

The three true believers looked attentively at their enemy, obviously interested in his answer. The knight, smiling to himself, took his time and began by translating the question into Frankish. His sergeant listened, nodded, and burst out laughing.

'Well now, all you have heard is really so,' the knight finally said, having delayed his reply to make everybody even more intrigued. 'We do have a *minbar* in the place we call Templum Salomonis and you call Al Aqsa. But then, it's not that special. Back in our Gaza fortress, we have a *majlis* every Thursday, which is the only possible day, and then the witness can swear by whatever text he holds sacred, be it God's Holy Scripture or the Torah scrolls or the Quran or, within reason, any other sacred text or object. And if you were the Egyptian merchants you claim to be, you'd have known of our many trading links with Egypt, where no one shares our beliefs. Al Aqsa, if you will, houses the headquarters of our Order. Our main problem is that the ships from Pisa or Genoa or the Frankish territories arrive each September, bringing new recruits full of eagerness to distinguish themselves. They may not want to get to Paradise straightaway, but they can't wait to kill unbelievers or at least give them a right good going over. This is a serious nuisance, and no September comes to an end without us having had to deal with riots in our part of the city. They are almost always caused by our raw recruits attacking people of your faith, and naturally we have to punish them quickly and hard.'

'You're prepared to kill your own on our behalf?' Fahkr exclaimed, almost breathless with surprise.

'Absolutely not!' the Templar knight replied with sudden anger. 'To kill a man professing the true faith is as grave a sin among us as it is among you. It's out of the question. But there's nothing stopping us from teaching these lads a good lesson,' he added after a pause. His good mood seemed to have returned. 'Especially if they won't listen to reason. I've had the pleasure myself on a couple of occasions . . .'

He leaned towards his sergeant and explained quickly what he had said. They began laughing together, and the others joined them in relieved, perhaps rather too loud, laughter.

A gust of wind from the slopes of Al Khalil, a last sigh of the evening breeze, suddenly wafted with it the stench from the Templar knight and his sergeant. The three true believers were again taken aback by such uncleanliness and couldn't quite hide their distaste. The knight understood, rose at once, and suggested a change of sides so that he and his sergeant should sit downwind from their companions. This was done without any impoliteness, after which Moussa served everyone mocha coffee in tiny cups.

'We all have our rules,' the knight said apologetically, once they had all settled down again. 'Your rules dictate that you should wash ever so often, and our rules forbid washing for almost any reason.

It's no worse than the different rules for hunting: you do it and we don't, except for lions. As for wine, we drink it and you don't.'

'Now, the matter of drinking wine is different,' Yussuf argued. 'There's a strict prohibition against wine and the like. It was part of God's words spoken to the Prophet, may peace be with him. But we are different from our enemies in that we enjoy good things. Listen to what God said in the seventh sura. "Who can forbid all that which is beautiful and given by God to His servants, or all the good things that He has provided for their sustenance?"'

'True, true,' the knight said. 'On the other hand, listen to the sixty-first sura, in the words of your own Prophet, may peace be with him. "Believers! Become God's helpers. As Jesus, son of Mary, said to the men wearing white robes: Who will help me for the sake of God? And they answered: We all want to help God! Among the children of Israel some came to believe in Jesus, although others denied him. But We supported those who believed in him against their enemies and the true believers were victorious." Of course I'm very fond of the passage about the white-robed men ...'

At this point Moussa dashed off in the direction of his sword but stopped halfway. His face glowed with anger as he accusingly pointed his finger at the knight.

'Blasphemer!' he shouted. 'So you speak the language of the Quran. Don't make free with it, don't twist the word of God into godless mockery! You deserve to die and you would, had not His Roy ... my friend Yussuf given his word.'

'SIT DOWN, Moussa! Behave!' roared Yussuf. Moussa obeyed, and Yussuf told him, more calmly, 'Those were the words of God and you'd do well to reflect on them. And don't imagine the phrase about "men in white robes" was a joke made up by our friend here.'

'Not at all,' the knight said hurriedly to pacify Moussa. 'It refers to people in white clothes who lived long ago and has got nothing to do with what I'm wearing.'

'So how come you're so well read in the Quran?' Yussuf asked in his usual pleasant tone of voice, as if no one had taken offence and no one had almost blurted out the secret of his high rank.

'Again, it's wise to know one's enemy – if you like, I'll instruct you about the Bible,' the Templar knight said easily, as if he wanted to get away from his intrusion into the world of the true believers and put a humorous gloss on the whole episode.

Yussuf was about to give a sharp response to the light-hearted suggestion that he should indulge in blasphemous studies, when he was interrupted by a drawn-out, terrifying howl. The scream faded into something that sounded like wicked laughter. The noise echoed between the summits and rolled down the hillsides. Moussa at once began rattling off the incantations that true believers use to keep the djinns of the desert at bay. The howling started up again, but now it seemed to come from several spirits from hell, telling each other about the small fire and the lonely human beings.

The Knight Templar leaned towards his sergeant and whispered a few words in Frankish. The sergeant nodded, and rose to fetch his sword. He then wrapped himself in his black mantle, bowed to his hosts and, without a word, walked away into the darkness.

'Please excuse this rudeness,' the knight said. 'We must look after our horses, though, and after today's work there's a strong smell of blood and a good deal of flesh about in our camp.' He seemed to feel that was all the explanation needed and held out his empty mocha cup towards Moussa, with a slight bow.

The guard's hand shook a little as he poured.

'You send your man out into the dark and he obeys at once?' Fahkr said wonderingly, his voice slightly hoarse.

'We must obey commands even when fearful,' the knight replied. 'Though I don't believe Armand felt any fear. The dark is a better friend to a man in black than to someone wearing white. Armand's sword is sharp and his hand strong and accurate. The wild dogs with their ghostly bark are well known to be cowardly, don't you agree?'

'But are you sure what we heard was only wild dogs?' Fahkr asked.

'Of course not. There's too much between heaven and hell for anyone to be sure,' the knight replied. 'But the Lord is our shepherd and we shall not want even when we walk through the valley of the shadow of death. That's the prayer that will sustain Armand now, when he's walking through the dark desert. At least, in his shoes I would pray it. We can do nothing if God decides that our allotted time has come to an end, but until then we'll cleave the skulls of wild dogs and human enemies. Surely you, who believes in the Prophet, may peace be with him, and deny the Son of God, think in the same way as we do about this. Isn't that so, Yussuf?'

'You're right, Templar knight,' Yussuf agreed. 'But where's the borderline between common sense and faith? Between fear and trust in God? And if a man must obey orders, as your sergeant must, does it help him if he's afraid?'

'When I was young – well, I'm not that old, I suppose,' said the knight slowly, as he thought about the question, 'I was constantly preoccupied with questions of this kind. It does you good to think.

One's mind becomes more agile from trying to work out these things, but by now I've slowed down, I'm sorry to say. Life has been reduced to obedience. To fighting evil and thanking God afterwards. That's all.'

'And if you fail to defeat the enemy, then what?' Yussuf spoke in a curiously mild voice, which the men close to him did not recognise.

'Death is the only alternative, at least, when it comes to myself and Armand,' the knight Templar replied.' And on the Day of Judgement both you and I will be measured and weighed. I don't know where you'll go, though I know what you yourself believe. As for me, if I die in Palestine, I know that I'll go straight to Paradise.'

'You truly believe this?' Yussuf asked, still speaking in that new, gentle voice.

'Yes, I do,' the Knight Templar replied.

'So tell me: is this promise written into your Bible?'

'No, not in these very words, not exactly.'

'But still you do not doubt it?'

'Well, no, the Holy Father in Rome has promised . . .'

'But when all's said and done, he is only human! Knight of the Temple, how come you believe a mere human can keep a place in Paradise for you?'

'But Muhammad was a mere human, too and you believe in his promises . . . sorry, peace be upon him.'

'Muhammad, peace be upon him, was God's messenger. Listen to the words of God. "But the messenger and his followers of the true faith who labour to support God's cause with their lives and all their possessions at stake will be rewarded with good things in this life and the next and all will go well for them." It could not be clearer than that, could it? And next, it says . . .'

'I know,' the knight interrupted him abruptly. 'That is the ninth sura and the next verse says that "God has prepared pleasure gardens watered by streams for them, where they will stay for all eternity. This is the great, the glorious victory". So, surely we should understand each other? There's one difference between us, though: I have no possessions and my life belongs wholly to God. When He decides, I die for Him. Your faith contradicts none of this.'

'You know God's words very well indeed, Templar knight,' Yussuf admitted but at the same time he was pleased at having trapped his enemy. His satisfaction was obvious to those who knew him well.

'As you said, everyone should get to know his enemy,' the knight

21

said, hesitant for the first time, as if he too realised that Yussuf had cornered him.

'But if this is what you say, then you cannot be my enemy,' Yussuf replied. 'You cite the sacred Quran, which I think contains the words of my God. As yet, you think not – my God is not a god. The Quran seems crystal clear to the true believers, but what does it mean to you? It is true that I don't know anywhere near as much about Jesus as you know about the Prophet, may peace be with Him. So, what did Jesus say about the Holy War? Did Jesus in any way assure you that you would go to Paradise if you killed me?'

'We mustn't argue about this,' the knight replied, dismissing the argument as minor with a gesture meant to look self-confident. It was obvious to all that he in fact felt ill at ease. 'Our faiths are truly different, even though similar in many things. But, different or not, we're living together in the same place. In the worst case, we fight each other. At best, we negotiate and trade. Let's change the subject. This is my wish, as your guest.'

Yussuf must have trapped his adversary, they thought. Jesus presumably had never said anything about God taking pleasure in Saracens being killed in His honour. The knight had got out of trouble by appealing to his hosts' unwritten laws of hospitality.

'In truth, you do know your enemy well,' Yussuf said. His feeling of triumph at having won the debate showed both in his voice and the expression on his face.

'Then we agree: Know thy enemy,' the knight replied quietly. His eyes were cast down.

For a while they sat in silence, staring into their cups of mocha. It was hard to think of anything neutral to talk about, but the silence was again shattered by a monstrous uproar. All of them knew that it was animals howling this time and not demons from hell. The creatures seemed first to be attacking and then fleeing, screaming in pain and the agony of death.

'As I told you, Armand's sword is sharp,' the knight mumbled.

'Why, in the name of everything holy, did you drag all these corpses along?' Fahkr asked. His mind had followed his companions' lines of thought.

'It would have been better to capture them alive, of course,' the knight replied. 'Alive, they're better riders and besides, they wouldn't have been smelling so badly. The heat will be back tomorrow, I'm sure, so we'll have to start early to get them back to Jerusalem before the stench becomes unbearable.'

Fahkr still didn't see the point. 'So, if you had taken them prisoners and brought them to Al Quds alive, then what would you have done with them?'

'We would've handed them over to our amir in Jerusalem. He is one of the highest-ranking men in our Order. He passes them on to the worldly authorities, the prisoners would have been stripped naked, apart from a cloth to hide their private parts and then hanged from the gallows on the city wall near the Rock,' the knight said simply.

'But in this case you've already killed them! Why not strip them here and now and leave the bodies to their fate. That's what they deserve, after all. Why even go to the length of defending their remains against wild animals?' Fahkr asked. He either didn't want to give in or was still genuinely confused.

'Dead or alive, their bodies will be on display,' the knight assured him. 'No one must miss our intention to punish with death anyone who plunders along the pilgrim routes. This is one of the sacred promises given by our Order. It must be fulfilled, so God help us.'

'What are you going to do with their weapons and their clothes?' Moussa asked. He sounded as if he, for one, wanted to talk sense. 'There must have been many precious things in their packs, too.'

'True, but all stolen goods,' the knight explained, his old self-assurance returning. 'I'm not speaking about their armour and their weapons, we've got no use for all that. But up there on the hillside, where Armand and I pitched camp, we found a cave packed with their loot. Tomorrow, our horses will be very heavily laden. Remember, these scoundrels have been plaguing this area for more than six months.'

'Interesting, but it's said that you're not allowed any possessions, surely?' Yussuf said, speaking in a gentle tone of voice but with his eyebrows raised. He seemed to think that he had again won a battle of wits with an adversary who could have struck him down like a babe in arms if they were to meet with sword in hand.

'Of course we're not!' the knight exclaimed, surprised. 'No possessions at all. You've got the wrong end of the stick completely if you assume that we're going to keep the booty for ourselves. Next Sunday, everything we recover will be on display outside the Church of the Sacred Sepulchre. The idea is that the people who owned these things should have a chance to claim them back.'

'Presumably most of the victims of theft are dead now?' Yussuf remarked quietly.

'Then we'll take account of the claims made by their surviving heirs. Of course, if no one comes forward, the goods come to belong to our Order,' the knight replied.

'This is such an intriguing sidelight on what your people have put about as being a sacred rule that the Knights Templar are too noble to loot as common soldiery do,' Yussuf said, and still he seemed sure of winning their skirmish.

'It's true though. We do not loot, neither on the field of battle nor afterwards,' the knight replied coldly. 'No problem, there's just more around for those who do. That's everybody else. Sadly. When we've been victorious, we turn at once to our God. Would you like me to quote what your own Quran says about plunder on the battle-field . . .?'

'Thank you but no, thank you,' Yussuf interrupted, and held up his hand as a warning. 'We would rather not enter into this. It could be that you, infidel, would turn out to know more about the commands of our Prophet, may peace be with him, than we do. Instead, may I ask you a straightforward question?'

'Yes, of course. Put it to me and it'll get the answer I think it deserves,' the knight replied, holding up both his hands palms outwards, in the way true believers do to show that a change of subject is quite in order.

'You mentioned our truce, but only to say you thought it would soon come to an end. What did you have in mind then? Brince Arnat?'

'Yussuf, you're well informed. You call him Prince but he's not. In our language, he's Reynald de Châtillon. Anyway, he's a thoroughly bad character but, unfortunately, an ally of the Knights Templar. He's started raiding again like the robber baron he is, and I wish I wasn't under orders to act on his side. But no, it's not de Châtillon who's the problem.'

'The other problem could be this new man from the land of the Franks – another prince? – who's arrived here recently, at the head of a large army. What's his name? Filius?'

'Not quite, because *Filius* would just mean he was somebody's son,' the knight said with a smile. 'Philip is his name, and his title is Duke of Flanders. But yes, his army is large and now I must warn you off this line of talk.'

'How so?' Yussuf asked, trying to sound relaxed and maybe a little surprised. 'I have your word of honour, haven't I? Surely you've never broken such a promise?'

'There's one thing I've sworn to do that I won't be able to carry out until ten years from now, if it's God's will. But so help me God, I have never gone back on anything else when I've given my word.'

'There you are. So, why should our truce be affected because this Filus chap from Flamsen is turning up in Palestine. He's just one more in the queue.'

The Knight Templar took his time to answer as he looked searchingly into Yussuf's eyes. Yussuf did not look away and so they stayed, locked in silent confrontation for a while.

Still fixing Yussuf with his eyes, the knight said, 'You're keeping your true identity secret. There are only a handful of men who'd know so much about military matters, and none of them are merchants trading with the Egyptians. If you tell me more than this, you'll have made it impossible for me to keep pretending that I've no idea who you are. It will be obvious that you're in a high position, a man in the know. Someone with access to a network of spies.'

'Remember, Knight Templar, I also have given my word.'

'Men of my Order trust you more than anyone else among our enemies.'

'You honour me. But if so, why break the truce between our two sides?'

'Please ask your men to leave us before we carry on discussing this subject.'

Yussuf did not reply at once. He pulled thoughtfully at his beard as he pondered the options. Now, if the knight felt sure about who his companion really was, then sending the men away would be a risk – the knight might decide to break his promise and try to kill his important enemy. But this seemed unlikely. Earlier that evening, the knight had proved himself. If he wanted to kill, he had no need to cheat. Attacking would have been enough.

His request was hard to interpret. It seemed both unreasonable and pointless. In the end, Yussuf simply could not resist his own curiosity and decided to throw caution to the winds.

'Leave us,' he commanded. 'You can go to sleep somewhere further away. Tomorrow we clean up the camp before leaving. Remember that battle orders apply.'

Fahkr and Moussa rose, hesitated, stopped, and looked at Yussuf. His stern gaze told them to obey. They bowed to the Knight Templar and withdrew. Yussuf waited in silence until his brother and the head of his guards had gone far enough away and he could hear the shuffling sounds of their bedding being prepared.

'Somehow, I don't think my brother and Moussa will fall asleep easily tonight,' he said.

'Indeed not,' the knight replied. 'But they're well out of earshot.'

'Why is that so important?'

'It isn't,' the knight said with a smile. 'But it is important that *you* know that they can't hear us. Once on your own with me, winning battles of words won't matter to you. Our talk will become more honest then. That's what I wanted.'

'You know much about human nature, don't you? More than one would expect from a man living in a cloister.'

'Cloisters are good places for finding out about human nature, much better than you might imagine. Anyway, let's talk. I cannot refer to anything that you wouldn't already know, of course. It would be treachery otherwise. That aside, this is what we know about the situation: a Frankish aristocrat has arrived with a big army in tow and he's going to stay here for some time. Back home, everybody who's anybody blessed his holy mission in the name of our Lord and so on. Now, what's he likely to do next?'

'Fill his empty treasure chests. His costs will have been great.'

'Exactly, Yussuf. You're so right. Will he march towards Damascus and challenge Saladin himself?'

'No. He'd risk losing everything then.'

'You're right again. We understand each other well. Now that your subordinates have left, we can leave both politeness and pretence behind us. So, to where will our new plunderer lead his men?'

'I've not worked it out. Some suitably wealthy but not too large city.'

'Of course. I don't know which one either. Maybe Homs or Hama? Aleppo is too far away and too well fortified. Homs or Hama seems obvious targets. Then what will our Christian King of Jerusalem do?'

'Not much choice for him, I shouldn't think. He'll let his men plunder too, even thought he should join forces with the new army and attack Saladin.'

'Right again, I'm sure. Yussuf, you seem to know everything and also understand everything. We're agreed about the situation facing us. What do we do about it?'

'For a start, both of us stand by our words of honour.'

'That goes without saying. What next?'

'We use this moment of peace to try to understand each other. Maybe I'll never talk to any other Knight Templar. And you, maybe you'll never again encounter . . . an enemy like me.'

'I think not. You and I seem destined to meet only once in our lives.'

'A strange whim of God's . . . but first, another question. Who or what, except our God, would we need to defeat you infidels?'

'Two things, but Saladin is already doing one of them. He's uniting all Saracens against us. The other means cultivating betrayal among the fighters for Jesus Christ. Betrayal or temptation into sins so gross that our God punishes us.'

'If we fail to make you sin or betray your cause, what then?'

'Then, Yussuf, I believe neither side will ever win. The main difference between you Saracens and us is that you can afford to lose. After a decorous interval to mourn your dead, you'll soon have raised a new army of men. All we Christians need is to lose one big battle and we're done for. We're not so stupid that we'd risk this. If things look bad for us we take cover in our fortresses. The warfare could go on forever.

'Eternal war, then?'

'It's possible. Some of us . . . do you know a Count Raymond de Tripoli?'

'Yes, I know him . . . I know of him. What about him?'

'If Christians of his calibre are in power in Jerusalem and you have leaders like Saladin on your side, then peace becomes possible. Many among us agree with Count Raymond. And, to touch on a current issue we talked about earlier, the Knights Templar never followed that 'Brince' and the royal army to Syria. The Knights of St John did, but not us.'

'So I gather.'

'You would have, because your name is Yussuf bin Ayyub Salah al-Din and, in our language, Saladin.'

'God be merciful to you, now that I know you know.'

'God has been merciful by giving us this miraculous opportunity to talk together during the last hours of peace between our sides.'

'And we'll both keep our promises.'

'Your worry on that score surprises me. You're the only one of our enemies who always keeps his word. I'm a Knight Templar. We can always be trusted.'

'So, what next, my dear enemy? The dawn is drawing close and when it comes, we both have duties to carry out. Yours is to escort your stinking corpses and I – well, I have things to do that I can't tell you about but which you'll surely guess.'

'Let's hold on to this one chance to talk. We are already agreed about one thing at least, you and I . . . but you must forgive me for addressing you so plainly, now that I know you're the Sultan of both Cairo and Damascus.'

'As you so wisely arranged it, no one but God can hear us. For this night only, you may address me as simply as you like.'

'You and I agree that we're fighting a war that neither side can win.'

'True – except I *must* win it. I've sworn that I'll win.'

'So have I. Eternal war, then?'

'It is a terrible prospect.'

'Then we must continue talking, even though I'm a lowly amir in my Order and you're the only one of our enemies whom we rightly fear. Can we turn the clock back and start again?'

The first issue they discussed then was the old one of pilgrims travelling in safety. This was, after all, the reason for their encounter, at least in the view of those who do not insist on tracing God's will alone in all that happens. Both Arn and Saladin claimed to see the hand of God in all things, at least when speaking within the hearing of others, but privately believed that human beings have free will, capable of bringing both great happiness and unspeakable disaster. Free will was in fact a cornerstone of both their faiths.

They spoke together almost the whole night through.

Dawn broke and Fahkr went to find his brother, who was a glorious prince and the leader of the true believers in jihad, Light of Religion, Water in the Desert, Hope of Islam, Sultan of Cairo and Damascus – and the man the infidels knew simply as Saladin.

The great man was sitting staring into the fading embers of the fire, his knees drawn up to his chin and his mantle wrapped tightly round his body.

The white shield with its red cross was gone, and so was the Knight Templar. Saladin seemed tired and almost bewildered, as if waking from a dream, when he looked at his brother.

'If all our enemies were like Al Ghouti we'd never win,' he said. 'But then, if all were like him, victory would no longer be necessary.'

Fahkr did not understand what his brother and his prince was muttering about. It sounded like the ramblings of an exhausted man. Fahkr had heard this kind of thing before when his brother had stayed awake pondering great issues of policy.

Saladin rose stiffly. 'We must get going. The ride to Al Arish is long and hard,' he said. 'The war is waiting. Soon, we'll be victorious.'

It was written that war was awaiting them. It was also written that Saladin and Arn Magnusson de Gothia would soon meet on the field of battle and that only one of them would leave victorious.

II

Jerusalem was in the centre of its own world. Even Rome was distant and the Frankish provinces were still further away. At the very edge of that world lay the cold and dark Nordic territories. They included a region called West Gothland that only few people had even heard about. Scholars would tell you that the land there was covered in deep forests, inhabited by two-headed monsters.

The true faith had found its way to these alien parts, mostly thanks to the holy Saint Bernard. Ever charitable and full of love for mankind, he insisted on offering the right of salvation to the souls of these isolated barbarians and dispatched the first missionary monks to wild Gothia, north of everywhere. It did not take too long before many Goths had been saved and the light of Truth was shining from ten cloisters.

One of these, a nunnery dedicated to the Virgin Mary, had an especially beautiful name: Godshome. It was situated on high land in the southern part of West Gothland. The views from Godshome took in the blue ridges of the Billingen Hills; beyond, almost out of sight, rose the twin towers of Skara Cathedral. To the north was the glittering expanse of Lake Hornborga, where the cranes went in the spring, just before spawning time of the pikes. The neighbourhood of the cloister was made up of cultivated land, dotted with farms and small oak woods. In other words, the landscape was very peaceful and pretty, with nothing to remind the traveller of dark, barbaric things. The elderly women, who had paid a substantial fee to end their lives in peace, found the name of Godshome a gentle caress and the area as beautiful as an ageing mind could wish for.

But Cecilia Algotsdotter had come to Godshome to be incarcerated for her sins. She was only seventeen, and to her it seemed barely a home and certainly well out of God's sight. She thought it more like Hell on Earth.

Cecilia already knew what living in a nunnery was like. She had spent two years of her life at Godshome, being educated among the *familiares*. These were usually high-born maidens, sent away to get a bit of polish before being married off. She had learnt to read, and could recite the Book of Psalms by heart after having sung all the hymns hundreds of times. There was nothing new or alarming about all that.

The difference this time was that she had been condemned and given a hard sentence. Her penance was twenty years in the nunnery. Her betrothed, Arn Magnusson of the Folkunga kin, had also been punished, and sent into exile. His penance was to serve for twenty years as a monkish recruit to God's Sacred Army in the infinitely distant Holy Land. The young couple had indulged in carnal intercourse before being wed in the sight of God, and so committed a mortal sin. Cecilia's own sister, Katarina, had been the hostile witness, and the proof of their sinning was there for all to see, because Cecilia was pregnant. The child was due in six months.

There was a carving of Adam and Eve in the sandstone lintel above the gate to Godshome cloister. It showed the first man and woman being driven out of Paradise for their sins, with only fig leaves to cover their nakedness. The image held a warning. Cecilia sometimes felt it had been chiselled into the stone just for her.

She loved Arn but had been forced to part with him less than a stone's throw away from that carving. He had kneeled before her and sworn with all the fire of a seventeen-year-old that he would stay alive, only for her. He swore on his blessed sword that he would go through war and pestilence to come back and wed her when their penance was done.

That was a long time ago now, and she had heard nothing from him since. This was bad enough, but the behaviour of the Abbess was terrifying. Mother Rikissa had grabbed Cecilia by the wrist and led her off as if leading a thrall to chastisement. It had been offensive and humiliating. Soon Godshome came to be a different place from the decorous cloister housing the young *familiares*. The place looked the same, apart from some new outbuildings, but the spirit was different. Cecilia had good reasons to feel fearful.

The ground on which Godshome stood belonged to the Abbess, who was of the Sverker kin. It had been donated by her kinsman King Karl Sverkersson. Almost all the blessed sisters and many of the *familiares* were Sverker relations too.

Then King Karl had been challenged by Knut Eriksson, whose claim to the crown rested on being the son of the former King, the Saint Erik Jedverdsson. King Erik had been murdered by the then Karl Sverkersson, who promptly became king instead. Erik's son had come out of his Norwegian exile to seek revenge as well as restitution. Knut and a small band of friends murdered King Karl just outside his own castle on Visingsö. Cecilia's beloved Arn Magnusson had been on that raid and was one of Knut's closest friends.

Killing the king had of course ignited a war outside the walls of cloisters and churches. The opposing forces were the Folkunga and Erik kins with their Norwegian relations on one side, the Sverker kin and their Danish allies on the other.

With good reason, Cecilia felt like a harmless butterfly caterpillar dragged into a hornet's nest. Since most of the sisters and almost all the pupils belonged to Sverker families, they hated her unquestioningly and made a point of showing it. The working lay sisters, who were called the *conversae*, took note, and did not dare do otherwise than behave as if they hated her too. Everybody turned their backs on Cecilia and no one spoke to her during the times when talking was allowed.

Mother Rikissa had ordered a bread and water regime for the girl from the first day and directed her to take her meals at an empty table in the refectory, where she sat alone, wrapped in a cloak of icy silence. As if that were not sufficient punishment, the Abbess also ordered her to work in the fields with the *conversae*. Apparently Mother Rikissa had decided to kill her off. Cecilia had arrived at the time when the turnips were due to be thinned – hard, hot work in which neither the sisters nor the well-born women took part. Now Cecilia crawled along the turnip rows, inch by inch, with her baby kicking inside her.

After a while Mother Rikissa must have become dissatisfied with the results of her severity, perhaps disappointed that Cecilia did not miscarry. She now directed that Cecilia must undergo bloodletting once a week. Bloodletting was regarded as good for health and also a way to cool carnal desires, obviously very much called for in Cecilia's case.

So Cecilia grew steadily paler as she crawled along the turnip rows, mumbling prayers to Our Lady. She asked incessantly that her sins might be forgiven, and that Our Lady would reach out with her gentle hands and protect her for the sake of the child she was carrying.

Autumn came and the turnip harvest was due, the hardest and dirtiest of all the tasks for Godshome's women. Cecilia's pregnancy was near its end now, but Mother Rikissa was unrelenting.

Cecilia nearly gave birth to her son while lying in a muddy field. One chilly day in November, when the harvesting was almost done, she suddenly cried out between clenched teeth and collapsed to the ground. The *conversae*, and the two sisters who saw to it that the picking crew worked virtuously and in silence, understood perfectly well what was about to happen. The supervisors seemed content to leave Cecilia where she was, but the lay sisters would have none of it. Quietly, they lifted her and hurried along to the *hospitium*, the guesthouse in the grounds of the cloister. There they bedded her down and sent for Lady Helena, one of the older pensioners and not only a wise woman but also a generous donor.

Lady Helena came quickly, showing mercy even though she belonged to the Sverker kin. Her decision, which no one dared to contradict, was that two lay sisters should stay behind in the *hospitium* and help. Rikissa, she said firmly and without using the title 'Mother', could take it or leave it. Women in this world of ours have enough to bear without adding to each other's burdens, she told the astonished lay sisters. They at once set to heating water, finding clean linen and washing the mud and filth off Cecilia, who by now was almost out of her mind from the tearing pain.

Our Lady herself had indeed been merciful when She sent Lady Helena, who had helped many women through this hard and solitary labour, and had herself borne nine children, of whom seven survived. At times like these, only other women can help, and Lady Helena frowned angrily at the very thought that this tormented girl was her enemy. Besides, as she pointed out to the lay sisters, the whole friends-and-enemies business could change overnight after just one silly little victory in the men's endless wars. Any woman who made a rash choice in the matter of friends would learn that lesson soon enough.

Cecilia did not remember much of the night she spent in labour, except that the pains felt like knives cutting into her sinful flesh. What she would never forget was the moment when she heard Lady Helena say that the child was a handsome boy with everything in its right place. His name would be Magnus, as they had decided long before. The memory of holding her little son for the first time to her aching breasts would stay with her always. It was all over by then and she was febrile. Then the night became wrapped in a fog.

Later, she realised that Lady Helena had had the wit to send a message to Arnäs. A large escort had come riding in to take the baby to safety. Birger Brosa, her beloved Arn's uncle and the most powerful of the Folkunga kin, had sworn that the little lad – he always expected Arn's first-born to be a boy – would become a full member of the kin and formally come of age as a Folkunga man, never mind his having been born out of wedlock.

Of all the trials that Our Lady demanded Cecilia should endure, the hardest was that she was not to see her first-born until he was a man.

Mother Rikissa's heart turned to stone in any matters related to Cecilia. She was ordered to join the hard work of the lay sisters soon after giving birth, even though her breasts were still painful, she suffered bouts of fever, and was very weak.

Near to Christmas time, Bishop Bengt of Skara made a visitation. He grew pale when he saw an apparently barely conscious Cecilia dragging herself along one of the cloisters. Afterwards, he arranged a meeting with Mother Rikissa behind closed doors and, that very day, Cecilia was given a bed in the infirmary. For several weeks, she was allowed daily *pitenseae* – gifts of food – from outsiders. The baskets for Cecilia came full of eggs and butter and fine white bread, fish, and even a little lambs' meat. They caused quite a lot of whispered speculation. There were some who thought Bishop Bengt was sending the food, some who thought it was Lady Helena, and others who argued the donor was Birger Brosa himself.

The torture of the blood-lettings was also stopped, and after a while some colour returned to Cecilia's face, together with a little more flesh on her bones. But still she seemed without hope, and mostly wandered about mumbling to herself.

When the cold of winter gripped West Gothland, all outdoor work came to a halt. That was a relief, but the nights brought their own terrors. During these early years of Godshome's existence there was no separate dormitory for the *conversae*, who slept with the *familiares* in a large room above the Chapter Hall. The rules dictated that the sleeping quarters must be left unheated, so it was crucial to get a bed well away from the two windows. Unsurprisingly, Cecilia was directed to a bed at the outer stone wall, immediately below a window where the cold came pouring in like icy water. The beds of the *familiares* were placed along the inner wall at the opposite end of the dormitory. The eight *conversae*, none of whom dared to complain, slept between Cecilia and the hostile worldly sisters.

The rules permitted one straw mattress, one pillow and two

woollen blankets. Even though everyone went to bed fully dressed, the nights could be so bad that sleeping became almost impossible, especially if you were actually shaking with cold. This was Cecilia's blackest time in Godshome.

Then Our Lady suddenly sent her a few words of comfort. They would have meant little in the outside world but in here they glowed like coals on a heating dish. It was as if Our Lady decided that Cecilia had suffered long enough without the slightest sign of an answer to her prayers.

One of the young women sleeping near the doorway had suddenly become notorious for something too awful to allow her to keep one of the best-placed beds. Mother Rikissa declared that part of her punishment was to move to the bed nearest to Cecilia's. The young woman turned up with her armful of bedclothes after compline that night. She stood there, her head bowed, until the lay sister realised that she was meant to get up and go to the warmer end of the room. The newcomer kept an eye on the supervisor while she made her bed. Once in bed, she met Cecilia's eyes and coolly broke the rule of silence.

'Cecilia, you're not alone,' she whispered almost inaudibly.

Thank you and praise be to Our Lady, Cecilia replied, in the sign language used at Godshome when speaking was not allowed. She dared not break the rule of silence there and then, but felt stronger, and even warmer, already. Her thoughts seemed to have found new paths rather than circling in hopeless longing and unhappy solitude. This had been going on for so long that she feared she would become insane. Now someone had not only spoken kindly to her, but at a time when all speaking was forbidden. She lay watching her unknown companion curiously. They smiled at each in the darkness. That night Cecilia did not shake and fell asleep easily.

When it was time for matins, the first service of the day, the unknown woman had to shake Cecilia out of her deep sleep. That morning, Cecilia sang heartily along in the hymns for the first time and her clear voice rose above all the others. In earlier years, when Godshome had been a place she could leave after a few months, singing had been her greatest pleasure.

She must have had much sleep to catch up with, because she slept again after matins and had to be woken for lauds, the morning service. After prime and the first Mass of the day, there was a gathering in the Chapter Hall, where Cecilia discovered that, like herself, her new dormitory neighbour had been told to sit down by the door. There really were two of them now. Cecilia was no longer alone.

Mother Rikissa took her seat under the middle window and waved condescendingly to the Prioress as a sign that she was to start reading the Lesson for the day. Cecilia was too preoccupied with speculating about her sister in misfortune to keep her mind on the text.

Afterwards a list of dead brothers and sisters in the Cistercian order was read out, and all joined in praying for their souls. Sometimes when that list was recited, Cecilia would stiffen with fear when she heard a name in Latin that might be that of a fallen Templar knight, who were regarded as honorary brothers. Today there were no such names.

In the past Cecilia had liked these mornings in the Chapter Hall. It was a beautiful room, with a ceiling made up of six equal-sized arches supported by six slender pillars of whitish stone. The walls were pure white and the floor covered with great, grey sandstone flags. The only decoration was the crucifix carved in black wood on the wall above the Abbess's seat. It seemed to be a room made for good thoughts, although Cecilia had to admit to herself that during this stay her thinking probably never deserved to be called 'good'.

Punishments were announced last in the morning gathering. The most common misdemeanour was breaking the rule of silence. Mother Rikissa had actually punished Cecilia half a dozen times for this, even though no one ever spoke to her nor she to anyone.

And now it is time to chastise Cecilia again, Mother Rikissa intoned. Her usual stern expression was replaced by what looked almost like a smile. The sisters sighed, bowing their heads, while the worldly maidens looked up and stared at Cecilia with curious malice.

Mother Rikissa paused, as if giving herself time to suck on a sweetmeat, and then resumed.

'However, this time it's another Cecilia,' she said. 'That is, not Cecilia Algotsdotter as usual, but Cecilia Ulvsdotter. As there seem to be two miscreants called Cecilia, from now on the red-haired Algotsdotter will be known as Cecilia Rosa and the light-haired Ulvsdotter as Cecilia Blanca.'

Mostly, and particularly during the time after the birth of the baby when Mother Rikissa had seemed determined to pester Cecilia to death, the punishment would be a couple of days of bread and water. Not this time, though. In a tone that sounded scornful and not particularly judgmental, she ordered the Prioress and one of the sisters to lead Cecilia Blanca to the *lapis culparum*, a post mortared into the floor at the far end of the room. They pulled off her woollen dress, leaving her in only her under-linen, raised her hands over her head and clamped them inside iron handcuffs attached to the post.

Then Mother Rikissa fetched a scourge and tested it lightly on her hand, as she went to stand next to the trussed-up Cecilia Blanca. For a while she stared out over her congregation, looking gleeful rather than pious, and then signed that it was time for the three Pater Nosters. Everyone obediently bowed their heads and started to run through the prayers.

Afterwards, she called on Helena Sverkersdotter, one of the worldly maidens, to come forward, take the scourge and hit the culprit three times, as the punishment due to her in the name of the Father, the Son and the Holy Ghost.

Helena Sverkersdotter was a plump and awkward young woman, who only rarely got an opportunity to show off. She looked pleased with herself as she turned towards her companions, who nodded encouragingly at her, some of them making gestures to signify 'a proper beating'. Helena did her best to oblige. She brought the scourge down, but not in the measured way meant to chastise the body while alerting the mind to the consequences of wrongdoing. Instead she hit out as hard as she could. After the third blow, two lines of blood had soaked through Cecilia Blanca's white linen shift.

Cecilia Blanca had moaned as the blows struck, but she neither screamed nor wept. In spite of almost hanging from the post, she turned as best she could and looked at Helena Sverkersdotter's excited eyes and rosy face. Then, her eyes black with hatred, she hissed between her teeth words so dreadful that an alarmed hush fell over the Hall.

'One day, Helena Sverkersdotter, you will regret beating me, more than you'll ever regret anything else in your entire life, I swear by the Holy Virgin Mary.'

This was outrageous. Cecilia Blanca had made threats in anger inside the holy walls of the cloister and used the sacred name of Virgin Mary in her sinful speech. Worse still, she had shown herself lacking in humility by refusing to accept that she had been rightly chastised, and that meant disobedience to Mother Rikissa.

Now everyone expected three times three beatings as an immediate response to the blasphemy and lack of respect. Helena Sverkersdotter lifted her hand with the scourge, but Mother Rikissa stepped forward and took it away from her.

From her seat down by the door, Cecilia Rosa thought she saw a red glow in Mother Rikissa's eyes, like those of an enraged dragon or some kind of demon. Except for the two Cecilias, everyone in the congregation bowed their heads – not in prayer but in fear of what would follow.

'Three days in *carcer*,' Mother Rikissa said slowly, as if after serious thought. 'Three days in *carcer* on bread and water, with only one blanket. You must seek forgiveness in prayer there, in silence and solitude!'

Cecilia Rosa had never heard this sentence uttered at Godshome. *Carcer* was the subject of ghost stories whispered in the dark, a small windowless earth cellar under the grainstore. It must be truly dreadful to endure being there in the dark and the winter cold, with only rats for company.

For the next few days Cecilia Rosa did not feel the cold, because she was too preoccupied with praying for her new friend. Her soul was on fire and her eyes brimmed with tears as she absently went about her daily tasks. She sat at the loom, she sang the hymns, she ate her meals, but her entire soul was devoted to praying.

On the evening of the third day, after the time for silence, Cecilia Blanca was led in, stiff and trembling, her face white and drained. Two sisters half dragged her to her bed, gave her a shove to tip her on to it and pulled her blankets carelessly over her.

Cecilia Rosa sought her friend's eyes in the dark. They were empty and cold. She must be frozen to the marrow of her bones.

Cecilia Rosa waited until the dormitory was silent and then she dared do the unthinkable. Clutching her blankets, she slowly and silently moved over to her friend's bed, crept into it and covered both of them with the blankets. Holding her friend's body close felt like hugging a lump of ice at first. But Our Lady protected them both in this grave sin, and, slowly, blessed warmth returned to Cecilia Blanca.

Cecilia Rosa did not dare keep up her act of charity after matins, but she left one of her blankets behind. Even with only one for herself she did not freeze during the last part of that bitterly cold night, when the stars glittered frostily against the black sky outside.

Their crime was never discovered. Maybe the lay sisters in the beds closest to theirs had observed them in the sinful act of sleeping together, but had decided not to tell tales. After all, if you did not have a heart of stone and did not hate the two Cecilias for kinship reasons, it stood to reason that you could not but pity someone who had suffered incarceration in an earth cellar for three nights during the coldest time of the year.

Winter was the time for spinning and weaving at Godshome, dull work for the lay sisters who were expected to produce as much cloth as possible. The material would be given away, or sold to enrich the cloister. For the young women of the world, these were skills to acquire that would also help to keep them busy during the dark and cold part of the year. In all cloisters, the second most important rule after obedience was *Ora et labora*: Pray and Work.

Should any of the young *familiares* be ignorant of such work, they had to sit by someone who was reasonably good at handling spindle and loom. It turned out that Cecilia Blanca did not know much of these things, while Cecilia Rosa could manage as well as any lay sister. Permitting the two Cecilias to share a loom was the only solution to this problem, because none of the six Sverker *familiares* were prepared to have anything to do with Cecilia Blanca. They all knew that her secret had been her betrothal to Knut Eriksson, and there was no one in the world they despised and detested more than the slayer of the late king and his bride-to-be.

It did not take long for Cecilia Rosa to find out that her friend was perfectly able to manage the weaving and most other crafts on her own. Cecilia Blanca showed it now and then, by undetected little signs. She had just acted ignorant so that they could get some time together. Even when talking was forbidden, they could exchange messages during the working hours using the sign language. Not even the most sharp-eyed supervisor could catch them out, and when her back was turned they even dared to whisper.

After a while Cecilia Blanca had passed on all she knew about the cause of the hatred that the others had against both of them, and about her hopes for the future. She insisted that things had changed out there in the men's world and the old simplicities had gone. You didn't just behead the old king when you fancied being his successor. Her betrothed, Knut Eriksson, would surely get there in the end, with the help of God and Saint Erik, his dead father and the former king. Still, it was not straightforward. That was why Knut had dispatched his betrothed into a nunnery. It was meant to be a safe refuge for her while the men fought it out. Her life would not be at risk there, even though it was run by an enemy. Granted, it would not be pleasant, but there were only a handful of nunneries in the country and all of them in hock to the Sverker kin. Incidentally, this was something they had better change in the future.

If the Sverker supporters won the war, times would be grim for them both. Then Cecilia Blanca might never get back outside to join her man and bear children; never run a household, wander freely over her own land, ride a horse, or sing ungodly songs. But should their side win, there would be great rejoicing at the dire prospect of a black future having turned shining white. Knut Eriksson would become King Knut, Cecilia Blanca would be the wedded wife of her beloved and his Queen to boot. The country would be at peace. This was the threat hanging over Mother Rikissa, the sisters, and the *familiares* too, silly, vicious geese that they all were. Helena Sverkersdotter was just the worst of a bad lot. All of them tried to pretend they did not care, though they lived in the shadow of possible doom.

Cecilia Blanca said the two of them must pray that the Erik and Folkunga side would be victorious for their own future happiness, and that perhaps their lives depended on that victory more than on anything else. No one could be quite sure what would happen, of course. Peace treaties could change everything and, besides, men often assumed that a marriage of state could bring in more land and wealth than a mere treaty. Maybe if the Sverker side won, the Cecilias would be hauled out of the nunnery one miserable day and handed over as brides to two ugly old men from the Sverker heartland round Linköping City. Bad enough, but better than drying up inside the walls and being whipped every time Mother Rikissa had nothing better to do.

Cecilia Rosa, who was a couple of years younger, felt bewildered at times by her new and only friend's tough-minded way of thinking. More than once she protested that all she wanted was for her beloved to come back for her, just the way he had promised. Blanca on the other hand found this sentimental talk hard to take. Of course love was a nice dream, but dreams don't get you out of imprisonment in Godshome. A wedding feast was one way out of Godshome, never mind whether the groom was a dribbling oldie from Linköping or a handsome young fellow. Nothing in their earthly existence could be worse than being forced to crawl to Mother Rikissa until you died.

Cecilia Rosa would protest that there was nothing worse in life than to betray your vow of love, but Cecilia Blanca could not see the point.

They were very unlike. Cecilia Rosa, with her mane of red hair, was quiet in speech and thought. She seemed to spend much of her time dreaming. The blonde Cecilia was hot-headed and spoke her mind. She thought a lot too, but her mind kept working out steely, vengeful plans about what she would do as Knut's Queen. She often repeated what she had sworn on the day of her beating: that stupid cow Helena Sverkersdotter would be made to pay and come to regret her blows more than anything else she had done in life.

Maybe these two would not have become so close if they had met outside as free women – as mistresses on neighbouring estates, for instance. But here in Godshome, locked in and surrounded by cowardly and malicious women who hated them, they were welded together by red-hot feelings. They would stay the closest of friends forever after.

Both of them wanted to rebel but neither could bear the thought of *carcer*, the cramped, ice-cold earth cellar teeming with rats. They liked the idea of breaking as many rules as possible, but being punished was irksome because it delighted the audience so much. With time and cunning, however, they managed to find low-key ways to annoy everyone.

Cecilia Rosa had a lovely voice, truer than anybody else's. Cecilia Blanca sang well enough, but used her singing to disrupt. She would hit false notes, go too slowly or, at other times, speed up the tempo. These tricks were especially effective during prime and lauds, the early morning offices when everyone was sleepy. It was quite difficult to disturb the singing without being obvious, but she quickly learnt how to become better at it to avoid getting caught out. They took turns. Sometimes Cecilia Rosa would sing so beautifully that everyone else felt ashamed. Next, Cecilia Blanca would subtly ruin everything. In the end the two friends managed to be irritating at most of the seven or eight daily services. Rosa would be submissive if she was admonished, mumbling her answers in a low voice, while Blanca responded in a loud clear voice with her head held high, but always using modest words to which no one could object.

Every day after sext, they ate their noonday meal. It was called *prandium* and was quite substantial. Bread was on the table and one of the different kinds of *pulmentaria*, usually soup made from lentils or beans. They were allowed to dunk their bread in the soup. The meal had to be eaten in silence, but a lesson would be read from texts considered improving for young women. Now and then, often at some critical point, Cecilia Blanca might slurp her soup audibly. At least a couple of the Sverker maidens would start giggling at this, occasionally so loudly that Mother Rikissa would hear it and notice Cecilia Blanca's naughtiness. Still, sometimes the giggling girls got a stricter telling-off than Cecilia did for slurping.

After the meal all the women processed from the refectory to the chapel, singing *Kyrie eleison* as they walked. It was meant to be a dignified procession, but it could happen that Cecilia Blanca stumbled, or stamped her feet heavily, like a man, or had to clear her throat. One way or another, the orderly line would get out of order.

Meanwhile, walking next to her with an angelic look on her face, Cecilia Rosa would be singing like a member of the heavenly host, her eyes fixed somewhere in the far distance.

The two girls would tell each other about the tricks they had played each day. It became a game. But because they were talking together all the time, even when it was forbidden, their cunning was not always enough to protect them from discovery. One of the women would spot them and tell tales during the Chapter Hall congregation, and Mother Rikissa punished them of course, though not as severely as many expected and hoped. She never again asked one of the *familiares* to carry out a beating, but handled the scourge herself, sometimes on Cecilia Blanca's back, sometimes on Cecilia Rosa's. Rosa would put up with the pain stoically, her head bowed and her face immobile, but Blanca would get up to her small acts of rebellion, scream suddenly or even break wind and then apologise with a barely hidden smile on her face.

They became obsessed with finding new ways to rebel and so show themselves as well as their hostile companions that nothing could break them. The odd thing was that the longer they carried on their private warfare, the less resistance was put up by Mother Rikissa. This was incomprehensible at first.

They both were convinced that Mother Rikissa was malevolent, set to force godliness in others. She was as ugly as a witch, with large protruding teeth and coarse hands. With looks like that it would have been hard to marry her off, even given a high rank in the Sverker kin. Influence from the bridal bed would never be hers to enjoy, so it had been easier for her to acquire power inside the walls. The two Cecilias were young women in their fairest years, full of life, with slender waists and clear eyes. They agreed, self-conscious but also wise, that the Abbess's resentment of them might well have something to do with these things.

When summer came and the Masses had been said for Ascension Day, Mother Rikissa changed again. Now she easily found new reasons to punish the Cecilias. Her hatred reached such a pitch that water and bread regimes were no longer enough and beatings at the *lapis culparum* for what she called their 'prankishness' became practically the order of the day. She often ordered Sverker women to swing the scourge, though never Helena Sverkersdotter. Although no one again hit them as hard as Helena had hit Cecilia Blanca, the constant beatings made their backs ache all the time.

It was Cecilia Blanca who, in the end, worked out a way to end this misery. Her ruse was based on her calculation that Mother

Rikissa's heart was as black and treacherous as one might guess from clapping eyes on the damned witch. It seemed reasonable to assume that she would not observe the iron rule of confidentiality and that she always tried to prise confessional secrets out of the Fathers who came to Godshome.

The Father Confessor who came most often was a young priest from Skara Cathedral. He heard the confessions of the worldly women as well. No one was allowed to see him, so he was ensconced behind a window opening into the cloisters but filled by a grid of wooden bars and covered by cloth. The woman sat outside in the passage.

One fine morning in early summer, Cecilia Blanca went to confession, feeling dizzy and almost feverish from sheer unease. Trifling with the sacrament of confession was a mortal sin.

'Father, forgive me for I have sinned,' she whispered so quickly that the words stumbled over each other. Then she drew a deep breath in anticipation of what was to come.

'My child, my dear daughter,' the priest said, and sighed on his side of the grid. 'Godshome is surely not a place where committing sins comes easily, but tell me anyway.'

'I have evil thoughts about my sisters here,' Cecilia Blanca said firmly. Now she had taken the leap into a sinful act. 'I cannot forgive them and even harbour thoughts of revenge.'

'Who has done things you cannot forgive, and what have they done?' the *vicarius* asked cautiously.

'The women of the Sverker kin and their hangers-on keep telling silly tales about me and my friend. When we're punished for whatever they've been accusing us of, one of them is picked to beat us with the scourge. Then I think, well . . . Father, forgive me, but I must tell you the way it is. I think that when I become Queen, I'll never be able to forgive them and not Mother Rikissa either. It's the truth. I can't help planning my revenge on them and how hard and cruel I'll be. I dream that their estates will burn one day and Godshome will be emptied of all its inhabitants. Not one stone will be left on top of another when I've finished with it.'

'Who is your friend?' the priest asked and now his voice seemed to tremble a little.

'Her name is Cecilia Algotsdotter, Father.'

'Ah, was she not betrothed into the Folkunga kin, to someone called Arn Magnusson?'

'Yes Father, that's my friend! She's very dear to Birger Brosa. My friend's tormented by everybody here, just the same as I am. I become overwhelmed by these unworthy, sinful feelings of revenge on her behalf too.'

'My daughter, for as long as you're at Godshome, you must follow the sacred rules of this house,' the priest said, in a voice he tried to make stern. It was obviously mixed with uncertainty, possibly fear, and Cecilia Blanca did not fail to notice this.

'I know, Father. I've been sinning and I'm seeking God's forgiveness,' Cecilia said in a low, modest voice. The priest saw as little of her as she of him and could not have guessed at the big smile that was spreading all over her face. He was slow to answer her, something she regarded as a good sign. Her medicine must be taking effect.

'Try to find some peace of mind, my daughter,' he said finally, but his voice sounded strained. 'You must accept what your life is offering you and everybody else here at Godshome. Consider your sinful impulses and understand that they are wrong. Say twenty Pater Nosters and forty Ave Marias and refrain from speaking to anybody else for a night and a day while you contemplate your sins with remorse. Have you understood what I have told you?'

'Yes, Father, I understand,' Cecilia Blanca said, biting her lower lip to stop herself from bursting out laughing.

'Then I forgive you in the name of the Father, the Son and the Holy Virgin Mary,' the priest said, sounding genuinely shaken.

Cecilia Blanca hurried along the cloisters, jubilant inside but with her head piously bowed. Cecilia Rosa was waiting, hidden behind the fountain in the *lavatorium*. When Cecilia Blanca got there, her face was flushed with excitement.

'That medicine should do a lot of good. I'm sure it worked, so help me God!' she whispered. She glanced around the empty *lavatorium* and then hugged her friend, as if they had been free women in the world outside the walls. The hug would have cost them dear if they had been seen.

'How can you be sure?' Cecilia Rosa asked, as she looked over her shoulder and anxiously pushed her friend away.

'My penance, that's how! Twenty Pater Nosters and forty Ave Marias, that's nothing. And just one whole day of silence – he was scared, don't you see? He'll run off and squeal to the old witch Rikissa. Now you've got to do the same thing.'

'I'm not sure I dare to . . .' Cecilia mumbled nervously. 'I can't threaten anything, I'm not going to be a queen and can't say I'll avenge myself. I . . . I'm sentenced to twenty years inside the walls, so what can I say?'

'Easy! Threaten with the Folkunga kin and Birger Brosa,' Cecilia Blanca whispered excitedly. 'I think something good's going on out there. Say you dream of the Folkunga vengeance for what you've had to endure.'

Cecilia Rosa envied her friend's courage. She had carried through a daring ploy that Cecilia Rosa would never even have imagined on her own. Now Cecilia Blanca had taken the risk on behalf of both of them and there was nothing else for it but to follow her example.

'Trust me, I'll do it,' she said. Then she crossed herself, pulled the hood low over her forehead and left the *lavatorium* rubbing her hands, as if she had just washed them at the fountain. Walking swiftly along the cloisters, she hesitated no longer, even though she was about to make a mockery of confession. She knew that friendship demanded that she do what they had agreed.

It was not clear to them which part of their plan had brought the results they soon saw. Although the blanket of silence stayed wrapped round the two Cecilias, for still no one in Godshome spoke to them, the open hatred disappeared from their companions' eyes. Now they were just glanced at surreptitiously, even fearfully. There was no more running along to tell tales, not even when they broke the rules of silence. They did this more and more often now and would wander along the cloisters, conversing freely as though they were outside.

It was a brief period of unexpected happiness, but marred by a creeping sense of insecurity. The people around them obviously knew and kept carefully to themselves quite a few things that the Cecilias could only guess at – things of importance, or the scourge would have been wielded on them both long ago.

Meanwhile, they had much joy of each other's company. They worked together at the looms, even though it was clear to everyone that Cecilia Blanca was far from a beginner and needed no help from Cecilia Rosa. Now that the winter was well and truly over, they worked with linen yarns under the supervision of Sister Leonore, who came from southern parts and had many ideas about dyes and patterns. The cloths she designed could not be used inside of course, but should sell well among ordinary people.

Sister Leonore was responsible for the Godshome gardens, both inside and outside the walls, and looked after all the roses along the cloisters. She taught the Cecilias how to care for a garden in the summer with regard to the characteristics of each type of plant, for instance by rationing the water correctly. They came to trust her more and more, for she had no friends anywhere in the Gothlands and no connections with any side in the battle.

Mother Rikissa allowed them to spend their time with Sister Leonore, because it meant that they were apart from their enemies even though they all still shared the same devotions. She stuck to one iron rule, though. They were not to go outside at all, except to walk between the gardens. When two of the sisters and all the *familiares* were allowed to go to the Midsummer's Market in Skara, the Cecilias were ordered to stay behind.

They were practically grinding their teeth with resentment and disgust at Mother Rikissa. At the same time, they realised that they were being kept in the dark. The others were aware of something significant they did not know.

Later that summer something happened that was as frightening as it was incomprehensible. Bengt, the Bishop of Skara, arrived in Godshome one afternoon, apparently in a great hurry. He immediately went to Mother Rikissa's rooms and the door was locked behind them. The Cecilias never found out what his errand was.

A group of armed riders was spotted only a few hours later. The cloister bells rang out a warning peal and the great gates were barred. The riders approached from the east and the Cecilias, alive with hope, ran upstairs to the dormitory to watch through its east-facing window. The colours of the riders' tunics, their banners and shields, ruined their joy at once, and Death's bony hand seemed to grip their hearts. These men all belonged to the enemy. Many of them had been bloodied and some must have been badly wounded, judging by the way they clung to their saddles. Others were unharmed but staring wildly ahead.

When they arrived at the closed gates, the leader started shouting a demand that the two Folkunga whores should be handed over. The two young women hanging half-way out of the dormitory window in order to hear as much as possible thought that they should kneel and pray for their lives immediately. Alternatively, they might as well hang on to hear as much as possible. Rosa wanted to start praying, Blanca definitely preferred listening. She pointed out that it made no sense for a small group of wounded men to try something as wild as stealing women out of a cloister. It was worth finding out more she said, and Rosa agreed. They stayed where they were and pricked up their ears.

After a while Bishop Bengt came out and the gate closed behind him. He spoke in such a low, dignified tone that the Cecilias missed some of the things he said. The message was clear enough though: disturbing the peace of a nunnery was an unforgivable sin and broke the absolute law protecting cloisters. They might just as soon cut down the Bishop himself. Then the tone of the exchange grew calmer and became too quiet for anything said to reach the dormitory window. At last the riders turned their horses slowly and unwillingly, and rode off southwards.

The two friends were quite overcome and sank to the floor, hugging each other tightly. They did not know whether they should pray to the Virgin Mary, offering up their thanks, or burst out laughing in relief. Cecilia Rosa prayed and Cecilia Blanca left her to it, while she herself thought hard about what had happened. Then she reached out, hugged Rosa even closer than before and kissed her on both cheeks, as if they had been outside together.

'Cecilia, beloved friend, my only friend in this dreadful place they've the gall to name Godshome,' she whispered and sounded wildly excited. 'I think we just saw a sign of our salvation!'

'But ... they were enemy soldiers, why do you speak of salvation?' Cecilia Rosa mumbled uncertainly. 'And they were trying to carry us off and if it hadn't been for the Bishop ... what's so good about that? What if they come back once our bishop friend has left?'

'They won't BE back! They were defeated, didn't you notice?'

'True, there were quite a few wounded ...'

'Of course! And who's inflicted these wounds, do you think?'

'Our men?!'

At the same time as she uttered this rather clueless answer to the simplistic question, Cecilia Rosa felt filled with pain and grief. She should have been joyous at the thought of a victory for the Erik and Folkunga armies, but it meant she would lose Cecilia Blanca. There were so many years ahead of her, all on her own.

A dark cloud of fear settled over Godshome that evening. Apart from Sister Leonore, who understood little if anything of what was going on, nobody dared look the two Cecilias in the eye. Mother Rikissa had withdrawn to her rooms and refused to see anyone until the following day. Bishop Bengt left in an even greater hurry than before. Once he had gone, the rigid order of work, song and prayer began to crumble. At evensong, the Cecilias sang together as never before, with not a single false note or break in the tempo on the part of Blanca. Rosa's voice rose more audaciously than usual, with almost worldly strength and subtlety of variation. Mother Rikissa was not there to snarl at her and no one else cared to admonish her for being jubilant.

Early the following morning a messenger from Skara rode in and was received by Mother Rikissa in the guesthouse. When he had gone, she locked herself in again after announcing that she would see no one until after prime, which would be followed by a Mass. Unusually, the Holy Communion would form part of the Mass, even though Whitsun was long gone and Christmas months away.

The Host had been blessed in the sacristy by some unknown priest from Skara and was handed out in the normal way, first to the sisters, then to the *conversae*, and last to the worldly maidens. When the sacred wine was carried in, the bells rang out to salute the miracle and the chalice was offered to each in turn by the Prioress, who also handed out a straw for each communicant to drink through.

When it was Cecilia Rosa's turn to drink God's blood, she did it with due piety and a sincere sense of gratitude for the fulfilment of their great hopes. Cecilia Blanca drank with an audible slurp, leaving precious little wine in the chalice. She seemed to be showing her contempt, if not for God, certainly for Godshome. The Cecilias never discussed the matter afterwards.

They were all so tense that they moved stiffly, like puppets, as they processed into the Chapter Hall. Mother Rikissa was waiting there, slumped in her great chair where she usually sat enthroned like an evil queen. The skin under her eyes was dark from lack of sleep.

The opening prayer was brief and so was the reading of the text, which was about mercy and charity. The choice made Cecilia Blanca wink cheerfully to her friend, because this made sense at this time, though mercy and charity certainly did not usually rank among Mother Rikissa's favourite subjects.

Afterwards a deep silence fell. Mother Rikissa broke it, speaking in a frail voice that was quite unlike her. She read out the names of brothers and sisters who now were walking over the flowering meadows of Paradise. Cecilia Rosa listened out for any names of Knights Templar, but there were none.

Silence. Mother Rikissa wrung her hands and, incredibly, looked close to tears, before managing to pull herself together enough to unroll a parchment scroll she had brought. Holding it open with trembling hands, she began speaking.

'In the name of the Father, the Son and the Holy Virgin Mary,' she said, rattling off the words in a dull tone. 'We must now pray for all the fallen, whether related or not, who are lying dead or mortally wounded on the blood-meadows, as these fields near Bjälbo will always be known.'

At the sound of the name Bjälbo, both Cecilias felt their hearts contract with dread. So there had been a battle near Bjälbo, which was the strongest fortress of the Folkunga kin and the home farm of Birger Brosa.

'There were many among the fallen, who . . .' Mother Rikissa had to steady herself before she could continue. 'Many fell in battle and among them were the Earls, by God's grace, Boleslav and Kol. So many of our kin followed the Earls into death that I cannot read out all the names. Now let us pray for the souls of the dead and mourn them for the week to come. We will sustain ourselves only with bread and water because our grief is great . . .'

Mother Rikissa stopped speaking. The hand holding the parchment sank into her lap. Someone in the Hall was sobbing aloud already.

Then Cecilia Blanca rose, holding her friend's hand and pulled her up too. This was daring but there was no uncertainty about her when she broke the rule of silence.

'Mother Rikissa, I beg your pardon, but Cecilia Algotsdotter and I must leave you to mourn your dead, since we cannot share your grief,' she said, without a hint of contempt or satisfaction in her voice. 'We will walk in the cloisters, pondering these events in our own way.'

This was an outrageous way to speak, but Mother Rikissa's only response was a feeble wave of her hand in acknowledgement. Cecilia Blanca took a few steps forward and made a worldly bow with a polite sweeping gesture with her hand. Her bearing was that of a queen, as she left the Hall hand-in-hand with her friend.

Well out in the cloisters, they ran swiftly on silent feet as far as they could get. Out of the mourners' earshot, they kissed each other most immodestly and then swung in circles, arms round each other's waists as if in a dance, all the way along the cloister.

Nothing needed saying. They knew enough. If Boleslav and Kol were dead, the war was over. If the Sverker forces had marched towards Bjälbo itself, then every Folkunga man would have gone into battle ready to fight to the death. Bjälbo meant everything to them.

Of course, if both the Sverker pretenders to the crown had fallen, most of their men must have died too. The great men always were the last to face death. If so, Knut Eriksson and Birger Brosa would have won a truly decisive victory. Some of the defeated army had clearly hoped to do themselves some good by taking the two Cecilias hostage.

The war was over and their side had won. As the two young women danced in the cloisters, this was all they could think of. Only later, it came back to both of them that the battle at the Bjälbo blood-meadows meant that they would soon be apart. Cecilia Blanca's hour of freedom would soon strike.

III

Armand de Gascogne, sergeant of the Knights Templar, did not lightly admit to fear or dread. This was not only because to feel fear would be against the Rules of the Order. It was also contrary to his idea of who he was and to his passionate desire to prove himself worthy of becoming a Knight Templar.

But when the tall walls of Jerusalem rose into his field of vision and he saw the centre of the world glowing in the rays of the setting sun, a deep, almost fearful sense of awe overwhelmed him. He shivered and the hairs on his arms prickled, although he was well covered and riding in the last warmth of the afternoon.

The whole long, hard day had been spent on horseback. Master Arn had only permitted one short break around noon. Otherwise they had stayed in the saddle, apart from the moments when they had to stop and adjust their awkward loads. The six dead men had stiffened into the most unlikely positions and, as the day grew hotter, the eager clouds of flies around the bodies had become larger.

Still, it wasn't the corpses that caused the real difficulties. Gradually, they could be bent and twisted to fit better. The big problem had been the robbers' loot from the cave, a quite sizeable haul ranging from Turkish weapons to Christian Communion vessels. They had found silk and brocade, jewellery and Frankish armour decorations, spurs made of silver or gold, and blue Egyptian – and other fine violet and bluish-green – stones that Armand could not name. There were small gold crucifixes attached to anything from hammered gold chains to straps of leather. The crucifixes bore witness to some twenty-odd faithful souls who by now must be in Paradise, peace be with them, because they had met a martyr's death on their way to or from the place where John the Baptist lowered Christ into the waters of Jordan.

During the day, Armand's tongue had swelled until it felt like a thick piece of leather in a mouth dry as the desert sand. Not that they had run out of water. With every step the horse took, Armand could hear the water slopping about inside the leather sack tied to his saddle. What stopped him from drinking was the Rule that said a Knight Templar must control himself and be prepared to endure what others would not. Anyway, a sergeant could not drink without his master's permission, just as he could not speak without being spoken to or stop unless ordered to do so.

Armand realised that Arn did not enjoy tormenting him and that his master was just as strict with himself. The harsh regime had surely to do with Armand's truthful reply that morning when Arn had asked if he wanted to be accepted into the Order and allowed to wear the white mantle. His master had nodded thoughtfully at his sergeant's answer, but had shown no emotion and ridden on without a word.

They had been on the move for eleven hours now, with only one brief rest, though they had stopped now and then to let the horses drink. The men never drank, although it was one of the hottest days of the year. During the last hour, Armand had observed how the horses' rump muscles shivered with fatigue at each new step. It had been a very hard day for the animals, but it seemed the Templar Rules applied to the horses, too. You never gave up. You obeyed orders. You endured.

As they finally approached the Lions' Gate in the city wall, a mist seemed to cover Armand's eyes and for a brief moment he had to grab hold of the saddle to stop himself from falling. He pulled himself together, helped by an awareness that something like a tumult had started when people spotted the two dusty riders with their strange baggage. He might also, mistakenly, have thought that he would soon get something to drink.

Most of the soldiers guarding the gate belonged to the King's regiment, but there was also a Knight Templar and his sergeant. One of the King's guards approached to grab hold of the bridle of Arn de Gothia's horse and inquire as to his business in the city, but the white-clad Templar knight placed his drawn sword in the soldier's way. At the same time he ordered the sergeant to drive the curious onlookers out of the way.

With a clear road ahead of them, Armand de Gascogne and his master rode unchallenged into the centre of the world. They belonged to God's sacred army and obeyed no king and no bishop, not even the King or Patriarch of Jerusalem – nobody except the

Holy Father in Rome. The Templar sergeant went ahead along the narrow cobbled streets that led towards the Temple and pushed away the people who came close to see the bodies. The Christians spat on the dead and the Muslims wanted to find out if they recognised anyone. The air was buzzing with languages; Armand recognised Armenian, Anatolian and Greek, but there were many more tongues that were strange to him.

At Templum Salomonis they rode down into the underground stables, which occupied the whole extent of the temple site. Templar sergeants guarded the arched entrance with its heavy wooden doors. Armand's master dismounted and handed the reins to one of the guards, who attended politely on him. After whispering something in the man's ear, Arn turned to Armand and in a hoarse voice ordered him to lead his horse in on foot.

Now a Templar knight had come hurrying along. The two knights bowed to each other and the whole caravan entered the huge stone arcades of the temple stables. At a table in a bay, green-liveried clerks recorded all comings and goings in ledgers. The knights conferred in low voices, out of earshot, and then ordered a couple of sergeants to start the unloading. This also meant showing the clerks every item and giving them time to describe them in writing. Arn signed to Armand to follow the two knights.

They walked through what seemed like endless stable arcades. Armand had been told that ten thousand horses could be kept here, though surely that wasn't true. On the other hand, it looked true enough that an arrow's flight-path had been used as the measure for both the length and breadth of the building. Everything was handsome, and very clean. There were no horse-droppings, or other muck or straw on the polished stone floors. The horses stood in long rows, dreaming or eating or being groomed and shoed by an army of stable-hands dressed in brown. Some sergeants and knights, wearing their distinctive black or white tunics, were working with their own horses. As they passed, Armand and Arn each bowed to members of their own rank, who punctiliously returned the greetings.

Armand was awed by this unimaginable display of military power and organisation. He had only visited Jerusalem once before, as a member of a group of recruits that had been taken to see the Holy Sepulchre. Of course he had heard rumours about the might of the Templar Order, but had never been inside the headquarters, and what he now saw was grander than anything he could have conceived of. These well trained and beautifully groomed horses of

Frankish, Arabic or Andalusian blood, would alone be worth enough to pay for a large army.

At the furthest end of the stables several steep spiral staircases wound their way upwards. Arn seemed to know this vast place like the back of his hand, and without asking anyone for directions he chose the fourth staircase. They walked up together, and in silence, in the dark of the stairwell. When they suddenly emerged into a large quadrangle filled with the evening light, Armand was almost blinded by the reflection of the sun in a large golden dome and a slightly smaller silver dome. His master stopped and pointed but said nothing. Armand crossed himself before taking a closer look at the holy sight. To his astonishment, he saw that the large dome was covered by rectangular tiles made of solid gold. The realisation that the entire roof was made of gold made him feel almost dizzy. He had always assumed that the builders had used ceramic tiles with a golden glaze.

His master still did not speak but, after a while, signed that they would set out again. The sergeant was conducted through a maze of buildings in every known style, arranged around hidden gardens with fountains. Some of the houses looked Frankish and some Saracen; some were covered in plain white lime-wash, others in blue, green and white Saracen tiles with very un-Christian patterns. Arn led the way towards a cluster of tiled facades crowned with small, while-roofed domes. They stopped in front of four identical wooden doors, painted plain white but for a red Templar cross, no bigger than a man's hand. Arn turned to look quizzically at his sergeant. Armand felt empty-headed and lost. He was obeying blindly, without the slightest notion of what it all meant, and was nearly crazed by thirst.

'Listen, my good sergeant,' Arn said. 'You must do what I tell you, nothing more or less. Go through this door. Behind it is a room, empty apart from a wooden seat. You ...'

Here he had to stop and clear his throat, for Arn's mouth was too dry to let him speak easily.

'You must take off all your clothes,' he continued. 'I mean *all*. Your tunic, chain-mail, hose, shoes – even the lambskin girdle which hides the impure part of a man's body. And more than that, the innermost lambskin pouch that you normally never remove. And the under-shirt under the chain-mail armour and the belt. You will be quite naked. Do you understand?'

'Yes, master. I understand,' Armand mumbled, and blushed. With his head bowed, he forced himself to speak in spite of his dry mouth.

'Master, you tell me to take all my clothes off, even though the Rule says . . .'

'Now you're in Jerusalem, the most sacred of all cities. The rules are different here.' Arn spoke sharply. 'Once you've undressed, you're to go into the next room. There are tiled pools full of water there, big enough for you to immerse your whole body. You will find oils and everything else you need to cleanse yourself. Which is what you must do. Clean every part of your body, your hair too. Understood?'

'Yes, master. But what about the Rule . . .?'

'So, while you're in that inner room you wash thoroughly,' Arn went on, more relaxed now and seemingly finding it easier to speak. 'Don't finish until darkness falls outside the windows. It's time to return to the outer room when you hear the muezzin, the man who recites the infidels' prayers, call out something about how Allah is great or whatever. You will find a new, clean set of sergeants' clothing waiting for you. Dress and come out to join me. I'll be waiting here. Understood?'

'Yes, master.'

'Good. Just one more thing, then. You will immerse yourself in water, lots of it. But you're not to drink a single drop. Obey!'

Armand was too amazed to think of a reply. In the next instant, his master had turned on his heel and taken one long step towards a nearby door. Just as he was about to disappear through it, he remembered something, smiled and stopped.

'Armand, please don't worry about whoever exchanges the clothes. They won't see you naked. They don't even know who you are and just do what they're told.'

Then Arn left his sergeant. The door closed firmly behind him. Armand stood stock still for a few moments, feeling his heart beating in his chest. The strange instructions had upset him. Then he pulled himself together and entered the first room. Just as his master had said, it was empty except for the wooden seat. Apart from the sky-blue wall tiles, everything was white. The floor was covered with plain white tiles and the ceiling lime-washed. The dome had little star-shaped openings.

He started by getting rid of his filthy mantle which, like his master, he had been carrying slung over his left arm. Undoing his sword-belt meant that he could remove the dirty and bloodstained tunic. So far, he did not hesitate, nor did he mind pulling off his chain-mail coat and hose, or the steel-clad shoes that were part of his body-armour.

Now he stood in his sweat-stinking undershirt and other under-garments. Suddenly he felt uneasy. Still, an order was an order. He bared the upper part of his body, hesitated again over the double layer of lambskin girding his lower parts, then shut his eyes and removed everything. When he was stark naked he did not open his eyes for a while. It was like being in a dream. He could not make up his mind if it was a good or a bad dream, but knew there was no turning back. He had to obey.

He pushed the door to the bathroom open with soldierly decisiveness, stepped inside, and stood with eyes shut for a few more moments. When he finally looked around, he was struck by how beautiful everything looked. The room had three arched windows, shaded by blinds made from wooden slats that allowed light to enter but prevented anyone from looking in. Outside were the domes and spires of Jerusalem. The sounds of the city could be heard in the distance. From closer by, the quiet of the summer evening was broken by the flapping noise of pigeons' wings.

Rather like the great church out there, decorative tiles in the blue, green and white Saracen patterns covered the walls. Slender, twisting pillars in white marble supported the arched ceiling. The square black and gold glazed floor tiles had been laid in a checkerboard pattern. Both on the left and right-hand sides of the room were steps leading down into water-filled basins, large and deep enough to hold two horses. Sets of silver bowls filled with differently coloured oils in pale shades were arrayed on two tables with mother-of-pearl inlays in the shapes of Arabic letters. Two small silver oil lamps were burning. Large white sheets of cloth, neatly folded, had been placed on almond-wood benches inlaid with red rosewood and the black wood from Africa called ebony.

Armand still felt very uneasy. He mumbled to himself that he must obey orders. Gingerly, he stepped into one of the basins, but regretted it and retreated quickly. The water was far too hot and wisps of steam could be seen rising from its surface. He left wet footprints on the golden floor as he walked across to the other basin, where the water turned out to be pleasantly cool. He immersed himself and just lay there, uncertain what to do next.

Then he started examining his naked body, surreptitiously at first. His hands were brown but from the wrists upwards and onwards, his skin was as white as the feathers of the gulls he remembered diving over the river back home in Gascony. The folds and hollows of his skin were outlined by dirt and dried sweat. He tried not to think of the Rule that forbade every kind of pleasure and felt he might try to float for a little while. It reminded him of swimming from the riverside below the fortress in Gascony. Life had been easy then, there were no clouds in the sky, and there was time to play in a world where war simply did not exist.

Impulsively, he dived under water but got water up his nose and emerged snorting in the middle of the basin. He tried swimming but hit the blue-tiled edge in one stroke. Then he pushed away with his feet, shot through the water and hit his head on the opposite edge because he had been silly enough to close his eyes. He whimpered but did not swear because there was a Rule against it. Suddenly he felt inexplicably happy. He scooped water up in his hands and splashed it in his face. Some went into his mouth, but he realised immediately what he had done and hurriedly spat it out. He tried to wipe away the last drop of water from his tongue with a finger, because he had been ordered not to drink.

Then he investigated the sweetly-coloured oils and smeared a little over the parts of the body that were not sinful to touch. He tried to find an oil that was right for his hair, and soon he had oiled himself all over. He stepped back into the cool water, washed his skin and his hair and his beard. When he had finished, he floated for a while, staring at the star-shaped apertures in the domed ceiling. He thought it was like the anteroom to Paradise.

Later, he changed to the hot-water basin, which had cooled down to a pleasantly warm temperature. It was like a part of his own body. He began washing the parts one must not touch and soon he found he was committing a sin. It was the first time for what seemed like years and he promised himself that he would confess immediately he got back to the city fortress called Gaza.

Then he lay quite still in the water for a long time, floating as if in a dream. He was in the anteroom of Paradise but, at the same time, far away in his childhood when the world was good and he played by the river in Gascogne.

Alarmed, he came to when he heard the shrill godless noise of the infidels screaming their prayers into the twilight over the city. He tumbled out of the water, feeling very guilty, and grabbed one of the white cloths to dry himself.

In the outer room, he realised that his old garments, even the felt protectors that he wore under his chain-mail, had all been taken away and replaced with new clothes that fitted him perfectly. His unknown brothers must know him very well. He dressed and went outside, his new black mantle draped over his arm.

His master was waiting. He had put on new clothes and had

fastened his mantle round his neck. The white mantle had a black border that showed his rank. Arn's beard was still damp, but like all the Templars, he had very short hair which dried quickly.

'Well, my good sergeant,' Arn said with an expressionless face. 'Did you find your bath agreeable?'

'I obeyed you in everything, master,' Armand said hesitantly. Suddenly he felt afraid that he had failed in some way and that Arn's blank face was a sign.

'My dear man, put on your mantle and follow me.' Arn slapped Armand's back with a little laugh. He wandered swiftly off along the corridor and Armand hurried after him, struggling to fasten his mantle at the same time and worrying about having broken some Rule or failing to understand a joke.

The two men wound their way through a vast network of corridors and stairs and courtyards and gardens with small fountains, past houses that looked like private homes, but Arn seemed utterly at home everywhere as he led the way to Templum Salomonis. They entered through a backdoor and suddenly emerged into a long hall. Its ceiling was very high and its floor covered with Saracens' carpets. At rows of pulpits green-clad clerks were busy entering the business proceedings of the Order into their ledgers and there were quite a few workers and tradesmen about in their brown clothes. Knights in their white mantles were everywhere, writing, reading or deep in conversation with visitors from many foreign lands. Arn led his sergeant past all this worldly business towards the most sacred part of the temple, the church itself. It was a domed rotunda floored with slabs of polished black and white marble forming star patterns and separated from the rest by white gates.

Furthest away under the dome stood the high altar in front of the crucifix. With water still dripping from their beards, they kneeled at the altar. Armand followed his master in everything. He received a whispered instruction to say ten Pater Nosters and add a special prayer of thanks to the Mother of God for bringing them back unharmed from their mission.

As Armand rattled off his Pater Nosters, a fiery thirst struck him with such force that he felt he might go mad or lose count of the number of prayers. Of the many men praying at different places in the church rotunda, none seemed to take any particular notice of them. Armand wondered vaguely why he and Arn alone were at the high altar but gave up. Everything was too new and strange, so he had better stop speculating and concentrate on praying for the right number of times.

'Armand, come with me,' Arn said, when they had finished and crossed themselves again in front of God's image. Off they went on another journey through labyrinthine passages, up a secret staircase, and along a huge corridor opening into another series of courtyards filled with lush greenery. A corridor so dark it was already lit by tar-torches, led them into a hall with lime-washed walls. This large space had clean, spare lines, free of any Saracen ornamentation. The only decorations on the walls were the banners of the Order and the knights' shields. The ceiling rose in tall arches, and the pillars of a cloister on one side reminded Armand of a monastery. He had no time to think more about the room, because next he found himself face to face with the Master of Jerusalem.

Arnoldo de Torroja, the Master of Jerusalem, was a tall, lean man with a severe face. His white mantle with two narrow black lines to show his rank was pulled back over the sword at his side.

'Do what I do,' Arn whispered to his sergeant.

They advanced towards the Master until they were the regulation six steps away, kneeled and bowed their heads.

'Master, Arn de Gothia and his sergeant Armand de Gascogne have returned from their mission,' Arn said briskly, his eyes fixed on the floor.

'Arn de Gothia and Commander of Gaza, can you assure me that you were successful?' the powerful leader of their order asked stiffly.

'We were, Brother Knight and Master of Jerusalem,' Arn replied in the same mannered style. 'We were pursuing six infidel highwaymen who had robbed both Christians and their own people. We ran them to ground and all six are now hanging from the city walls. Tomorrow their loot will be displayed at the Rock.'

The Master of Jerusalem looked at them in silence. Arn and Armand continued staring fixedly at the floor.

'You have washed, I trust, as our Rules for Jerusalem prescribe? And then prayed in Templum Salomonis to Our Lord and the Holy Mother of God, who is the protector of our Order?' the Master finally asked.

'Yes, Master of Jerusalem. That is why we now are ready to humbly request the only wage we have earned, a bowl of water,' Arn said in a loud, expressionless voice.

'Commander Arn de Gothia, Sergeant Armand de ... Gascogne, wasn't it? That's right, Gascony. Rise and embrace me,' the Master said.

Armand followed his master's example, rose quickly and when

his turn came, embraced the Master of Jerusalem. Unlike Arn, he was not kissed.

'Arn, this is truly good news. I knew it! I was sure you'd deal with these people!' the Master said and sounded completely different. The loud, doom-laden voice had gone and he was more like someone receiving friends to a feast.

Now two white-mantled knights came up to them, each carrying a large silver bowl full to the brim with cold water. With a bow, they handed Arn and Armand the bowls. Following his master's example, Armand drank deeply and carelessly so that water dribbled down over his tunic. Afterwards he found to his surprise that the knights were still in attendance and ready to take the bowls away. Armand had never been served by a knight before, but the man seemed to understand his confusion and nodded encouragingly. Armand handed him the bowl and they exchanged bows.

Now the Master of Jerusalem put his arm round Arn's shoulders and they walked along together, chatting as pleasantly as any men of the world, towards the far end of the hall where servants were laying a table. Armand dared to follow them after another helpful nod from the serving knight. The Master had arranged the seating so that he and Arn were together, then the two serving knights with Armand on their other side.

The table had been set with dishes of fresh cooked pork and smoked lamb, vegetables, white bread and olive oil. There was wine to drink as well as great silver bowls of cold water. Arn read a prayer in the language of the Church while the others sat quietly with bowed heads. When the praying was done, everyone ate and drank heartily. The Master and Arn were soon deep into very personal talk of old times, places and friends. These two powerful men seemed not only to know each other well but also to like each other, something that didn't always follow in the Order, Armand reflected. He kept watch on himself so that, unlike worldly men, he would show due moderation and not eat or drink any faster than his master.

He had suspected that the meal would be brief and it was. Suddenly the Master of Jerusalem wiped his knife clean and rose from the table. Immediately everyone else stopped eating and the servants began clearing the table. However, they left the Syrian glass beakers, the bowls of water and the wine in its clay carafes.

Arn read another prayer of gratitude for the food and the other gifts of the table.

'There, dear brothers, I'm sure it was well deserved,' the Master of

Jerusalem said when Arn had finished. Then he contentedly wiped his mouth with the back of his hand and turned to Armand.

'Now, we'd like an account of how you got on, young sergeant,' he said. 'My brother and dear friend Arn here has told me good things about you, but you should speak for yourself!'

The Master seemed friendly enough but Armand thought there was a searching look in the great man's eyes. This was surely one of their endless tests. He reckoned the most important thing was to be modest.

'There's little to be said, Master of Jerusalem,' Armand began slowly. 'I followed my master Arn and obeyed his orders. Our Lady was merciful and so we succeeded,' he mumbled. He kept his head bowed.

'Ah, yes. You take no personal pride in your exploits, just follow your master and do what you're told. If Our Lady is merciful that's all to the good. And so on and so forth,' the Master said in a rather heavily ironic voice. But Armand did not dare respond to the irony.

'Yes, Master of Jerusalem, that's the sum of it,' Armand replied shyly, still staring at the tabletop. He didn't look up until he heard the unmistakable sound of barely suppressed laughter from the far end of the table and saw that Arn was grinning broadly at him. It seemed almost rude and Armand could not think of anything he had said or done that made such serious matters cause all this amusement.

'Well, well, well,' the Master of Jerusalem said. 'You clearly have a set opinion of how sergeants should speak to higher-ranking brothers in the Order. Is it true, as my Brother Arn tells me, that you want to become a Knight Templar?'

'Yes,' Armand replied with sudden intensity. Now he could no longer stay modest. 'Master of Jerusalem, I'd give my life to . . .'

'Please don't,' the Master said and laughed outright. 'Dead, we've little use of you. Don't you worry, death will come soon enough anyway. You must remember one thing, though. If you're to become one of us, you must never lie to a brother. You realise, don't you, that once Brother Arn and I were young recruits just like you? We understand your dreams very well. Of course you're proud of this mission you're just back from! I'm told you did as well as any knight. Just don't forget always to speak the truth. Shame about too much pride is a good thing, but you can always confess sins of pride. Truth is simply more important!'

Now Armand's head drooped again and his cheeks were aflame. However kindly and humorous the Master had been, he had just delivered a telling-off. It didn't seem fair. After all, Armand had behaved very well by any standards.

'So, where were we?' the Master said with a rather false-sounding little sigh. 'Tell me, what happened, and how did you handle yourself in the fighting, young sergeant?'

'Master of Jerusalem . . .' Armand began. His thoughts were away in full flight, like a flock of disturbed birds. 'Well, we'd been after the robbers for over a week, studying their tactics and . . . we reckoned it'd be hard to catch them on the run, so we planned to meet them head on instead. It was just a matter of finding the right place . . .'

'I see,' the Master said helpfully when Armand lost his grip on what he was trying to say. 'You arrived at a good place in the end, did you?'

'Yes, we did.' Armand went on with more courage now, because it began to feel like producing an ordinary field report. 'They were chasing three Saracens up a wadi, hoping to trap their prey inside it. The robbers had done the same thing before, so we kept an eye on them from higher up and then moved down to meet them, master Arn first and me following behind him, as the Rules instruct. Master Arn signed to me what he was going to do – a feint to the left that would open up a good gap for me to push the lance in.'

'Were you afraid at all, at that moment maybe?' the Master asked with suspect gentleness.

'Master of Jerusalem!' Armand said in a loud indignant voice. Then he stopped. When he spoke again, he was much quieter. 'I admit . . . I was afraid then.'

He glanced round the table. None of the other men showed any particular reaction to a sergeant's confession of fear on the field of battle.

'I was afraid but determined to do what I should,' Armand resumed. 'We had been waiting for this opportunity for a long time and what mattered most was getting it right! That's how I felt,' he said, feeling now so awkward and uncertain that he almost stumbled over his words.

At this point Arn started gently thumping his glass beaker on the tabletop and the others joined him, first the Master of Jerusalem and then the two knights. They were all laughing but the laughter was kind and unchallenging.

'My dear young man, trials like this are commonplace in our Order, you know,' the Master said with a little smile. 'You've just got to put up with things like being made to confess to fear. Fear, now how about that? Listen, anyone who's not a *little* afraid at times is a fool and we've no use for fools. Arn, when are we meant to admit him?'

'Quite soon,' Arn replied. 'Very soon, actually, but I've yet to start the talks as set out in the Rules. I will, as soon as we're back in Gaza but . . .'

'Excellent,' the Master said, cutting Arn short and turning to Armand. 'I'll come for a visitation after the ceremony and be second only to Arn in giving you a kiss of welcome!'

The Master drank a toast to Armand and the knights joined in. Armand rose, his heart hammering in his chest, and saluted his four brothers. He was almost bursting with happiness.

'The trouble is, the situation is critical just now and it might be difficult to set aside the necessary three days for the ceremony,' Arn said soberly, just as the tone of their talk was about to become very cheerful. The others settled back to hear what Arn had in mind.

'As you know, we managed to extract three Saracens from a dangerous trap. Well, one of them was none other than Yussuf ibn Ayyub Salah al-Din,' Arn began brusquely and apparently taking no notice of the buzz of excitement round the table. 'We broke bread together and talked over our shared evening meal,' he continued calmly. 'The talk suggested to me that the war will soon engulf us.'

'Broke bread with Saladin, did you now?' the Master of Jerusalem said in a hard voice. 'Ate a meal in the company of the greatest enemy of Christianity? And then you let him go?'

'Yes, that's right,' Arn replied. 'There is much to tell you about this, but the easiest thing to explain is that I let him escape with his life. In the first place, we have agreed a cease-fire and in the second, I gave him my word.'

'You gave Saladin your word?' the Master asked. His eyes had narrowed but he sounded more astonished than anything else.

'Yes, I gave him my word, though that was before I knew who he was. But there are more important things to speak about.'

The Master of Jerusalem sat in silence for a few minutes. All the time he rubbed his chin with his clenched fist. Then Armand, who was staring at Arn with wide open eyes in utter terror at the thought of their Saracen companion, caught the Master's eye.

'My dear sergeant, it's time for you to leave us,' the Master ordered. 'Brother Richard Longsword here will take you for a short tour of our enclave and our part of the city. Afterwards he'll show you the sergeants' night quarters. God be with you! And I hope soon to have the pleasure of giving you that welcoming kiss.'

One of the knights got up immediately and gestured to show

Armand the direction to take. Armand rose and looked at Arn, but got a dismissive wave from the Master and realised he had to leave at once. The massive gate of wood and iron slammed behind them.

At first none of the three men at the table said anything. Arn broke the heavy silence.

'Who's to start speaking?' he asked, in the relaxed voice of someone talking to friends.

'I will,' the Master said. 'Now, you know Brother Guy, don't you? Same rank as you and our Armoury Commander here in Jerusalem. This matter concerns all three of us. First, why did you break bread with an archenemy?'

'Good question,' Arn replied lightly. 'But think about it: what would you have done? Our cease-fire may well be fragile – Saladin knew that as well as anyone – but the robbers were our targets, not peaceful travellers of whatever faith. I had given him the word of a Knight Templar and he gave me his in return. It was only later that I realised whom I had promised free passage. What would you have done?'

'If I had given my word, that would've been that, of course,' the Master of Jerusalem concurred. 'Surely you were working here in the house when Odo de Saint-Amand was around, weren't you?'

'That's right. Philip de Milly was the Grand Master at the time.'

'So he was. Anyway, you and Odo became good friends, didn't you?'

'Yes, we did. Still are.'

'And he's Grand Master now, which is all to the good. For one thing, it solves this problem about supping with the archenemy of Christianity. Some people might have got quite tense about that, you know.'

'Naturally. But what do you think?'

'I'm on your side; you're a Knight Templar, so you kept your word of honour. Besides, if I've understood you right, you learnt a thing or two, didn't you?'

'That's true. Like when the war might start. At the earliest two weeks, at the latest about two months from now. Or so I believe.'

'Tell us more! What do we know and what can we conclude?'

'Saladin was very well informed. He knew about the advance of Philip of Flanders towards Syria with his worldly army reinforced by the Hospitallers. He knew roughly where they were going, probably to Hama or Horns, but probably not threatening Damascus and Saladin himself. The interesting thing is that, knowing this, Saladin travels southwards, swiftly and without an escort, I think to

Al Arish. He said Cairo, but I don't believe him. Now, this is not because he's in a hurry to escape a Christian army marching down from the north. On the contrary, his aim is to attack us from the south precisely because he knows that a large part of our forces are engaged in the north. At least, that's my conclusion.'

The Master of Jerusalem glanced towards Brother Guy who nodded in response to the unspoken question. They all realised that the war was closing in. Saladin counted on his forces in the north being strong enough to prevent the enemy from going further south. If, at the same time, he could march northwards through Outremer with an Egyptian army, he might get a long way before he met any serious resistance, and might indeed reach Jerusalem. This was an appalling thought, but they must not shy away from it.

And if these conclusions were right, the first battle would be for the occupation of Gaza where Arn commanded the fortress. It was not particularly well defended, with its allocation of forty knights and two hundred and eighty sergeants. A decent-sized army with good equipment would take Gaza, no doubt about it. Unlike really strong fortresses such as Krak de Chevaliers and Beaufort, Gaza was vulnerable to siege, but it was unlikely that Saladin would stop there. Battering its walls down would be a bloody business. It would cost him more than he would gain in the end, because no one takes a place manned by the Knights Templar without the heaviest possible losses and it was, of course, pointless to take Knights prisoner. The whole thing would be a waste of time.

It stood to reason that Saladin would march past Gaza, although he might possibly leave a small siege contingent outside its walls. But what if his next goal was Ashkelon? After twenty-five years, returning Ashkelon to the fold would be a good move. Gaining it would be seen as a great Saracen victory and it could become a strong staging post on the coast north of Gaza. Also, it would cut off the defenders of Gaza from Jerusalem. When all was said and done, Ashkelon was a likely target for Saladin.

But then, if he met no serious resistance, what would stop him from going for Jerusalem itself? Nothing.

This was an uncomfortable conclusion but it could not be avoided. Saladin had recently united Syria and Egypt under one army general and one sultan, just as he had declared he would. The other oath he had sworn was to take command of the sacred city that the infidels called Al Quds. The time for decisions had come. First, the Grand Master Odo de Saint Amand, currently away in Acre, had to be informed. Brothers must be called up and sent to reinforce both

Jerusalem and Gaza. The King, a sad boy plagued by leprosy and surrounded by a scheming Court, must be informed. Messengers must be dispatched at once and at full speed.

Everything was decided quickly. Making great decisions is often easier than agreeing on minor changes. In the early hours of the morning Guy, the Armoury Commander, left the other two alone to finalise the plans.

Arnoldo de Torroja, the Master of Jerusalem, had stayed seated at the table until now. When the heavy door had finally closed behind Guy he rose slowly, beckoned Arn to follow him, and crossed the large empty floor of the hall to reach a side door into a cloister with a view of the entire city of Jerusalem. There they stayed for a while, leaning on the stone balustrade and looking out over the dark mass of houses. The warm summer wind carried the smells of the city, cooking odours laden with spices, rotting waste, perfumes and incense, excrement from camels and horses. It was a mixture reflecting that which God had made of human life: high and low, beautiful and ugly, appealing and disgusting.

'Arn, what would you have done? If you'd been Saladin, I mean. And please forgive the offensive comparison,' Arnoldo de Torroja finally asked.

'Don't ask for my forgiveness! Saladin is a magnificent enemy, you know that as well as anyone,' Arn replied. 'But I see what you're after, because both you and I would have acted differently in his position. Our strategy would have been to draw the enemy as far as possible into our territory. We would have tried to make him lose time by avoiding direct confrontation but harassed him with ambushes and little attacks by Turkish riders to disturb the men's sleep at night. We might have poisoned the wells and water holes along the route of his army and used other Saracen tactics too. And if it finally came to battle with a large Christian army, we would've waited until spring and then marched towards Jerusalem.'

'Saladin, whom we know well as an enemy, will surely do something completely different and unexpected,' Arnoldo de Torroja said. 'He might deliberately risk leaving Homs or Hama to their fate in order to gain something more desirable.'

'It would be a daring but logical plan,' Arn replied, appreciating his friend's line of thought.

'Indeed, yes. Still, thanks to your unusual ... intervention, or whatever it was – may God have mercy on you – at least we are better prepared. And that might make all the difference between holding and losing Jerusalem.'

'In which case I think God might just have mercy on me,' Arn said a little irritably. 'Why, the clergy might well start praising the Lord for sending His enemy right into my arms, because the Lord wanted to save Jerusalem!'

Arnoldo de Torroja was not used to having his subordinates snapping at him and turned in surprise to his young friend. But looking into Arn's eyes in the dark of the cloisters did not help. He could not interpret the other man's feelings.

'Arn, you're a friend of mine but don't trade on our friendship or it will cost you dear one day,' he said crossly. 'Odo won't be the Grand Master for ever, you know.'

'I trust that if Odo falls in battle you'd become Grand Master, and you're my friend, aren't you?' Arn said lightly, as if he had been talking about the weather.

The sheer cheek made Arnoldo de Torroja drop all pretence of being the stern leader of men and burst out laughing instead. It would all have seemed most improper to anyone watching them talking at this difficult moment for Jerusalem.

'Arn, you've been here since your first youth,' he said. 'You're practically one of us but there are times when you take liberties. Is this something Nordic or weren't you flogged enough as a lad?'

'I was flogged enough, Arnoldo,' Arn said calmly. 'Maybe we're rather too straightforward in the North, unlike these fussy Franks. But what a Knight Templar says and how he acts should surely be considered together?'

'I still don't hear anything sounding like reverence for your superiors, Arn. Watch it, my friend.'

'Just now I'd better watch Saladin. We'll take his first attack down in Gaza. How many new knights will you let me have?'

'Forty. No more but you will get another forty under your command.'

'That's eighty knights and less than three hundred sergeants against an army. I'm pretty sure Saladin won't move without something like five thousand Egyptians on horseback. I'll plan a reception for him as best I can, but just don't order me out to meet him lance against lance on a flat field!'

'Ah, you're afraid to die for a sacred cause, are you?' Arnoldo asked teasingly.

'Arnoldo, that's a cheap jibe!' Arn hissed angrily. 'It's dying for nothing in particular that I don't like. It happens far too often in Outremer when newcomers who fancy going to Paradise just run at the enemy and get killed before they've been of any use to anyone. It seems like blasphemy. Or just very stupid – so stupid it's a sin in its own right.'

'If you're breathless from dying too soon when you knock on the heavenly gate, you think you might get a nasty surprise, eh?'

'I do, you know. Though I wouldn't tell any Brother except my closest friends.'

'You're right there. Go to Gaza and manage as best you can. That's my only order to you.'

'Arnoldo, my friend, thank you. I'll obey to the last, as you know.'

'I do. We shouldn't have given you such a high post so early, you know. I'm glad for you, of course, but you're too good a fighting man to be stuck inside a fortress.'

'So . . . why did you?'

'Odo has been looking after you and seen to your advancement. I've done the same, in my modest way. The Gaza command seemed a good idea at the time, even if it was wasteful use of an outstanding horseman or turcopole, as they say in the order of St. John's.'

'Now the enemy may well be marching towards Gaza, of all places.'

'God's will must not be questioned. When do you go there?'

'At dawn. We've a lot of building to do in Gaza and very little time.'

The town of Gaza and its fortress was the southernmost Outremer possession of the Templar Knights. Their fortress had never had to endure a siege and any passing armies had always been their own men marching to war in Egypt. It seemed a sign of the changing times that Gaza was now under threat. The Christians had a new enemy that they feared more than any other, for all the terror and fire and military success of men such as Zenki and Nur al-Din. None of these older Saracen leaders could compare with the commander who had taken charge now: Saladin.

The young commander in Gaza was faced with the unaccustomed task of organising defence. Arn de Gothia had spent the last ten years in the field and fought hundreds of battles, but almost always as part of an attacking force. He had commanded groups of turcopoles, the Turkish cavalry mercenaries who travelled light on fast horses and specialised in harassing the enemy. Well directed, they could be used to hem in whole army units so that the heavier Frankish soldiery could move in and crush them. Arn had also ridden with the knights in armour who, in massed array, could land blows like an iron fist on the enemy cavalry. Sometimes he had been in the thick of battle. At other times he had been held in reserve on the sidelines, waiting to be deployed either in delivering the final, fatal attack or – worse – to provide a diversion by attacking the best of the enemy units in order to allow his own side to retreat in reasonable order. There had been sieges laid to the two fortresses he had served in previously, first as a sergeant in the Order's castle at Tortosa in County Tripoli, and later as a knight in Acre, and both had meant months of passive resistance followed by the retreat of the enemy forces.

The situation here and now in Gaza was different to anything he had experienced and he knew it was necessary to rethink from the beginning. The township of Gaza included some fifteen Palestinian villages and two Bedouin tribes. The commander in Gaza was the master of these people and could claim all they owned, including their lives. He controlled taxation, raising higher taxes in good years and keeping them low during bad times.

Gaza had done well this year, in spite of poor harvests elsewhere in Outremer. This added to the difficulty of persuading the villagers to allow their produce and animals to be taken away, even though the idea was to offer protection against plundering Egyptian soldiery. The farmers disliked very much being ordered about by hard-faced knights at the head of empty wagon-trains. It looked like plunder, whatever anyone said, and it made no difference to the Palestinian villagers whether they were robbed by Christians or Muslims.

Arn rode from village to village, indefatigably trying to explain and giving his word that this was neither taxation nor confiscation. Everything would be returned when the army they expected had marched away again. The enemy would go all the sooner, he told them, the less they found to loot.

When, to his surprise, he found that no one seemed to believe him much, he introduced a system of accountancy, handing out receipts once every single item had been noted down. It slowed the whole process, and if Saladin had attacked early the delays would have cost the people of Gaza dear. But there was time to gradually clear the countryside of food and animals. Everything was moved by long, noisy transports into the increasingly crowded city.

It was worth the trouble, the new commander reflected, since planning supply lines was by far the most important part of preparing for battle. Not that he admitted such subversive ideas to the knights from other fortresses, who came and went while he was waiting for his promised permanent reinforcement of forty knights.

The next most important stage was to complete defensive building works, especially the widening of moats and the strengthening of the city walls. It would only become necessary to take everyone into the fortress itself if those first lines of defence were broken. He inspected the building sites daily, where all his sergeants and every able-bodied man in the Order's employment, including clerks and customs men, worked all day and even in torch-light at night.

Saladin took his time. No one understood why he delayed, especially since Arn's Bedouin spies had located the army in Sinai, near Al Arish and just one full day's march from Gaza. It might have something to do with what was happening in far-away Syria. The Saracens had a near-miraculous ability to find out what was going on anywhere in the country. The Gaza Bedouins believed that the Saracens knew how to get birds to carry messages, but that seemed incredible to the Christians, who relied on smoke signals from fortress to fortress, but Gaza was too far south to be part of the system.

Arn's spies had reported that Saladin's army was large, an estimated ten thousand men, and that most of them were Mamelukes on horseback. This was extremely alarming, for such an army would be almost unbeatable on the field of battle. Still, it was possible that the information was exaggerated, since bad news meant better tasks and better pay for the spies than when there was nothing very serious to report.

When a month had passed without any attack, the atmosphere in Gaza grew calmer. Most of what could be done had been completed and, besides, the aftermath of clearing the countryside kept everyone busy. The farmers stood in long, irritable queues outside the produce magazines. They wanted some of their crops and animals back, but couldn't read the clerks' entries on the receipts and stirred up endless arguments. The young commander came to speak to the queuing men, listened to their complaints, and tried to sort out errors and misunderstandings. He wanted everyone to have what his family needed for a week. Should the enemy arrive, they were to bring everything edible with them into the city so that nothing but empty stores and barns met the invaders. Slowly, people began to believe him. This was not confiscation but a sensible precaution against looting and famine.

There were those, including his own armourer Brother Bertrand, who thought Arn spent far too much time negotiating with peasants, but the commander did not give an inch. A promise from a Knight Templar could not be reneged on.

During this calm before the expected storm, Arn finally gave himself time to think about his 'sergeant in preparation', as Armand de Gascogne had become from the moment the Master of Jerusalem agreed to his knighthood. Instead of preparing himself, Armand had found himself working as a stonemason on the city walls, but now he was called in and ordered to wash and put on new clothes. His commander would see him after the midday meal. He felt happier than he had for some time. Maybe his initiation into the Order had not been forgotten after all.

The commander's *parlatorium* in the western part of the fortress had two large, arched windows facing the sea. Armand found his master was looking tired; his eyes were bloodshot but he was in a thoughtful, gentle mood. The beautifully proportioned room with its white, plain walls was lit by slanting beams of afternoon sunlight. It was simply furnished and dominated by a large table, which was covered by documents and maps. A door between the windows led to a balcony.

When Armand entered, the knight's white mantle lay carelessly thrown over a chair, but Arn immediately put it on with practised hands. Only then did he return Armand's salute with a slight bow.

'Armand, you've been digging for weeks. You must be feeling more like a mole than a sergeant in preparation, don't you?'

Arn's tone was joking, which put Armand on his guard at once. The high-ranking brothers had a habit of sounding particularly amiable when they planted verbal traps for you.

'Yes, we've done a lot of digging, but it has to be,' Armand replied cautiously.

Arn looked at him searchingly without showing what he thought about the answer, then his face became very grave. He gestured Armand to a chair and then cleared a corner of the table for himself to sit on. Leaning on his right hand, he bent towards his sergeant.

'First, there are some questions and answers that will be quickly dealt with,' he said briskly. 'You must of course answer truthfully. If your answers are acceptable, there will be no formal obstacle to your joining the Order. If not, it may be that you'll never become one of us. Have you prepared yourself by saying the prayers that our Rules prescribe?'

'Yes, master,' Armand replied. Then he swallowed nervously.

'Are you married or betrothed to a woman? Can any woman claim you?'

'No, master. You see, I was the third son and . . .'

'I see. You need only answer Yes or No. Next. Are you born by a married woman and conceived by parents wed in the sight of God?'

'Yes, master.'

'Is your father or your uncle or your paternal grandfather a knight?'

'My father is a Baron in Gascony.'

'Excellent. Do you owe money or property to any worldly person or persons, or to any brother or sergeant in our Order?'

'No, master. Indeed, sir. How could I possibly owe a brother or . . . ?'

'That's enough.' Arn raised a hand to stop him. 'Just reply, don't argue. And don't question!'

'Master, forgive me.'

'Is your body sound and intact? I know the answer, of course, but the Rules state that I must ask.'

'Yes, master.'

'Have you paid anyone, in gold or silver or any other currency, to gain favour within the Templar Order? This is a very serious question. The crime it refers to is called simony. If it is discovered at any time, your white mantle will be taken from you at once. The Rules say that we might as well know sooner rather than later. What do you answer?'

'No, master.'

'Are you prepared to live in chastity, poverty and obedience?'

'Yes, master.'

'Are you prepared to swear by God and the Holy Virgin Mary that you will, always and in any circumstances, do your utmost to live according to the traditions and customs of the Knights Templar?'

'Yes, master.'

Are you prepared to swear by God and the Holy Virgin Mary that you will never leave our Order, whether at its times of weakness or strength, that you will never betray us or, indeed, never leave except by the express permission of the Grand Master?'

'Yes, master.'

Arn seemed to have run out of questions and sat silent and thoughtful for a while, as if already lost in other concerns. Then he suddenly smiled, leapt off the corner of the table and embraced Armand. He kissed his sergeant on the forehead and on both cheeks before addressing him again.

'This procedure has to follow what the Rules state, from paragraph 669 onwards, and the instructions are now known to you.

You have my permission to go and read the Rules again, ask the chaplain to let you see it. Anyway, let's go outside on the balcony!'

'Actually, all that was part of the preparation,' Arn explained, sounding a little tired now. 'You'll be asked the same questions at the initiation ceremony but more as a formality. We know what you'll say already, of course. This question-and-answer session was decisive. I can tell you now, you'll be a knight as soon as I can arrange it. From now on, you'll be wearing a white ribbon round your right arm.'

Armand was swept away by a wave of happiness and was lost for words.

'We've a war to win first,' Arn mused. 'Not an easy task, as you know. If we die, well that's it. If not, then we'll hold that initiation ceremony for you. Arnoldo de Torroja and I will lead it. Right. Does this make you happy?'

'Yes, master.'

'I confess I wasn't very happy when I was accepted. It had to do with the first question, the one about women.'

Arn made this earth-shattering confession absentmindedly. Armand had no idea what to say. Maybe he wasn't meant to say anything.

They stood together for a while, watching the hard work of unloading two cargo ships which had arrived earlier that day. Then Arn seemed to come back to reality from his reveries.

'I have decided to make you our *confanonier* for the time ahead,' he said. 'I needn't tell you what an honour it is to carry the banners of the temple and the fortress at a time of war.'

'But mustn't it be ... a knight? A sergeant can't ...' Armand stammered, overwhelmed.

'That's true, it's usually a knight, but then you would have been one if the war hadn't got in the way. This is my decision and nobody else's. Our current *confanonier* has suffered quite severe injuries, and I visited him in the sickbay to talk to him about you. Come, let's go back inside. Tell me what you think about the war.'

They settled down and Armand tried to express his opinions about the war. A long siege would be bad, but probably endurable. He was convinced that riding out would be a disaster. Barely four hundred men against maybe seven or eight thousand Mameluke riders might well be brave, but very foolish.

Arn nodded in apparent agreement. Then he said, in what sounded like an aside, that were Saladin's army to pass Gaza on its way towards Jerusalem then questions of what was brave or foolish or wise would become immaterial. Only one course of action would be left – they would have to fight and put their trust in a miraculous intervention by the Lord.

A long and bloody siege was the best they could hope for, because only then could they help to save Jerusalem, the paramount task of any Knight Templar. A siege then, with all its horrors.

Two days later Armand de Gascogne rode with a squadron of horsemen, fifteen knights and one sergeant in tight formation, led by the commander himself. It was Armand's first day as *confanonier*. They were travelling south towards Al Arish.

According to the Bedouin spies, Saladin's army was on the move but in two wings, one following the coast northwards and the other swinging eastwards in a circular course to Sinai. The intention behind this strategy was obscure and the information needed checking.

At first they rode along the coastline, which gave them a wide field of vision towards the southwest. Later, when Arn felt they might end up behind the enemy's lines, he ordered a change of direction. Now they climbed into the inland mountain ranges to their east to reach the route caravans took when seasonal storms made the coastal road unsafe.

Once arrived on the caravan route, they changed course again in order to follow the high ridges and in that way keep a long view over the road below. Then, as they emerged from behind a huge rock outcrop that hid the road, they encountered the enemy.

Each side discovered the other at the same time and was equally taken by surprise. From their vantage point on the hillside, the knights saw an army of horsemen, four abreast, filling the road for as far as the eye could see.

Arn lifted his right hand to indicate regrouping into attack formation with all sixteen riders in line facing the enemy. His men obeyed instantly, but many looked concerned and anxious. Down the slope from them were at least two thousand Egyptian riders, their yellow uniforms and banners glowing like gold in the sunlight. They were all Mamelukes, the best horsemen and soldiers on the Saracen side.

Just after the knights on the hill had taken up an attacking position, the valley filled with the sound of shouted orders and the noise of horses' hooves on the stony road. Longbow-men on horseback were moved into the first line facing the knights.

Arn silently watched the enemy. He was hopelessly outnumbered and had no intention of giving the order to attack. It would only lead to the loss of sixteen good men with minimal returns. On the other hand, fleeing did not appeal either.

Meanwhile, the Mameluke commander also seemed to be hesitating. From his position down on the road, he saw a small group of men who would be easy to deal with. On the other hand, these were the unbelievers' most fearsome riders, the ones with the red cross on their shields and they just stayed up there, watching calmly. Having noticed the commander's banner held by Armand, the Mamelukes must have suspected a trap with the sixteen visible armed men as bait and a much larger army – maybe five or six thousand knights – ready and waiting somewhere out of sight.

The mere thought of being downhill to an attack from thousands of armoured Frankish horsemen was enough to put the fear of death into any Saracen. Soon new orders echoed between the hillsides and the Egyptian army was ordered into retreat by its officers, who also sent fast riders fanning out into the mountains to locate the position of the enemy's main force.

Arn had immediately ordered an about turn, a new close formation, and the little troop disappeared in a slow trot out of sight of their bemused enemies.

As soon as they could no longer be seen, Arn issued a new order: return to Gaza at top speed and by the shortest route.

As they came closer to the town the road filled up with refugees travelling away from plunder and towards safety. In the eastern distance plars of black smoke rose towards the sky. Soon Gaza would be packed with people in full flight from the advancing army.

Finally, the war had come.

IV

Finally, the war was over. Cecilia Rosa and Cecilia Blanca had a long lesson teaching them that the end of war is not the same as a peaceful, orderly state of affairs and wars do not end at a stroke. The last men to fall in the field do not herald the end of all conflict, and peace does not mean that life at once becomes calm and plentiful, not even on the winning side.

One night, well into the second month after the bloody battle outside Bjälbo, when the first storm of the autumn tore at the windows and wooden slats on the roofs of Godshome, five riders arrived and hurriedly took away five of the Sverker *familiares*. The whispers said that they were fleeing to Denmark, where they hoped to be taken in by relatives. Not long afterwards, three young women from the defeated side arrived at Godshome, seeking some peace and safety away from Erik and Folkunga rule.

Their arrival brought news of the world outside. The last of the new Sverker girls told the story of Knut Eriksson, spoken of now as the King, riding into Linköping itself with his earl, Birger Brosa, at his side. The city had sworn allegiance to King Knut, confirming that he could dictate the conditions of peace.

The two Cecilias were delighted. Now Cecilia Blanca's betrothed was King and the dearly loved uncle of Cecilia Rosa's betrothed was his Earl. The worldly power was concentrated in their hands. Still, a large black cloud of uncertainty remained for as long as King Knut did not come to claim his Cecilia.

But then, nothing was certain in the world of men. A betrothal could be annulled, either because the man's side had won or because it had lost. When men fought for power, nothing else mattered. A marriage could mean alliances for either the winning or the losing families, and usually the only sure thing was that the brides-to-be were the last to know.

Cecilia Blanca agonised about the future constantly and so remained in a humble, anxious mood. The good thing was that she did not antagonise any of the unhappy sisters. Cecilia Rosa also carefully avoided being scornful or triumphant.

Their restraint and gentleness helped to heal wounded souls in Godshome. Mother Rikissa, who was a great deal more astute than the two Cecilias gave her credit for, realised the need for calming her charges and made a series of decisions. She changed the rules for the conversations held in *claustrum lectionis*, the collection of stone benches in the north part of the cloisters. In the past the conversational fare for the *familiares* had consisted of readings and rote-learning from the few books of worldly wisdom kept in Godshome, rounded off by improving talks about sins and their punishments. Now Mother Rikissa asked Mistress Helena Stenkilsdotter to speak several times during the last months of the summer on the subject of worldly power games and, in particular, on the role of women.

Mistress Helena was very well qualified, and not only because she was of royal blood and very wealthy. She had seen out five previous kings, had had three husbands and lived through many wars. What she didn't know about women and power would probably not be worth knowing.

Her first rule was that women must stick together, in so far as it was at all possible.

In the first place, women trying to keep up with the men's shifting allegiances when it came to choosing their own friends, would soon enough be left alone in life with enemies all around. Being triumphant when a sister's family suffered a defeat was plain silly, because your own family might be struck down soon enough. Though it was very pleasing to be on the victorious side, it was correspondingly wretched to share the fate of the losers. Anyone who had as long a life as she – and this she wished all her listeners – had gone through the cycle of black despair and delighted elation many times.

It was worth thinking about how many pointless wars would be prevented if women only had the sense to support each other. Conversely, how much evil wasn't caused by women hating each other for no particular reason?

Initially, Mistress Helena's tone had been cautious, but in the third talk she threw discretion to the winds and spoke plainly. So plainly that the young listeners were duly horrified at first and then started thinking for themselves – so fast that their heads seemed to be buzzing.

'Let's play with what is possible,' she began. 'One obvious possibility is that Cecilia Ulvsdotter will become King Knut's Queen. Another is that Helena Sverkersdotter will soon get wed to one of the former King's Danish relatives. Now, would either one or both of you want war? What might be the future consequences of the few short years at Godshome when you hated each other's guts? Alternatively, what if you were friends instead? I can tell you what kind of difference it makes – it's the difference between life and death for your relatives and many others too.'

She paused to catch her breath and change position, peering all the while at her audience with her small, bloodshot eyes. Everyone sat stock still, not even glancing at each other to show what they felt. Cecilia Blanca herself appeared unmoved but she was thinking that, for one thing, she'd like to pay back Helena Sverkersdotter's whipping, three-fold at the very least.

'I must say, you all look like silly little geese to me,' Mistress Helena went on. 'You're surely thinking that I'm preaching the usual Gospel, more or less, telling you to be just and peaceable, turn the other cheek and show forgiveness, abhor anger and pride, and all the rest of the good instructions the dear sisters here at Godshome are trying to bang into your empty heads. But no, it's not that simple, my dear young friends and sisters. You see, you believe that you have no power of your own and that the important decisions are only made at the point of a sword. Wrong and wrong again. You're badly mistaken on both counts and so you keep trotting off in this direction and that, like a flock of geese in the farmyard. Calm down. No sensible, decent man – and the Holy Virgin knows that I wish you all wise and fair-minded husbands – will fail to listen to his wife, the woman he has chosen to be the mother of his children and keeper of the keys to his house. At your age, you still think that a wife's power affects only little things and that the only way she can exert influence is by shedding a few pretty tears or tugging a man's beard and giving him a cuddle. Little girls' wiles like these are sure to get round the most cross-grained of fathers and make them suddenly buy you that lovely little brown pony. But as grown-up women you mustn't believe you're still sweet little fools, and you'll anyway find that such tactics are not enough. Indeed not. Set out to shape things your own way, using your strong and free will just as the Scriptures bid you. Use it well. Like men, you must take responsibility for life and death, for peace and war. It would be sinful to back away from these decisions.'

Then Mistress Helena indicated that she was tired. Her runny eyes were signs of poor eyesight, so two sisters helped her back to her house outside the walls. She left her young listeners alive and hot with the excitement of new thoughts.

Mother Rikissa sensed a new conciliatory atmosphere growing stronger and acted both swiftly and wisely.

Four young women had arrived from Linköping and only one of them had any experience at all of nunneries. They were in mourning over family members who had died, and were badly frightened. They all cried themselves to sleep most nights and clung to each other during the days, going everywhere together like orphaned ducklings who fear a pike lurking among the reeds.

But it might be possible to turn their suffering into something that was good, thus making a virtue of necessity, thought Mother Rikissa grimly. First, because none of the newcomers knew their sign language, she ordered that the rule of silence would be lifted in Godshome, for the immediate future at least. Because the hard-working sisters were already carrying enough responsibility, the two Cecilias would teach the young ladies the cloister rules and its sign language, and also some singing and crafts, especially spinning and weaving.

Cecilia Blanca and Rosa were called to attend on Mother Rikissa in the Chapter Hall. The instructions they received were amazing. Suddenly they could speak when they wished, and were given almost unimaginable freedom to decide their own working day. True, they would be forced to spend their time with members of the Sverker tribe, and Cecilia Blanca for one wanted as little to do with them as possible. Admittedly, there was no longer a requirement to hate them individually because of their appalling families, but even so it was odd being with them. Cecilia Rosa pointed out that if the Bjälbo battle had ended otherwise, everything would have been against them both and, besides, they simply had to obey.

The air was heavy with embarrassment when the six young women met for the first time in the cloisters after the midday rest. Since no one could think of anything much to say, Cecilia Rosa, who knew the order of hymns exactly, decided that they might as well practise singing. She knew what was due at the *nones* in three hours time and sang the hymns one by one. The others practised with her until everyone could make a good account of themselves.

The cloisters grew cold and draughty in the late afternoon and Cecilia Blanca went to get permission to teach sign language in the Chapter Hall. The group spent a few hours in there, working on the basics of Godshome's secret language: *yes* and *no*, *bless you* and *thank you* and *may Virgin Mary protect you*, and of course *come here, go there* and *watch, sister is watching*.

The two novice teachers realised that they had to teach by easy stages and decided to spend some time in the weaving sheds before sext. The *conversae* reluctantly moved over to let them have a couple of looms to themselves and as they got on with the work they started joking and laughing together.

It turned out that Ulvhilde Emundsdotter, the youngest and smallest of the new girls, already knew a lot about weaving. No one had realised it, perhaps because she had said very little since she arrived in Godshome. Now she was eager to tell them what she had learnt, especially about a new way to mix wool and linen yarn to make a cloth that was as warm but much softer than pure wool. It was perfect for both men's and women's mantles, which were of course needed for everyday use in good families as well as for religious and worldly ceremonies.

At this point the talk faded and they all felt rather shy of each again, for the mantles were red in the families of four of the girls and blue in the families of two.

Not long after this incident, Cecilia Rosa realised that little Ulvhilde seemed to be trailing her, not like a hostile spy but anxiously, as if there was something she hardly dared to express. By now the two Cecilias had divided up the teaching, apart from the sign language tuition which they did together. Cecilia Rosa gave singing lessons and Cecilia Blanca taught weaving. To be alone with Ulvhilde, Cecilia Rosa simply ended the singing lesson a little earlier one day and asked Ulvhilde to stay behind. The other girls left so swiftly and discreetly it seemed they already knew what was up.

'Ulvhilde, you must speak frankly about what is on your mind . . .' Cecilia Rosa began in the authoritative tones of an abbess. Then she felt silly and started again. 'Ulvhilde, I've had a feeling you wanted to talk to me face to face. That's right, isn't it?'

'Yes, dear Cecilia Rosa,' the girl replied, clearly fighting to keep her tears back.

'What's the matter?' Cecilia asked uncertainly. She sensed impending doom.

The answer did not come for a while and they were both unable to break the silence.

'You may not know that Emund Ulvbane was my father, may his soul rest in peace,' Ulvhilde finally whispered, her eyes fixed on the limestone pavement of the cloisters.

'I don't know anyone called Emund Ulvbane,' was Cecilia Rosa's cowardly reply. She regretted it at once.

'I think you do. Arn Magnusson, your betrothed, met my father in hand-to-hand fighting and what went between the two of them is common knowledge all over West and East Gothland. My father lost the fight and his sword hand.'

'Yes of course, I do know of the battle at Axevalla Thing,' Cecilia Rosa admitted. 'Everybody does, just as you say. But Arn wasn't even betrothed to me at the time, I wasn't there and had nothing whatever to do with it. Neither did you, so why bring it up? Do you feel it forms a barrier between us?'

'Much, much worse than that,' Ulvhilde said, weeping openly now. 'Knut Eriksson killed my father at Forsevik. And that was after he'd promised to let father go unharmed and follow my mother and my brothers. And then, at the blood-meadows . . .'

Ulvhilde could not speak for tears and bent over as if pierced by a sudden pain. Her older companion felt at a loss, but hugged the weeping girl and caressed her cheeks gently.

'There, there,' she said. 'You have to tell me this, if only because it is a good thing to let bad thoughts out. Tell me about what happened on the blood-meadows. I truly have no idea.'

Ulvhilde fought her grief, catching her breath to speak.

'At the blood-meadows both my brothers died, slain by Folkunga men . . . and then a band of armed men went to my mother's farm . . . she was there. They burnt it down, with everyone still inside, my mother and her people and the farm animals and everybody!'

Ulvhilde's wild grief spread to Cecilia, who felt it as a chill spreading through her body. They kept hugging each other, but couldn't think of anything more to say at first. Then Cecilia Rosa, rocking Ulvhilde like a tired baby, said the only thing she thought right.

'My dear, dear friend, just remember that I could have been suffering as you do if your side had won.' She whispered hoarsely. 'We are both innocent and I shall do everything I can to comfort you. I'll always support you and be your friend. Living in Godshome isn't easy and believe you me, here you need friends more than anything else.'

Helena Stenkilsdotter fought death for ten days. During all this time she was mostly quite lucid. This complicated things for Mother Rikissa, who had to send messages far and wide.

Mistress Helena could not be given the same burial ceremony as the rest of the pensioners at Godshome. In normal peacetime her funeral would have been splendid, with a large following, because she was of royal blood and had married into the kins of both Sverker and Erik. Now, when the Bjälbo wounds were still raw, only a small, determined group turned up. Almost all the clan groups of guests arrived in good time before the death and were forced to find lodgings, either in the *hospitium* or in houses outside the cloister.

The two Cecilias were the only *familiares* who were allowed to sing in the cemetery and that had nothing to do with family ties and everything to do with their lovely voices. Bishop Bengt of Skara, in his light blue, gold-embroidered Episcopal hood, had come to read over the grave. He was left standing alone, clinging to his staff, in the empty space between the hostile groups. Members of Sverker and Stenkil kin in mantles of red, black and green were on one side and on the other, their old enemies wearing sky-blue, the Erik mantles decorated in gold thread and those of the Folkunga in silver. Outside the cemetery wall, two long rows of lances had been driven into the ground, a shield fastened to each one. Some shields showed the impact of sword and lance, just as some of the mantles were torn and bloodied, for the weather and wind had not yet had time to blur the marks of war. The emblems on the shields were clear enough: the Folkunga lion, the three Erik crowns, the black Sverker griffin and the Stenkil wolf's head.

The Cecilias sang with real dedication, for they had come to respect and trust Mistress Helena during the short time they had known her. When the singing was over and the great lady's coffin lowered into the black soil, there was no question that they or the sisters would be allowed to stay outside the walls. Funeral meats would be served in the *hospitium* but, apart from the worldly guests, only Mother Rikissa and Bishop Bengt were to attend. The occasion was likely to be tense, for the guests would come face to face more than they seemed likely to bear easily.

The hostility and distrust among the guests became clear when Bishop Bengt and his Canon began moving, seemingly to start the slow procession to the *hospitium* in the northern corner of God-shome. The Erik kin started off first, but the Sverker people noticed this and hurried on to at least get in front of the Folkunga.

The two Cecilias had been slow to leave because they wanted to watch the colourful, theatrical crowd. Mother Rikissa discovered this and walked over to tell them off in no uncertain terms. It was entirely unbecoming for Christian maidens to hang about and stare. They were to get packing at once and go inside the walls.

Then Cecilia Blanca replied, in tones so mild she amazed herself, that she had been thinking about something that would be good for both the peace and Godshome. So many of the guests had worn and stained mantles and Godshome was well placed to do something about this.

At first Mother Rikissa looked as if she was about to lose her temper instantly in her usual way, but then she seemed to change her mind and turned to look at the long procession of hard-faced men and women.

'Even a blind hen can find the odd grain,' she said, thoughtfully and not at all unkindly. Then she pushed the two young women along as though she were herding geese.

Mother Rikissa had so far kept two serious problems to herself. One was linked to a coming great event, as unavoidable as one season following another and promising a big change, at least for Cecilia Blanca. The other was rooted in the finances of Godshome and very much harder to understand.

Even though only one human generation had passed since the chapel at Godshome had been blessed and the first sisters moved in, the cloister was wealthy. The problem was that the wealth was in endowments of land, which had to be turned into food and drink, clothes and buildings. The produce of the land holdings arrived from near and far: packs of dried fish and barrels of salted fish and grain and beer, bales of woollen yarn, sacks of flour and fruit. Although a proportion was kept for use in Godshome, most of the goods were carted off to marketplaces, especially the large Skara market, to be sold in return for silver coins. The silver was needed mainly to pay the wages of the many foreign artisans working on the building projects of the cloister. When the turnover was less than brisk, and that was becoming more and more common, the resources of silver dwindled quickly.

This troubled Mother Rikissa a great deal. The *yconomus*, one of Bishop Bengt's junior clergy with poor grasp of theology but a good head for business, always seemed able to produce smart answers to Mother Rikissa's questions, however thoroughly she tried to prepare herself. If the cereal harvest had been good, there was a glut on the grain market and a bad year for sales; if it had been a bad harvest, the idea was to hold back in anticipation of rising prices. And, of course, it was important to spread trade over the whole year and not

84

sell all at once. Every autumn the stores were filling to bursting-point and every summer they stood empty. *Yconomus* said that this was the proper procedure.

Once or twice, Mother Rikissa had tried to speak of these matters to Father Henri, her opposite number at Varnhem monastery and her senior, for Godshome sorted under Varnhem. Father Henri was not much help. Running a cloister with men or with women made a difference, he said, looking concerned. At Varnhem, much silver arrived as direct income from works. Varnhem had twenty-odd stone quarries, mainly producing millstones, with smithies making every kind of implement as well as noblemen's swords and other weaponry. Then again, most of the building was carried out by lay brothers and naturally not paid for in silver. Godshome, Father Henri concluded, needed to start manufacturing products to sell.

This had seemed easier said than done, but now that Mother Rikissa had taken in Cecilia Blanca's observation about the guests' worn mantles, she had an idea that she would always think of as her own. Woollen and linen cloths were made at Godshome, step by laborious step, from wool and flax. Sister Leonore, the gardening sister, was skilled in dyeing cloth, although other than black, none of her rich colours was of any use inside the cloister.

Mother Rikissa felt that her mood heralded a new dawn. After the funeral meats had been eaten, and that was as quickly as any meal shared by victors and vanquished, she came out carrying two selected mantles, one red and one blue, both worn and carelessly mended.

All this new work would surely bring hope for Godshome. Mother Rikissa also saw it as important for a reason other than shortage of coin, and this concern she confided in no one. She was running out of time for her attempt to calm hostilities between her worldly charges.

The worldly maidens bore most of the responsibility for this new task. This suited Mother Rikissa in many ways. The obvious advantage was that, as autumn drew nearer, the heavy labour of harvesting would fill every day for the lay sisters, leaving little time or strength for other tasks. Besides, these women all came from simple families and lacked understanding of the traditional use of clan colours for ceremonies, feasts and visits to church or market-place. Usually they were surplus females in families too poor to find the wherewithal for a decent dowry and were sent to a nunnery to work for their living rather than growing old at home. Mother Rikissa, who harboured a poorly concealed contempt for such humble origins, was convinced that you had to know from your own experience about proper mantles – like most of the blessed sisters, the *familiares* and the two Cecilias – to be of any use for her new scheme.

It soon became obvious that the project was alive with problems, and just getting the new cloth right would take many trials. Still, the endless snags only seemed to stimulate the women, who hurried to work each day with almost vulgar eagerness. Walking past the weaving room, Mother Rikissa would now and then hear them chattering and giggling in a most ungodly way. She disapproved, but left them to it for the time being. Once the great event had come and gone, there would be time enough to reinstate order.

Ulvhilde Emundsdotter had persuaded everybody that her idea of a wool-and-linen cloth was worth following up. It should work, because linen alone was too floppy and thin for mantles while, on the other hand, woollen mantles were too heavy and fell clumsily over shoulders and thighs. They quickly realised that the proportions of the materials and quality of the yarns were crucial. Dealing with things like fluff from wool spun too loosely, or hardness in linen thread too tensely spun, also meant much experimentation.

Dyeing the material also turned out to be problematic. Sister Leonore was struggling with her mixtures of herbal extracts and going through endless test pieces of cloth. Red was easier than blue, but they agreed that beetroot gave too bright a purple and St John's Wort a shade that had too much brown in it and anyway was too pale. Mixing alder root with St John's Wort darkened the colour, and after some more trials a true, bright red emerged from one of Sister Leonore's many earthenware jugs.

So it was that they worked long hours without having made one single new mantle. Worse still, they had to find answers to what the mantles would be lined with and where the skins were coming from. The best – the winter coats of squirrel, marten and fox – were also the most difficult and expensive to buy. Instead of bringing in silver, the new project looked like costing a great deal. Mother Rikissa ordered *yconomus* to go to Skara market for the skins, and if that failed to travel on to Linköping. He whined about the cost, complaining that it was excessive to spend that much good silver when the time was so long between the expenditure and any possible profit. Mother Rikissa, who had her own reservations but wasn't going to let on to such a low-ranking man, pointed out that silver didn't multiply if left piling up in the chests. *Yconomus* sounded sour when he replied that the likelihood of profit and loss should be assessed before rushing into a new venture.

Mother Rikissa might have taken his protestations more seriously if only the times ahead for Godshome had looked calmer. These days, it was even more important to keep the *familiares* happy than to hoard silver in the treasury chests.

One clear, quiet autumn day, the first sign of the coming great event arrived at Godshome in the form of a convoy of ox-drawn carriages. The men started unloading the laden vehicles and setting up a tented camp outside the walls. No one seemed to question this, even though the goods were unusual, to say the least. Apart from the tents and wooden tent-props, there were animal carcasses that had to be hung in the cool rooms, roasting spits, and barrels of beer and mead and wine from Varnhem. The language of the men was most improper, especially when used inside the cloister.

The air in the weaving room was buzzing with speculation. These days, the Cecilias and the Sverker women spent much more time than strictly required in what was now solemnly known as the *vestiarium*. Surely the reason for this sudden outburst of activity must be that one of them was going to be taken away to be married? These were clearly preparations for some kind of festivity and a wedding feast seemed the likeliest. The idea caused much excitement, but it was mixed with dread. Who would it be and what kind of deal had been struck? The risk of ending up with some drooling, lecherous old man from Skara or Linköping was just as horrid a threat to everyone, and the girls fantasised as if there was no enmity at all between them. By now they were speaking of each other as 'red' or 'blue' and had, half in jest, started wearing a red or a blue piece of yarn tied round one arm. Regardless of kin, anyone might have to bed some man who'd done the new King a good turn in exchange for a virgin bride. The more they talked round the possibilities, the more upset they became. A new life outside the walls sounded wonderful, but what if . . .? The political per-mutations were endless: a man from the victorious side might pick one of the Cecilias but then, so might someone from the losing side. Maybe a winner had wanted to consolidate his good fortune by marrying into a Sverker family? Or maybe a loser had decided to stick with his own kind.

This kind of talk made Cecilia Rosa feel as if an iron hand was clutching at her heart. She broke out in a cold sweat and felt so breathless that she had to go out and walk round the cloisters,

87

breathing the chilly air in deep, spasmodic gasps. What could she do if they'd decided to marry her off? She and her beloved Arn had sworn to be true to each other, but such promises mattered little to those who were negotiating settlements to end a war. Her promises, her will and her love were of no account to men in power.

Then she recalled that it was the Holy Roman Church itself which had condemned her to twenty years of penance and that no worldly power could change this. It was strange that she should feel comforted by the harshness of her sentence, but at least no one could demand to marry her against her will.

'Arn, I'll love you always. May the Holy Mother of God always protect you wherever you are, fighting the infidels in the Holy Land,' she whispered. Then she immediately prayed to the Holy Virgin, assuring Her that, although she'd been overwhelmed by her worldly love, she loved God's Sacred Mother best of all. She added three Ave Marias and, restored to her usual calm, went to join the others.

Although it should have been a time for rest, there was a great commotion after the midday meal and thanksgiving the next day. Messengers hammered on the gate and sisters ran back and forth. Mother Rikissa came out of the chapel wringing her hands in distress and called on everybody to join a procession. Once lined up in the right order, they walked slowly through the great gate under the carving of Adam and Eve, processed round the walls three times, and finally came to a halt outside the southeastern wall. To everyone's surprise, the worldly maidens had to join the blessed sisters to form a group on their own.

They were facing the tented camp, which was being hurriedly tidied by the brown-clad working men. After having removed all waste and arranged a row of poles with pennants on top, the men lined up and stood to quiet attention.

It was a beautiful clear day, with no premonition of the hard winter to come. Only a gentle breeze was stirring the canopies of the trees in their full autumn colour.

Gradually, all the women looked southwards. At first they could only see flashes of light, which turned out to be the reflections of the sun in a forest of raised lances. A large contingent of riders was advancing towards Godshome and as they came closer, everyone could see the dominant blue of their mantles.

'They're wearing our colours. They are our men,' Cecilia Blanca whispered excitedly to Cecilia Rosa, but was immediately silenced by a stern glance from Mother Rikissa.

The riders were coming closer and the emblems on their shields became visible. The leaders all had either three crowns or the rampant Folkunga lion on a blue background, but behind them were shields carried by men in mantles that were green or red or black with gold trim, and behind them rode yet others in colours belonging to less important families.

As they approached, it was clear for all to see that one of the three leaders wore no helmet, and the sun was gleaming in a golden crown. Later, the spectators spotted another one among the three also wearing a crown, but a smaller one than the first.

When they were less than an arrow shot's length away, everyone was able to recognise the three leaders. First rode Archbishop Stéphan on a slow-stepping fat, brown horse. It was well known that prelates as they grew older tended to become very cautious riders and the Archbishop's mount was a nice old mare with thoughtful eyes.

Knut Eriksson followed, on a lively black stallion. His crown was that of a king. Next to him rode his earl, Birger Brosa, with the smaller crown of the king's commander-in-chief on his head.

Mother Rikissa's back was so straight that she looked almost impertinently haughty, but as the riders came close enough for greetings to be exchanged, she kneeled as she must, confronted by this combination of worldly and religious power. Behind her, the sisters, the *conversae* and the *familiares* also sank to their knees. When all the women were kneeling with their eyes fixed to the ground, the waiting rows of men followed suit. King Knut Eriksson had arrived at Godshome on his first royal progress round his realm.

The three first riders stopped only a few paces away from Mother Rikissa, who kept staring at the ground in front of her. The Archbishop, making heavy weather of dismounting, had to pull his disordered clothing into place before reaching out his right hand to Mother Rikissa. She kissed it humbly and he gave her permission to stand. As she rose, so did everyone else, still in complete silence.

Now King Knut, like the young warrior that he was, leapt easily off his horse. Then, without looking over his shoulder, he raised his right hand and immediately a man came galloping along from the back and handed over a blue mantle with three crowns embroidered in gold thread and lined in black and white martens' skins. It was a mantle like the King's own, fit only for royalty.

King Knut draped the mantle over his left arm and walked slowly towards the group of worldly maidens. Everyone was still and silent, every eye following him. Without saying a word, he went and stood behind Cecilia Blanca, raising the mantle with straight arms so that everyone could see it, and then wrapped it round her. He took her hand, and with a queen's mantle over her shoulders, Cecilia Blanca was led towards the royal tent. Four banners with the Erik emblem flew from poles in front of the tent. Cecilia Rosa had time to be annoyed that she had not noticed the banners being raised, and then to become more irritated still because she was thinking about such pointless things.

When King Knut had wanted to lead his betrothed away, Cecilia Blanca had been holding Cecilia Rosa's hand. They had reached for each other the moment they recognised Knut Eriksson. The woman who would soon be crowned Queen of all Sviars and Goths would not let go of her dearest friend at once, and turned to kiss her on both cheeks.

A cloud seemed to darken the King's face, but he brightened up again when he saw who it was. Then they walked together towards the royal tent, watched by the silent crowd.

Once they were inside, there was a great outbreak of noise as the armed men dismounted and led their horses away to the meadows where bales of hay and water troughs were waiting. The Archbishop turned to Mother Rikissa, blessed her, and then dismissed her with a wave of his hand as if swatting a fly before walking off in the direction of the royal tent.

Mother Rikissa clapped her hands as a sign that everyone was to return to the cloister. Back there, the women would not be stopped from talking, no matter how strict the rules might be. Even the blessed sisters were chatting away, almost as loudly as the worldly maidens. Mother Rikissa had to be as hard as only she could be in order to get everyone to process with dignity and in due silence into the chapel.

She watched thoughtfully as Cecilia Rosa sang, with more strength than usual, although tears were streaming down her cheeks. That young woman was dangerous now. Everything had worked out just as badly as Mother Rikissa had feared in her worst moments.

Cecilia Rosa was thinking that everything had worked out as well as she could ever have hoped, but also feared. Her dear sweet friend would become queen – that much was clear to all. It was a great joy, but meant that she would be left alone for many hard years to come. The grief this caused had to be balanced against her joy for her friend, and as yet she could not decide which was the more powerful feeling.

Inside the cloister walls the rest of the day followed its prescribed order, even though it was different from all other days. The arrival of the King and his following had been news to everyone except Mother Rikissa, who had received many messages about it weeks ago but kept it all to herself. She had not even told Cecilia Blanca, to whom the King had sent his special greetings. Cecilia Blanca could well have become impossible to control if these greetings had been delivered. She was perfectly capable of causing any amount of disorder among the worldly young women and was better left in ignorance for as long as possible.

The King's progress had been different from the established route. He travelled from Jönköping towards Eriksberg, his own and his father's birthplace. King Erik was now known as Saint Erik almost everywhere and the Erik kin had built a church at Eriksberg, decorating it with the finest murals known in West Gothland. This passage through the heartland of the Erik kin had been the most pleasurable part of Knut's journey.

Inside Godshome, the events outside reached the women only as noises and aromas. The coming and going came across as sounds of rattling armour and horses' hooves, while the cooking smells told them that meat was roasting on many spits. Working in the *vestiarium*, they fantasised about the busy world outside, but despite all the chatter there was always a distance between Cecilia Rosa and everyone else. Now she was the only one with a length of blue yarn round her arm. Alone among Sverker kinswomen, some of the old hostility towards her seemed to come creeping back, though mixed with due caution. She might have been left on her own but she was still the dearest friend of the queen-to-be.

After vespers, Mother Rikissa was to join the feast outside and she wisely refrained from sharing the refectory supper of lentil soup and black rye bread. However, the Prioress had hardly time to read the prayer of thanks before Mother Rikissa returned, spreading fear all around because her face had gone white with barely restrained fury. Through clenched teeth, she ordered Cecilia Rosa to come along at once. She was obviously going to be punished for something unimaginable, possibly even sent off into the *carcer*.

But as Cecilia Rosa walked with her eyes fixed on the floor behind Mother Rikissa, she was filled with hope rather than fear. Sure enough, her Abbess was not taking her to the *carcer*, but towards the gate leading to the *hospitium*. Jolly voices and the other sounds of feasting came from inside.

The *hospitium* was too small to hold any more than the most honoured guests and in the tents outside the smithy and the stables, the working men were drinking beer and eating meat. At the oak table inside were the King himself, Earl Birger Brosa, Archbishop Stéphan, Bishop Bengt of Skara and four more men, whom Cecilia Rosa didn't think she could recognise. At the short end of the table opposite the King, sat Cecilia Blanca in her blue, ermine-lined mantle embroidered with three golden crowns.

Entering the room, Mother Rikissa pushed Cecilia Rosa brusquely in front of her, grabbed her neck and made her curtsey, as if she'd never have thought of it herself. Knut Eriksson lifted his eyebrows at this and stared angrily at Mother Rikissa, who pretended not to notice.

Then the King raised his right hand, at once silencing all talk in the room.

'Cecilia Algotsdotter, we wish you welcome to our feast here at Godshome,' he said, looking at Cecilia Rosa with friendly eyes. Looking less friendly, he turned to Mother Rikissa although he was still addressing Cecilia Rosa.

'It is the wish of my betrothed lady that you should join us. She also wants Mother Rikissa to be here, should it be my pleasure to invite her.'

He gestured towards the still empty seats near Cecilia Blanca and Mother Rikissa at once grabbed Cecilia Rosa's arm in a hard grip and marched her along as if she had been unable to walk on her own. As she took her seat, the Abbess reached out for the blue length of yarn round Cecilia's arm and ripped it off. The she returned to her own place at the other end of the table.

Mother Rikissa's contemptuous treatment of the blue colour had not escaped anyone in the room and an awkward silence fell. Under the table, the two Cecilias held hands to comfort each other. The King's anger was clear to all.

'Mother Rikissa, you must feel uneasy about being with us tonight, given this aversion of yours to blue yarn?' he said with a politeness made suspect by his gesturing towards the door at the same time.

'Here at Godshome we've got our own rules, which not even kings can change,' Mother Rikissa replied brusquely. 'Our maidens must not wear the colours of their kin.' She was looking pleased with herself, as if she felt telling the King what's what in her nunnery would silence him.

But Earl Birger Brosa had got to his feet, and banged his fist on the tabletop so hard that the tankards jumped. Everyone crouched instinctively in their seats. The quiet was that of the interval between a flash of lightning and a rumble of thunder. The Earl pointed at Mother Rikissa but spoke in a more restrained voice than anyone had expected.

'Mother Rikissa, you must remember that we Folkunga have our rules too,' he began. 'Cecilia Algotsdotter is a dear friend and betrothed to someone still more dear both to the King and to myself. It is true that she has been sentenced to serve long and hard in penance for a sin most of us have committed without being punished at all. Be that as it may, I want you to know that in my view she is one of us!'

He had been raising his voice towards the end and, when he finished, he walked with determined steps along the table until he was standing behind the two Cecilias. Taking off his mantle, while keeping a steely eye fixed on Mother Rikissa, he placed it slowly and almost tenderly over Cecilia Rosa's shoulders. He glanced at the King who nodded briefly. Then he walked back and sat down heavily, after having raised his tankard to the two Cecilias.

For quite a while afterwards, the conversation was slow and halting. The cooks came in carrying new supplies of beer as well as dish after dish of venison, pork, sweet vegetables and white bread, but the guests only took as much food as they felt politeness demanded and ate hesitantly.

The two Cecilias were bursting with eagerness to talk about everything that had happened but had to behave themselves. In such a sombre atmosphere women's chatter would have been out of order. Instead they sat quietly, their eyes modestly fixed on the table and picking decorously at their food. After endless months of refectory meals, they would actually have liked to devour everything at once.

The cooks had provided Archbishop Stéphan with a special dish of mutton and cabbage and, unlike the others, he drank only wine. The great prelate had completely ignored the heated exchange between Mother Rikissa and the Earl in favour of the worldly pleasures of the table. Now he lifted his glass to examine the colour of the wine, than raised it to his lips, inhaled its scent and rolled his eyes.

'Ah, *mon Dieu*, it's like being back home in Burgundy again,' he sighed, after having drunk deep. 'This wine certainly wasn't harmed by its long journey. Which reminds me ... as it were ... your Majesty, how are your dealings with the Lübeck merchants progressing?'

Just as the Archbishop had planned, although appearing to think of nothing in particular, Knut Eriksson enjoyed being asked and his face lit up with enthusiasm. This business was close to his heart.

At that very time Eskil Magnusson, Birger Brosa's nephew and Arn's brother, was acting as the King's chief negotiator in Lübeck. Soon a treaty would be signed, sealed and delivered, forging a link between Knut Eriksson and none other than Henry, the Lion of Saxony. It would mean that for the first time the Gothlands could trade across the Baltic Sea and as many goods as possible would be switched to the routes linking East Gothland with Lübeck. The merchants of that great city had generously reassured their new partners that ships would be provided, should there be any shortages of cargo space. From the Lübeck side, there was particular interest in a new product, dried fish from Norway. Eskil Magnusson, who had discovered its potential, was already buying up large quantities and transporting the fish from the shores of Norway, across Lake Vänern, then by river and smaller lake systems to Lake Vättern, and then on to the East Gothland harbours. There were of course other goods to sell, such as iron from Sviarland, and furs, butter, cured herring and salmon. But then there was much to trade these things against, not least solid silver.

Soon, all the men were happily and noisily engaged in talk about what the link with Lübeck would mean. The general feeling was that trade was all to the good and would open up new and excellent prospects. Many voiced their conviction that horses bite when the manger is empty and, conversely, everyone would become more peaceable and content with plenty of silver in circulation and plenty of goods in the markets.

Beer was being served at an increasing rate and the noise was reaching the level you would expect from a great feast. At last the two Cecilias could start speaking cautiously between themselves, hoping that no one could hear what was being said at the far end of the table.

Cecilia Blanca began by explaining how Knut had sent messages long ago, saying that he would arrive in Godshome on this very day to bring her a queen's mantle. In other words, Mother Rikissa had known this all the time but was too wicked to tell. Obviously, that woman's only pleasure was to torment the people around her.

Cecilia Rosa quietly said that surely the happiness was all the greater now the waiting and worrying had at last come to an end. And then, imagine how hard it would have been to keep counting the days and months, fearing that there might be a sudden change of plan after all.

They did not get much further than this before the conversation about the wealth that trading with Lübeck would bring was getting repetitive and Bishop Bengt decided to start on a new tack. He thought that his own contribution sounded suitably modest as he said that he had been fearing for his own life and praying to God for courage, when he had realised the danger to the two Cecilias from the would-be hostage takers. God had heard him and aided him in his instant resolution to rescue the two young women from becoming victims of the worst of crimes, robbing a house of God. He rambled on, telling his story in the most pointless detail.

The Cecilias couldn't chat while the Bishop was holding forth, talking about them as well as – mostly – himself. They lowered their eyes becomingly and conversed in sign language under the table instead.

True enough, he sent some clodhoppers packing – so what's so brave about that? Cecilia Rosa signed.

It would've been brave if the Sverker lot had won on the blood-meadows, Cecilia Blanca replied. *Then his life would really have been at risk.*

It seems his courage amounted to not risking his life, Cecilia Rosa commented, causing both of them to giggle discreetly.

King Knut, who was not yet too drunk, kept a sharp eye on everyone and spotted their amusement. He asked them loudly if Bishop Bengt's story was not quite true as told.

'Yes, of course, true in every detail,' Cecilia Blanca replied without the least hesitation. 'Armed strangers turned up demanding that we should be handed over in language so coarse I cannot repeat it here. Cecilia Algotsdotter and I could've been forced to leave the protection of Godshome if Bishop Bengt hadn't stepped forward and so sternly admonished the soldiery that they rode off at once.'

There was a short pause while all the assembled men pondered the angelic words pronounced by the King's betrothed lady. The King said that this act must be rewarded and the Bishop assured him that nothing of the sort was in his mind. Being at peace with his conscience and having done his duty as bidden by Our Lord was more than enough for him. Were the Church to gain in any way, well then, that was a different matter. Such gifts were always gratifying to the servants of Our Lord and caused much pleasure in Heaven.

The general talk started up again and Cecilia Rosa asked in sign language why the lying Bishop had been let off the hook quite so easily. Cecilia Blanca replied that it would have been unwise for the queen-to-be to antagonise a Bishop of the realm by shaming him in front of other men. The king would be told the truth soon enough. By now their signing had begun to slip up over the edge of the table and they suddenly realised that Mother Rikissa was watching them with far from kindly eyes. Maybe she'd understood what they had been telling each other.

Birger Brosa preferred to stay quiet at feasts, watching and listening. He too had been observing them. He was sitting back easily with a contented smile on his face, as always, carelessly resting his tankard on one knee. Now he suddenly leant forward and put the tankard down on the table hard enough to make the talk die down. Everyone knew that this was the Earl's habit when he had something to say and when Birger Brosa spoke, everyone – including the King – listened.

'This seems as good a time as any,' he said thoughtfully, 'to consider what we can do for Godshome, now that we're all here and also have heard of Bishop Bengt's heroic deed. Rikissa, you must surely have ideas of your own?'

The Earl was well known to expect direct answers to his questions and all eyes turned to Mother Rikissa. She thought carefully before speaking.

'Cloisters always receive gifts of land,' she said. 'Godshome too will get more as time goes by. Just now we need skins more than anything else, the best grey squirrel furs and also the winter coats of foxes and martens.'

She was looking quite pleased with herself, because she knew exactly how amazed everyone would be by her choice.

'Requesting gifts of the winter coats of squirrel and marten suggest that worldly temptations have entered the lives of yourself and your sisters, but this cannot be the case, surely Rikissa?' Birger Brosa asked pleasantly, with a bigger smile than usual.

'Of course not,' Mother Rikissa snapped. 'But as you gentlemen are boasting of how well you manage affairs, it's worth your recalling that the servants of the Lord also need to trade these days. Noticing the worn and soiled mantles most of you and your men are wearing, I've seen to it that in Godshome we'll manufacture better, finer mantles than you've ever seen. They have to be paid for in silver, so the trade should profit Godshome in the long run. We women can't quarry stone, after all.'

Her answer was surprising but everyone murmured sympathetically. After all their talk of trade, there was nothing for it except to try looking wise and register approval of Rikissa's hard-headed approach.

'What would be the colour of the mantles you plan to provide?' Birger Brosa asked, his still pleasant tone barely hiding the sly intent of his question.

'Dear Earl, need you ask?' Mother Rikissa replied, with as much pretence at surprise in her voice as Brosa's had held mock innocence. 'Why, red embroidered with black griffins, naturally ... and blue, with three golden crowns ... or with a golden lion, such as you usually wear, I believe. And so on.'

Birger Brosa stared at her for a moment and then burst out laughing. A moment later Knut Eriksson joined in and soon all the men were laughing heartily.

'Mother Rikissa, you don't only have a sharp mind but also your own way with words,' Knut Eriksson said after drinking a mouthful of beer. 'The furs you request will arrive at Godshome soon, we promise you this,' he continued. 'Anything else, while we're still in a good mood and eager to do clever deals?'

'Well, my King, there's indeed something else,' Mother Rikissa answered, uncertainly at first. 'If we could use gold and silver thread for the embroidery, maybe buying it from the Lübeck merchants, the finish of the emblems would be much improved. Cecilia Blanca and Cecilia Rosa can confirm this. They're both most accomplished in all these new skills.'

Everyone looked at the two Cecilias, who shyly agreed that Mother Rikissa was right and that such rich embroidery would enhance the mantles a great deal. The King gave his word that there would be thread from Lübeck as well as plenty of fine furs arriving at Godshome. He added that not only did this seem a more useful thing than endowing land but also that there would be gains all round. His own coronation would benefit, because the ceremony would look all the better with kinsfolk turning up wearing Godshome mantles.

Soon afterwards Mother Rikissa rose and said that her duties called but that she was deeply grateful for the fine fare and the royal promises. The King and the Earl nodded as signs that she had permission to leave, but she stopped and stared sternly at Cecilia Rosa. When Knut Eriksson noticed this silent demand, he looked at his betrothed and she shook her head quickly in response. He took his cue at once.

'We bid you goodnight, Mother Rikissa,' he said. 'And you need not concern yourself with Cecilia Algotsdotter. Our decision is that she's to spend the night with my betrothed so that no one can ever say that Knut shared a room, let alone a bed, with his wife-to-be.'

Mother Rikissa froze. Apparently she couldn't quite believe her ears and so make up her mind about whether to leave quietly or stand her ground.

'We all know, only too well, what appalling consequences can ensue if a Cecilia isn't kept properly apart from her betrothed until the wedding feast,' Birger Brosa amiably pointed out from his corner. 'I'm sure, Rikissa, that you'd find it most gratifying to keep *both* Cecilias in the austere service of the Lord for twenty years, but I've a feeling our King would be less than pleased.'

As always, Birger Brosa was smiling but his words were oozing poison. Mother Rikissa was a combative woman and by now her eyes were flashing with anger. The King intervened before any unforgivably hard words were exchanged.

'We're sure you can sleep in peace tonight, Rikissa,' he said. 'Trust that what we've decided has got the blessing of your Archbishop. Isn't that so, my dear Stéphan?'

'*Comment*? Ah, now ... *naturellement* ... indeed, *ma chère Mère Rikissa*, it's just as His Majesty has said, nothing serious, just a minor matter ...'

Then the Archbishop turned his attention to his third helping of mutton and cabbage, keeping an eye on his refilled glass of wine. As far as he was concerned, the matter was settled – whatever. Without another word, Mother Rikissa walked towards the door, her heels clattering across the oak planks.

Finally the company was rid of the most severe inhibition on its talk and manners. Now everything could move more freely. As the need to go outside and relieve oneself on the fir branches at the back door was becoming urgent, the constraint of having an Abbess present at a feast had begun to feel intolerable. Still, the two well-born young women at the far end of the table didn't help. Their fair ears would be burning soon enough, once the talk got going among the men.

The King declared that a bedchamber should be arranged for them upstairs and a guard detailed to stand by the door all night to protect them and stop tongues wagging. As much as the men now wanted to see them gone, so were the Cecilias eager to withdraw. This would be their last time together for goodness knew how long and there was so much they wanted to talk about. They politely said goodnight and were about to leave when Birger Brosa stopped them, pointing at his mantle. Cecilia Rosa blushed and as the Earl turned his back to her, replaced his mantle of office with its golden Folkunga lion where it belonged.

Once in their bedchamber, they stayed quiet for a long time, holding hands and thinking with awe about everything that had happened. The splendid mantle of a queen was lying next to the bed as a reminder of the incredible events of the day. From downstairs rose the laughter and general uproar of men, freed of women's presence, setting about having a feast fit for a king while the night was still young.

'The Archbishop will surely have got started on his fourth helping by now!' Cecilia Blanca said, giggling at the thought. 'I don't think he's as silly as he seems, don't you agree? Did you notice how he dismissed Rikissa like she'd been a fly drowning in his glass of wine?'

'I don't think he's anywhere near as stupid as he pretends to be,' Cecilia Rosa replied. 'He had to make some quick decisions and couldn't afford to be seen obeying the King's every whim. He didn't want to take the whole thing too seriously, so he got out of trouble by pretending the whole thing was negligible – nothing more than a fly in the wine. Arn always spoke well of him, even though the Archbishop punished us both so hard.'

'Dearest Rosa, you're always so good and think the nicest things about people,' Cecilia Blanca sighed.

'How do you mean, my sweet Blanca?'

'You must learn to think more like a man, Rosa. It's important to know how they think, these men who wear an earl's crown or a bishop's mitre. There was nothing at all good or fair about yours and Arn's sentence. Birger Brosa put it well: many have committed the same sin without any punishment at all. Of course you were made examples of, don't you see?'

'No, I don't. Why would they punish us especially?'

'For a start because Rikissa wanted it. She's a rotten schemer. I was at Godshome when your no-longer-so-dear sister Katarina was there and Rikissa was starting to spin her net, mean old spider that she is. Your beloved Arn was a Folkunga man and Knut Eriksson's friend, and Rikissa reckoned that by using you she could get at Arn and so harm Knut. Then again, your Arn was known to be an outstanding swordsman. There were many stories around of how good he was. That's what the Archbishop was after.'

'What could the Archbishop and his friend Father Henri possibly want with a swordsman?'

'My dear, come on!' Cecilia Blanca said impatiently. 'Don't be like these silly geese Mistress Helena used to scorn. Why, the clergy keeps talking all the time about sending men to fight in the Holy Land, as if they weren't occupied enough with our own wars. You know how they say that followers of the Cross go straight to Paradise and so on, but that for all the talking they do they don't get many takers. I don't know of anyone who's gone willingly, do you? But they had Arn in the bag. I'm sure they were giving heartfelt thanks for months afterwards. If Arn Magnusson's skills with sword and lance had been average and if he hadn't become famous after the battle at Axevalla, your punishments would've lasted two years at most, not twenty.'

Cecilia Rosa contemplated this, visibly shaken by what she had just heard.

'You've begun to think like a queen, is that it? And you're practising now,' she asked.

'I am, as best I can. And of the two of us, I seem the best suited to be queen. You're far too kind and good, darling Rosa.'

'Was that how you made them agree to have me join you tonight at the feast – by thinking like a queen? You should've seen Mother Rikissa when she came to get me! She was nearly bursting with sheer hatred.'

'Serves her right, the mean cow. That'll teach her that what she wants isn't the same as God's will on Earth. I did try to persuade Knut by being all sweet and loving, but to be honest, he didn't seem the least bit impressed. Instead he went off to ask his Earl for advice. That's how far I got with my female cunning. I've got a lot to learn still.'

'So it was Birger Brosa who said I could come?'

'He alone. You must take care not to lose his support, which you've got now. When he wrapped you in the Folkunga mantle it surely wasn't just to keep you warm.'

They lay in silence for a while, mostly because of the noisy, drunken laughter shaking the floorboards. Both of them also felt suddenly troubled by the way hard statecraft had crept into their talk, almost as if that royal mantle next to their bed had forced them into being something other than just the closest of friends.

But though the night had only just begun, it would come to an end as all nights do, even those in *carcer*. Afterwards they would be apart for a very long time, if not forever. There must be other things worth talking about now.

'Do you think he's a handsome man, to you I mean? Does he look the way you've remembered him?' Cecilia Rosa asked.

'Knut Eriksson? Yes – and no, I suppose – it's true that I've been thinking of him as younger and better looking. We didn't see much of each other even when we met and that was a few years ago. He's tall and strong enough, but now his hair is thinning on top. He'll look like a monk soon, though he's not that old. No old man from Linköping of course, but ... he could be handsomer. And he's not as wise as Birger Brosa. All in all, I could've done better, maybe, but much worse too. I'm quite content.'

'Is that it? Quite content?'

'Yes. It's my confession to you. Not that it's very important. What matters is that he's the King.'

'You don't love him, do you?'

'As I love Virgin Mary? As people love in fairy tales? No, of course not. Why should I?'

'Haven't you ever loved a man?'

'Not a man, exactly, but there was a stable lad, once ... I was barely fifteen then. My father caught us and all hell broke loose. The stable lad was soundly whipped and thrown out. He was furious, promising to return with a following of herdmen and all sorts. I wept for days and then I was given a new pony.'

'When I get out I'll be thirty-seven years old,' Cecilia Rosa whispered, rather loudly, through the festive roaring from downstairs.

'Then you'll have half your life in front of you,' Cecilia Blanca said. 'And you'll come to live with the King and me. You and I are friends for life and nobody, not all the Rikissas in this world, can do anything about that.'

'But I'll only get out if Arn comes back for me. He swore he would. If he doesn't I'll dry up and become an old maid inside the walls.' Cecilia Rosa was speaking up now.

'I know you'll pray for Arn always and so shall I, for your sake. If we keep praying we'll convince the Holy Virgin, believe me,' Cecilia Blanca said, squeezing her friend's hand tightly.

'Oh, yes I do! I've heard some truly beautiful stories about Virgin Mary's heart being softened by the prayers of constant lovers.'

'So you would answer "Yes" to the question "Do you love Arn Magnusson?", would you? He's not only a means of getting out of Godshome – you do love him as you love the Holy Virgin? Fairy-tale love?'

'Yes, all that. I love him so much I fear sinning through loving a man more than God himself. I'll love Arn as much after these wretched twenty years are over. I'll love him forever.'

'You mightn't understand, but it's true that I envy you that love,' Cecilia Blanca said, twisting quickly round and hugging her friend. They both wept now, holding each other close.

In the end they had to let each other go, for the simple reason that affects everyone after a feast. Cecilia Blanca had to get up and relieve herself in the wooden bucket thoughtfully placed under their bed. Once back under the sheepskin rugs, Cecilia Blanca decided that now was the time to ask what she had not dared ask before.

'This is something you could only ask your dearest friend. Tell me, what's it like to have a son who's not yours to mind? And what's giving birth like? Is it as bad as they say?'

'That's a lot of questions at one time,' Cecilia Rosa replied, smiling rather bleakly for a moment. 'It's unbearably hard to have seen my little boy Magnus, who was so small and so perfectly beautiful, and then let him go. Birger Brosa and his Brigida are bringing him up and I have to stop myself from thinking about him, except in my prayers. But in the middle of my unhappiness I'm feeling happy that he's growing up with someone like Arn's uncle, a truly good and great man. It's all very confusing.'

'Believe me, I understand. What was giving birth like?'

'Are you worrying about that already? There's time enough – why, there's still someone standing guard outside your bedchamber!'

'Don't laugh at me, I'm really upset about it. I won't get out of bearing children, you know. What's it like?'

'What do I know, I've only had one birth after all. Does it hurt? Yes, it does. Badly. Do you feel happy once it's over? Yes, you do. Did this experienced lady tell you anything you didn't know?'

'I wonder if it hurts less if you love the child's father?' Cecilia Blanca asked a little later and only half in jest.

'Yes, I do believe that.'

'Nothing for it then, I'd better start loving our King at once.' Cecilia Blanca said in a self-mocking voice. They both burst out laughing and their laughter freed them to feel completely easy again. Hugging each other almost as tightly as the night when Cecilia Blanca had been brought back from *carcer*, they whispered together for a little longer and soon came to reminiscing about how they had felt that awful night.

'I shall always believe, as I did then, that you saved my life,' Cecilia Blanca whispered into her friend's ear. 'I was frozen to the marrow of my bones and felt like the last blueish flame flickering in the embers of a fire.'

'I think your flame burns stronger than that,' Cecilia Rosa mumbled sleepily.

They slept but woke in time for lauds. Crawling out of bed, it took some time before it dawned on them that they were in the *hospitium*. There was still some drunken shouting below, and now they were fully awake and couldn't go to sleep again, although the candle had burnt down and the night outside the oxeye window was still dark. Instead, they started where they'd left off, speaking of eternal friendship and eternal love.

V

Saladin was not caught out by any of the defensive traps set for him in Gaza. He had fought too many wars, defended as well as besieged too many cities, to believe the first evidence of his eyes. To all appearances Gaza was easy to take, in fact practically undefended. Its fearful citizens seemed ready to surrender their city to its attackers. But on top of the gate tower, with its wide open doors and its drawbridge down, flew the black and white banner of the Knights Templar and their standard bearing the image of Jesus' mother, whom they worshipped as though she had been divine. This alone was significant, since the pretence that the knights would give in without a fight was ludicrous. Indeed, it was almost insulting that the commanders should even think of trying to get away with such a simple trick.

Saladin waved away the amirs, who came riding along one after another to suggest idiotic instant raids. His orders remained the same, regardless of the seemingly open city gate and the thin rows of defending soldiery with no white-clad knights to back them up.

In the company of his armourer, Guido de Fatamond, and his *confanonier* Armand, Arn was observing the enemy army keenly from one of the watchtowers. The city of Gaza had been cleared of anything that would burn easily, all windows that had been covered by wooden shutters or tightly framed hides soaked in vinegar. Refugees had been herded into the masonry grain stores – the contents had been transferred to the magazines inside the fortress itself – and the citizens were organised into militias ready to deal with fires and house-to-house resistance.

Gaza was built on a hill, which sloped down to the seashore where the fortress and the harbour lay. Besiegers had to attack uphill to break through the city gates. Beyond the gates, the main road to the fortress was as open as an arena for practising horsemen. Turkish archers, commanded by a handful of black-uniformed sergeants, defended the walls. The rest of the sergeants, some two hundred men with crossbows at the ready, waited out of sight, below the parapets. Arn, with a single command, could double the visible defence on the walls. Behind the fortress doors, which were closed but not bolted, eighty mounted knights were waiting to ride out at any instant.

Arn had hoped that the enemy's men would arrive gradually, in isolated groups, and that some ambitious amir would be incapable of resisting the temptation of a glorious, daring attack. Saladin would richly reward such bravery, or so they might imagine. Thoughtless excitement tended to reach its greatest heights at the outset of a siege.

Now, if some four hundred Mamelukes on horseback had ridden in through the open gate and the doors swung shut once the crowding had become serious, then the knights could have cut down the invaders almost at will. The Saracen skills of swift horsemanship would be of little use in the narrow lanes of the city, and the sergeants could finish them off by turning round and completing the slaughter with their crossbows. The enemy army might then have lost almost a tenth of its strength in one hour – quite a blow for its commanders to contemplate.

But it was true that this had been more a fond hope than a cunning plan. Saladin was not the kind of enemy commander to be easily trapped.

'Maybe it's time our knights got on with other tasks?' Guido the armourer asked tentatively.

'Yes, all right. But they must remain on high alert. Who knows, there might be another opportunity soon,' Arn replied, without revealing whether he was disappointed or hopeful. The armourer nodded and left.

'Come on,' Arn said to Armand. Together they went to look over the parapet near the gate tower, standing just under the banners and fully visible to the enemy. Arn was the only white-clad knight to be seen among the defenders of the city.

'Now what do we do?' asked Armand. 'They didn't take that bait.'

'We wait. Saladin is going to demonstrate the strength of his army first. Once that's done . . . games played by armed men . . . our first day will be calm but a man – just one man – will die.'

'Who?' Armand asked, looking worried.

'A young man, someone of your age.' Arn sounded almost sad. 'A brave young man, believing that there's honour to be won. Now that he's part of a great siege, maybe for the first time, he'll believe, too, that God is on his side, but God will have chosen him to die.'

Armand could not bring himself to ask any more questions about the man who would die. His master's voice had anyway sounded as if his mind was far, far away – deep in thoughts of his own, seemingly the way many of the great knights spoke.

Soon Armand's attention was caught by the spectacle outside the wall. Just as Arn had predicted, Saladin was showing off. The Mamelukes rode their beautiful, lively horses in parade groups of five by five, the sunlight gleaming in their golden uniforms. On cue, they raised their lances and bows, shaking them in the air as they passed the tower where Arn and Armand were watching. The display lasted almost an hour and although Arn lost count in the end, it was clear that the enemy numbered over six thousand riders. As for Armand, this was the greatest army on horseback that he had ever seen. It seemed invincible, especially in view of his conviction that Mamelukes were just about the best of all Saracen fighting men. He noted that his master seemed curiously unconcerned.

When the parade finally came to an end, Arn smiled and looked at Armand. He rubbed his hands together either with pleasure at what he had seen, or perhaps to exercise them before using his longbow, waiting in the gate tower with a barrel containing more than a hundred arrows.

'A fine display, wouldn't you say Armand?' Arn said, sounding distinctly pleased.

'It's the largest enemy army I've ever seen,' Armand replied cautiously, not wanting to say that 'fine' was the last word that came to his mind.

'That's true. Still, we're not going to get down there to chase them, as they might have been hoping. We'll stay inside the walls and their horses won't get anywhere. But Saladin hasn't shown his real strength yet. You'll see. All this riding up and down keeps everybody happy. The show of strength will come after the next episode.'

Arn leaned over the breastwork again and Armand silently followed suit. He didn't want to admit that he had no idea what was coming next, nor what Saladin's real strength might look like.

What followed was a completely different show of cavalry skills. The bulk of the army had dismounted and was busy looking after horses and setting up tents, while some fifty-odd riders moved towards the city gate. Suddenly, these shouted a resounding call of war and started galloping at full speed towards the open gate, holding their weapons high.

There was only one way to cross the moat and that was near the gates. Along its eastern side, the moat was edged with sharpened poles pointing forward. Anyone trying to cross would only impale himself and his horse, dying quickly or slowly as luck would have it.

Just before reaching the gate, the Saracens came to a halt and began a noisy argument. Suddenly, one of them spurred his horse and rode at full speed towards the gate, standing in his stirrups and tensing his bow, a skill mastered by the Saracen riders and hardly anyone else. Arn stood quite still and Armand, who was watching his master, noticed a slight, sad smile on his face. Then Arn sighed and shook his head. The solitary white-clad knight was an obvious target, but he didn't move at all. The rider took aim and drew his bow. The arrow whistled past Arn's head.

The rider turned instantly and galloped swiftly back to his companions who greeted him with encouraging shouts and back-slapping. Then the next rider started out, much as the first one had, but coming daringly closer. His arrow fell even more widely off the mark.

While he rode back to join the other young amirs, as fast as if his life depended on it, Arn ordered Armand to fetch his bow and a couple of arrows from the tower. When Armand came panting back with the weapon, a third rider was storming forward.

'Cover me from the left with your shield,' Arn ordered, and at the same time readied his bow. Armand waited until the rider was close enough.

When the young Mameluke amir came thundering across the drawbridge, ready to fire his shot, Armand lifted his great shield and Arn calmly let his arrow fly. It hit the rider at the base of his neck. He was thrown off his horse backwards, a spray of blood erupting from his mouth. Watching the convulsions of the man's body in the dust, they concluded that he had probably been dead before hitting the ground. The fallen warrior's horse ran on down the main street towards the fortress.

'That is the man I was talking about,' Arn said quietly. He seemed to be feeling grief rather than triumph over his deed. 'It was written that just that man would die, almost certainly the only one today.'

'Master, I don't understand what's going on,' Armand said. 'You've told me always to ask you when I don't. Please, explain all this.'

'It's wise never to be too proud to ask,' Arn said. 'Besides, you'll soon be one of us and brothers always reply truthfully to each other's questions. These young amirs know that Al Ghouti has a reputation as a reasonably good archer. It's regarded as brave to ride within my range, and if you do so and survive, then God is favouring you for your courage. That's how these people think. They also believe that the third time is crucial, so the third rider is the bravest. Not that there could be a fourth one in this case, because it's impossible to come any closer than the first three and the game is no longer worth playing. The many different ways people feel about courage make it an even greater mystery than honour, I think. Look at them now! To the men down there indecision is cowardly, but you can see how much at a loss they are. They wanted to shame us and instead they've landed themselves in a nasty hole.'

'What's in their minds? Do they want revenge for the dead man?' Armand asked.

'Not if they have any sense. And if they think it'd be safer advancing as a group to pick up their comrade's body, we'll kill them all or as near as damn it. Get the crossbows ready for action!'

Armand gave the order at once. The sergeants armed their crossbows and rose to crouching position, ready to respond to the next order with a deadly rain of arrows. The amirs were still hesitating, possibly because they suspected a trap. The scattered Turkish archers on the walls must have looked too improbably weak a line of defence.

When a renewed approach seemed unlikely, Arn ordered the Mameluke horse to be taken to the city gate. He took the reins, leading it through the gate and on to the dead man. The mounted amirs were watching tensely, ready to attack. Behind the parapets, the sergeants were waiting for the equally tense Armand's order to shoot.

Arn lifted the corpse onto the back of the horse, securing it with the stirrup straps. Then he turned the horse towards the silent, waiting men and slapped it across the rump. The animal ran off, and Arn walked slowly back into the city. He did not once turn to look over his shoulder.

No one shot at him nor made any move to attack him.

Once back on the wall, Arn was obviously in a very good mood. His armourer had joined them and he, too, seemed delighted, shaking Arn's hand and hugging him. The Mamelukes were riding off with their comrade's body to bury it according to their own rites. Arn and the armourer watched with satisfaction as the dejected group retreated.

Armand was completely baffled. Why were the two high-ranking brothers so pleased? Arn's gesture seemed senseless. Courageous, yes, but given his responsibility for all their lives, did he have the right to risk his own in this way?

'Forgive me, please, but there's something else I don't understand,' he said after much hesitation.

'Carry on! Something about my way of going about this recent business that you don't get the hang of?' Arn sounded positively jolly.

'Yes there is, master.'

'Meaning that I was risking my life in a really idiotic way?'

'It appeared strange to me, master.'

'But I wasn't doing anything of the sort, you know. If they had started riding towards me, they would've been killed by our crossbows long before their arrows could reach me. Also, I'm wearing double layers of felt back-panels under my chain-mail, so any arrows hitting me from behind would just have stuck in the padding. I would've looked like a hedgehog, which might have been quite amusing.'

'There are still things I don't understand though,' Armand pleaded. The two older men looked fatherly and smiled at him.

'Armand, you'll soon be one of us and it's important that you learn about our enemies,' the armourer said. 'This lot is made up almost entirely of Mamelukes and they're special. You must recognise both their strengths and their weaknesses. They're skilful horsemen and very brave, but the main flaw lies in the way their minds work. They have no established faith and instead believe in all manner of spirits and souls meandering about between bodies or inhabiting stones in the desert and suchlike. A man's courage is thought to be the essence of his true soul and they're convinced that the bravest men will always win in a war.'

'I see,' Armand said, obviously still confused.

'The number three, as I was saying, is almost a sacred number,' Arn said, taking over the explanation. 'It's not so hard to understand that – think of the third blow in a sword-fight, for instance. It's well known to be the most dangerous. Now, what happened this time? First their third rider dies. Then Al Ghouti, their enemy, shows greater courage than they did. The conclusion must be that I'll win the war, not Saladin. The rumours will be circulating all round the camp tonight.'

'But master, what if they'd all come riding towards you ...?'

'Most of them would've died there and then. The few who'd seen

110

me getting hit without falling would have started a rumour about my immortality. That might've been even better. Still, the next move is Saladin's. He should be showing his hand before the evening.'

Arn decided that there was no risk of an attack that day and sent almost all the defenders off for a meal and some rest. Then he sang at the vesper service held in the fortress and led the prayers with the knights. After an evening meal, half the knights went to rest, while the remainder stayed on alert. The gates of Gaza were still wide open but there was no sign that Saladin was about to take up the challenge.

Later that evening, laden carriages brought the wheels, beams and mighty ropes of the enemy's heavy siege equipment. Groups of men began constructing the catapults and other machinery that could throw big rocks or fireballs at the fortifications. Arn climbed to the top of the watchtower the moment a message about this development reached him. Apart from the construction site, the scene appeared peaceful. A thousand campfires were burning between the tents as the army cooked food and prepared to rest. The precious siege machinery and its engineers seemed to be guarded only by about a hundred foot-soldiers.

If appearances did not lie, this was a golden opportunity. Saladin surely wouldn't have taken this risk with his equipment if he'd known about the eighty knights in the fortress. If all the knights attacked now, they might kill the engineers and set fire to their machines. It could, of course, be that hundreds of Mameluke cavalry were kept in readiness somewhere in the deepening darkness, out of sight from the observers on the city walls. After all, the enemy commander was far from stupid, whatever else might be said about him.

Arn ordered the drawbridge to be lifted and the gates barred. The first day of war had passed in a battle of minds and the outcome was a draw. No one had fallen into the other's trap and only one man had died. Arn went off to sleep, reckoning that this might be his last night of sound rest for a long time to come.

At early dawn the next day, Arn was back on the walls. Throughout the night the machinery site had been resounding with hammer blows. As the impenetrable darkness was slowly thinned into a grey haze by the first light of the rising sun, he was able to pick out the outlines of the force waiting in a valley to the right of the site. His suspicions had been right. The force was large, possibly as many as a thousand men on horseback. If Arn had taken Saladin's bait and attacked during the night, his men would have rushed straight into a deadly trap.

The knight smiled at the thought of the men who had been on watch, having to control their horses and keep their eyes on the drawbridge that might be lowered any moment. Then he reflected that in the future – if he had a future – he must never underestimate Saladin.

At present, his single objective was to delay Saladin by keeping him busy with Gaza for as long as possible. If the city held out for long enough, it could save Jerusalem and the Holy Sepulchre of Our Lord. The plan was that simple, at least in words.

It was time for the changing of the guard. Rested men came to take the place of the cold, sleepy archers of the night watch. Arn was wondering how long they all had to live. Certainly, if all went according to plan, he and his brother knights would be dead in about a month's time. He had never felt so close to death before. Of course he'd been wounded in battle, and at times only luck had saved him. And of course he'd taken risks, more often than he could remember. But until now he had always felt sure of surviving. No incident in the past had ever made him feel in the presence of his own impending death, as he did now. The promise of Paradise to come had meant little to him, because he believed that he wasn't meant to die. His fate was to live and, after twenty years, return to his betrothed as he had promised on his honour and his blessed sword. It simply couldn't be God's intention that he should break his word.

Now, it was different. Saladin's grip on Gaza became clearer as the light grew stronger. Like a fantasy turning into reality, the imagined threat had turned into armed men. From occasionally hearing horses snorting and armour rattling in the dark, Arn could now see the reflections of the first sunbeams on golden uniforms. This was his death. Gaza could not resist such a force for long unless the Lord himself intervened. A miracle was unlikely, for God showed little mercy towards those who believed in Him.

The image of Cecilia appeared in his mind. He saw her as he had last seen her, his eyes full of tears, when she walked through the gate into Godshome. Life had been so different then, that after all these years in the Holy Land he couldn't quite believe in the reality of his past.

'God, why did you want me? I'm just one more knight who serves You. Why me? And why do You never answer me?' Then he felt deeply ashamed that he should be thinking in this way about God, who knew all his thoughts. This was to insist on his own interests above the great cause of God's rule on Earth. And he thought himself fit to be a Knight Templar? His regret was sincere and he kneeled at once to ask God's forgiveness.

Below the walls the enemy's lances and banners were catching the glow of the rising sun. Arn called his armourer and six squadron leaders to a council of war.

It was agreed that they'd done well to avoid Saladin's trap. Nevertheless, a successful raid on the machinery site would have been good. Gaza couldn't resist a continuous bombardment of rocks and Greek fire for long, and once the walls were breached the entire population and their animals would have to crowd into the fortress.

Saladin didn't know how many knights he had to deal with and had only received reports of the sixteen men who had met his advancing army. The absence of a raid on the siege machinery might have persuaded him that the force facing him was not much stronger than that. The best time for an attack would be when it was least expected, maybe during a working day and at midday prayers. But what might it achieve, and would any gain be worth the likely cost in fallen brothers?

The armourer thought they had a good chance of setting fire to the machinery. It was being assembled quite close to the city walls, halfway down the slope. An unexpected raid could get there and do much damage before the enemy was ready to hit back. He reckoned that it might cost the lives of twenty brothers, which seemed reasonable given that the destruction of the machines would bring at least a month of precious breathing space.

Arn agreed, deciding that the armourer should take command in the city while he himself led the raid. He also said that all the brothers would be ordered out, even those who might have been spared due to minor injuries. This morning, the sergeants should start preparations at once, fill sacks with tar and soak tow in Greek fire, so that everything was ready for an attack at noon, the hottest time of the day and also the time when the infidels were busy at their midday prayers.

After this meeting, Arn returned to the walls to be seen both by the defending and besieging men. After a while he ordered the drawbridge to be lowered and the gates opened. This caused just as much agitation in the enemy camp as he had planned, but when nothing more happened, the excitement died down and everybody went back to work.

He walked round the full circumference of the walls, which joined the harbour and the fortress in the north and the south. Both western ends of the moat were deep and filled with seawater, making them the strongest parts of Gaza's defences. Attacking here would be wasteful and it was towards the weaker, eastern sections that Saladin had massed his siege machinery.

For as long as the walls held, the entire army of riders was almost useless and the Mamelukes were likely to become increasingly impatient as time went by. The most important stage in the battle would be directed towards the city gates, where Gaza's archers would confront the attacking foot soldiers and, above all, the siege engineers, with their various skills in blasting, tunnelling and generally undermining the walls. It was only a matter of time before they would succeed.

Arn was well aware of what awaited them all. Soon the stench of dead Saracens cooking in the sunshine would lie like a pall over the city. The wind was mostly westerly though, so the enemy camp would suffer more than they from the odours of the corpses.

No relief could be expected from Jerusalem, or from Ashkelon northwards along the coast. Gaza depended entirely on God's mercy.

At noon Chamsiin, Arn's favourite horse, was saddled and covered in a felt blanket with chain-mail on top. This raid would be more dangerous for the horses than the men, but even so Arn wanted to ride Chamsiin, who made up in speed and mobility for what he lacked in sheer weight. Soon or later they would part company anyway and who died first was not important. The brothers were ready and praying by the gate. They knew that many would die – or all, if the enemy was on the alert or if it so pleased God.

But the enemy seemed unaware of any danger. In the full light of the day, Arn could not see any groups of men on horseback nearby. Instead, in the distance, a large contingent was busy going through exercise routines. Most of the horses were unsaddled and stabled. It was truly looking like the right moment to strike. Arn kneeled and prayed to God for help in this perilous task, which might help to save the sacred city. Leaving his life in God's hands, he rose. Chamsiin was impatient and his restless movements told Arn that the animal knew something difficult was afoot.

It was at that moment he saw a group of men approaching the gates. They were riding in tight formation behind the banner of Saladin's own command. After lining up a short distance away from the moat, one rider came forward with the banner lowered as a sign that he was a negotiator. Arn quickly ordered that no one was to shoot.

He ran down to the waiting Chamsiin and galloped out to meet the approaching amir. The Egyptian lowered his banner down to the ground and bowed his head.

'I greet you in the Name of God the Merciful and Charitable. You're Al Ghouti, who speaks the language of God.'

'My greeting to you. I also wish you God's peace,' Arn replied impatiently. 'What is your message and who has sent you?'

'My message for you was sent by ... he told me to say from Yussuf, although his honours and titles are very numerous. The men you see behind me are prepared to be held as hostages during the negotiations.'

'Wait here! I'll return with an escort,' Arn said, and rode back into the city at full speed.

Once inside the gate he reined in his horse to a slow trot. He thought hard as he rode down the cleared main street towards the fortress, where eighty mounted knights were waiting. A surprise attack launched at this moment would have maximum effect. They couldn't have a better opportunity to destroy the siege machinery.

One Christian line of argument was to the effect that betrayal simply didn't exist in the crusade against the infidels – a promise to a Saracen was worthless by definition. The fact that he had entered into negotiations would therefore be of no account. But then, there were others who disputed this view. Hadn't the Master of Jerusalem himself sanctioned that agreement to keep the peace during the meeting with Saladin on the arid, stony land near the Dead Sea?

Or was his pride in his own honour sinful? His honour was being weighed against the fate of the Sacred City itself. What was one betrayal of the Saracens against their taking of Jerusalem? No, he thought. All I'd gain by reneging on my promise would be a little time. Machinery can be replaced, but never the loss of trust when a word of honour has been broken. And Saladin wasn't planning any treachery, he felt sure of that.

Arn ordered one squadron of knights under the banner of the Order to accompany him and the other brothers to dismount and rest. The small group of knights with the *confanonier* at their head rode out at a swift pace and, as they approached Saladin's messenger, lined up in attack formation like the waiting Saracens. The two sides closed in on each other at a slow trot until there was only a length of a few lance-throws between them. Then they stopped, except for a group of five Saracen riders. Arn and his *confanonier* moved out to meet them.

Arn recognised Saladin's brother Fahkr among the five hostages and greeted him.

'So we meet again, maybe sooner than either of us thought, Fahkr,' Arn added, when Fahkr returned his greeting.

'True, Al Ghouti, and under circumstances I'm sure neither of us would have wished. Only He who sees all and knows everything foresaw this moment.'

Arn nodded. Then he sent the other four hostages away and ordered Armand to escort Fahkr, treating him as an honoured guest in every way and seeing to it that everyone else did – though there would be no guided tours of the fortifications and no opportunities to count the knights. Then the two groups re-formed around their charges and rode off in opposite directions.

Saladin honoured his visitor with a much grander display than a simple fortress commander could have expected. Five hundred pairs of mounted men accompanied Arn to Saladin's tent and not a single piece of abuse was uttered on the way. Along the passage leading to the doorway of the commander's tent two lines of Saladin's personal guard formed an arch of honour with their swords and lances. When Arn unbuckled his sword, as custom demanded, intending to hand it to the guard who had hurried up to lead Chamsiin away, the man refused to take it. He explained that the sword was to be carried as usual and Arn, rather surprised, did as he was told.

Inside the tent Saladin rose to meet him, taking both his hands as if they were the closest of friends. Watched by the curious eyes of Saladin's advisors, Arn returned the greeting as warmly. He was shown to a seat exactly matching Saladin's own, a camel's saddle decorated with gold and silver inlays and studded with precious stones. They bowed to each other, sat down and only then did the other men settle on the rugs covering floor of the tent.

'If God were to allow us a meeting at another time, Al Ghouti,' Saladin said, 'you and I would have much to talk about.'

'I agree with you. But at present, *al Malik an-Nasir*, victorious King, you have brought your army to besiege my fortress, so I fear our conversation will be brief.'

'However, you agree to hear my conditions?'

'Naturally. I will refuse them, but my respect for you demands that I listen. Speak without diplomatic sweet-talk, for you and I both know that the other can see through such words and phrases.'

'I'll give you and your men – your *Frankish* men, that is – free passage. You can ride off to Jerusalem or one of your northern fortresses in Palestine or Syria or wherever you want. Not a single arrow will be shot at you. No such mercy will be shown the traitors, who while claiming to believe in the true Faith have been working for you in return for silver. Those are my conditions.'

'I cannot accept them,' Arn declared. 'As I was saying, our negotiations won't last long.'

'Then you will all die. You're a warrior, Al Ghouti, and you know that's the truth. For reasons only you and I know, I think highly of you and trust you. My offer of free passage would not have been made to anyone but you, and I assure you that my amirs don't think much of it. Refusing this offer means that you'll be shown no mercy once you've been defeated.'

'I know that, Yussuf,' Arn replied, with almost teasing stress on the simple first name he used to address the greatest of the Saracen commanders. 'Indeed, I know all the rules well enough and they demand that you must take Gaza by force and that I must defend it to the last man. If any of us is taken prisoner, we'll expect nothing but execution. Yussuf, I believe there's nothing more we can say to each other now.'

'At least tell me why you take this foolish course!' exclaimed Saladin, his face twisted with grief. 'You know I don't want you dead. We'll defeat you, you know that too. Why not save yourself and your men?'

'Because there's something else to save that's more worthy still. I agree that, short of a divine miracle, this siege will end in about a month's time with the death of Gaza's defenders – all of us, sooner or later.'

'Why, Al Ghouti, why refuse the gift of life for you and your people?' Saladin was obviously pained.

'It is surely not so hard to understand – and Yussuf, I believe you do,' Arn said, with a small hope growing in his mind. 'We agree, Gaza will be yours. But we both also know it will cost you dear in time and men, maybe as many as half your army. If that were the outcome, I would have died not for pride or folly but something much greater, as I'm sure you too realise.'

'Then we've nothing more to say to each other,' Saladin said, with his head regretfully bowed. 'Go in God's peace. Pray today, for tomorrow there'll be no more peace.'

'I'll leave you now. I wish God's peace be with you too.' Arn rose, bowing deeply and with great respect to Saladin.

On the way back he met Fahkr, who asked what the outcome had been. Hearing Arn's account, Fahkr shook his head and mumbled that he'd warned his brother that even the most generous offer was likely to be rejected.

'Al Ghouti, I want you to know that I too grieve for what must be. I bid you farewell.'

'I share your regret,' Arn replied. 'At least one of us will die but only God knows who it will be. Farewell.'

They rode on slowly, both deep in thought. Arn was feeling quite hopeful. Saladin might be so angered by having his generosity thrown back in his face in front of his amirs that he'd feel compelled to stay and sack Gaza. It saddened him to think of all the deaths it would bring, but he also felt joy at the thought of being instrumental in saving Jerusalem. Maybe this was God's way of balancing his grief at never going back home; at least he could think of himself as part of a great endeavour, he who might have died in any kind of small conflict.

As Saladin had foreseen, Arn decided to pray that evening and night. He would also lead all his brothers into Holy Communion in preparation for the day to come.

In the morning Saladin's entire army broke camp and started marching northwards, one long column after another, along the coast towards Ashkelon. Not even a small contingent was left to maintain the siege of Gaza.

The entire population of Gaza watched the enemy leave. Everyone gave praise to whatever gods he or she believed in – only rarely the true God – and lined up to walk past Arn, bowing, and thanking him for their deliverance. Arn acknowledged the people's gratitude with mixed feelings. It was rumoured that the commander of the fortress had managed to frighten Saladin away somehow, most likely by using magic. Another possible explanation was that Arn had threatened him with the revenge wrought by the evil counterparts of the Knights Templar, the legion of men called The Assassins. All this made Arn snort with derision, but he did not go out of his way to stop the talking.

His disappointment was actually greater than his relief. Intact, Saladin's army was large enough to occupy Ashkelon, a much larger and more important town than Gaza, and at worst maybe even Jerusalem. His sense of failure overshadowed his pleasure at seeing his people saved.

In order to make sensible decisions about the deployment of his knights, Arn needed information about what was happening in the north. Orders might arrive by ship, and with a good wind, sailing between Ashkelon and Gaza did not take long.

While waiting for the moment to take big decisions, Arn threw himself into activities that required him to make lots of smaller ones. The refugees must be directed back to their villages to plant their burnt and ravaged land. They had to rescue what they could before the winter rains arrived. Returning them to normality meant doling out grain and letting them take their animals with them. Dealing with such matters with the help of his Head of Clerks and several scribes kept him busy for the best part of a day and a half.

Towards the end of the second day a message arrived by ship, as he had expected. He immediately called the high-ranking brothers to a meeting in the *parlatorium*.

The young King of Jerusalem, the leprous Baldwin IV, had come out of Jerusalem to meet the enemy in the field with a force of no more than some five hundred knights. It was a poor strategy, for the flat plains near Ashkelon suited the Mameluke riders only too well. It would have been much wiser to keep close to the walls of Jerusalem.

Once the Christians had discovered what kind of force they were confronting, they doubled back into Ashkelon and there they stayed, locked in by the superior enemy army. Saladin left a siege contingent behind, large enough to isolate the city. Any attempt at a break-out by the heavily armed knights would be easily defeated on these open fields by the fast Mameluke cavalry.

Arn was given no room for making decisions on his own. The Grand Master of the Knights Templar, Odo de Saint Amand, was among the knights besieged inside Ashkelon and he had sent explicit orders about what must be done.

Arn was to ride swiftly towards Ashkelon with his knights and at least a hundred sergeants, all heavily armed and without any foot soldiers to defend their horses. The plan was to attack the besieging force the following day, one hour before sunset. Once Arn's men were engaged in battle, the army units inside Ashkelon would move out and the enemy would be squeezed between two shields, as it were. This was all, but it was an order from the Grand Master and so beyond dispute.

One independent decision, though, was made by Arn. He needed to use his mounted Bedouin spies to scan the territory ahead, which was under the control of the large enemy army. Information was the only means he had to protect his men. The Bedouins were always on the move, riding fast horses and camels. Chasing them was usually pointless, since nobody could tell from a distance which side they were acting for. Arn had paid them well in silver and told them that the plunder would be rich, so they were likely to stay loyal, at least for the time being.

There was no point in speculating about the final outcome. Their small force was very vulnerable, especially without foot soldiers to defend them against ambush by Turkish archers. All they could do was to move at the highest possible speed, throwing caution to the wind.

The Bedouins had been fanning out ahead, and the column of heavily armed knights and sergeants was less than half way to Ashkelon when a moving cloud of dust turned out to be one of their advance guards approaching at top speed. Still breathless, he told Arn of how he'd seen four Mameluke horses tethered outside a mud hut at the edge of an abandoned village. Sheep and goats killed by arrows were lying all around it, but that was no reason why four riders would want to stop in such a wretched hovel.

Arn's first thought was that they had no time to waste on four stray riders, but his armourer, Guido Faramont, said that these men might be enemy spies, taking time off from their proper task. Catching them could mean that the enemy would learn less soon about the Christian force advancing from the south. Arn agreed and thanked his brother for speaking up. After dividing his men into four groups, they rode towards the village from all four directions.

Once on the outskirts of the village they surrounded it completely and rode in at a slow trot, past the dead animals and the silent, apparently empty dwellings. Then they heard the heartbreaking wail of women coming from within one small hut. Four horses in expensive tack were standing outside, tossing their heads from side to side to keep off the flies.

Arn detailed a party of knights to move in. The men silently drew their swords and, after a short fight, four half-dressed Egyptians were thrown out in the dust, screaming about the large sums of money they'd be worth alive.

As the grim-looking knights stepped back outside, Arn went into the hut and saw roughly what he had expected. There were three women inside, half-naked and bleeding from being beaten round the head, but apparently not mortally wounded. Once they had covered themselves as best they could with their torn rags, Arn tried to question them although only one of them understood a little proper Arabic.

'What is the name of this village? To whom do you belong?' he asked slowly. After much stopping and starting it became clear that the women and the animals belonged to a man from Gaza and that they had fled rather than handing over the animals at the start of the siege. In trying to escape one danger, they had ended up facing a worse one.

They calmed down a little once they realised that Arn and his men were not about to carry on where the Egyptians had left off. He told them what would happen next. Since their entire family had lost face after the violation of its women, they would have to decide themselves on how best to take their revenge. They would have the four tied-up rapists to deal with as they saw fit, and he would also let them keep the horses and their tack as a gift from Gaza, provided that none of the captives survived. His only alternative was to have them beheaded there and then. The women fervently promised not to leave anyone alive and Arn left it at that.

He and his men set off again on the forced march towards Ashkelon. They had to get there before sunset. It could not be helped if there was no time for preparation, for this was the order of the Grand Master. They managed to approach close to Ashkelon without any further incidents and without being detected. It might have been due to almost incredible luck in getting through the net of enemy spies at the one point where it had broken down, or else the Holy Virgin Mary had been guiding them.

Now their spies came riding back with information about the disposition of the siege troops outside Ashkelon. Arn dismounted, flattened a piece of ground with his iron-shod foot and used the point of his dagger to draw a plan of the city and its fortifications in the sand.

It became clear that there were two main lines of attack. The wooded land to the east meant that they could get close to the enemy before having to attack at speed. On the other hand, it meant riding straight westwards into the light of the setting sun. The other possibility was to move in a long arc around the enemy and attack from the north, but that would increase the risk of detection. Arn decided to put up with the problem of the sunlight. The enemy outnumbered them ten to one and attacking them depended on surprise, weight and speed. The eastern route would also allow them to stay where they were for an hour or so – time for resting and praying.

Afterwards they rode slowly and silently through the woodland, which narrowed and grew sparser near the city. When Arn did not dare rely any longer on the tree cover, he called a halt and his armourer rode up to join him in inspecting the lie of the land. The enemy was encamped along the whole eastern wall of Ashkelon, with the horses in fenced fields further away on the flanks.

This meant that deciding how to attack was straightforward. Arn called his eight squadron leaders and gave his orders. After praying one last time to their High Lady Protector, Her banner and the banner of the Order of the Temple were raised.

'*Deus vult*! It's the will of God!' Arn cried, and the men behind him repeated the cry.

Then the group of knights round Arn moved forward slowly while the rear was brought up on either side at a brisker trot. Thus, when they emerged from the wood, the centre looked almost still while the two huge wings of riders in black and white were unfolding. By the time the whole force was in a single line their speed had increased so that the sound of horses' hooves had risen to a mighty thunder. Galloping full tilt downhill they crashed into the enemy camp along almost its entire extent.

Their first targets were the few mounted enemy riders and the unsaddled horses. The paddock fences were ridden into the ground and the panicking animals driven at lance-point into a stampede towards the camp, which, in a few moments, turned into a chaotic mass of terrified horses, running soldiers, collapsing tents, and trampled fires scattering embers and sparks in all directions.

Then the gates of Ashkelon swung open and the royal army of worldly soldiers moved in two columns towards the centre of the besieging force. Arn shouted immediately at Armand de Gascogne to ride southwards with the banners to guide the Templar knights in that direction, leaving space for the King's men to attack. Soon they were again in tight attack formation, sweeping across the enemy lines and stabbing, cutting and trampling on everything in their path.

The Mamelukes had no time to regain their nerve and regroup after their initial fear and confusion. The few mounted men had been isolated and eliminated before they had a chance to survey the scene and so realise quite how small a force they were facing.

The bloodbath lasted well into the evening. Over two hundred men were taken prisoner and marched into Ashkelon. The battlefield was left to darkness and to the Bedouins, who arrived from nowhere as swiftly as vultures and in remarkably large numbers. The city gates then closed on the plunder that would go on in the light of torches through the whole night.

Arn lined up his men on the biggest square and made a

headcount, squadron by squadron. Only four men were missing, a low enough cost by any standards. His first task was to find the dead or wounded brothers and bring them back for care or a Christian burial. He detailed sixteen uninjured men to get hold of reserve horses and set out to search. Then he went to the small Templar headquarters to deal with his own injuries.

Arn's wounds were all minor and, after washing, he presented himself to the Grand Master. As he had expected, the great man was in the chapel dedicated to the Holy Virgin, giving thanks for the splendid victory. Arn joined him and they prayed together.

Afterwards, they walked together on the city wall to find a seat as far from the guards as possible. They needed peace, away from the celebrations in the city below where the only dark and silent buildings were the Templar headquarters and the brothers' dormitory in a grain store. There, only a few flickering lights showed where someone was looking after the needs of the wounded men.

'Saladin may be a great tactician, but he can't have guessed how many of you were holed up in Gaza. If he had, he'd hardly have left just two thousand men to keep Ashkelon quiet,' Odo de Saint Amand said speculatively. This was his first remark after leaving the chapel, as if the battle itself needed no further comment.

'All the knights were inside the fortress. At most there were two men in white mantles on show,' Arn explained. 'But whatever happened today, Saladin has got some five thousand Mameluke riders left. How's Jerusalem faring?'

'As you know, the King is here. Arnaldo is in Jerusalem with two hundred knights and four or five hundred sergeants. That's all, I'm afraid.'

'Then there's nothing for it, we must attack Saladin's army. Harassing it is all we can do and we should start as soon as possible – and that's tomorrow,' Arn said grimly.

'Tomorrow's unlikely, at least as far as the royal army is concerned; they'll be recovering from today's events. Not on the battlefield, but in the inns where they're feasting tonight.' Odo de Saint Amand sounded distinctly angry.

'We won a victory and they celebrate. The usual division of labour, in other words,' Arn muttered, at the same time glancing quite merrily at his august friend. 'Anyway, it might be a good idea not to rush into things. With any luck, none of the retreating or fleeing men out there will get through the Bedouin marauders and, if so, Saladin won't learn of today's battle until many days from now. And that would be very useful.'

'Let's see what happens tomorrow,' Odo de Saint Amand replied, and rose. Arn, too, stood, and the two men kissed, first on the left and then on the right cheek.

'Bless you, Arn de Gothia,' the Grand Master said, sounding very solemn. Then he put his hands on the knight's shoulders and looked into his eyes. 'I'm sure you cannot imagine how I felt, standing in the watchtower and seeing you and our brothers come sweeping down in attack formation, as if you'd been two thousand men and not two hundred. I had promised the King and his worldly officers that you would come, just at that moment. You kept that promise for me, in every way. Arn, it was a splendid victory but we've still got a long way to go.'

'Yes, Grand Master,' Arn replied quietly. 'Today's victory is already in the past. In front of us is a very large army of Mamelukes. May God protect us once more.'

The Grand Master let go of Arn and took a step back. Arn at once knelt in front of his Master and waited with his head bowed as his most senior commander walked away along the fortifications and disappeared into the shadows.

Arn stayed where he was for a while, looking out over the parapet and listening to the occasional cries of the wounded in the night. His entire body was aching, a pounding but almost pleasurable ache. Except from a cut on his cheek, he wasn't bleeding from any wounds. His knees were the sorest parts of his body, because they received most of the hard blows when he rode close to an adversary on horseback or struck a man down by riding over him.

Nothing much happened in Ashkelon during the next few days. The Mameluke prisoners were chained together and ordered to bury their companions on the battlefield. Small groups of Bedouins arrived from time to time, dragging prisoners for sale behind their camels. They had been meticulous in their work, apparently mopping up all escapees, which was not to say that they wouldn't do exactly the same thing for Saladin in different circumstances.

The Bedouins also brought information about the Saracen army's activities. Saladin had decided on a course directly opposite to what anyone might have expected. Instead of moving swiftly towards Jerusalem, he had let his army free to loot the entire stretch of country between Ashkelon and Jerusalem. It could be that he thought it more advantageous to plunder now rather than later, when he would have won a glorious victory. The troops would be less prone to desecrate the Holy City once some of their hunger for loot had been satisfied. He must have been quite certain that he had his enemies nicely bottled up inside their fortresses and walled cities. Whatever his thinking might have been, it was mistaken, and he would regret his error for a decade to come.

They were holding a council of war in the Ashkelon fortress. King Baldwin was there, a blurred shadow inside his sedan chair, which was covered by thin blue muslin. The court gossip was that the King's hands had practically rotted away and that he would soon be totally blind. Odo de Saint Amand was sitting on the King's right, with three Templar fortress commanders behind him. Apart from Arn of Gaza, the commanders of Toron des Chevaliers and Castel Arnald were there. The Bishop of Bethlehem sat on the King's left. The King had managed to entice some of the Palestinian barons into joining him in his desperate act of war and these warlords were arrayed on seats along the wall.

The True Cross, heavily ornamented in gold, silver and precious stones, was placed behind the Bishop. Many believed that Christians carrying the True Cross in the field never lost a battle. This raised crucial questions, which needed a lot of debating.

The highest-ranking barons in the room, the brothers Balduin and Balian d'Ibelin, were arguing that it was blasphemous, indeed sinful, to drag the cross on which Our Saviour had suffered and died into a battle that was doomed from the start. The Bishop countered by saying that nothing could more clearly express their awareness that a divine miracle was their only hope. The True Cross would embody exactly what they were praying for.

Balduin d'Ibelin replied that, as he understood it, you mustn't try putting pressure on God when your back was against the wall. It would be almost like holding God to ransom or like negotiating with a party bound to lose. In the battles ahead, the Christians could hope for nothing more than making Saladin's life very uncomfortable and dragging out the warfare until the autumn. Then the rains would turn the mountains around Jerusalem into mounds of slippery red mud, sleet and winter winds would follow, and with any luck the siege would be lifted. The reasons would have nothing to do with the bravery and pure faith of the defenders.

The Bishop pointed out that of present company he was the best fitted to talk to God and he had no use whatever for the advice of laymen in this matter. The True Cross would be their salvation in a battle that required one of God's miracles to secure a good outcome for the Christians. What relic, anywhere in the world, could compete with the True Cross?

Arn and his two colleagues did not enter into this debate. Arn felt he couldn't speak when his Grand Master was there and, besides, both the other commanders were of higher rank than he. Had anybody thought of asking him, he would have found answering difficult. On the whole, he felt the Bishop was wrong and the d'Ibelin brothers right. In the end, the young leprous King intervened and ended the discussion in the Bishop's favour. He did this just in time before everyone despaired of any decisions at all being reached.

As it was, smoke from endless fires was rising in the east. Saladin's army had marched to Ibelin, sacked the city, and moved on towards the east and Jerusalem. Judging by the billowing smoke and the tales of the few refugees who managed to get through, Egyptian army units were moving through the area near Ramle, ravaging everything in their way. This was the land belonging to the d'Ibelin brothers and they immediately asked to be given command of the worldly army, since they had the most to avenge. The King agreed at once.

Because the Grand Master was in Ashkelon, there could be no question about who would lead the Templar force. However, the leadership was more complicated than it seemed at first glance, as he explained when he met with his three commanders. Odo de Saint Amand had decided that he and a special guard of twenty knights should be at the centre of the Christian army, guarding the True Cross and the Templar banner.

Consequently, another commander had to lead the knights and the Rules dictated that it should be Arnoldo de Aragon from Toron des Chevaliers, who was the eldest. Siegfried de Turenne from Castel Arnald came second in rank, but the Grand Master felt that Arn de Gothia had been under the Holy Virgin's protection when he trounced the much larger Mameluke army. To deny Arn the command would be to refuse Her clearly shown preference.

The faces of the three men were quite unmoved as they listened to their Master's instructions. They only bowed to show that they would obey unquestioningly. The Grand Master then left them to plan the campaign on their own. The small and very plainly furnished *parlatorium* in the Templar headquarters was silent for a long while after the great man had left. Arnoldo de Aragon spoke first.

'It's rumoured that our Grand Master is fond of you, Arn de Gothia. This decision would appear to confirm what people are saying,' he said sourly.

'Maybe so. It's certainly true that both your fortresses are in the region where we'll meet Saladin and that you therefore know the area very well,' Arn replied, speaking slowly and seriously, as if weighing each word.

'But it seems that tomorrow we may all ride towards our deaths,' he went on in the chilly silence. 'Nothing would be worse than if we were preoccupied by lesser things. We must do our best and not let personal matters distract us.'

'Arn is recht, we must join forcez and decide what's the best, not strife,' Siegfried de Turenne agreed between clenched jaws that made his German accent sound even stranger than usual.

Now they all pretended to have forgotten the Grand Master's irregular decision. They were short of time and had a lot of important decisions to make. Some matters were relatively easy to resolve. No question but that the knights should ride as heavily armoured as possible, including protection for the horses' heads and chain-mail covers for their bodies. Provisions must be kept to a minimum so as not to increase the load. All this was self-evident because their only hope of success lay in attacking when the Mamelukes' mobility was for some reason restricted, allowing the weight and power of the knights to be exploited fully. In any other situation the knights were at the mercy of the fast Mameluke riders – even with the knights riding lightly loaded, the enemy's speed would remain superior.

They had to spend some time discussing the disposition of the Templar force in relation to the worldly army. Should the knights be in front or at the back? In a frontal attack from the enemy, which was the most likely, more Christian lives would be saved if the most powerful unit was in the vanguard. On the other hand, their entire army was not large, and if the Saracens saw that the Christian front lines were under worldly banners, they might assume certain victory and attack with a smaller number of their presently scattered units. If the Templar knights marched forward when the Mamelukes were moving at speed and too close to turn back, it could be decisive.

The commanders agreed that keeping the Templar force at the rear would be the wisest. This would also give them greater scope for fighting off flanking attacks. But when Arn insisted on using as large a contingent of Bedouins as they could muster, his two colleagues objected. Both said contemptuously that their fortresses had no use for these nomads, infidels with filthy habits and no idea what loyalty meant.

Arn agreed that he, too, found them untrustworthy in defeat. If the

Christians lost they might well end up, all three of them, being dragged after camels to be sold to Saladin. It was likely that the Bedouins hadn't yet realised that Templar knights, unlike the worldly barons, were useless as prisoners because they could not be traded. On the other hand, the Bedouins were good spies for as long as they gained by it. They rode horses as fast as the wind, and camels, which could find their way over the worst terrain. Using them, the Christians would have a constant supply of information about the enemy and it seemed certain that such knowledge, next to God's mercy, would be their most important aid in the battles ahead.

Reluctantly the other two gave in. It was obvious that Arn would not yield over the matter of Bedouins, and in the end the final decision was his. This was what the Grand Master himself had sanctioned.

When the Christian army marched out in the early November dawn, it looked almost invincibly great to anyone who had not, like Arn and his *confanonier*, Armand, been watching while the Mameluke riders paraded by for a full hour.

The weather was raw and damp. The northwesterly breeze was too feeble and uncertain to shift the clouds of mist. The poor visibility was both bad and good news for both sides, but more advantageous to the Christians, who knew this part of the region well. This was particularly true of the brothers d'Ibelin and also the commanders from Toron des Chevaliers and Castel Arnald. The army was marching along a route lying between these two fortresses.

Nobody could work out how the Bedouins managed to navigate though the mist, but from the first hour onwards they came and went, delivering a stream of messages to Arn de Gothia. Towards midday, the Christians began encountering groups of heavily laden Egyptians, who always rode off with their plunder rather than stopping to give battle. This was still a bad omen because it meant that soon Saladin would get to hear of the enemy being on the move and could pick the time and place for a major confrontation.

It did not, in fact, take long. Near the fortress of Mont Gisard, not far from Ramle, they suddenly faced a well-organised Muslim army of men on horseback, coming straight towards the advancing Christian lines. The worldly commanders decided to move forward and engage in battle at once, even without a clear idea of the size of the opposing force. They left their centre behind, including the King, the Bishop of Bethlehem, and the banners with their guard. The knights were bringing up the rear, but Arn gave no order to attack. Heading into the mist to fight an ill-defined enemy seemed unwise both to him and his two fellow commanders.

What worried them most was that the Mameluke force was giving way almost at once, apparently in full flight. This was a well known Saracen tactic. Those who chased the fleeing riders would suddenly find new contingents of attackers closing in from the flanks. Once the pursuers were almost encircled, the fleeing units would suddenly turn back and fight too.

Arn's Bedouins soon brought news confirming their suspicions, though this time the new Saracen units were coming from one direction only. They came streaming down from the north and must have been crossing the lands of Castel Arnald. Siegfried de Turenne knew these parts like the back of his hand. Arn ordered the knights to halt and called a quick council. Siegfried drew a map in the sand, which showed that Saladin's men had to pass through a ravine that started wide in the north but narrowed towards the south.

They swiftly agreed what they must do. Arn sent a sergeant with a message to the Grand Master, who was organising a circular defence for the centre, to tell him what the main body of knights was doing, then ordered his men to follow Brother Siegfried at a fast trot.

They arrived at the ravine where, from the top of a gentle slope, they could see it narrow to a pass like the neck of a Damascene bottle. If the enemy troops were coming down by this route from here, they would soon reach the worldly army. But no sounds were heard through the damp veils of mist, which would sometimes lift and sometimes close in so that no one could see even one arrow-shot away.

They contemplated two possibilities: either God had shown them a place from where they might be able to save the Christians, or else they had ridden off and left the worldly army to its fate. Arn ordered a moment of prayer.

They all dismounted as silently as they could and kneeled by their horses. When the prayers were over, Arn ordered that all mantles should be rolled up and secured behind the saddles. It was chilly, and to become stiff with cold was dangerous for fighting men, but if the enemy arrived suddenly the mantles would be a terrible encumbrance.

Then they sat silently listening into the mist. Sometimes sounds were picked up, only to be dismissed again as imagination. The waiting was hard to bear and made worse by the thought that their comrades were being routed in a battle the knights should have joined. If nothing happened soon they would have to turn back and try to save the True Cross, which was being defended by far too few men. If the True Cross were lost to the infidels, the fault would be Arn's more than anybody else's. Exchanging glances with his fellow commanders, who seemed to spend most of their time in prayer, Arn realised they all had the same fears.

But then he suddenly felt as if the Mother of God was filling him with confidence and sending him knowledge. He ordered his commanders to outer positions on the flanks. The men needed clear colours to follow through the mist and the side covers of the commanders' horses had a distinctive broad black band under the red cross. The white Templar tunics and mantles, although causing alarm and despondency among the enemy, were normally a disadvantage because they were visible from far away. Today they merged with the white, whirling mist.

The knights began quietly to change into the linear attack formation, as if they already knew where their enemy would be. Maybe the Mother of God truly was guiding them for they suddenly saw the first golden uniforms down below. They were worn by Mameluke lancers, the troops that led in the field. In long columns, they came pouring downhill on the far side of the ravine, sometimes hidden in mist. It was impossible to reach a reasonable estimate of their number. Depending on the size of the retreating unit that had served as bait for the Christians, it could be anything between one and four thousand men.

Arn allowed one or two hundred men to pass undisturbed through the bottleneck of the ravine, ignoring his *confanonier*, Armand de Gascogne, who was in an agony of impatience. Then a dense bank of mist obscured the enemy and Arn ordered an advance at a slow trot to keep in a line while approaching the enemy unseen. Time enough to spur the horses into a gallop once the enemy spotted them. Attacking at such an unreal pace felt at though they were riding in a dream. Further down, the sounds of snorting horses, their hooves rattling across stony ground, reverberated around the ravine, making it impossible for any mere listener to work out whether one or two armies were on the move.

Soon, Arn knew, he would have to attack into the unknown. He bowed his head in prayer to the Holy Virgin, but She showed him something distant from war: in his mind's eye he saw Cecilia on horseback, her childlike, freckled face glowing and her mane of red hair flying as she looked back at him with shining, smiling eyes. The image was very vivid, but in the next moment he encountered a

Mameluke within the reach of his lance. The man was staring in utter astonishment, his jaw dropping when he looked around to find himself surrounded by bearded riders as white as ghosts.

Arn lowered his lance, howling out the order to attack – *Deus vult!* – and heard it repeated by hundreds of voices from near and far. The next moment the entire valley was filled with the sound of heavily-laden stallions galloping and soon, with the cries of wounded and dying men.

The iron fist of the knight's attack hit the advancing columns just at a point where they were crowded together side by side to get through the pass. The wave of heavy horses and sharpened steel threw the Mameluke riders sideways on to each other, then backward as they tried to avoid the onslaught. The Egyptian archers who followed behind had no time to arm their bows before riderless horses rushing back in a panic overwhelmed them. At the same time new units, hearing the noise of battle, were trying to force their way forward.

The Templar knights held every yard of the narrow passage as, knee against knee, they slashed their way through the crowded enemy lines. The Mamelukes found it practically impossible to mount a defence against the long swords of knights wielded at close range. They were cutting through the enemy lines like scythes during harvest time.

The men who got through the bottleneck tried to come back to help their trapped comrades, but Arnoldo de Aragon had foreseen this and made an independent decision to move twenty-five knights forward to form a front in that direction.

Where the fighting was at its heaviest, no one could see much beyond the tip of his lance. This was something of a comfort to the knights, who were aware of how few they were and knew that all they could do was to slaughter as many as possible in the still tightly packed mass of enemies. But for the Mamelukes, bearing the brunt of heavy Christian cavalry, this was the worst imaginable situation and the ultimate nightmare for men of the true faith. Finally, some of the officers leading the Mameluke advance controlled their dread and blew the signal to retreat – straight backwards, since using the slope of the ravine seemed a bad idea.

Arn called his men and ordered returning fighters to regroup rather than chase the enemy in the misty valley. A breathless Siegfried de Turenne came thundering up and stopped next to Arn. At first the two men stared at each other in astonishment and dismay, both thinking they were looking at a mortally wounded brother. Their white tunics were soaked in blood to such an extent that the red cross was no longer visible against the white cloth.

'Brother . . . are you truly not injured?' Siegfried panted.

'Nor you? The fight has gone our way so far. Now what do we do? Did you see which way they fled?'

'Let's regroup, new formation in line, slow trot until we find them. The valley ends over there so we'll have them trapped,' Siegfried said, recovering his calm with remarkable speed.

Nothing more needed saying. It was important not to lose their orderly formation, and a slow advance on a broader front was necessary as the valley widened towards the northern exit. The wind was blowing more strongly now and there was a risk that the mist which had served the Christians so well might soon be dispersed.

The Mameluke lancers and archers had also tried to get into an orderly formation while trying to escape down the ravine, but when they realised that they were hemmed in by steep rocky slopes they took a long time to turn round. Once that was accomplished, they decided to ride into attack quickly before they were herded together again in the narrowing part of the valley. The signal for rapid attack was given and the valley filled with the noise of fast, light horses moving at speed.

However, there had been a misunderstanding of the signal by the slower train carrying provisions, reserve horses and loot, which had been following the troops into the ravine. The result was more confusion as the retreating and advancing bodies of men and animals collided, crashing into each other as if they were enemies. Once Arn heard that sound he again ordered a rapid attack, and the Egyptians who saw the long line of knights multiplied by the mist, panicked and tried to flee back through their own ranks.

The slaughter took hours to complete and did not really end until darkness fell. Never had the Knights Templar won such a glorious victory.

Much later, they were told that the worldly army had caught up with those Saracen units serving as bait and forced them to take a stand and fight without any expected troops turning up. Once they realised that they were trapped with no hope of support, the Egyptian defence had cracked and turned in disorderly flight. While the worldly army of Franks settled down to celebrate what they thought of as their own single-handed victory, the slaughter at Mont Gisard was still going on.

In the end, Saladin's army had been almost totally scattered and demoralised. Even though, strictly speaking, there were enough

Mamelukes left to fight another day in better circumstances and better weather, the groups of uninjured fighting men could no longer locate each other and organise themselves.

The result of their disorientation and the rumours of the bloodbath at Mont Gisard was a wild flight southwards, a loss of discipline that was to cost as many lives as the battle of Mont Gisard. There was a long way to go from Ramle to the safety of Sinai, and all along the way Bedouins were waiting and ready to murder, plunder and take useful prisoners.

Among the many prisoners who were dragged behind camels with their hands tied behind their backs into the fortress at Gaza, were Saladin's brother Fahkr and his good friend, Moussa the amir. They had been riding close to Saladin when the great warrior was nearly taken prisoner by a group of Knights Templar, and had willingly sacrificed themselves so that he would go free. Not even at the bitter moment of defeat did they doubt that Saladin had been selected by God to lead the true believers to victory.

The Knights Templar had forty-six wounded and lost thirteen men. Young Armand de Gascogne was one of the dead who were found and brought back to Gaza. He was among those who had tried to capture Saladin and had been only a lance's length away from changing the course of history.

VI

In all her years of penitence, the darkest time for Cecilia Rosa followed the loss of Cecilia Blanca, her friend who had been taken away by King Knut Eriksson to become his wife and Queen. Honouring his promises to his betrothed had taken much longer than he had planned, as with so many other things. Their coronation service, though held by Archbishop Stéphan, failed to be quite as big an affair as he would have wished. Instead of East Aros Cathedral, it took place in the chapel of the fortress at Näs, on the Island of Visingsö in Lake Vättern.

But though the lack of grandeur annoyed him, he was the crowned King by the Grace of God and Cecilia Blanca, who had decided to keep that name, was now his Queen by the Grace of God. The arrangements had taken a year to complete, and that year turned out to be the most miserable in the entire life of Cecilia Rosa.

King Knut and his following had hardly moved off to continue the royal progress before every recent change of regime in Godshome was cancelled. Once again the rule of silence held everywhere in the cloister and special conditions seemed to apply to Cecilia Rosa, who was often whipped whether she had been talking or not. Mother Rikissa was the source of cold winds of hatred blowing around her and, with one exception, the Sverker women were quick to take the lead from their Abbess in this.

There was one person who would not be induced to hate Cecilia Rosa and who refused to run with the herd. Ulvhilde Emundsdotter never cheated or told tales, though it must be said no one thought what little Ulvhilde did mattered one way or the other. Her entire family had been wiped out at the time of the Bjälbo blood-meadows and she had inherited nothing. Nobody of any consequence would want to wed a maiden so impoverished, especially since her family

135

name was now practically worthless. Still, Mother Rikissa didn't let cousin Ulvhilde taste the scourge, maybe because she felt that blood had some value after all.

As the first storm of the winter was roaring round Godshome, Mother Rikissa declared to her discreetly gloating audience that it was time to send Cecilia Rosa to *carcer*. The Folkunga whore, she sneered, was obviously fancying herself a wearer of the family colours, free to be rude and overbearing to others.

This early in the winter there was still plenty of grain in the store overhead and the dank cellar was swarming with fat black rats. In addition to learning how to keep the cold at bay by fervent prayers, Cecilia Rosa had to train herself to wake from drowsing the moment she was touched by a rat. If during the second or third night her exhaustion made her fall asleep she'd be bitten, as if the rats wanted to taste a piece to find out if she was really dead or not.

Her only source of warmth during these repeated stays in *carcer* was her praying to the Holy Virgin, not so much for her own sake but to entreat the Mother of God to hold her hand over Cecilia's beloved ones, Arn and Magnus, protecting them both against evil.

Her prayers for Arn were not entirely unselfish. Although she realised that, unlike Cecilia Blanca, she couldn't yet think about games of power in the way a man does, it was crystal clear that she'd never be let out of the frozen hell that was Godshome unless Arn Magnusson returned uninjured to West Gothland.

When spring came, her lungs were still sound despite Mother Rikissa's attentions. The Abbess had half hoped and half feared having to watch her awkward charge coughing herself to death. During that summer the weather was so hot that incarceration came to mean a refuge of cool solitude, by then free from rats after the last grains in the now empty store had been eaten. Even so, Cecilia Rosa knew the past winter's hardships had weakened her and that she might not endure another like it unless the Holy Virgin sent a miracle to save her.

It seemed that She was not prepared to do something miraculous, but instead She sent a Queen by the Grace of God and that had quite a splendid effect.

At harvest time, just as the turnips were ready for pulling, Queen Cecilia Blanca arrived at the head of a rich following and commanded rooms at the Godshome guesthouse as if it had been her own to dispose of. She issued orders in all directions and demanded food and drink. Then she sent for Rikissa, whom she spoke of without the *Mother*, just as the King and his Earl did. Rikissa was to meet with the Queen and her companions immediately. Wasn't it a Godshome rule to treat all guests as if they'd been Jesus Christ Himself? Surely the same would apply to the Queen?

When Mother Rikissa could think of no further excuses, she went to the *hospitium* burning with anger and ready to tell that rude woman to behave herself, queen or no queen. As an abbess, Rikissa was in charge of a piece of God's Realm on Earth and wasn't beholden to any worldly powers.

She lost no time in making this point once she had taken her seat at the Queen's dining table, ill-temperedly noting that her placing was lowly. For a start there was nothing to be done about Queen Cecilia's request to see her dear friend Cecilia Rosa. It had been Mother Rikissa's decision to punish that sly woman for her sins in an appropriate way and hence she was not available to amuse herself by visiting royals or anybody else. The Queen had no say here. Godshome was under God's law – as Queen Cecilia Blanca had every reason to recall.

The Queen listened to the self-assured, arrogant discourse about the laws of God and mere men without showing any uncertainty and without ceasing to smile sardonically.

'I believe you've finished your evil chatter for now, which *we* indeed remember only too well as *we* have suffered under your version of God's order in there for long enough and not for one second do we believe your protestations of godliness, so we suggest you keep your sharp beak shut and listen to your queen.' Cecilia Blanca spoke in one long, smooth sentence and in a mild tone that belied the harshness of her words.

Mother Rikissa seemed to respond to the words and waited silently, actually keeping her mouth tightly shut. She felt absolutely sure of her own position and equally certain of her ability to deal with the maiden just let out of a nunnery. She soon learnt how much she had underrated Cecilia Blanca.

'Now Rikissa, let me tell you a thing or two,' she went on in her calm, almost drawling tone. 'You insist that you're one of God's representatives and I'm but a worldly ruler. We have no say in the order at Godshome, you say. Maybe so, but I'm not so sure any more. There have been a few changes and one is that your relative, Bengt, is no longer the Bishop in the Skara diocese. He's banned, you see. I've no idea where he's holed up with his woman and don't much care. The ban is a fact and you cannot expect any more support from that quarter.'

This was bad news for Mother Rikissa, but nothing in her face and posture revealed the grief and fear she felt. She chose to stay silent rather than to answer the Queen, who started speaking again, even more slowly than before.

'The next thing you should know, Rikissa, is that we very much value Archbishop Stéphan and that both my husband King Knut and I regard him as a trusted advisor. Naturally, it would be utterly wrong of us to say anything like "the Archbishop is eating out of our hands" or to suggest that he is likely to obey whatever we might want in order to keep the state and church together in unity and peace. To say anything like that would be to embarrass one of God's servants on Earth. Let me put it this way: the King, the Archbishop, and I have got an excellent understanding. It would be such a shame if you, Rikissa, were to be banned, too. Did I mention that our Earl, Birger Brosa, is deeply interested in matters of the Church and keeps telling us about the new cloisters he's planning to endow and the huge quantities of silver that he's prepared to spend on these holy places? Am I making myself clear, Rikissa?'

'You're telling me that you want to see Cecilia Rosa,' Mother Rikissa replied between clenched teeth. 'I'd now reply that there's no problem about that.'

'That's good, Rikissa! You're not as stupid as you look,' the Queen said in a jolly tone. 'Just to clarify things a little further, I should tell you that you'd better mind your manners or you might get into trouble with my good friend the Archbishop. There, now – off you go and bring my guest along at once!'

Now the Queen clapped her hands together to send Mother Rikissa on her way, hustling her out as uncaringly as the Abbess herself used to treat the two Cecilias.

When Cecilia Rosa entered the *hospitium* she was so weak and emaciated that no words were needed to describe what horrors she'd been subjected to ever since the hour King Knut's following left Godshome. The Cecilias fell into each other's arms. Neither could stop the tears from filling their eyes.

It pleased Queen Cecilia to stay for three nights and three days in the *hospitium* at Godshome, and during that time the two friends were not apart for a single hour, day or night. Afterwards, Cecilia Rosa was never again sentenced to time in *carcer* and for several months she received so many excellent gifts of food that the flesh returned to her body and a healthy colour to her cheeks.

Cecilia Rosa and Ulvhilde Emundsdotter spent the years that followed developing their skills in the art of weaving and dyeing cloth. They learnt to sew and stitch lordly mantles, embroidered on the back with the most splendid emblems. It had not taken long before the orders arrived in Godshome from near and far, from powerful families and from distant, unknown clans.

The two young women worked peacefully together, often chatting quietly, for the rule of silence no longer applied to them. Their work soon brought more silver straight into the Godshome treasury chests than any other activity. *Yconomus*, the failed curate, was growing old and mellow. He took such a delight in the diligent maidens that he hardly ever missed an opportunity to let Mother Rikissa know how well they were doing, and she would nod silently in agreement. She never forgot that she had her own version of the Sword of Damocles suspended over her head. Mother Rikissa was malicious but far from stupid.

Every year Queen Cecilia Blanca found occasion to visit. She took over the guest quarters for several days each time and always insisted on being served by Cecilia Rosa and Ulvhilde Emundsdotter. Not that she actually asked them to do anything, because she brought her own retinue of servants. These were glorious days for the two 'prisoners', as they called themselves. It was clear to all, Mother Rikissa not excepted, that the two Cecilias truly were friends for life. Mother Rikissa took note and behaved accordingly, though with ill grace.

Cecilia Blanca brought especially pleasing news on her third visit. She had decided to arrange for Sister Leonore of Flanders to learn more about the world of the plants that she loved so much from Brother Lucien, the gardener and physician at Varnhem cloister. On her way past Varnhem, the Queen had called on Father Henri to discuss how this could be done while observing all the rules of respectable behaviour. But Father Henri had begun with some important news. Arn Magnusson had been first sent to a strong Templar fortress called Tortosa in the part of the Holy Land called Tripoli. He had distinguished himself and been called to Jerusalem itself to serve one of the highest men in the Order. Hearing this Cecilia Rosa hugged her friend hard, her whole body shaking.

Afterwards, she went walking alone in the cloister. It was summertime and the apple trees between the buildings were in full bloom. Walking alone would have meant a punishment of at least a week in *carcer* during the worst time, but now Cecilia Rosa did not give it a thought. In this moment of happiness, Godshome simply did not exist.

He's alive, alive, alive! The news was sweeping her head clean of everything else. Then she had a vision of Jerusalem, the holiest of cities. She saw the streets paved with gold, the churches of white stone and the gentle, God-fearing faces of the people who lived in this peaceful place. Then her beloved Arn came walking towards her in his white mantle marked with the red cross of the Lord. This was a dream that would sustain her for many years to come.

Time at Godshome moved almost imperceptibly. Nothing much happened. Everything stayed as it had always been. They sang the same hymns in slow rotation, sold mantles made according to the same patterns, and watched the familiar seasons come and go. The sameness of almost everything hid the discovery of changes until they became truly momentous.

Brother Lucien began teaching Sister Leonore about the greatness of God reflected in nature, and what in nature was good for people to eat and drink or to treat illness. After a while, the sight of the two of them working together in the gardens seemed not particularly noteworthy and soon Father Lucien came to be regarded as part of Godshome. Everyone forgot that when he first came visiting, he was not left alone with Sister Leonore for a minute. Eight months into the second year of Father Lucien's comings and goings, there was not a hint of suspicion in any eye watching the two gardeners wander around together, deep in conversation, something which in other circumstances would have been most improper.

Cecilia Rosa and Ulvhilde were seeking out Sister Leonore's company more and more, because they realised how much she could teach them of all the things she herself was learning. A new world was opening in front of them as they understood what miracles skilled hands, with the help of God, could create in a garden. The Godshome fruit grew larger and juicier and was keeping better in winter storage. The rules forbade foreign spices but home-grown herbs were acceptable, and the eternal supper soups suddenly acquired new, more interesting flavours.

Increasingly, Cecilia and Ulvhilde would go to work in the garden or collect fruit and vegetables to bring back. This was how it became established that they could move freely in and out of the enclosed area of the cloister, excursions that a couple of years earlier would have been punished by the scourge or a stay in *carcer*.

Twilight was gathering one evening in late summer when Cecilia Rosa made herself an errand to the garden. All she wanted was to walk there on her own and enjoy its ripe loveliness. The apples were swelling with new sweetness under the late, blushing moon and the air was heavy with the smell of moist, rich soil. No one else was likely to be there and maybe that was why she did not discover the sinful secret until it was too late to shy away.

Between a couple of spreading berry bushes, Brother Lucien was lying with Sister Leonore on top of him. She was riding him lustily and without shame. It was as if they were man and wife in the world outside. This was the second thing that came to Cecilia Rosa's mind, after the first shock at the terrible sin, and she felt as though she had fallen under a spell – unable to move or scream or close her eyes or run away.

Then all other feelings gave way to a strange tenderness that made her almost want to share in their lovemaking. Her longing for Arn swept over her and she remembered their lovemaking, although they had never done it in this especially very sinful way. As she watched, the dusk between the trees deepened and the muffled sounds from the lovers ceased. Sister Leonore had rolled off Brother Lucien but stayed close to him. They were holding each other, caressing each other gently. Sister Leonore's clothing was in such a state that her naked breasts were exposed and she let Brother Lucien stroke them and play with her, while he lay on his back catching his breath.

Cecilia Rosa did not have it in her to condemn this appalling sin as she should. To her it looked like love. She tiptoed away, careful to make no sound. She asked herself if she was sinning too, and that night she prayed for a long time to Our Lady. As far as Cecilia Rosa knew, it was Our Lady who, more than anybody else, helped people who loved each other, and she prayed again for her beloved's life, but also for forgiveness on behalf of Sister Leonore and Brother Lucien.

She kept her secret to herself all through the autumn. When winter came, the garden was closed and Brother Lucien would not return to Godshome until the spring. Instead, Sister Leonore often worked with the others in the *vestiarium* and Cecilia Rosa would steal glances at her now and then. It seemed to her that Sister Leonore was lit from the inside by a light so strong that not even the dark shadow of the Abbess could blot it out. Sister Leonore smiled as she worked and hummed hymn tunes to herself. It seemed that her sin had brightened her eyes and made her more beautiful.

At the beginning of Lent, when only those who wanted to worked late, Cecilia Rosa found herself alone with Sister Leonore one night in the *vestiarium*. They were dyeing cloth red, by now a well practised process that went smoothly when they helped each other.

Without being quite certain why. Cecilia Rosa decided that she had better say something.

'Please, Sister, you mustn't get upset by what I'm going to tell you. It's just that I happened to see you and Brother Lucien together once in the orchard. I fear that your secret might be discovered by others and then you'd be in danger.'

Sister Leonore grew pale and covered her face with her hands. It took some time before she dared to look up.

'You won't betray us?' whispered Sister Leonore in a voice that was barely audible.

'Of course not!' Cecilia Rosa replied indignantly. 'I know that you know the reason why I am in Godshome. I sinned like you and, like you, for love. I'll never betray you, but I felt I must warn you. Sooner or later you'll be seen by someone who'll tell tales to Mother Rikissa, or she might find you herself. Either way, she's too malevolent to leave you alone.'

'I do believe the Holy Virgin Mary has forgiven us and is protecting us,' Sister Leonore said slowly and a little uncertainly.

'But you've promised her a lifetime of chastity – how can you believe that she'll just ignore the breaking of your vows?' Cecilia Rosa was more confused than shocked by the immodest way Sister Leonore spoke of her sinful thoughts,

'Because She has been helping us so far. The only one who's seen us is you and you're the only one here who can understand and forgive. And because love is a wonderful gift that makes life worth living, more than anything else!' Sister Leonore said, raising her voice defiantly, as if she were no longer afraid of anyone.

Cecilia Rosa was speechless. She felt suddenly transported to the top of a tall tower, looking out over great new vistas, but she was fearful, too, because she knew there was a risk of losing her balance and falling. It had never even occurred to her before that a blessed sister, wedded to the Sacred Bridegroom, could renege on her vows. Sister Leonore had sinned in the same way as Cecilia Rosa, but with a monk, also breaking his vows – not with her betrothed in the world outside. Cecilia Rosa's sin was a lesser one by far. Love could lead to the worst of sins, yet the Holy Scriptures confirmed that love was God's gift to mankind.

An old story came to her mind and she began telling it to Sister Leonore. She wasn't sure of all the details, but it was about Gudrun, a maiden who had been sent away to marry an old man, even though she didn't want to live with him because she loved a young man called Gunnar, who loved her back. The lovers never gave up hope or stopped praying to Our Lady. She must have listened for, in the end, she sent them a most wonderful deliverance and, as far as anyone knew, Gudrun and Gunnar were still living together in great happiness.

Sister Leonore had heard the story already from Brother Lucien, because it was apparently told and retold at Varnhem. Our Lady had actually chosen a young Varnhem monk, no more than a boy, to encounter Gudrun's intended and his companions, who were bad men, and given him the strength to kill them all. The monk-boy was innocent and without guilt because he killed in self-defence. The story proved that if you believed in God's gift of love and never faltered, all sins could be forgiven. Even manslaughter could be nullified when Our Lady took mercy on lovers who prayed to her.

So far the story seemed to make beautiful sense, but in truth Cecilia Rosa had to add something that made it less easy to understand and less comforting. Our Lady's chosen monk-boy was Arn Magnusson, and not that many years later he paid a heavy price for his love for Cecilia, who had been punished as hard, of course. This made Our Lady's intervention difficult to interpret. Cecilia Rosa had been pondering it for almost ten years and was still bewildered.

Sister Leonore, who had had no idea that Cecilia's Arn was the little monk in the story, was dumbstruck by this sad addition to the tale of Gudrun and Gunnar. Brother Lucien had never mentioned it, but he knew that the youngster had grown up to become a brave knight in God's own army and was now away fighting in the Holy Land. This had seemed to fit in with the idea that Our Lady had made everything end in the best possible way. There was no hint of lovers sentenced to live apart.

This conversation was followed by many more, and talking together made Cecilia Rosa and Sister Leonore very close. After a while, Cecilia Rosa convinced her new friend that there was nothing to fear from letting Ulvhilde Emundsdotter in on the secret. The three of them worked long hours in the *vestiarium* with such dedication that even Mother Rikissa had to praise them.

In a never-ending dance, their talk circled around the magic subject of love. Sister Leonore had fallen in love for the first time when she was Ulvhilde's age, but it had ended in misery. The man she loved had been forced by his family to marry an ugly old widow for reasons entirely to do with the widow's wealth. Leonore's father would have none of her weeping and wailing. He thought women were useless in business dealings and young women particularly witless about marriage. Besides, Leonore was too young to know what she wanted after just one romance.

Sister Leonore said that she had been convinced she'd never love another man and that she must spend her life wedded to the Sacred Bridegroom. She had given her vows eagerly as soon as her first year as a novice had ended. Now she felt that if the Holy Virgin had showed her anything beyond doubt, it was that the grace of love could come to anyone, anywhere. It must be said that the dour old man with his belief that no romance need be the last had also been proven right in a way. They all giggled delightedly at the thought of the mixed feelings of Leonore's father, had he ever learnt of the way in which he was right.

During all this talking, Cecilia Rosa and Ulvhilde seemed to be drawn deeper into sharing Sister Leonore's sin. Their cheeks glowed and their breathing came faster every time they were alone and able to talk of their secret subject. The forbidden fruit was divine, even when talking about it rather than tasting it. But forbidden it was, and one of them had already been punished for her love. Sister Leonore's sentence would be harder still, for she would be banned if discovered.

Ulvhilde had never before had any reason to believe that love existed in real life and listening to the whispered confidences of her friends changed her entire life. Stories and songs of love had seemed to Ulvhilde to be no more believable than tales about mythical creatures like gnomes and spirits. All such things, she thought, were fantasies to while away the time by the fireside during long winter evenings.

She had been a small girl when Knut Eriksson killed her father, Emund. She remembered leaving home in a sledge with her mother and two little brothers. Some time later a high-up man had ordered her mother to wed somebody and Ulvhilde had never seen anything remotely like love in that marriage. While in the cloister, Ulvhilde had come to the conclusion that she might as well take the vows, because being a blessed sister at least gave you more standing than living as an ageing maiden among the *familiares*. Cecilia Rosa would leave one day and, once she'd gone, there'd be nothing left for Ulvhilde except to love God. The only thing that had made her hesitate was the thought of promising to obey Mother Rikissa for all eternity. Then again, Mother Rikissa couldn't last forever. Alternatively, there might be a chance of moving to one of the new cloisters that Birger Brosa was planning to endow.

Ulvhilde's minimal expectations of life horrified her two friends.

Both entreated her not to take the vows. It was possible to live as a free person while loving and venerating God and God's Mother. When Ulvhilde protested that she'd never have anywhere else to live because all her relatives were dead, Cecilia Rosa said hotly that nothing was impossible with a friend like Queen Cecilia Blanca.

In her eagerness to persuade Ulvhilde, Cecilia Rosa found herself uttering things she hadn't been aware of even thinking. She kept to herself the realisation that there was a measure of selfishness in what she was saying; she couldn't bear the thought of losing another friend in Godshome. Now that she had promised, she would have to bring up the subject with Cecelia Blanca during her next visit.

Another exciting chain of thoughts had to do with age. Cecilia Rosa had been seventeen when she went into Godshome and unable to imagine herself at thirty-seven except as a bent, dried-up old woman. Looking at Sister Leonore, glowing with the youthful strength given to her by love, Cecilia was amazed to learn that her friend was exactly thirty-seven years old. If she trusted to Our Lady maybe she would be as radiant at Leonore's age.

The spring that year was to be unlike any other at Godshome, before or after. As work started in the gardens, Brother Lucien's visits began again and Sister Leonore's need of instruction was seemingly endless. It seemed reasonable to allow Cecilia Rosa and Ulvhilde to spend a lot of time in the garden so that no one could say that either the sister or the maidens were ever left alone with a man. But the two young women were, of course, spectacularly ill-suited as guardians. Instead, they kept watch to protect the law-breakers and gave Sister Leonore and Brother Lucien many more delightful trysts than they could ever have hoped for.

One annoyance was that the results of their winter labours disappeared before the summer, bringing in a lot of silver but also forcing Cecilia Rosa and Ulvhilde back into the *vestiarium*. Brother Lucien had a solution which, because he never spoke to the two maidens, Sister Leonore explained to them. The goods they made sold so quickly, Brother Lucien argued, because the prices they charged were too low. Raise the prices and the rate of sales would slow down but they would also bring in even more silver.

This sounded like white magic, but not too hard to grasp after some thought. It helped when Sister Leonore brought pages of writing explaining how it would work, telling them at the same time of Brother's Lucien's many jokes about the *yconomus* at Godshome.

The useless ex-curate apparently understood so little about money and counting that he didn't even keep the books properly.

Cecilia Rosa became very interested in this talk of keeping proper books, of using an abacus for counting, and turning trading goods made by busy hands into numbers to be understood by the mind. She started pestering Sister Leonore, who in turn got at Brother Lucien, and he brought account books from Varnhem with notes to help explain the system.

A whole new world was opening up to Cecilia Rosa and she was so absorbed by her insights that she tried to tell Mother Rikissa. At first the Abbess snorted with derision at these silly innovations, but with Lent almost over and Queen Cecilia Blanca's visit soon due, she became more amenable, at least in her behaviour, if not in her heart. Books and parchment were ordered from Varnhem and the ever-willing Brother Lucien was very helpful. It did not take him long to persuade Mother Rikissa that it would be very beneficial to the business of running Godshome if he were to instruct both Jöns, the *yconomus*, and Cecilia Rosa. Her only condition was that Brother Lucien must not speak to the maiden. He must direct all his teaching to *yconomus*, who would then address Cecilia. The arrangement infuriated Cecilia Rosa, who learnt much faster than the slow and resentful Jöns.

According to Brother Lucien, who was actually no more expert than any of the Varnhem brothers, the state of affairs at Godshome reminded him of a particularly messy rats' nest. The problem was not lack of assets, not at all, but the absence of balances between saved and owed silver, and between stores and ordered but unsold goods. *Yconomus* Jöns couldn't even say how much silver was in the chests, because his chief measure was 'a fistful'. Another tried and tested method, he declared, was to reckon that ten fistfuls would keep things going for a good long while and that less than five fistfuls was a cause for moderate alarm. The income from land was no better accounted for, and many tenants had not paid their dues for so long that they had been forgotten about.

Cecilia Rosa picked up everything Brother Lucien was saying very quickly. She was as able as Jöns was stubborn and stupid. His opinion, much repeated, was that the old ways were the best and that working by the sweat of one's brow created wealth, not newfangled tricks done with numbers and books. Brother Lucien only shook his head at this and insisted that Godshome's finances would be greatly improved with good book-keeping. To Mother Rikissa he also pointed out that it was sinful to manage God's realm on Earth quite as badly as was done at Godshome and she took the point. It was just that she couldn't see what might be done about it.

Brother Lucien and Sister Leonore had many moments to themselves that spring and the effect on Sister Leonore's waistline eventually became noticeable. It was only a matter of time before her crimes would be obvious to all. She wept and agonised until not even Brother Lucien's visits could comfort her any more. Her two friends had seen what was coming long before anyone else and felt that they carried some of the guilt. The quick sales of their handiwork meant that all three of them had a lot of time together in the *vestiarium* and Cecilia Rosa was determined to think hard about the problem rather than just moaning about it. She wanted to be like Cecilia Blanca in this matter and remember that doing nothing except sitting about crying might just lead to still more grief.

There was nothing for it: it would become known that Sister Leonore was pregnant and the immediate consequence would be a ban. A man had to be involved and that meant that Brother Lucien would also be banned. The two of them simply had to escape before they were forced to leave.

Sister Leonore pointed out that escape would mean banishment anyway, but Cecilia argued that it was still better to get away before they were found out and that they must concentrate on working out the details. It was better for the two of them to leave together, for a run-away banned nun would need all the protection she could get.

After a long discussion, Sister Leonore went off to talk to Brother Lucien, who told her of whole cities in the south of the Frankish lands where people like themselves, true believers in all except the meaning of human love, lived peaceably together. But it was a long way to walk, without money and dressed in their cloister habits.

They could easily make reasonably worldly clothes in the *vestiarium*, but getting silver was more difficult. Cecilia Rosa said that the state of Godshome's finances was such that no one would miss a fistful or two of its silver, but of course stealing from a cloister was an even worse sin than anything they'd done to date. Sister Leonore was desperately upset by this and pleaded that no one should steal for her sake. She'd rather wander the roads without a single coin in her pocket. They would surely be given asylum in the wonderful southern places. A theft from a house under the protection of the Blessed Virgin would never be forgiven.

Then Queen Cecilia Blanca sent a message to announce her visit. The three friends who guarded Godshome's gravest secret were

147

deeply relieved to hear that the Queen was coming. By now Sister Leonore was three, maybe four, months gone.

On the other hand, Mother Rikissa took the announcement of the visit badly. The old Archbishop had died but the new man, Johan, seemed to be just as much in the King's pocket as Stéphan had been. This meant that the Abbess saw nothing for it but to obey every whim of the Queen's. Cecilia Rosa, may she rot forever, was still as much of a threat. She was not worried about vengeful acts – Mother Rikissa knew a thing or two about taking revenge – but the threat of being banned was terrifying.

Cecilia Rosa, who understood her Superior's mind perfectly well, decided that it was time to have a serious talk. She requested an audience and without beating about the bush told Mother Rikissa that *yconomus* should be retired from most of his duties and Cecilia Rosa put in charge. She would manage business at Godshome and could give assurances that it would be better done than ever before. Jöns could devote himself to the journeys to markets, where at present he spent so much of his time that little seemed to be left for his other tasks.

Mother Rikissa stared at her, and objected feebly that she'd never heard of a woman *yconomus* – and besides, the word had a masculine ending. Cecilia Rosa countered this by saying that it was surely reasonable for women to do the tasks required in a nunnery that did not actually require physical strength to lift a horse or heave masonry about. As for the word, what was wrong with giving it a feminine ending? In the future she wanted to be known as the *yconoma* at Godshome.

The Abbess seemed unable to think of any other objections and Cecilia Rosa moved to the next stage. Obviously, it must be the *yconoma* who decided what her servant Jöns was given to do, but in the main he would be sent on errands. No decisions to trouble his head with, of course, since using his head had not proved one of his strengths.

This demand almost made Mother Rikissa lose her temper. She sat very still, rubbing her left hand with her right – in the past, a sure sign of impending bad moods, with much screaming about scourges and incarcerations. Finally she got herself under control and spoke quite calmy.

'God will no doubt show us if these decisions are wise or not. Do as you wish at present but pray humbly that it does not go to your head. Remember that I'm still your superior and can take away in an instant what I have given.'

'Indeed, Mother, you're *still* my Abbess. And may God protect you.' Cecilia Rosa pretended a humility she did not feel so that the hidden threat should not sound obvious. She left the room with her head bowed, and only just stopped herself from slamming the door. But she was hissing under her breath: so far and no further, you old witch.

When the Queen arrived she was accompanied by her first-born child, a boy called Erik, and she was obviously pregnant again. Now that they were both mothers, the meeting of the two Cecilias was even more warm and intimate than before. It added to the happiness of them both that Cecilia Blanca brought good news of both Arn and Magnus Magnusson.

Magnus was a brave and tough little boy, who climbed trees and rode horses. He had had his falls but was never seriously hurt. Birger Brosa insisted that he was already showing encouraging signs of becoming an outstanding archer, so there was no doubt whose son he was. According to Father Henri's sources, Arn was still in Jerusalem, mingling with kings and archbishops and other great men of the world. This delighted them both, because among such people he couldn't come to any serious harm, as Cecilia Blanca put it.

Then she inquired if Mother Rikissa was still behaving herself and Cecilia Rosa replied that it wasn't too bad but the peace and quiet would soon end. She added something vague to the effect that a serious problem was building up and might mean real danger to some people – but about these things she would only speak to the Queen in private.

The two friends climbed the stair to the *hospitium* bedchamber where they had spent their last night as prisoners together. Lying down on the bed and holding hands, they were silent for a while reliving their memories.

'Well then,' Cecilia Blanca finally said. 'What's the problem that's only for my ears?'

'I need silver coins.'

'How much and for what? Surely coins cannot be a real problem, of all the things you lack at Godshome?'

'How much? About two fistfuls, as our daft *yconomus* would say – by the way, I'm to replace him and become the *yconoma* – anyway, enough to finance a journey for two to the Frankish lands. Maybe about a hundred Sverker coins. This is a dear wish of mine and I promise to repay you and more, as soon as I can.'

'Are you and Ulvhilde about to run away? Don't, please, I don't want to lose you! And remember, we aren't at all old yet and half your penitence has already past.'

'No, it's got nothing to do with me or Ulvhilde,' Cecilia Rosa said with a little laugh. She had a vision of herself and Ulvhilde climbing the wall and walking away, hand in hand, to the distant Kingdom of the Franks.

'Swear that it hasn't,' The Queen said doubtfully.

'I swear, truly.'

'Please, can't you tell me what it's for?'

'No, I don't think I should. It's to finance something that in some people's eyes is a great sin, and if it was said that you might have helped, then wicked tongues might also say that you were part of the sin. If you don't know, you're without sin, you see.'

Silence fell again. Then Cecilia Blanca giggled and said that it wasn't much and she could easily take it from her travelling allowance, but she would hand over the coins only on condition that she was told of this dreadful sin that she was innocent of and still had to pay for. At least she wanted to be told later on, when everything was settled one way or the other. Cecilia Rosa promised her that. She went on to say that since the other thing she wanted to talk about affected Ulvhilde, it would be better if all three of them met up.

Then they kissed each other and went down to enjoy the Queen's table. Cecilia Blanca said that since wining and dining with her Queen seemed to cause Rikissa such pain, the Abbess might as well stay behind her walls that night. It would mean that everyone else would have a better time watching the amusing buffoons who travelled with the royal entourage. The entire party that night was composed of women, because the Queen had told her guards to keep an eye on the doors and otherwise eat and drink in their tents. As she said, it had not taken her long to find out that men became too noisy when they were drunk and always showed off to women, especially when no king or earl was present.

Not that the women spared the food and drink that night or kept their voices down. Their jokes became as wild as any man's, Cecilia Blanca taking the lead with her old tricks from the Godshome whippings, like burping or farting at will. She scratched her ears or her behind to imitate men she knew and all the women found this mightily funny.

But when the food was finished, she asked that some mead be left on the table and then ordered her ladies-in-waiting to leave. She and her closest friends at Godshome were going to talk of serious matters, that much she had guessed already. Everything concerning Ulvhilde Emundsdotter was serious.

Cecilia Rosa began the story by reminding her listeners of the stormy times when Ulvhilde arrived at Godshome, and of how the blessed Helena Stenkilsdotter had warned them to be wise and steady in their friendships and not rush about like frightened geese when the politics looked like turning against one faction or another. Ulvhilde's close family, and most of her distant relatives too, had died. For her, unlike the Cecilias, the tidings of the Bjälbo blood-meadows were the cause of the blackest grief and despair. Ever since, Ulvhilde had been forgotten and there was no one out there to speak for her. True, Rikissa was loath to throw a kinswoman out, but one day the fee would have to be paid somehow.

Time then to do something, Cecilia Rosa said. Then she reached out to get at her tankard and her elbow slipped off the table. They all burst out giggling.

'When you've stopped trying to wash the table in mead maybe we can get back to the matter in hand,' Cecilia Blanca said. 'And both as your queen and your friend I'd like to know what this long speech of yours is meant to achieve?'

'Simple, really,' Cecilia Rosa said, after calmly swallowing a mouthful of mead. 'Ulvhilde's father died and her small brothers and her mother inherited. Then her brothers died and then her mother too, so the whole inheritance of the family should be ...'

'Ulvhilde's, indeed,' the Queen said crisply. 'This is the law, as far as I can understand. Ulvhilde, what was the name of the estate that burnt down?'

'Ulfshem,' Ulvhilde replied. All this was quite unexpected and it scared her.

'The estate has been taken over by a Folkunga family now, I know them,' the Queen said thoughtfully. 'My dear friends, we must move carefully about this. We want to win and the law should be supporting us. But the law is one thing and men's notions of what's right and proper another. I can't promise anything, but I will try. First of all, I must talk with Torgny Lawman in East Gothland. He is a Folkunga man and related to the great Torgny Lawman. Then I'll ask Birger Brosa for advice, and once that's done I'll go a round or two with the King. I give you my word!'

Ulvhilde was sitting bolt upright, looking very pale and suddenly completely sober. Her older friends had been thinking ahead of her, but now she understood that her life could be changed as if by magic. Then it struck her that she'd have to leave her dearest, dearest friend Cecilia Rosa and burst into tears.

'I won't ever leave you alone with that evil troll Rikissa, not now when Sister Leonore . . .' she sobbed, but was interrupted at once by Cecilia Rosa who placed a warning finger across her friend's lips and then hugged her.

'There, there, remember that I was left behind once before and that was by Cecilia Blanca, who's sitting right here. Anyway, soon enough I'll be out of here too. Now, not another word about all this in front of your queen.'

Cecilia Blanca rolled her eyes and lifted her eyebrows to let them know she hadn't missed a thing. Then she left them, muttering that she'd be back soon but had to go and get some bits and pieces. While she was away Cecilia Rosa tried to comfort Ulvhilde who had started crying again.

'I know,' she said, 'I've felt as you do. But time's on our side, my side, too.'

'But . . . you'll be alone . . . and that witch . . .' sobbed Ulvhilde.

'I'll deal with her, I'm stronger now. And remember how strong love is – isn't it one of God's miracles? Our Lady will help people in love who never give in and lose hope.'

All this seemed to comfort Ulvhilde a little and she drank some mead, although she'd actually had more than enough already. Then Cecilia Blanca returned and put a leather purse on the table with a thump.

'Two fistfuls, or thereabouts,' she said laughingly. 'Whatever sly schemes you're planning see that you succeed, damn it!'

At first they stared at her in astonishment – this was a man speaking! Then they all burst out laughing.

They hid the leather purse full of silver in a cracked section of the garden wall and described the place to Sister Leonore. They also sewed the clothes when they had time to themselves and gave them to Leonore to hide as best she could. Summer was drawing to a close, and Brother Lucien visited often to give invaluable advice about the harvest.

He also brought a little book he had drafted, which contained most of the things he knew. It was a gift for Cecilia Rosa from a brother who had never spoken to her but who still wanted her to have a gift of thanks. Using Sister Leonore as go-between, Cecilia slowly learnt to understand the contents of the cryptic little book.

One evening late in summer, when the apples were almost ripe and the moon glowed red and Sister Leonore's habit could no longer hide her blessed state, Cecilia Rosa and Ulvhilde accompanied her to the small gate leading to the garden, unlocked it with the keys from the familiar hiding place and opened it carefully to prevent any squeaking. Brother Lucien stood waiting outside, in worldly dress and carrying a bundle of clothes for Sister Leonore.

The three women hugged quickly and blessed each other, but did not cry. Then Sister Leonore wandered off into the moonlit night and Cecilia Rosa slowly closed the gate behind her. Ulvhilde turned the key and the two friends went back to the *vestiarium* and calmly carried on working as though nothing had happened.

Sister Leonore had left them forever. Quite apart from the recriminations that would follow, she had left a huge space in their lives. Cecilia Rosa, who both hoped and feared to be left alone again in Godshome, missed her most of all.

VII

In the Holy Land, autumn and winter was the time of rest and healing. It was as though the land itself, as well as its warring inhabitants, needed respite to build up strength while hostile forces were unable to march and fight. In the region round Jerusalem the roads were no better than ditches deep in mud, and on the bare hills the wind blew over sodden drifts of snow. A besieging force would have suffered more than the besieged.

The climate was better in Gaza. It was cool, though no worse than a Nordic summer, and rained almost all the time, but snow was unknown in those parts. After the miraculous victory at Mont Gisard, Arn was back in command in Gaza and very busy, with two tasks in particular dominating his daily life. One was dealing with the hundred-odd Mameluke prisoners that had been brought there, more or less badly mauled. The second was caring for almost thirty wounded knights and sergeants hospitalised in the northern wing of the fortress.

Two of the prisoners held the sort of rank that made locking them into a grain store impossible: Saladin's brother Fahkr and his amir Moussa. Arn prepared space for these two in his own living quarters and took his midday meal in their company every day instead of eating in the refectories with his brothers. He was aware that his behaviour caused consternation, but then he had not let it be known quite how important Fahkr was.

In all of Outremer and the neighbouring countries, everybody behaved in the same way to prisoners, regardless of whether they were followers of the Prophet, or Christians, or of any other persuasion. Important prisoners like Fahkr and Moussa were either exchanged or returned against ransom. Prisoners without a price were usually beheaded.

With a few exceptions, the Gaza prisoners were Mamelukes. The most straightforward way was to sort them into those who were still slaves and those who had served for long enough to have been given their freedom and some property. The slaves might as well have their heads chopped off because, like the Knights Templar, no one would pay ransom for them. Also, keeping them alive would lead to overcrowding and disease, so elimination was the best policy from all points of view.

Financially, the greatest asset was Fahkr ibn Ayyub al Fahdi. He alone would be worth more than the greatest ransom ever paid for a Saracen thus far. Moussa, too, was a great bargain. Naturally, both men were taken completely by surprise when Arn suggested something different, namely that Saladin should exchange each prisoner for the same price, five hundred gold besants. Fahkr protested that most of the prisoners were not worth a single besant, in gold or not, and that Arn's suggestion was actually insulting. Arn clarified further – he had counted on five hundred besants per prisoner including Fahkr and Moussa.

This was utterly astonishing. Were they being humiliated by this unbeliever? He was, after all, Al Ghouti, the first of all Franks in the eyes of right-thinking men. Maybe he was avoiding too heavy a charge on Saladin. The possibility that a Knight Templar might be rather unworldly about business did not seem worth considering. They spoke carefully about the matter every time they met for the midday meal.

Arn only served fresh, clean water with the food and when he left them alone in his quarters, he provided the Holy Quran for them to study. But even though he treated his two noble prisoners with regard, there was no doubt that they were in captivity and during the first days they were cautious about what they said. Arn found their circumspection excessive, and by the fourth day he seemed almost impatient.

'I don't understand you at all,' he said, sounding mildly exasperated. 'What's the problem? My faith demands that I should be merciful towards prisoners. I could go on elaborating the point, were it not for thinking it unfair to preach my own faith to you now that you're not free, but it shouldn't be hard to grasp, for your own faith makes the same demand. These are the words of the Prophet, peace be with him: "When you meet those who deny the true faith on the battlefield, direct your swords towards their heads until they fall before you; then capture the survivors alive. The time will come when you free them and let them go or exchange them for ransom, so that the burden of war is made lighter for you. This is what you have to observe." You recognise it, don't you? What if my Scriptures tell me the same?'

'It's your liberality about the price that we cannot understand,' Fahkr mumbled uncomfortably. 'You know full well that asking a mere five hundred besants for my freedom sounds laughable.'

'I know, and if you were my only prisoner I'd happily demand fifty thousand besants from your brother. But what about the other prisoners? Am I supposed to cheerfully hand them over to our Saracen executioners? Fahkr, is your life worth more than that of every other man? And how much *is* a good man's life worth?'

'To claim that one's life is worth more than another man's is to go beyond what is right. It is also blasphemous, for God makes no such distinctions and that's why the Holy Quran declares each life to be precious,' Fahkr replied quietly.

'Exactly so. Indeed. And Jesus Christ said as much, so there's no dispute between us in this. Let's talk about something more interesting instead. The total cost to Saladin for all the prisoners here is fifty thousand besants. Moussa, I would like you to travel to your master and give him this message.'

'You send me as your messenger? Setting me free?' Moussa asked, clearly completely baffled.

'Yes, because I can't think of a better man for this errand. I trust you, as I would trust myself, not to think of your own freedom only and run away. Now, we've got ships sailing to Alexandria every day, as you may know – or not? Anyway, that might be the wrong direction, so maybe I should ask you to go to Damascus instead.'

'Going to Damascus is the harder journey and it doesn't matter much where in Saladin's lands you go, a message would reach him from any city within a day.'

'Really, from any city . . . and in one day?' Arn sounded dubious. 'I've heard it said, but how is it done?'

'Simple. We use homing pigeons. Pigeons bred in one place, Damascus, say, are carried in cages to another, for instance Alexandria. Or Baghdad or Mecca. Tie the message to one of the legs and let the bird go. They always fly home and along the shortest distance, too.'

'How miraculous,' Arn said, obviously very impressed. 'So I could converse with my Grand Master every day? How long would a pigeon take to fly to Jerusalem? Half an hour?'

'Certainly, if you had trained the pigeons and looked after them properly,' Moussa said, with an expression suggesting that he thought all this was a lot of fuss about nothing.

'Extraordinary . . .' Arn muttered dreamily. Then he pulled himself together. 'That's agreed then. Tomorrow you'll sail for Alexandria with one of our ships. Don't worry about the company, most of the sailors are Egyptians and I'll anyway give you a document of free passage. I'll try to arrange that you get some of the wounded prisoners to escort. Now, let's change the subject!'

'Yes, I agree. There are many things to talk about,' Fahkr said. 'For instance, I pleaded with my brother that we should take Gaza, but he wouldn't listen. Things would've been very different if he had.'

'I would have been dead, that's for certain. You would have been masters of Gaza after having lost about half your army. But He, who sees everything and He, who hears everything – as you say – ordained differently. He must have wanted the Knights Templar to win the victory at Mont Gisard, even though we were just two hundred men against several thousand. It is proven, because it took place. It must have been His will.'

'Two hundred! You were only two hundred men?' Moussa exclaimed. 'By God! I was there myself of course . . . I could've sworn . . . one thousand, maybe. But two hundred?'

'Yes, that's right. I was in charge and led the attack, so I know. Instead of dying defending Gaza, as I thought I would, I was chosen to win a miraculous victory. Now you understand why I must be humble and magnanimous towards the defeated, don't you?'

They agreed on the folly of investing human pride in successes that were in God's gift only, and that God would harshly punish such hubris – that much was common ground between their faiths. After great victories, modesty and restraint was in order, but the great questions about the balance between human sin and God's will were still left open to debate.

They also accepted as given that Saladin could have taken Gaza. Why had God punished his conciliatory behaviour? And why had God let Saladin suffer such a brutal defeat at the hands of Al Ghouti, after having shown such mercy precisely to Al Ghouti? All three of them pondered these questions and discussed the meaning of it all.

Moussa at last concluded that God must have forcibly reminded His most beloved servant, Saladin, that Jihad could not be directed according to the wishes of one man alone. Saving an entire city on account of a debt of gratitude to one inhabitant just wouldn't do. The argument was based on the conviction, shared by Moussa and Fahkr, that Gaza would have been sacked had it not been for

Saladin's high regard for its commander. But this was a sin and God had meted out his punishment at Mont Gisard.

Unsurprisingly, Arn did not agree. In his view, God had decided to protect the people whose belief in Him came closest to His true nature. So many things had come together at Mont Gisard that the only explanation must be His direct intervention. Saladin had left Gaza alone because he thought taking it would waste time that should be spent going for a greater prize. He had left too small a force besieging Ashkelon and allowed his invincible army to disintegrate into plundering units. The misty morning gave the greater advantage to the smaller force and – as if all this weren't enough – Arn and his men had had the incredible luck of arriving at just the right place at the right time, when the Mameluke army was marching with the least room for manoeuvre. Taken together, all this surely confirmed the teachings of Jesus Christ? Muhammad, may peace be with him, was but a divinely inspired prophet. How else could anyone understand the wonderful victory at Mont Gisard?

Moussa tried to explain how it could be otherwise. God, he argued, had observed that the true believers were on the brink of crushing the Christians, whose beliefs are the closest to the true faith, and turned His back on them all. As a consequence the war was conducted only by human minds. Certainly, men of the true faith had committed many errors of the kind that come from over-estimating your likelihood of success. Bravado is always punished in warfare, regardless. Any experienced professional soldier has observed the deadly outcomes of foolish or risky decisions thousands of times. Wasn't it misplaced pride to imagine that God would bother to get involved in every little skirmish fought by His children? Couldn't Mont Gisard be most simply explained by it having slipped God's mind, as it were, so that man's pride and the luck of war become decisive?

Neither Arn nor Fahkr liked this explanation. Fahkr thought it was nothing short of blasphemous to suggest that God might turn His back on His warriors fighting Jihad for His sake. Arn pointed out that the Christian side was actually fighting for God's Grave and surely could expect at least His attention.

Again they returned to the unanswerable question of which faith was the true one. In the end Fahkr, a seasoned negotiator, steered the discussion to an area of possible agreement. Man would never know whether God had punished the Jihad fighters who threatened Jerusalem in His name, or protected those who defended the Holy City, also in His name. If they were unclear about who was punished or protected, how could they be certain whether the Prophet, peace be with him, or Jesus Christ, peace be with him too, proclaimed the true faith?

Siegfried de Turenne, or Thüringen in his own language, had been wounded at Mont Gisard and Arn persuaded him to be cared for in Gaza, rather than at his own fortress, Castel Arnald. Arn never explained exactly why this was preferable, because it seemed unwise at the time to tell the ailing Knight Templar that he would be treated by Saracen doctors.

Employing Saracens in hospitals was considered positively shameful by some knights, though typically they were new arrivals in Outremer. Indeed, the new recruits usually believed that all Saracens should be killed at sight, no questions asked. Some of the worldly Franks held the same views and, in both cases, the reason was lack of experience. During his first year, Arn himself had been as stupid but for one thing, he had come to share the high opinion of the local medical men held by almost all the long-serving brothers. In comparison with the Franks, the Saracen doctors had by far the larger proportion of surviving patients. A joke, with more than a little truth in it, said that if wounded, your best hope was a doctor from Damascus and the next best was no doctor at all, but a Frankish medic meant all hope was gone.

The question of whether it was a sign of faltering faith to allow oneself to be looked after by an infidel was sometimes debated in worldly circles. It was even suggested that relying on a Saracen was a sin, even though he was the better doctor. Arn always countered this by saying humorously that to reward purity of faith by death and punish a sin by life seemed unreasonable, and that being allowed into Paradise if you died on the battlefield was one thing, but going to heaven for refusing good treatment quite another.

Siegfried complained about 'impure hands' in the beginning but stopped soon enough, His doctors, Utman ibn Khattab and Abd al-Malik, had managed to remove the arrowhead buried in his chest, even though the tip went in so deep that it touched his shoulder blade. Their herbal concoctions had stilled his fever and their cleansing spirit had stopped the wound suppurating. After only ten days Siegfried could see for himself that the wound was healing and could even move his arm, though this was against doctor's orders.

When he grew better, Siegfried was able to observe the differences between the infirmary in Gaza and the fortress hospitals he had encountered elsewhere. Here, the spacious rooms for the ill and wounded were situated several stories up and kept cool and well aired though the arrow-slits. Wooden shutters protected against wind and rain. The patients, bedded down among woollen blankets and sheepskins, had their linen constantly changed and taken away to be washed in the town laundries. The beds stood so far apart that it was hard to talk to your neighbours. The whole thing was a pleasant change from the usual converted grain store, even though it was not obvious what it had to do with healing.

The absence of incessant prayers was also agreeable, as was the lack of medical fuss. When the Saracen doctors had cleaned and bandaged the wound, they tended to leave it alone instead of fiddling with poultices, warming pads full of cow dung and more of that sort. Only rarely was it necessary to cauterise persistently suppurating wounds with white-hot irons, and then Arn himself came along, accompanied by two sturdy sergeants to hold the unfortunate patient down. Arn anyway came every day to lead a brief prayer before going round with the doctors to translate their, and their patients', comments.

This was all new to Siegfried, but soon his common sense overcame his initial suspicion. Most of the men recovered and left well enough to return to more or less normal service, while in Siegfried's previous experience at least half the hospitalised men either died or left as cripples. During his time in Gaza only one man died in the infirmary and he had suffered deep stomach wounds, known to be almost always deadly. The obvious conclusion was to immediately employ a Saracen doctor in Castel Arnald, even though it went against the grain. Any other decison would be unthinkable, because it would betray his wounded brothers.

The doctor Abd al-Malik was Arn's oldest friend in Outremer. They had met when Arn arrived as a shy, innocent eighteen-year-old on his first posting to the Templar fortress in Tortosa, far up the coast. He had pleaded with the doctor to teach him Arabic and the lessons had continued over two years, until Arn got orders to move on.

According to Abd al-Malik, the purest Arabic was found in the texts of the Quran, for it was God's own language transmitted through one Messenger, may peace be with him. Arn provoked his teacher by pointing out that it was likely to be thought correct if only because it had always been used as the universal guideline. These little arguments amused both teacher and pupil, and Abd al-Malik was unfazed by other people's faiths. He had worked for Djuk

Turks, Byzantine Christians, the Shia Caliph in Cairo and the Sunni Caliph in Baghdad – whoever offered the best pay at the time.

When Arn and Abd al-Malik met again by chance in Jerusalem, Arn had just been given the command in Gaza. He persuaded his former teacher to come and work for him as a doctor for old friendship's sake, but with a princely income for good measure. It would be worth it, for to repair an experienced knight so he could get back in the saddle again was infinitely preferable to training a newly arrived lad from scratch.

Not that the Templar order was short of gold. At this time there was probably no wealthier organisation in the world and some said that the contents of the Templar treasure chests amounted to more than those belonging to the Kings of the Frankish lands and England combined. It might have been true, and it was certainly true that the Knights Templar knew how to trade for profit.

Gaza itself was not just the southernmost outpost on the Christian frontline against invasions from Egypt, but also one of eight trading harbours along the Palestine coast. It had the advantage over other harbours, such as Acre, of being wholly controlled by the Templar Order. This made it possible to continue trading with Alexandria, war or no war. Besides, nobody could know the extent of the shipping between the two neighbouring cities. The hundreds of merchant ships that made up the large Templar fleet in the Mediterranean also linked Gaza with cities such as Venice, Genoa and Pisa. By using the camel trains of its own two Bedouin tribes, Gaza was a node in a network linking Pisa with Tiberias and Pisa with Mecca.

Of all the goods manufactured under Templar control and sold on to Franks, Germans, Britons, Portugese, Castilians and many others, the most important was pure sugar. Camels brought sugar from Tiberias, where the canes were grown, harvested and the sugar extracted, to nearby ports or, preferably, all the way to Gaza, where the transfer to ships was fast. Sugar was a very sought after commodity, paid for weight by weight in silver.

Immense sums passed through the hands of the Gaza commander, his quartermaster, and the clerks who served them. The temptation to fraud was constantly confronting them and never more than when shipments of gold arrived. When one ship from Alexandria turned up laden with eight huge chests containing fifty thousand gold besants, it would have been easy for someone in Arn's position to change the account to, say, thirty thousand besants. He could have kept the difference and gone back home to buy up the entire country he came from with his newly acquired wealth.

It seemed that few of the worldly men who served under the banner of the Cross hesitated to enrich themselves in the Holy Land, but during Arn's long service in the Templar order such crimes were unheard of among the brothers. There was a story about a brother, found in possession of a gold coin, which he insisted he had kept because it brought him luck. He was immediately deprived of his white mantle, so his claim was patently not true.

Arn was deeply convinced that his promise to live in poverty was crucial and would not even accept the five horses the commander was allowed, rather than the four allotted to ordinary brothers. The sight of the fifty thousand besants did not cause his heart to skip a single beat and he felt certain that he was no different from other brothers in this.

It was a relief for him to dispatch the hundred Egyptian prisoners, as it was a relief – though mixed with regret – to say farewell to Fahkr and Moussa and escort them on board the waiting ship bound for Alexandria. Moussa had returned in person with Saladin's ransom. They parted as good friends, exchanging merry jokes about what a pleasure it would be for Arn to be a Saracen prisoner next time. Arn laughed, and reminded them that it would either be a very short or a very long imprisonment, because no ransom would ever be paid. The pleasure might be in anticipation alone.

What He who sees all and He who hears all had in store for them, none of them could have anticipated, not even in their wildest dreams.

When Siegfried de Turenne was well enough to take up riding again, he immediately insisted on weapons practice as well. He approached Arn, because he preferred to train with a friend of the same rank as himself. Sword-fighting seemed the best to start with and they wandered into the armoury to choose weapons and shields. The equipment was arranged by numbers, indicating size. The tall Siegfried needed a size nine sword and took a number ten shield, while Arn selected size sevens for both sword and shield. The arms used for training were the same as for battle, but their cutting edges were blunted by grinding and the unpainted shields had been covered by extra thick layers of soft leather to endure being hit more often.

As soon as they had entered the training arena, Siegfried leapt at Arn and hit out with furious energy. He was clearly intent on going at full tilt from the start. Arn laughed, parried, and stepped out of reach easily. He pointed out that it was the wrong way of going about practising and could only end with aches and pains and more damage. With slow, deliberate movements, he went on to direct a series of blows at Siegfried's shield-side, keeping an eye on his friend who was finding it difficult to raise and lower his shield with his injured arm. To ease the pressure, Arn shifted to another exercise that involved moving close and drawing back, forcing Siegfried to reach out and then retreat, stretching his injured thigh again and again.

After some more of this Arn stopped the session, saying that it was clear enough what Siegfried's weaknesses were and surely unwise to continue testing his strength at present. Siegfried protested that pain was something knights should endure for their own good, and Arn countered that it might be true enough for healthy men but not for the recovering wounded. He would rather order Siegfried to be tied to his bedposts than allow him to carry on like this. And by the way, he'd pull rank and forbid Siegfried to practise with anybody but himself. Siegfried muttered angrily but followed his friend to the chapel to sing in the evening service.

Afterwards, Arn was due to officiate at a *majlis* outside the eastern wall of the fortress. Every Thursday, accompanied by the learned doctor Utman ibn Khattab, he sat in judgement over disputes and sentenced criminals. He asked Siegfried to join him, since it might be of interest to a northern commander to observe what kinds of problems turned up in the south. The only condition was that he had to wear full knightly dress, complete with mantle and sword.

Siegfried came along to this alien form of justice mostly out of curiosity. He tried to tell himself to be fair and not too hasty in condemning what was obviously a pretence, certainly eccentric and potentially degrading, of allowing Saracens the justice accorded to equals. Even though he reminded himself of how much he had come to admire the Saracen art of medicine, he found the *majlis* a distasteful spectacle at first. It seemed to make a mockery of sacred texts that the Quran was placed next to the Holy Scripture on the pulpit at which he sat with Arn and the Saracen doctor. In front of them, a large crowd of people had gathered behind a boundary marked by a rope and guarded by armed, black-clad sergeants.

The whole performance began with Arn saying the Pater Noster, although very few in his audience seemed able to join in the prayer. He was followed by Utman ibn Khattab, who said a prayer in the language of the unbelievers. Most of the people present began hitting their foreheads on the ground. Then a Palestinian peasant from one of the outlying villages stepped forward to present the first case. A heavily veiled woman was walking slightly behind him, and another woman with her hands tied behind her back was made to walk ahead. In front of the tribunes, the man pushed the bound woman down in the sand. Then he bowed to the three judges, raised his arm and rattled through a long incantation, apparently in homage to Arn.

Siegfried, who had found it all quite incomprehensible so far, listened to Arn's mumbled translation of the Palestinian's case with increasing interest. The mistreated woman was his wife. She had been unfaithful, but the husband had nobly given up the right to kill her there and then, although it was his according to the true faith. He had been merciful only because, like everybody else in Gaza, he had promised to obey certain laws in exchange for the protection of the fortress. However, now he'd discovered his wife sinning in a major way and had brought a respectable woman, who was his neighbour in the village, as a witness.

Arn interrupted the monotonous pleading and asked the respectable woman to speak. The audience was silent as she shyly came forward and, when questioned, confirmed that the man's account was true in every detail. Arn asked her to put her hand on the Holy Quran, swear that she'd burn forever in hell for any falsehood in her testimony, and then make her statement again. Trembling, as if told to touch a red-hot stove, she put her hand on the sacred book and repeated all she had said. Arn told her to move away while he discussed the matter with Utman ibn Khattab.

Once the two judges had nodded in agreement, Arn rose and spoke in the infidel language, apparently from one of their texts. Siegfried was intrigued to learn from the brief translation that four witnesses were required to prove adultery and that the accusation in this case was invalid. Then Arn unsheathed his dagger and walked toward the bound woman. There was a collective intake of breath in the audience, but Arn only used the knife to cut her ties. Then he told her that she could walk free from the *majlis*.

The next stage in the proceedings surprised Siegfried even more. The witness was told that she had sworn a worthless oath and must be punished. She was to serve the falsely accused woman for a year or go into exile from the village. If she didn't obey, she would be executed in punishment for her perjury. As for the man, who had dragged along a single witness and wasted everybody's time, he would be given eighty lashes for making mock of the law, as the Holy Quran prescribes.

The judgement was heard in petrified silence, soon broken by the man's lamentations as he was dragged away by two sergeants. The two women, the accused who walked free and the respectable witness who became a slave, disappeared into the crowd, which had started to debate the outcome of the case. Siegfried, with the hubbub filling his ears, looked out over the scene and spotted a small group of elderly bearded men with white turbans. They were apparently some kind of Saracen priests and he was relieved to see that they seemed to be calmly nodding approval at Arn's extraordinary decisions.

The next case had been called once before but postponed so that the evidence could be brought. The evidence was a horse. Two men, who seemed to be almost fighting to keep a grip on the reins, led it into the enclosure. Both claimed the animal as his own and each accused the other of being a horse thief. Arn made them swear on the Holy Quran and while one made his oath, the other had to hold the horse. The audience found the whole performance immensely amusing so far.

Both men took the oath with apparent conviction, even though one of them must be perjuring himself. After a long consultation with his Saracen colleague, Arn muttered an order to one of the sergeants and soon afterwards a butcher's carriage turned up. Meanwhile, he told the men sternly that one of them would burn in hell for the sake of a horse and that there was only one possible judgement. He drew his sword, making a theatrical show of lifting it high above his head. Both men were alarmed but neither reacted in a way that helped to spot the liar.

With a single, one-armed blow, Arn severed the horse's neck and leapt quickly sideways to avoid the jets of blood and kicking legs. Then he wiped the blade, sheathed it and raised his hand to stop the noise from the agitated crowd. The butchers would carve the horse in half, he declared. The man who had lied would get half a horse he didn't deserve, but his punishment in hell would be all the worse. The truthful one would be deprived of half a horse, but his reward in heaven would be all the greater.

Once the horse had been butchered and the enclosure spread with clean sand, the hearings resumed. Most of the disputes were about money and were resolved by compromise, and Siegfried was getting bored. Only one proven liar was taken away to be whipped. The last case seemed more exciting, at least judging by the reaction of the crowd. Everyone was whispering and looking curiously at a handsome young Bedouin couple, an unveiled woman and a very well dressed man.

Their submission contained two requests: asylum in Gaza to

protect them from vengeful parents and permission to be made husband and wife according to the true faith by one of the city's *khatibs*. Arn immediately granted them asylum, but the second request seemed to be more difficult to meet. After an earnest exchange with Utman ibn Khattab, they finally came to a conclusion. When Arn rose, the noise of the crowd died away at once.

'You Aisha, with a name like the Prophet, may peace be with him, belong to the *Banu Qays* and you Ali, with a name like a holy man whom some call a caliph, belong to *Banu Anaza*, two Gaza tribes which are both ruled by the Knights Templar and therefore by me. The case is, however, not easy to settle, for your families are enemies and for me to grant you the right to wed might lead to war. I cannot permit this now, but promise you that your case is still open. Meanwhile, go in peace and enjoy the asylum of Gaza.'

As Siegfried learned the details, his first reaction was to marvel at seeing a brother in the army of God descending to the level of these natives and taking their family rows seriously. But then, he had to give Arn credit for the dignified way he handled all this. Also, everyone in the mixed audience seemed to accept Arn's judgements respectfully.

There was no time to discuss these interesting matters afterwards, because they had to attend vesper and then take their meal in the refectory – in silence, as always. Later on, before compline and the handing out of orders for the following day, there was a quiet time when they could talk.

Siegfried didn't want to start by questioning whether it was reasonable to treat Saracen slave peoples as if they were worthy of Christian justice, and was completely bemused when Arn told him that the whole thing was an elaborate charade to maintain his own standing as Gaza's ruler. Utman ibn Khattab, who understood the situation perfectly, was the true judge. Unlike Arn, the doctor was experienced in legal matters and also something of an expert in the interpretation of the infidels' Sharia law.

Siegried took this in and decided he had better stick to discussing individual cases. In the first case it was likely, Arn said, that the would-be respectable witness had been the adulteress and that both she and the man had perjured themselves. Be that as it may, they couldn't be tested with immersion or burning irons in the Frankish way, because it was against the local law and generally regarded as barbaric. There was no point in using methods that nobody trusted.

As for the man's belief that the Quran sanctioned the husband's right to kill an unfaithful wife, that was just wilful ignorance. The law wisely insisted on four witnesses. When Siegried protested that it was surely hard to find four observers of adulterous goings-on, Arn agreed. Presumably Muhammad had worked this out, too, and decided that his ruling would stop these complicated cases from being brought in the first place.

When Siegfried had stopped laughing, mostly because his chest-wound had started to hurt, he turned to the matter of the decapitated horse.

'What was all that about?' he asked.

'Blood and death are important,' Arn replied gravely. 'These courts are partly theatre, of course, but mustn't be seen just as an afternoon's entertainment. If one of the men had been caught out in perjury, *his* head would have been rolling in the sand. Everybody knows this. The idea is to instil fear of the law, but with justice seen to be done.'

'All very well, but what about the way you let these people get away with their own ungodly practices? This swearing on the infidels' book, which is nothing but the Devil's own work, looked more than a little blasphemous to me.'

'Maybe so, though at times the Devil's way of putting things sounds remarkably like the words of Jesus Christ,' Arn sighed. 'Anyway, it's essential that they swear on something they believe in. Would you feel bound by an oath you'd been forced to swear on the Quran?'

Siegfried replied that he wouldn't, naturally. After a pause, he added that this kind of court procedure would never happen under his command and probably nobody else's either. Still, he added mildly, other fortresses didn't have as many native folks to deal with and some of them must be very strange indeed. Bedouins, for instance.

Arn promptly invited him to join tomorrow's trip to visit the families of the young runaway couple. When Siegfried muttered something to the effect that surely it was rather distasteful to get involved in their couplings, he was firmly told that this was no minor matter. As he would see. Siegfried couldn't resist his own curiosity and the following day they set out on their own towards the Bedouin camps. Riding out with no escort worried him, however.

'Why not take a couple of sergeants at least?' he asked. 'You know how pleased the infidels are when they get a chance to ride about with Christian heads stuck on the tips of their lances. And we're high-ranking prey.'

'True. The worst might happen one day and both our heads will be on parade. They do like the heads of Templar knights; maybe it's got something to do with our beards. At least ordinary Franks are clean-shaven, so their heads probably look less impressive.'

'Don't be ridiculous, it's got nothing to do with beards,' Siegfried said sourly. 'We are their most feared enemies, so that's why they want to show off having killed us.'

Arn dropped the subject, but still insisted there would be no escort.

After only an hour at a slow pace, they saw the black tents in the camp of the tribe called *Banu Anaza*. At that moment, about twenty men came running out of their tents, leapt on their horses and rode out at a gallop, shouting wildly and brandishing their swords and lances.

Arn drew his sword and Siegfried followed suit, pale with sudden fear.

'Please, could you speed up for a bit?' Arn called out and spurred his horse. Arn's face was looking absurdly cheerful, Siegfried felt. He nodded grimly, as he urged his horse on towards the war-like horde.

'Do what I do and for God's sake, don't use your sword on anybody!' Arn shouted, and stormed off towards the Bedouin camp, swinging his sword threateningly over his head. After a second's hesitation, Siegfried followed his example.

When the two groups of riders met, the Bedouin swung round and they all galloped on together until Arn, with Siegfried at his heels, pulled up his horse next to the largest tent in the camp. Outside, an elderly man with a long grey beard and dressed in black waited while Arn and Siegfried leapt off their horses and greeted him with their swords held high. Then they saluted everyone else and were greeted from the saddle by the riders, who were taking their horses at a slow trot in a wide circle round the old man's tent.

When the formalities were complete everybody sheathed their swords, the riders dismounted and Arn spoke warmly to the old man, introducing Siegfried as his brother. They were led into the tent and given fresh water to drink before being invited to sit among the piles of cushions on the richly carpeted ground.

Arn's conversation with the Bedouin chief started as a polite ritual, full of mutual respect and requiring each man to repeat much of what had been said by the other. Later, there was a point when the chief seemed angry and upset and needing to be soothed by Arn, whose almost humble manner seemed to calm the old man. A little later he became very thoughtful, mumbling to himself and pulling at his beard.

Suddenly Arn rose and began to say farewell, only to be met by effusive, persistent protests. Siegfried stood up to support Arn in refusing what he took to be offers of food and they left, but only after Arn and the chief had exchanged more polite phrases. The final greeting involved grasping the chief's hands, which Siegfried found off-putting but steeled himself to do not to let Arn down. They were accompanied out of the camp by the riders who had received them, and at the same furious pace. They reined in their horses to a slow trot when they were on their own again, so that Arn could explain what had been achieved.

'First though, never arrive at a Bedouin camp with any kind of escort, armed or not,' he began. 'They just conclude that you're either a coward or an enemy. Riding alone, they take you to be a brave man with honest intentions and that's why the warriors welcomed us.'

'Do we own these people?' he went on thoughtfully. 'Strictly speaking we do or, at least, that's how our Christian authorities see it. But the Bedouins believe that no one can enslave them. They can't be imprisoned either, because they simply die in captivity. If I were silly enough to treat them as servants – or worse, as slaves – they'd melt away into the desert overnight. To fellow Saracens, the Bedouins are symbols of irrepressible freedom.'

Arn went on to explain the treaty, based on mutual trade and security, that made Gaza's relationship with its local tribes so profitable in every way. He wouldn't hesitate to order his entire force of knights to ride out in defence of the Bedouins against their enemies among the Saracens. In return, he had first call on the information they gathered and could rely on safe transports of merchandise from the Arabic hinterland, since it was the Bedouin camel caravans that brought them the fine building materials, sugar, spices, scented oils and blue stones.

They had just visited the tribe of Ali, the young man who had technically stolen a woman from another tribe. Technically, because at the same time the woman had run away. The result was that they would be rejected by everyone, and if they tried to live with either family, the relatives from the other family would attack. It was all a question of honour. Worse still, these tribes had been enemies since time immemorial and only agreed to a truce under the rules of the Gaza treaty.

'I asked the chief if he couldn't let Ali wed Aisha under the Gaza laws. It would be symbolic of a peace between the two tribes. The old man, who is Ali's uncle, said that he didn't believe it for a moment, the enmity was too ancient. The only hopeful thing is that he would consider the idea if the other side agreed. It might come off, because they all know how much richer they've become as a result of the Gaza treaty.'

Siegfried pondered this in silence. Any threat to the caravan trade was of serious concern to the Templar order. As for the tribes getting richer, the wealth of Mameluke armoury and saddles in the camp was enough to remind one of the rich pickings of war.

'Mont Gisard must've been a fabulous source of loot.'

'It certainly was,' Arn said and sighed. 'Every one of them wishes us well. Besides, the reverse wouldn't be so profitable, since there's no money in taking Templar knights prisoner.'

'How have you managed to learn all this – their language, which sounds no better than animals' snorting, and even their barbaric habits?' Siegfried asked suddenly.

'I've always enjoyed finding out about things, I suppose. When I was a boy I had to learn Latin and philosophy and so on, but here in the Holy Land I wanted to know about more practical subjects. Arabic, of course, but also warfare and trade. They're not that barbaric, are they? You can't complain about their medical skills anyway.'

Siegfried opened his mouth to reply, but closed it again. It was true that he had healed remarkably well and besides, there was much to think about before he took on any more arguments with his alarmingly well-informed brother.

The following day, Arn rode out alone to negotiate with the *Banu Qay* tribe in their camp near the road to Al Arish, where the huge sweep of the bay meets the mountains. He was away the whole day but brought good news when he returned. There would be a peace settlement between the Gaza Bedouins.

When spring arrived, the Gaza infirmary was emptying at a rapid pace. Only two patients were left in the end and one of them would have a bad limp for the rest of his life. Arn told his armourer to employ the man as a blacksmith. Siegfried had recovered completely and returned to Castel Arnald several weeks previously.

Arn hardly missed his friend for this was always an intensely busy time, particularly with the upsurge in harbour traffic after the quiet winter months when few dared to risk their ships in the storms at sea. Apart from his usual duties, going through the accounts with the quartermaster and studying the Quran with the two doctors, Arn spent much of his time at riding practice. His beloved Arab stallion Chamsiin took the place of human friends. They talked together and the animal understood everything the man said in words or gestures and tones of voice.

The brothers were not surprised by Arn and Chamsiin's love for each other, only by the way the horse, an easy target for arrows, had survived all these years. After all, Arn rode like a turcopole, fast but within range of the enemy's mounted archers. Ardent, his Frankish stallion, was not as important to him but was always in heavy armour for massed attacks.

Then the shiploads of new recruits began arriving. They were always miserable, pale and shaky after weeks in transit, often from as far away as Marseilles or Montpellier. Arn and his armourer took turns to arrange receptions for the newcomers. These days the Frankish recruitment officers accepted practically every volunteer for the knighthood without insisting on a trial year as a sergeant. This meant that there was always a quota of useless novices wearing white mantles and expecting to be treated as fully fledged brothers. This required more than usual tact, because their ideas about their own skills and courage tended to be wildly inflated. The new sergeants were easier to deal with, often tough, older men with soldiering experience but not the noble ancestry required to become a knight.

The last week at sea had apparently been particularly awful for the first load of seasick sergeants that spring. In spite of this, there were two men who were quite unperturbed. Both were tall, one had bright red hair and the other was blonde and bearded. The Saracens would be interested in his head, because a blonde beard inspired greater awe than a dark one.

Watching the two men, surrounded by trembling, bent figures with sick, green faces, chatting amiably with each other, Arn was curious and studied the lists of names to try and work out where they came from. One name aroused faint memories from his youth as a lay brother in cloisters.

'Sergeants of our Order, who is Tanguy de Bréton?' he roared. The red-haired man immediately stood to attention.

'And you, standing next to de Bréton, what's your name?' The tall man with his mane of long blonde hair was obviously not from Brittany.

'Now my name is Arad d'Austin,' he answered in heavily accented Frankish.

'Austin? What land is that?'

'Is no land. My other name ... not to be said in Frankish.'

'Tell me what your name is in your own language then,' Arn said pleasantly.

'In my own language, Harald Øysteinsson,' said the man, noticing that his commander seemed dumbstruck.

Arn searched for the right words. He wanted to say in the Norwegian tongue that it was the first time he'd met a kinsman from the Nordic countries in the Holy Land, but in trying to get away from speaking Frankish, only Latin or Arabic came to mind. He gave up and launched into his normal, somewhat stern introductory speech. Then he introduced the sergeant who would record the arrivals and find them quarters. As he left, he told the sergeant quickly that he wanted to see Arald d'Austin in the *parlatorium* afterwards.

When sext had been sung, Harald duly presented himself. Norwegians could take storms at sea in their stride, but he looked vaguely resentful because his long hair had been cut short. Arn pointed to a chair and was obeyed, although the man clearly needed more discipline.

'Tell me now, kinsman ... for so you must be,' he said haltingly. 'Who are you, who is your father, and exactly to which Norwegian family do you belong?'

At first Harald stared at him uncomprehendingly, but his face lit up when he realised that he could speak his own language and he began the long tale of why he had turned up in Gaza. Arn at first found him hard to follow, but gradually the old language trickled back into his mind as he listened.

Young Harald was the son of Øystein Møyla, who was the son of King Øystein Haraldsson, of the kin called the Birkebeinar. Over a year ago now, the kin had lost a crucial battle near Re in Ramnes, a place just outside Tønsberg. Harald's father Øystein had fallen in the battle and the times had become hard for all Birkebeinar. Many of his kin had fled to West Gothland where they had friends, but as King Øystein's son, Harald felt that vengeful men would search him out unless he travelled very far away. And if death was following him, why not meet it in another land, fighting for a greater cause than simply being his father's son?

'Who is King of West Gothland now, do you know?' Arn asked, trying hard not to show how excited he was.

'For many years now, the King has been Knut Eriksson, who supports us Birkebeinar. So does his Earl, a man called Birger Brosa.

Good men, both of them, and our closest relations in West Gothland. But Knight, tell me who you are and why you're so interested in me.'

'My name is Arn Magnusson, of the Folkunga kin. Birger Brosa, the Earl, is my uncle and Knut Eriksson is a dear friend from the time when we were both children,' Arn replied. He was deeply moved but tried not to show it. 'When God led you to join our brotherhood, he took you along a road leading to a kinsman.'

'When you speak you sound more like a Dane than a man from West Gothland,' Harald remarked in a hesitant tone.

'That's easily explained. I spent many years in Denmark as a child, being brought up by the monks in a place called Vitae Schola – I've forgotten what the local people called it – but what I tell you is true. I'm a Knight Templar and brothers never lie. Tell me, why did they give you a black mantle and not a white one?'

'They were asking if my father was a knight or something. I didn't quite understand, but tried to tell them that my father was a king. It cut no ice though.'

'Kinsman, they made a mistake. Still, I need a sergeant and you would do well to have a relative to trust in this place, so far from Norway. You'll do more and learn more wearing a black mantle than a white one. Just remember one thing. Back home, the Birkebeinar and the Folkunga are friends and kinsfolk, but here in the Holy Land I'm the commander and you're a sergeant. It's rather as if I had been an earl and you a member of his hird. That's how it is and it doesn't matter that you and I can talk together in the same language.'

'When you flee from your own land, you pay for it,' Harald replied sadly. 'But it could've been worse. The choice between serving a Frankish master and a Folkunga man is easy.'

'Well said, my kinsman,' Arn said, and rose to show that their talk had come to an end.

When summer and the time for war returned, the training of the new recruits took up most of the time for the command at Gaza fortress. The new knights were taught to ride tactically, recognise the signs that stood for different orders and, above all, accept the harsh field discipline. For instance, any knight who left his formation for reasons of his own risked losing his white mantle in a humiliating ceremony unless he could prove that the reason was that of trying to save a Christian life.

The wealthy family connections of the men selected for knight-hood usually guaranteed that they were good horsemen, and cavalry training was the easiest and least strenuous exercise for the newcomers. Weapons training was another matter because, by Templar standards, they were all useless and needed hours of labouring in hot training courts if they were not to be killed in their first skirmish. It did not help that all these new 'softies', as the sergeants called them, were convinced of their own superior skills with sword, battleaxe, lance and shield. They had to be taught just how bad they were and their teachers went about the lessons with a will. During the first months, the softies felt that they really deserved the nickname, because their bodies were aching and covered in bruises.

Harald Øysteinsson was a wild fighter, but no good. Arn had decided to train the Norwegian himself and Harald started by selecting a sword that was far too heavy. Then he rushed at Arn, brandishing his sword and looking for all the world like a witless Nordic berserk. Arn made him hit the ground again and again, felling him with sword or shield, kicking him down and tripping him up. The exchange of blows always ended with the blunted edge of Arn's sword leaving huge bruises on Harald's arms, shoulder and thighs, despite his covering of chain-mail.

But Harald was both brave and stubborn. That fighting like a Viking in the Holy Land meant certain death was a lesson he found hard to take. The more body-hits Arn scored, the keener the battered Harald was to leap into another attack. This made him unlike other novices, who usually could be hammered into meekly accepting that they had a lot to learn. After a week of tormenting his young opponent, Arn decided to give him a talking-to one evening, when they were walking along one of the harbour piers after vesper.

'You realise by now, don't you, that you'll get killed unless you start learning a new kind of swordsmanship?'

'Nothing wrong with my swordsmanship, I'd say,' Harald muttered sourly.

'Is that so?' Arn was truly baffled. 'So how come you're one aching mass of bruises from your collarbone to your shins?'

'The reason is that I've been fighting a swordsman whom even the gods couldn't defeat. I know what I'm talking about. I've slain quite a few men.'

'You'll get killed in your first fight here, for as long as you trust to your "knowing-what-I'm-talking-about". You're far too slow, unlike the Saracens who're very fast. Their swords are lighter than ours but just as sharp. The other thing is, you're wrong about me. Here in

Gaza we are five knights who are more or less equally good, but three of us are better than me.'

'I don't believe it,' Harald said hotly.

'Very well. Tomorrow you'll fight Guy de Carcasonne, the day after tomorrow Sergio de Livorne, and the next day our best swordsman, Ernesto de Navarra. When you begin to be able to move your arm and legs after meeting that lot, you can come back to me. That medicine should've cured you by then.'

It was nasty medicine, but it worked. For several days Harald could not raise his arm without groaning with pain or take a step without almost falling over. Even coming close enough to get in a blow had been nightmarishly hard, like being stuck in ship's tar, he said. Every movement of his had seemed mistimed and misdirected.

Arn was pleased. This tough offspring of Norwegian Vikings was finally seeing sense. They started from the beginning again and Arn helped Harald pick a new practice sword, gently pointing out that it wasn't weight that mattered but how well it was balanced in your hand. Then he ordered Harald to spend the next two days recuperating and learning by example from Arn's own practice sessions with Gaza's best, Ernesto de Navarra.

The two knights alternately went about their business swiftly and seriously, or slowly and demonstratively to let the young softy see how particular moves were made. They seemed about equal, but Ernesto hit his opponent more often. Harald found it bewilderingly hard to follow what happened as the two men, neither ever staying in the same place for a moment, exchanged lightning-quick series of strikes and counter-strikes. Also, their endurance amazed him. Both took blows in the passing, which would have made most people crumble with pain. In between their furious attacks, they politely acknowledged each other's successful moves, making complimentary bows when a blow struck home.

Young Harald's journey towards a new world of war had begun. Now he patiently accepted Arn's insistence on repeating single points of technique over and over again. Slowly he felt that he was changing for the better and he was determined to reach the level of Arn and Ernesto in the end.

But Harald's trials had only just begun, for next his master told him that he didn't know how to ride either. It didn't matter that he had been going about on horseback since childhood, because, as Arn put it, there was a huge difference between riding and sitting on a horse. Like most Northerners, Harald also needed convincing that horses were of any use in war in the first place. They still believed that you rode to the battlefield, tied up your horse, and then ran at the enemy on foot. Now Harald had to bear the humbling judgement that he was no good as a cavalryman and had to join the infantry. It took some time before he accepted that infantry had its important role to play in the new kind of warfare he was learning about.

But Harald was still proud of his archery skills. He had been renowned as a longbowman among the Birkebeinar and their enemies, but it took only a few sessions of shooting with Arn to humble him. Later Arn reflected that he might have left Harald despairing for too long before cheering him up with well-deserved praise. As it was, the young man hadn't even understood the significance of the audience of knights and sergeants that began to turn up every time he and Arn were practising together. The reason was that everyone was becoming interested in the new recruit, who was handling longbow and arrows almost as well as the comman- der. Arn's skills were rated very highly, outshining even most Turks.

'Listen, I've got something pleasant to tell you for once,' Arn said at the end of their fifth day of practice. 'You're truly the best archer I've come across here in the Holy Land. Where did you learn?'

'I hunted squirrels as a boy ...' Harald begun. Then his face brightened. 'Do you really think I'm any good? But you're better than I and so is everybody else, I fear.'

'Come on,' Arn said. Then he looked quizzical. Calling out to a pair of passing knights, he asked them what they reckoned he should do about his young sergeant, who thought himself a poor archer because his master did better. They simply burst out laughing, slapped Harald encouragingly on the back and wandered off, still laughing.

'Now you know the truth,' Arn said. 'The fact is – no Templar knight should ever boast, but this is the truth – among us I'm the best shot in the Holy Land, possibly in the whole Order. You're very good indeed. Be grateful, for one day it may save the life of others and yourself.'

Sooner than they thought, Harald Øysteinsson's chance to save his life by using his longbow arrived when the Gaza force was ordered to go northwards, taking the archers on foot as well as both heavy and light cavalry.

Saladin had certainly learnt the lessons of Mont Gisard, for this was how he always approached defeat – not as a sign that God had abandoned Jihad or himself, but as an instructive example of how plans could miscarry. In the spring he had led a small army of Syrian and Egyptian units into the northern regions of the Holy Land. It had defeated the forces of King Baldwin IV in the far north near Banyas and moved on to plunder and burn the fields in Galilee and South Lebanon. When he returned on another campaign in the summer, everyone assumed that it was the same army. It was an assumption that would cost the Christians dear.

The King had mobilised a worldly army but thought it too weak to go against Saladin on its own. He turned to the Grand Master of the Templar Order and was promised every support. When the Gaza force moved off northwards, Harald Øysteinsson learnt what it meant to march every day for ten days in what seemed to him quite inhuman heat.

When they finally joined in battle with the Saracens he thought their thundering hordes of riders were as terrifying as the stories of Ragnarök, the disaster that destroyed the world of the gods. Any one rider was no harder to hit than a Norwegian squirrel, but however many he shot they kept storming forward in wave after wave. He soon realised that his side was losing, but not that he was taking part in the most catastrophic defeat that had ever befallen the Christians in the Holy Land, worldly or Templar knights alike.

Arn did understand what was happening and the experience was all the more bitter for him. The Grand Master, Odo de Saint Amand, had taken command of the Templar units on their way to join King Baldwin's army, which was fighting a small contingent of plunderers returning from the coast of Lebanon.

In Upper Galilee, between the River Jordan and the River Litani, they had encountered Saladin's main force. He had marched it off, leaving the small unit to pin down the enemy in a deliberate manoeuvre to prevent the knights from reaching the royal army. Odo de Saint Amand must have misunderstood, assuming at the first sight of Saracen riders that they were just stray plundering units or possibly a small diversionary force to slow Christian progress.

In retrospect, it was crystal clear that he should have refrained from attacking and at almost any cost attempted to lead his knights, foot soldiers and turcopoles on to join Baldwin's army. If the situation had got completely out of hand, his only option would have been to stand fast. Instead, he took the monumentally wrong decision to send his entire heavy cavalry of knights in armour towards the enemy. No one ever had the opportunity to ask him why.

Arn commanded a contingent of light mounted archers, positioned high up on a slope near the right flank, and was reflecting that his was the best view. From up there the men saw the large army, vastly outnumbering their own, advancing under Saladin's own banners. Down on the plain, Odo de Saint Amand had started arranging his knights into line for a full frontal attack and at first Arn thought the Grand Master was preparing a cunning mock manoeuvre to give the infantry time to escape. His despair was all the greater when he saw the black and white banner raised and lowered three times, the signal for full-scale attack. From their vantage-point, he and his men watched transfixed as the main Templar force rode straight into the jaws of death.

Following the usual Saracen tactic, the light Syrian cavalry kept retreating in front of the knights until the speed of the attack was slowing of its own accord without having met any resistance. By then the knights were surrounded and the slaughter began. Following the development of the battle below, the turcopoles started shaking their heads and spreading their arms wide to show that as far as they were concerned, this was the end of the fighting and it was now each man for himself. Soon Arn was alone with a handful of Christian mounted archers.

He stayed a little longer, trying to spot any Templar units trying to fight their way out of the trap. When he saw a group of about ten knights slashing their way toward the infantry lines, he rode into attack with his small following of terrified men, hoping at least to cause some local confusion and provide an easier escape route for the knights.

His tactic had exactly that effect, but only briefly. Soon, enemy soldiers were vigorously pursuing him and his remaining men. Everyone who had recognised Al Ghouti was gripped by the idea of presenting Saladin with the head of the victor at Mont Gisard stuck at the tip of a lance. The reward would surely be great.

After a while, Arn found himself alone, his followers having ridden off towards the infantry and the rest of the army. Arn steered his horse in a wide arc in the opposite direction towards a rocky slope that was an obvious trap. When his men were safe he reined in his horse, because by now it could get no further up the increasingly steep hillside. Seeing his predicament, his pursuers lowered their bows and advanced more slowly, their grinning faces showing that they were positively looking forward to this last stage of the chase.

Then a high-ranking amir came storming along, pushing his way through the riders, pointing at Arn, and shouting various orders that he didn't catch. The Syrian and Egyptian archers greeted him by raising their bows, swung their horses round and galloped off in a big cloud of dust. It seemed a miraculous event, but he decided that it was probably not God but Saladin who had decided that his life should be saved.

He shook off the stillness with which he had forced himself to await his death and rode down to find the remains of the army. The surviving knights were wounded to a man, some seriously. The turcopoles, all mercenaries, had fled, and the only fighting men left were about a hundred archers on foot. There were twenty-odd reserve horses and about as many packhorses. Some three hundred knights lay dead, an unprecedented and terrible loss. Arn was highest in rank among the survivors and took command.

The most important thing now was to safely join the royal army. That Saladin had not taken the trouble to kill off every man and horse they had, must mean that he had achieved his main intention – to separate the knights from King Baldwin's force. Now he presumably intended to march back north and meet the weak worldly army without its expected reinforcements. Speed was of the essence.

They jettisoned the loads of the packhorses to get enough suitable animals to carry the wounded, allowed the eldest sergeants and archers to ride the reserve horses, and made the younger men run alongside. This sad remnant of the Templar force set out for the River Litani, because Arn assumed that the royal army would be under pressure and its only way out would be to cross that river.

He was partly mistaken. King Baldwin's army was beaten already and had scattered into fleeing groups, which were eliminated in turn as larger enemy contingents caught up with them. Baldwin and his personal guard had managed to cross the river; now the crossing had also to be attempted by the exhausted army units which, like Arn's, were trying to follow the King.

Arn had ordered the best of his archers, including Harald Øysteinsson, to line up on the riverbank, covering the desperate mass of men, both wounded and well, and animals in the water against attack by the enemy's mounted archers and lancers. The archers kept shooting until they ran out of arrows and then threw themselves into the river. Arn and Harald were the only survivors among this last lot, because they knew how to swim under water and drift with the currents.

On the other side of the river there was only a short respite to get back into order. To Arn's almost immodestly demonstrative joy, his stallion Chamsiin suddenly came galloping through the disorder to join his human friend and master. The beaten Templar force was received by knights and foot soldiers from the Order of St John's, who escorted their brothers from another Order to the fortress of Beaufort, only an hour's ride away. Many of the fleeing royal army had sought refuge in Beaufort already. It did not take Saladin long to get a siege force in place, but no one cared too much, because Beaufort was known to be impregnable.

Worse was that, though technically brothers, the members of the Order of St John's were no friends of the Knights Templar, for reasons Arn had never understood. The Hospitallers, as Knights of St John were called, would often fail to support the Templar knights in battle. This time, only a token force of Hospitallers had ridden out from their safety behind the walls of Beaufort.

The Templar knights called the members of the Order of St John's 'black Samaritans'. The nickname referred to their black tunics with a white cross, but also to the Order's origins among men serving in field hospitals giving free care. No insults were exchanged now that the members of the rival order would care for the wounded Templar men.

It was a hard night for the many wounded in the Beaufort fortress. Although exhausted, red-eyed from lack of sleep and weighed down with grief, Arn forced himself to walk around in the morning. He wanted to observe and learn.

Beaufort was high up on a hill and from its western walls you could see the sea glittering in the distance. To the north lay the rich Bekaa valley and to the east, range after range of snowy mountains. The position of the fortress made it practically impossible for siege towers to be built high enough to allow men to climb the walls. The rocky precipices meant that there was nowhere to park catapults and other siege machinery. Long sieges had little hope of success, since the fortress was so abundantly supplied with water from its own spring, that they had had to construct a channel to lead away the excess, and the grain stores were generously proportioned and constantly topped up. Standing outside the wall and howling insults, as the enemy was doing now, was completely pointless.

It was true there were disadvantages. The steep slopes made mounted attacks on besieging forces almost impossible. The three hundred knights and as many sergeants holding Beaufort could have wiped out the shouting idiots outside the walls if the ground had been more favourable. But there was no raid and the men outside were left in ignorance of how many were inside and what they could do. Like all fortresses, Beaufort kept its secrets.

Arn began his day by going to see Chamsiin, tell him of his great sorrow, and meticulously investigate every part of the large gleaming body for injuries. When he was sure his horse was as well as he was himself, Arn went to the quarters for visiting sergeants and said a prayer with the wounded men. He then sought out Harald Øysteinsson and took him for a walk around the walls to show the young man how a fortress functioned.

Along the eastern parapet, they saw a hideous procession slowly moving toward Beaufort. It consisted of several squadrons of Mameluke lancers, each man carrying his lance upright with a bloody head speared on the tip. Almost all the heads were bearded.

They stood very still and silent, trying to keep their faces from showing what they felt, Harald finding it difficult to behave as calmly as his mentor. The triumphant Mamelukes were lining up in front of the eastern wall and shaking their bloodied lances so that the heads jumped up and down. Then one of them moved in front of the rest and began a wailing prayer.

'What's that he's saying?' asked Harald.

'He says that he's grateful to God because the shame of Mont Gisard has been avenged, that what took place at Marj Ayyoun was a more than just settlement, that soon we'll all have our heads stuck on lances, and more of that sort,' Arn said in a level voice.

Just then, the armourer of Beaufort came hurrying along, accompanied by several Knights of St John. He shouted an order forbidding any shooting at the enemy. The sergeants on guard, who had been aiming their crossbows, put their weapons down.

'Why aren't we allowed to shoot?' asked Harald. 'Why not pick a few of these fellows off to teach them not to boast – in this barbaric way, too.'

'There's a reason,' Arn replied in the same level voice. 'True, at least the man in front should be killed. Look, he's wearing a blue silk ribbon round his right arm to show that he's an officer. He's claiming that he's a great victor, God's favourite, and many other ridiculous things. He will be dead before nightfall, but we'll sing the evening service first.'

'Why not take revenge now rather than singing hymns?' Harald asked with barely hidden impatience.

'Well, that's one way of looking at it,' Arn said. 'Still, no point in rushing at it. Look, they've lined up at what they think is a safe distance ...'

'But I can shoot ...'

'Quiet! You're not to interrupt me! Remember you're a sergeant. I know you could take one of them out from here. So could I, but the screaming fellow down there doesn't know. We don't make up the rules here in a fortress owned by the Hospitallers and the order given by their armourer was a wise one, anyway.'

'What's so wise about it? For how long must we put up with this performance?'

'Until after the service, as I said. By then the sun will be sinking in the west and shining straight into their eyes, so they won't see our arrows until it's too late. It was also wise because we mustn't show our despair and shoot in vain. It'll only cause contempt and more jeering, something we definitely don't want.'

Then Arn took his sergeant along to greet the armourer and, after exchanging polite bows, asked that the two of them should be allowed to kill some Mamelukes after the service. Naturally, no one would shoot beforehand. The armourer agreed, but reluctantly because he thought it a waste of time and effort given how far away the enemy front line was. Arn bowed again and said humbly that he and his sergeant would need to borrow longbows and arrows, having lost their own during the river crossing. It would be useful to practice with the new weapons before the time came to use them in earnest.

Whatever the reason, maybe the black line on Arn's mantle, perhaps the seriousness of his manner, the armourer suddenly softened and granted the request. Soon they had set up two bales of straw as targets, setting them as far away as the godless spectacle outside was from the walls. They practised with grim determination and the Hospitallers, who had been coming along to urge their guests condescendingly not to exert themselves too much in their despair over the defeat, were soon silenced by the sheer skill of the shooting.

After the singing in the large fortress chapel, Arn got some of the brothers to walk up and down on the walls with himself and Harald. They all wore their black and white mantles to rouse the demonstration below back to fever pitch. The enemy needed livening up after their long wait. As the ghostly parade came closer, the watching men recognised faces of their brothers: Siegfried de Turenne was one, Ernesto de Navarra was another. Now the amir who reckoned he had a special relationship with God was riding forward again, shouting about the great victory at Marj Ayyoun and waving his bloody trophy.

'He's to go first,' Arn said, 'Let's both aim at him, you high and I low. Once he's dead we'll see what we can do about the rest of them.'

They stood close together, outlined against the setting sun but with the glinting arrowheads hidden behind their bodies.

'You first, then I,' Arn ordered.

The amir had just begun a long tirade, bending his head back and wailing prayers alternating with military boasts, when one arrow struck his chest exactly where the ribcage divides and another pierced his open mouth. Soundlessly, he fell off his horse. Before the men around him had grasped what had happened, they, too, fell to well-aimed arrows and a tumult was created as everybody tried backing away at the same time. They were bombarded with a shower of arrows because all the guards on the walls had been ordered to shoot.

Everyone praised Harald afterwards, because his was the shot that had plugged the yelling mouth of the Mameluke amir. His feat would be remembered for a long time.

Harald confessed to Arn afterwards that his shot had been a bit of a fluke and that he'd actually aimed at the man's neck, just below the chin. Arn told him to keep his own mouth shut. Now the Mamelukes were busy minding their own dead and unlikely to start any more offensive displays. And so it was. The next morning, the riders outside were all gone.

There had had been a question of inviting Arn for an evening meal of wine and bread, but the Hospitaller's commander had been told not to by the Count Raymond III of Tripoli, who was well known to detest Templar knights. When the commander heard of Arn's brilliant shooting from the walls, he thought it unreasonable to withhold the invitation.

Arn arrived full of innocent expectation, because all he knew was the Count Raymond was the most prominent of the worldly knights in Outremer. He had no idea of the Count's hatred of Knights Templar, but learnt soon enough when the Count, alone among all the knights present, worldly and monkish, refused to greet him. Once the bread and wine had been blessed, the guests settled at the table in a tense atmosphere and began eating and drinking in silence.

Count Raymond asked in a scornful tone of voice what that madmen's business at Marj Ayyoun had been all about. Arn was the only one in the room who did not know who the Count was referring to by 'madmen' and so did not realise that he was meant to answer the question. Count Raymond explained, with heavy irony, that he was interested to find out if this was what always happened when Knights Templar went to the rescue of their king.

Arn simply told the story of the battle and the fundamental

mistake that had led to the disaster, without any attempt to hide the truth. He added that at the time he'd been in a good position to observe the plain, an advantage unfortunately denied his Grand Master when he gave the last order of his life. The brothers of St John, who were well known for their reckless attacking, were silenced; they could only too easily imagine what had happened.

Not so Count Raymond. Without paying the slightest attention to the sad tale of bravery and loss, he began a loud and insulting speech about the Knights Templar, capable of winning battles at times but also of losing disastrously. Best to have nothing to do with them; useless allies, mad enough to befriend assassins, ignorant fellows who knew nothing about the Saracens – their ignorance alone would be fatal for the whole Outremer enterprise.

Raymond was a tall, heavily built man, whose long blond hair was turning grey. He always spoke abruptly and brutally, in a local Frankish dialect that his countrymen called *subar* after a cactus fruit, prickly on the outside but sweet and delightful inside. This was because *subar* speech used many Saracen words and was hard to understand for newly arrived Franks.

Arn said nothing, because he had no idea how to get out of the situation. He was a guest forced on his hosts and being insulted by another invited guest to the Hospitallers' fortress. On one hand, he should draw his sword in response to this abusive challenge to the honour of his Order. On the other, the rules of his Order forbade any brother to draw his sword to fight a Christian, on pain of losing his white mantle. Arn was stymied, since neither swords nor words were permissible.

His submissive silence did nothing to stop Count Raymond, who had lost a stepson in the battle and was as desperately saddened by the defeat as everyone else in the room. Now he had a hateful young Knight Templar at his table, a perfect target to hit in order to lessen his pain. He started raving again about the ignorance of the Templar knights about the Saracens.

'Your ill-educated, unwashed soldiery wouldn't recognise the Quran if they fell over it.'

'In the Name of the Merciful and Charitable one,' Arn began in Arabic, for suddenly an idea had arrived into his perplexed head. 'Honoured Count Raymond, consider the words of God, now that we're drinking together. "The fruits of date palm and vine give both nourishment and wine, a message that should be contemplated by those who use them wisely."'

Arn drank some wine and then put his Syrian glass down, calmly meeting Count Raymond's eyes.

'Is that so? The Quran says that bit about drinking wine?' Count Raymond asked after a long pause.

'It does indeed, in the sixteenth *sura* of the sixty-seventh verse. True, it comes just after a few lines in praise of milk, but it's worth thinking about.'

'Knight Templar, where did you learn the Saracen language? I learnt it when I spent ten years imprisoned in Aleppo, but you've presumably never been a prisoner.' Count Raymond was looking searchingly at Arn and addressing him in Arabic.

'I took lessons from learned natives working among us,' Arn replied in the same language. 'You're right about imprisonment, of course. As you saw so bloodily demonstrated today, a Knight Templar isn't taken prisoner. It hurts me grievously to hear you speak ill of my dead brothers. They died for God and His Grave and the Holy Land, but also for you.'

'Who's this Knight Templar?' Raymond asked the fortress commander in Frankish.

'Sir, he's Arn de Gothia. He led two hundred knights to victory over three thousand Mamelukes at Mont Gisard. The Saracens respect him and call him Al Ghouti,' the commander replied quietly. 'I would appreciate it if you moderated your tone.'

Count Raymond was accustomed to dominating all gatherings he attended and rarely felt uncomfortable about his manners for any reason whatever. This night, he knew he had overstepped the mark and resolutely set about making up for his error.

'I've been a complete ass,' he sighed. Then he smiled and rose from his seat. 'My only defence is that at least I know when I've misbehaved, unlike most asses, and now I must do something I've never done before in my life.'

He crossed the floor in a few long strides, hugged Arn and then knelt in front of him in apology. Arn blushed, stammering something about all this being quite uncalled for. In this strange way, the two ill-matched men began a long friendship that was strengthened by both of them being closer to the Saracens than most other Christians were.

Raymond insisted on sitting close to Arn and speaking only in Arabic, at first as a device to send the rest of the guests packing. Once they were alone and had ordered more wine, he continued in the language. As he put it, all over Outremer the walls have ears, which are particularly keen to pick up the things he wanted to speak about now. Some malevolent souls might even call his talk seditious.

'Malevolent' was actually a perfect description of the people in charge in the Kingdom of Jerusalem now, and this state of affairs would soon lead to the catastrophic end of Christian rule. Unlike the events at Marj Ayyoun, such defeats were commonplace if you looked back at the many years of war in the Holy Land. Raymond himself had lost about half of the hundred or so battles he had fought.

'Of all the evil crew at the Court in Jerusalem, the worst is the King's own mother, Agnes de Courtenay.' Raymond said. 'She's the most powerful, too, and sees to it all her lovers get senior positions. She picks up newcomers, softies who become as proud as the cock on the dungheap and behave with as little wit. Prettily dressed and devising new plots every day God gives, they'd do better at the courts back home in Paris or Rome. When they have nothing else to do they sin unspeakably – picking up little boys in the slave markets is their least offensive habit.' The Count drank heartily and continued his instruction in politics.

'Courtenay's latest lover is a young cad called Lusignan. He spends most of his time trying to persuade everybody that the King's sister Sibyl should marry his younger brother Guy. Why is he so keen? No need to ask: the leprous King's days are numbered, there aren't many left, so next we'd find Lusignan junior on the throne of Jerusalem.'

Arn found Raymond's saga of intrigues at Court almost incredible. The Count kept their glasses filled and produced more tales from a world in which the Grave of God was surrounded not by the devoted faithful, but by deceivers who'd enjoyed sodomising asses and little boys. He was reminded of the Prophet, may peace be with him, looking down from the heavenly ladder on the rock at Templum Domini saying that he saw Hell below.

Finally it dawned on Count Raymond that this honest young man was clearly too inexperienced to grasp half his tales of Court intrigue and began analysing the lost battle at Marj Ayyoun instead. Now that everybody else was out of earshot, the two men agreed unreservedly that it was Saladin's brilliant command of the situation which had won the day. As at Mont Gisard, luck had probably played a role, but Saladin had seemed almost supernaturally certain about the course events would take. He had diverted the attention of the King and his commanders, found and crushed the Templar force, and finally beaten the isolated royal army before reinforcements from Tripoli had had time to reach the scene. The likelihood was that the whole campaign had been planned in the spring, when Saladin made his first destructive forays with a relatively small number of men, only to return in the summer with an army five times the size, something the Christians didn't realise before it was too late.

Yes, it was a just victory for a great commander and Arn, whose head was spinning from the unaccustomed quantities of wine he'd drunk, felt unable to think of any objection to this conclusion. Instead, he asked Raymond why he hated the Knights Templar so much.

'Well, not all – and from tonight, Al Ghouti, certainly not you. Of those I value, I think Arnoldo de Torroja, your Master of Jerusalem, must come first. He for one knows that an honourable peace with Saladin is the one single condition needed to keep a Christian presence in the Holy Land. That, and dividing Jerusalem between the faiths, the Jews too, of course. If justice is done for once, de Torroja should be your next Grand Master now that Odo de Saint Amand has presumably gone to Paradise. He could be in prison but it's not likely, as we know.'

Raymond argued that a negotiated peace was the only alternative to a war with Saladin that would inevitably end with Christian defeat and Jerusalem being taken by violence. Then he launched into an account of the way Court intrigues, useless and immoral 'friends' and false alliances had weakened the Order of the Temple. That scoundrel Raynald de Châtillon was among the worst. He had now wormed his way into Court circles and found himself a rich widow, Stéphanie de Milly, with alarmingly powerful connections. By marrying her, Raynald hadn't just bagged the two fortresses of Kerak and Montreal, he had gained the support of the Knights Templar. Why was that? Because his Stéphanie was the daughter of the ex-Grand Master – or should he say ex-ex?

The villains were hovering like hopeful vultures over the Court in Jerusalem. Take a certain Gérard de Ridefort now, as crooked as de Châtillon himself, as dangerous a friend to the Templar Order as the Assassins and, all in all, a name for Arn to keep in mind.

Talking of the Assassins reminded Raymond of how these shadowy murderers had killed his father, Count Raymond II, just outside the gates of Tripoli. He started on a long digression, aimed at showing why for this and other reasons, he would never forgive the Templar Knights for their alliance with the Muslim agents of terror.

Then Raymond returned to his interrupted line of thought concerning Gérard de Ridefort, describing how this man also became associated with the Order of the Temple. He had arrived, a common adventurer, by ship to Tripoli and found employment with Count Raymond's household. The two men liked each other and all had gone well in the beginning. In a weak moment Raymond promised Gérard a wealthy marriage and they settled on Lucia, a young lady with prospects of a sizeable inheritance. But she caught the eye of a rich merchant from Pisa who, overwhelmed with love, offered Raymond the lady's weight in gold. Lucia was very plump and Raymond found the offer irresistible, but Gérard was furious. His honour had been abused, he claimed, and he had no intention of waiting for the next young lady to be shoved his way. Instead he'd sign up with the Templars to seek revenge on Raymond.

Arn, opening his mouth after a very long silence, said that for sheer oddity, this beat all other reasons he had heard for joining the Knights Templar. Raymond paused, but only for a moment. Soon the flow of talk started again and continued all night, until the first rays of sun came through the great arched, east-facing windows, pricking their eyes. By then Arn's head was whirling as much from Raymond's endless stories about evildoings in the Holy Land as from the wine he had drunk. Later that morning, the knight was forcibly reminded of what it had been like once, a long time ago, as a very young man in West Gothland, when he had drunk too much beer and felt terrible the morning after.

A week later, Arn and his sergeant Harald were riding unaccompanied along the coast towards Gaza. They had had all their wounded transferred from Beaufort to the quarters of the Knights Templar in Saint-Jean d'Acre, as they called the city of Acre. From there, Arn had organised a larger, more comfortable transport to get his men to Gaza and under the care of Saracen doctors as soon as possible.

Travelling ahead of the transport, the two men were deep in their own thoughts most of the way. They had ridden out with forty knights and one hundred sergeants, but only two knights and fifty-three sergeants were returning. Among those who lived no longer – on this Earth at least – were some of the best and truest knights that Arn had ever met. Surviving them gave him little joy and a bitter sense of life's injustice. Harald had tried to joke at one moment about how his early training in defeat, part of his Birkebeinar heritage, had come in handy in the Holy Land, but Arn neither smiled nor spoke.

The heat of summer was at its most punishing and Harald found it almost impossible to endure. He had taken off as much clothing as he could and was mercilessly fried in his armour of red-hot chain-mail. Arn, who was looking almost like a Saracen, was insisting that his layered head-cloth and the thin summer mantle wrapped round his body helped to protect him.

When they reached Ashkelon, they stopped and went their different ways, for knights and sergeants never shared night quarters except in the field. Arn did not sleep that night. Instead he spent it praying to the Holy Virgin. He did not pray for his own welfare but begged for the protection of his beloved Cecilia and of his little boy or girl. Again and again he come back to a prayer for understanding – an answer that would lead him towards the gift of being able to distinguish between truth and falsehood. Much of what the despairing, angry and drunken Raymond had spoken of was festering in Arn's mind and he felt in need of clarity more than anything else.

Maybe the events of the following day were part of Virgin Mary's answer to his prayers. If so, Her way of offering insight was cruel or, as Raymond might have said with a raucous laugh, lucid in a ruthless manner he wouldn't have expected from Our Lady.

The next day, when Arn and Harald were close enough to Gaza to see the black tents of the *Banu Anaza* camp, they realised that something was very wrong. No warriors rode out to meet them, and between the tents women, children and old people were praying with their foreheads touching the sand. On top of a low hill nearby they saw three Frankish knights apparently preparing themselves to attack.

Arn immediately spurred Chamsiin into full gallop, riding towards the camp with Harald behind him, trying to keep up. The people at first crouched more deeply into the sand at the sound of thundering horses' hooves, but when Arn entered the camp at a slower pace, they looked up cautiously and recognised him. A few of the Bedouin women began a long, ululating call of welcome and soon everyone was thanking God for sending Al Ghouti to help them in their hour of need. The cry of 'Al Ghouti' was taken up all over the camp, until the old chief, whose name was Ibrahim, like the father of all men, stepped forward. Arn dismounted and greeted the old man courteously.

'Ibrahim, what has happened? Where are the *Banu Anaza* warriors and what are the *franji* up to on the hill there?'

'I thank God for having sent you, Al Ghouti. He is indeed great. Our men are all away on a *razzia* in Sinai; there's a war on and we don't need them here since we're under Gaza's protection. These *franji* just turned up from the north, maybe from Ashkelon. They threatened us, saying they're going to kill us all and we might as well pray because today is our last day.'

'I can't ask you to forgive them on account of they don't know what they're doing,' Arn said angrily. 'All I can do is get rid of them.'

He bowed to Ibrahim, leapt up on Chamsiin and galloped off, slowing when he came near enough to the Franks to observe them more closely. They were undoubtedly new arrivals, softies to a man, dressed in very colourful tunics and wearing the newest style in helmets, the kind that enclosed the head completely apart from a narrow cross-shaped slit for the eyes and nose. When they saw the Christian rider, they took off their helmets with obvious reluctance.

'Who are you? Where do you come from and what's your business?' Arn roared in his well-practised commander's voice.

'Who're you? A Christian dressed like a Saracen, as far as I can see,' one of the Franks replied. 'Whatever you might be, you're interfering. We're preparing for a sacred task, so you'd better get out of our way. Or else you'll get treated a bit roughly.'

Arn stared at them, praying silently for the lives of these three fools. Then he pulled his mantle back to show his white tunic with the red cross.

'I'm a Knight Templar, my name is Arn de Gothia and I'm the commander in Gaza,' he told them slowly. 'You are on Gaza land and the Bedouins down there belong to Gaza. Lucky for you that their warriors are away on business, as it were, or you'd be dead by now. Now, answer me. Who are you and where do you come from?'

They told him that all three of them had recently 'taken the cross' in Provence and counted themselves lucky to have found a whole camp full of Saracens so soon after arriving in the Holy Land. Dispatching that lot to hell was their God-given duty.

'Given by the Pope, rather,' Arn corrected them ironically. 'But as you should know, the Knights Templar are the Holy Father's own army and we take our orders from him. In other words, as commander of Gaza, I'm as close to the Holy Father as you're going to get for a long time. You're welcome to the Holy Land and I wish you well and so forth. Now, I order you to get off my land and return to wherever you came from.'

This cut no ice with the Franks, who seemed not to grasp what Arn had told them about his Order and his position, and repeated their insane notion of having a sacred duty to kill Saracens. Arn's attempts to persuade them that it was unholy work to kill defenceless women, children and old people fell on deaf ears, as did his warnings of how dangerous it was to fight a Knight Templar with only three men against the one.

Indeed, this warning seemed if anything to cheer them up. One of them said that killing a Saracen-lover would be an excellent start to the rest of the day's tasks. Still Arn tried to convince them of their folly, saying that anyone who knew the Holy Land would tell them not to take on a Knight Templar lightly, but nothing made them see sense.

Arn rode back downhill and demonstratively kneeled next to Chamsiin in the middle of the camp. He drew his sword, lifted it to the sky three times, kissed it and began on the required prayers for an attack.

Old Ibrahim began walking towards him, sinking into the sand with each step. From the other direction, Harald approached on horseback. Arn explained to each in turn what had happened and that he had to deal with these dangerous fools. Ibrahim left at once, but Harald stayed, bravely putting his horse next to Chamsiin and drawing his sword.

'Move over, you're in my way,' Arn said in a low voice, without looking at his sergeant.

'As if I wouldn't stand by a kinsman facing an uneven fight!' Harald said hotly. 'You can't make me leave you, earl or no earl.'

'You'll die and I don't want that,' Arn said. He kept his eyes fixed on the three Franks, who were kneeling in prayer. They were clearly deluded enough to carry on preparing for an attack. Harald had not moved an inch.

'Once more and for the last time, move over. It's an order,' Arn went on more loudly. 'They'll use their lances and you'll be speared if you get in the way. You're to lead that horse away, now. Help me if the fight's continued on foot. If you can find a bow and arrows anywhere, use them. But I forbid you to ride against the Franks.'

'You haven't got a lance!' Harald exclaimed in despair.

'Doesn't matter, I fight like a Saracen. My tactics will be news to these three. Now go!'

Harald finally obeyed, trundling away dejectedly. At the same time Ibrahim was coming back, stumbling in the sand with a bundle in his arms. When he reached Arn, he had to catch his breath before explaining. Meanwhile the Franks on the hill were putting on their helmets, the brightly coloured plumes standing out against the sky.

'God is indeed great, but His ways are inscrutable,' the old man panted as he unravelled his bundle. '*Banu Anaza* has treasured this sword since times immemorial. The sacred Ali ibn Abi Talib lost it when he was martyred outside Kufa. It's been our duty to hand his sword on from father to son until He comes who can save the true believers. You're that man, Al Ghouti! He who fights for a holy cause with a pure mind and wielding this sword can never lose. It was written that it should be yours!'

The old man was holding an old-fashioned, blunt-looking sword in his trembling hands, offering it to Arn.

'My very dear friend, I cannot believe that I'm the right man,' Arn said, and had to smile despite the seriousness of the moment.

But the old man insisted, still holding the sword in his outstretched hands and shaking from the effort. Arn's face darkened as it suddenly occurred to him that not only was it against Templar rules to kill or injure a fellow Christian, but also that his sword, blessed in Varnhem chapel, must not be raised to commit a sin. If that promise were broken, he would be struck down. He reached down and took the old man's sword, letting a finger run over its dull edge. The Franks were on the move now and lowering their lances. He had to decide at once.

'Take my sword Ibrahim,' Arn said. 'Drive it into the sand in front of your tent, pray in front of its cross. I'll use your sword. Let's see how great God is!'

Then he spurred Chamsiin, who had been trampling up and down with excitement. They stormed towards the approaching Franks, while Ibrahim stumbled back to his tent to do as he had been asked.

Harald, who had been looking in vain for a bow and arrows, was watching in bleak terror as his earl, with only a sword in hand, rode straight at the three knights with lowered lances. A few moments later, he had understood what Arn's unkind criticisms of the Norwegian style of riding had been all about.

Compared with the other horses, Chamsiin was obviously the faster by far. A split second before Arn would have been pierced by a lance, Chamsiin turned right so sharply he was almost lying down in the curve. The lances missed and the three knights, looking through their narrow eye-slits, were slow to take in the new situation. Now Arn was coming at them from behind, striking one of them across the back of his neck. The knight collapsed, sliding off his horse apparently lifeless, as Arn was already attacking his second man, who was trying to use his shield in defence while the third rider was manoeuvring into a new attacking angle. Arn cut the nearest horse over the small of its back, paralysing its hind legs. When the rider lost his balance, Arn's sword hit precisely the eye-slit of his helmet and he fell, leaving only two men on horseback facing each other. Arn seemed to hold back, as if to argue with his opponent, but the only response was an attack with lowered lance. In the next moment, the attacker's head, inside its handsome helmet, was flying through the air and hitting the ground with a thud, while his body, spurting blood, sagged to the ground.

At this point Arn reined in Chamsiin and tested the edge of his sword in surprise. Then he shook his head and steered his horse toward the nearest living Frank. The man's face was bloody but he clearly was not seriously injured. Arn dismounted, reached out his hand and helped the fallen man to his feet. When Arn turned to inspect the third Frank on the ground, the man he had just helped drew his sword and drove it straight into Chamsiin's belly. With a wild scream of terror, the big horse reared. The sword had been driven into its body to the hilt.

Arn stood absolutely still for a moment. Then he killed the Frank. The man was kneeling and holding up his hands pleading for mercy but received none. Afterwards Arn did what had to be done. He stuck the sacred Saracen sword in his belt, took his own sword, and called Chamsiin who, in spite of his fear and pain, came limping towards his master. The Frankish sword was moving with each step and the stallion's terrified rolling eyes were almost all whites. Arn caressed and kissed him, and then beheaded his old friend with a single blow of furious strength.

Then he dropped his sword on the ground, went into the camp and sat down on the ground alone.

Suddenly women and children came out and started digging in the sand, taking down tents and rounding up camels, horses and goats. Harald understood nothing of all this, but knew better than to disturb his earl with questions.

Ibrahim went to pick up Arn's sword. When he had cleaned it, he walked with slow determined steps to Arn's side and sat down. Arn's withdrawn face told the old Bedouin of a sorrow that he understood very well. Ibrahim was prepared to sit there in silence for two days and two nights, for custom dictated that the grief-stricken man had to speak first.

'Ibrahim, I know I must speak first. In this your rules and mine say the same,' Arn said in a low, pained tone. 'The sword you lent me was truly miraculous.'

'Al Ghouti, that sword belongs to you now. It happened as it was written. It's all the proof I need.'

'No, Ibrahim, no. Do I have the right to ask you a favour?'

'Yes, Al Ghouti. Whatever you ask, I will grant you if it is within my power and that of *Banu Anaza*'s,' the old man whispered.

'Take the sword and ride off to give it to the man who is its rightful owner. Go to Yussuf ibn Salah al-Din, whom we simply call Saladin. Give him the sword. Tell him that it was written and that Al Ghouti said so.'

Silently Ibrahim took the sword, but did not leave Arn at once. The two men sat together, looking out over the sand dunes towards the sea. Arn's grief was hanging over him like a cold shadow. Although Ibrahim was sure he understood, Arn's feelings had their roots in many things that the old man did not know.

'Al Ghouti, you are the *Banu Anaza*'s friend for all eternity,' he said after some time, Arn could not tell how long or how short the interval had been. 'The favour you ask will be done, but it's too small. First we must do what we have to. We bury horses like your Chamsiin, because they are great warriors. Come with me.'

This persuaded Arn to rise and when they walked together towards the campsite, it was clear that everyone was waiting for them. The camp had already been packed up and loaded on the backs of camels. The three dead Franks and their horses had somehow disappeared into the sand. All the *Banu Anaza* people were gathered round an open grave, watched from a little further away by a bewildered Harald.

The Bedouin burial ceremony is brief for horses and people alike. Chief Ibrahim said a prayer, which told of their belief that Chamsiin was now running free forever on fields always covered in green plants and watered from many springs. Arn prayed for this too, but very quietly to himself, for he knew it was blasphemous. But Chamsiin had been his friend since his youth, and for him alone Arn was prepared to offend his God. He was so deeply moved that he felt he wanted to share the Bedouin belief that Chamsiin, tail lifted high, was running over green meadows in Paradise.

Then they all set out for Gaza. Three Franks had died in their camp and the *Banu Anaza* people knew that they had to move closer to the walls of Gaza or even inside the city. The women and children were as practised and skilled as their menfolk in rounding up animals and moving camp.

Harald was riding next to his earl, who had some slight problems controlling his borrowed, nervous horse. Harald dared not say anything during the whole ride, completely taken aback by the unimaginable sight of a man like Arn Magnusson weeping and, worse still, showing his childish grief in front of a lot of wild natives.

Admittedly, they seemed unsurprised at the warrior's abject sorrow over a dead horse, but then, their faces were immobile and unemotional as if embossed on leather. They were Bedouin and Harald had not the faintest idea of what they were like.

Arn showed them a campsite when they arrived. The site was close to the wall and given that the wind was almost always westerly, the odours of the city would not affect them there. Then he jumped off his borrowed horse and began undoing Chamsiin's tack. Ibrahim rode up to him, leapt off his own horse with remarkable agility, and took Arn's hand.

'Al Ghouti, my friend, I want you to know one thing. The *Banu Anaza* tribe breeds the best horses in Arabia. Everyone knows it, but no one – not a sultan, not a caliph – can buy one. Rarely, we may give one away. The young stallion you've ridden now is not schooled yet. I know you noticed that he hasn't yet felt a master's hand, but he's our best, his blood is the purest, and he was meant for my son. You must have him. The favour you've asked me isn't great enough, although I will do it.'

'Ibrahim, you cannot give away . . .' Arn began and then broke down, his eyes overflowing with tears. Ibrahim, like a father, caressed the bowed head.

'Of course I can, Al Ghouti. I am the chief, the elder of the tribe and what I say goes. You've been my guest. You cannot insult me by refusing my gift.'

'That is true. You must know that in the eyes of my own people, I'm as weak as a woman or even a fool, mourning so bitterly for a horse. But you know better, Ibrahim – you know that such grief never leaves you and to you alone can I admit this. Your gift is truly great. I accept it with a gratitude that I will feel for the rest of my life.'

'I'll give you a mare as well,' Ibrahim said with a cunning smile. At a gesture of his hand, the mare was lead up to Arn by Aisha, the young woman who but for Arn would have died for her love of Ali ibn Quays.

It was nicely planned by Ibrahim because, according to custom, Arn could not refuse a gift from Aisha, whom he had made happy and who bore the name of the most beloved wife of the Prophet, may peace be with him.

VIII

Within only a few years, Cecilia Rosa's life in Godshome had taken on a completely new shape. Under her control, the business side of the cloister had changed out of all recognition and income had more than doubled, even though there had been few sizeable additions of land. When Mother Rikissa, or anyone else, pestered her with questions about how she had managed it, Cecilia Rosa would reply that it was just a matter of being orderly – and raising prices a bit. Nowadays a Folkunga mantle cost three times as much as it had at the outset and, as Father Lucien had predicted, the mantles now sold steadily instead of vanishing off the shelves in a week. The work became easier to plan and *familiares* could be left to do regular sessions in the *vestiarium* without undue pressure.

The investment in skins had helped as well. The most expensive ones were sold only in a few of the spring markets, and when the stock forecasting had gone wrong in the past they had ended up with too many orders and not enough skins. Now everything ran smoothly and the treasure chests would have been bulging with silver if Mother Rikissa had not begun so many new building projects. She built expensively and beautifully, hiring French and English master masons. Godshome's wealth was on show and one of its most visible signs was the new church tower. Its bell came from England and had a lovely sound that rang out over the whole region. The new vaulted cloisters and circle of inner walls were also great works.

Two large stone-built rooms had been added next to the sacristy, the central offices of Cecilia Rosa's realm. In the outer room, wooden racks covered the walls, providing hundreds of compartments to hold the documentation of all donations to Godshome. Cecilia Rosa kept them in rigorous order according to principles that she alone fully understood. In response to requests for information from anyone with the authority to ask, she could immediately find the details of a tenancy or the value and nature of a particular estate. If tenancy payments were late, she wrote letters for Mother Rikissa to sign and stamp her own personal seal. The letters were addressed to the bishop in the local diocese, whose duty it was to have bailiffs visit the sluggish tenant promptly and extract what was owed, one way or the other. No one slipped through Cecilia Rosa's net.

She was not unaware of how much power her position as *yconoma* gave her. Although obliged to provide answers to questions, no business decisions could be made without her, and without the income streams she controlled, Godshome would have gone under. It did not surprise her that Mother Rikissa no longer treated her with the condescension or the cruelty that she had once shown. They had established a way of coexisting that allowed both worldly and divine affairs to proceed calmly.

The more practised Cecilia Rosa had become with her abacus and her account books, the more time she could set aside for other things. Much of her spare time was spent with Ulvhilde, either in the gardens or, during the dark, cold seasons, in the *vestiarium* where they sometimes sewed and talked late into the night.

A long time had passed without any resolution in the matter of Ulvhilde's inheritance. Cecilia Blanca, who still visited Godshome regularly, brought no answers, reporting that it was all very difficult but surely would get settled in time. Meanwhile, Ulvhilde's hopes for the future were fading and she seemed to have almost resigned herself to a life inside the walls.

Because it was part of their new relationship to see as little of each other as possible, it surprised Cecilia Rosa to be asked to attend on the Abbess in her private rooms. The reasons for the request were obscure.

Fairly recently, Mother Rikissa had begun mortifying herself with uncharacteristic devotion and harshness. She was using the scourge regularly and wore horsehair shirts next to her skin. Cecilia had taken note of this, but was not unduly concerned – it happened from time to time that nuns were overwhelmed by religious fervour and did quite strange things – but when they met face to face, she thought the Abbess looked quite unlike her usual self. She seemed to have shrunk and her eyes were bloodshot from lack of sleep.

Mother Rikissa at once started speaking in a frail voice, wringing her hands incessantly and humbling herself in front of Cecilia, both by her words and the posture of her emaciated body. She said that she had been seeking forgiveness, first begging the Holy Virgin and then pleading with the people to whom she had been most cruel during the past years. She had been examining her heart to find the demon from hell that had driven her to wickedness, she said, for it must have taken domicile in her without her own knowledge.

By now, having prayed and mortified her flesh, she felt that Our Lady might be taking pity on her. Could Cecilia Rosa ever forgive her? She would gladly endure all the time Cecilia had spent in *carcer* and all the blows of the scourge, twice or three times over, if only she could reach reconciliation with her former victim.

She spoke of her youth, when she had suffered because she was ugly. From her very earliest days, she had known that God hadn't created her in the image of fair maidens in courtly love songs. Her kin were of royal blood, but her father hadn't been sufficiently well off to give her the kind of dowry that would bring hope of a wedding feast. Everyone agreed that Rikissa was doomed never to marry. Her mother had tried to comfort her by saying that God had a purpose for everything. Girls who were not made for the bridal bed, which after all was the goal of all sorts of little fools, were intended for higher callings, and Rikissa should aspire to the Kingdom of God. The girl liked people, and was particularly fond of riding and hunting. This got her nowhere, for these were not considered suitable interests for a young lady.

Her father had been very close to old King Sverker, and together they worked out a scheme that involved the King in giving Rikissa responsibility for a new nunnery, which the Sverker kin intended to finance and call Godshome. She had, of course, no leg to stand on in an argument with her father and her King, and after completing her year as a novice she was made Abbess immediately. God alone knew how strongly she had felt her lack of experience and how frightened she had been. Obviously, if a kin invested in a cloister, they wanted to keep it in the family and not let go of their property. Trying to walk the narrow path between the Church and the worldly powers, she had learnt that it was near impossible for the King and his henchmen to change anything once an Abbess or an Abbot was in charge. Still, there was much covert outside manipulation of the world behind the walls of cloisters. She had seen it all and felt that she could not reject her calling, be it as much from her own kin as from God.

At least some of Rikissa's harshness towards Cecilia Rosa was explained by the recent war, which saw both Folkunga and Erik men defeating the Sverker side. Of course, it was unfair to make a fragile young maiden into a scapegoat, especially in the cloister where the storms of war should not be felt. It had been deeply unjust and Mother Rikissa, knowing how badly she had sinned, admitted it and bowed her head in grief.

The longer the confession went on, the more Cecilia became aware that, among her mixed feelings, the chief one was pity. This was unexpected, but she felt vividly what the ugly maiden would have experienced when she realised how men and youths were sniggering behind her back – just as, much later on, the Cecilias and Ulvhilde had giggled together at her appearance and called her a witch. The young Rikissa surely had the same hopes and dreams for the future as other girls, but unlike most she had watched them crumble all too soon when she was forced into a life she had never wanted.

And it's so dreadfully unfair, Cecilia Rosa thought. No man or woman can choose how they look. Beautiful parents can produce ugly offspring, and the other way round, too. God had made Rikissa look like a witch, but it wasn't her fault. So, when the heartbroken woman was sobbing and begging her forgiveness, Cecilia Rosa's first impulse was to hug her and give her all the support she needed. At the last moment she remembered Cecilia Blanca, and had an inner vision of how her friend would react when she reported this affecting scene. Cecilia Blanca would have no kindly, understanding words to say.

Now Cecilia Rosa had to think of another way of dealing with the situation; she desperately tried to imagine what Cecilia Blanca or Birger Brosa would have said and done.

'It's a very sad story you're telling me, Mother,' she finally said. 'It's true that you've sinned, and I myself have known just how badly on my own skin and during long, icy winter nights. But God is good and forgiving to those who feel true remorse, as you do. My forgiveness, now – I don't think it matters much because my wounds are long since healed and the chill has gone from the marrow of my bones. Mother, you must seek God's forgiveness, for I cannot offer anything of real worth.'

'So, you won't forgive me,' Mother Rikissa said, sobbing. She was bent over as if in a spasm, her twisting causing the horsehair cloth under her clothes to creak and crack.

'I would wish for nothing better, Mother,' Cecilia said, pleased that she had managed to slip off the hook. 'Come to me the very moment that you feel sure of God's forgiveness and we'll kneel together and thank Him for His mercy.'

Mother Rikissa straightened up from her crouching position and nodded thoughtfully, as if she had found much spiritual sustenance in what Cecilia had said, even though she had not been forgiven. She wiped her eyes, sighed profoundly, and began the sad story of how things had been just after the news of the double escape from Godshome and Varnhem had got out.

It had been dreadful for both the elderly Father Henri and herself to be chastised so severely by the Archbishop for a grave sin that, at least to some degree, had been their fault. To how great a degree Mother Rikissa for one couldn't say, because she, of course, had had no idea of what had been going on behind her back. Now, after such a long time, surely dear Cecilia Rosa could take mercy on her and share her understanding of what was the truth in this matter?

Cecilia Rosa felt herself turning as cold and hard as ice. Looking into Mother Rikissa's face, she saw the Devil's own eyes. Had not the pupils in that woman's red eyes turned into vertical slits like the eyes of goats and snakes?

'No, Mother Rikissa, in this matter I know as little as you do. How could I, a sinful young penitent, have any understanding of the lives of a monk and a nun?' Cecilia said stiffly, and left the room without kissing Mother Rikissa's hand.

She controlled herself until she reached the cloisters. They looked particularly beautiful now, with Sister Leonore's roses in full bloom. Climbing up every pillar, the flowers were as messengers from Sister Leonore and Brother Lucien and their child, surely living happily and without sin in the lovely Occidental lands. There had been no news, which must be good news, or there would have been tales of punishments and penitence and bans. Cecilia walked slowly, inhaling the scent of the red roses and caressing the unscented white blooms, but despite the warm summer evening, she found herself shivering from an inner chill.

She had been facing the Snake, which had appeared like a little lamb. For a moment, Cecilia Rosa had believed that the snake was a lamb, and she was now terrified to think of what might have happened if she had been taken in by its pretty bleating. Such great misery would have befallen so many, such dreadful punishments meted out, if she'd persisted with her childish pity. It was important to see people clearly for what they were and to try at all times to think like a man of power – or, at least, like Cecilia Blanca.

A possible explanation soon emerged as to why Mother Rikissa had been so brimming with remorse, and why she had made her determined but fruitless attempt to trick Cecilia Rosa into admitting that she had sinned most grievously against the very principles of the cloister. A message arrived that the Queen would not be travelling alone on her next visit to Godshome. Earl Birger Brosa would be accompanying her. This was most significant news.

The Earl was not a man to go traipsing off to visit a cloister just because he had taken it into his head to spend time chatting to a distantly related penitent. However friendly he had been towards Cecilia Rosa in the past, for him to make a special visit meant that something serious was afoot. She had been told immediately, because these days the Abbess had to inform her *yconoma* in good time of any unusual expenditure. Errands to market had to be run in order to purchase all the food normally not eaten in Godshome. It was all very well to forbid the consumption of four-footed animals to monks and nuns, but earls and their retinue would have none of these restrictions. It was a fact that many male orders, for instance the Cistercians who owned Varnhem and had their roots in Burgundy, did not follow these rules to the letter. Under Father Henri, the cooking at Varnhem had become the most famous in all the Nordic lands and they could receive Birger Brosa without advance notice.

Cecilia Rosa didn't even try to imagine what the Earl's intentions might be. Her time as a penitent was drawing to its close, but until then all anyone could do for her was to keep Mother Rikissa in fear of God or, at least, of man. Instead she was happily curious about how this unusual visit from her dear friend Cecilia Blanca would turn out.

When the Earl arrived with a large following, they came from Varnhem and had already been properly wined and dined. Inside the inner walls, the women listened excitedly to all the unaccustomed sounds of horses' hooves on the newly cobbled outer courtyards, men's voices talking and shouting, and the noise of ropes and pulleys as the tents were raised. Cecilia Rosa, who now could go to the *hospitium* any time she liked, stayed calmly in her counting chambers, finishing the accounts of all the costs that the splendid visitation had demanded. She was content to complete her daily tasks first, like the worker in the vineyard, rather than rush off to join in what was for her the most joyful event of the year. She felt her satisfaction in work well done was something she would take with her, for now her penitence had so little time to run that she often thought of how life would be on the outside.

Her dreams of the future were very vague, because the most

important part was still unknown. It had been many years since Father Henri had heard anything about Arn Magnusson. She felt sure he could not be dead, but that was all. He apparently had risen to such a high office in the Order of the Temple that the whole Cistercian world would have read funeral Masses for him.

It was news of Arn that was Birger Brosa's first errand. Once Cecilia Rosa had stepped into the *hospitium* and hugged Cecilia Blanca, she bowed her head to the Earl because she did not dare hug him too. Her cloister years had marked her in many ways, more deeply than she was yet aware of. Greetings done, Birger Brosa sat comfortably back in his seat with one leg across the other as was his habit, raised his tankard and looked at her with a shrewd glint in his eyes. Cecilia Rosa was looking down and pulling her dress into place.

'Well, my dear kinswoman, the Queen and I have many things to tell you,' he said amiably, and paused as if to tantalise her. 'Some of these matters are more important than the rest, but what I think you'd like to hear first is the latest news of Arn Magnusson. He's led the Knights Templar to one of their greatest victories, a tremendous battle at some place called Mount Gizzard, it seems. Fifty thousand Saracens slain by the ten thousand knights riding out with Arn right in front. May God protect such a Christian warrior and bring him back home soon. That's the Folkunga wish as much as your own, Cecilia!'

Cecilia Rosa immediately lowered her head, praying in gratitude with tears streaming down her cheeks. Cecilia Blanca and Birger Brosa looked fondly at her and left her to it.

'Now, may I carry on and talk of another subject close to all our hearts?' Birger Brosa asked, with one of his familiar broad smiles. Cecilia Rosa nodded shyly and wiped her tears, with a happy glance at Cecilia Blanca who needed no other word or sign to understand what the news of Arn had meant to her friend.

'I'd like to talk to you about Ulvhilde Emundsdotter,' the Earl went on, once Cecilia Rosa had pulled herself together. 'This is no easy matter, as you know. Let me go through the arguments for and against, one by one.'

And so he did, calmly and systematically. It was true that the inheritance should be Ulvhilde's by law. The three Lawmen were in complete agreement about her right to Ulfshem, her childhood home. One complication was that King Knut Eriksson had been no friend of her father Emund. 'No friend' in this case meant that the King insisted that nothing would please him more than if Emund, like the mythical pig, would come to life every day ready to be slaughtered again. Emund had killed a king, but worse, he had been the cowardly slayer of Erik, Knut's father, a saint as well as a king. So exactly why, Knut had asked, should any mercy be shown to that vile man's offspring?

Birger Brosa had pointed out that this was what the law stated and that the law is not subject to anyone's rulings, not even the king's. The realm must be founded on the rock of law. But even if the king had to accept that, other problems remained. One was that Ulfshem had been burnt down and the land had been given to a Folkunga family led by Sigurd Folkesson, who had served with distinction at the battle of Bjälbo. Sigurd had two unmarried sons and he himself hadn't married again after the mother of his boys died in labour. They had devoted much effort to building up Ulfshem again and could always claim their right to a royal gift.

At this point the Earl was interrupted, to his obvious astonishment, by Cecilia Rosa. She rather tartly pointed out that the land was worth more than any buildings on it, especially if they had been constructed in the new method, using wood on top of the old masonry foundations. As likely as not they had used this method, and if so, what were a handful of wooden houses against land and foundations? The Earl did not take kindly to being corrected in this way, but since no one except Cecilia Blanca had been listening, he just lifted his eyebrows and said, pleasantly enough, that he was very impressed by Cecilia Rosa's acumen in property dealings.

Then he went on with his own thoughts about how to get out of this foxes' hole. There were ways and means, of course. One was to pay, in solid silver. Another was to arrange a wedding. If Ulvhilde would agree to marry one of Sigurd's sons, it would bring her at least half her inheritance, for something had of course to be handed over as a dowry. Cecilia Rosa was about to interrupt again, but thought better of it.

The Earl smiled, wagging his finger to show that he was going on and turned to the option of buying out the Folkunga family. He was prepared to put up a reasonable amount of silver and wanted to explain why. The reason was a promise made to God during the last of his two crusades to the territories on the other side of the Baltic Sea. A local force had ambushed Birger Brosa and his men in an awkward spot. Praying to God for rescue, he promised three churches in return. It didn't help much at first, so he added an assurance that he'd help little Ulvhilde. God clearly approved, for they had fought their way out soon afterwards.

Now, he had already built the churches, but couldn't regard his debt to God as properly settled until Ulvhilde's life was in order. The question of how it should best be achieved wasn't something he could discuss in the girl's presence, which is why Cecilia Rosa had been asked along on her own. In her view, would it be better to solve the problem expensively and buy out the Folkesson men, or simply, by having Ulvhilde married into the kin somehow?

'These are indeed difficult questions and finding the best answer will take yet more time,' she replied thoughtfully. 'If Ulvhilde's nearest and dearest hadn't been killed in war, her father would surely have married her off long ago, probably into the Sverker kin. As it is, she has no immediate reason to accept anybody. True, if her two closest friends, and above all, the Earl himself, told her what her best course would be, she'd be foolish not to follow it.' Cecilia Rosa paused for a while to think.

'Wouldn't the simplest decision be to let Ulvhilde have her old home back, with no promises made to anyone?' she asked in the end. 'Sigurd and his sons could help her settle in and explain the duties of a housewife. Learning everything would take time anyway; remember that she knows nothing except hymn-singing, sewing and a bit of gardening.'

'Probably the more expensive solution, then,' Birger Brosa muttered. 'What if she doesn't like either of the Folkesson lads?'

Both Cecilias attacked him for being mercenary and reminded him that he had made a promise to God without specifying any cost limit. Besides, Cecilia Blanca observed, his crusades in the eastern territories had enriched him a great deal, by all accounts. He might have been angered by these admonitions in male company, but now he only nodded and asked Cecilia Rosa to bring Ulvhilde to the *hospitium*.

Before she left, Cecilia Blanca called out asking her to remind Ulvhilde that this would be the last time she walked out of Godshome. She would stay in the *hospitium* and in a few days' time, she would come with them on the journey northwards.

'If there's a reasonably good Sverker mantle in stock, best give it to her now,' Cecilia Blanca added. 'The Earl here will surely not mind paying, would you? If he does, I'll pay.' Then both she and Birger Brosa burst out laughing.

Blushing and with pounding heart, Cecilia Rosa went quickly back into the cloister. She expected to find Ulvhilde in the *vestiarium*, and when she wasn't there, decided to pick up a Sverker mantle before looking for her friend. There was a fine mantle, in deep clear red.

The black griffin embroidered on the back had been stitched with silk and gold thread. She bundled it under her arm and hurried on, because a sense of anxiety had suddenly gripped her. As if directed by her fears, she did not consider other likelier places but went straight to Mother Rikissa's rooms. She found them both there, kneeling side by side and weeping. Mother Rikissa had put her arm round Ulvhilde, who was shaking with sobs.

To Cecilia Rosa it looked as if what she had most feared was happening, or worse, might already have happened in spite of all her warnings.

'Ulvhilde, don't let her lead you astray!' she cried, running up to the two women and pulling the girl out of Mother Rikissa's claw-like grip. She hugged Ulvhilde, stroking her trembling back and trying to unwrap the Sverker mantle.

Mother Rikissa was hissing with anger when she sprang to her feet.

'No one must interrupt the sanctity of the confession!' she screamed wildly, her bloodshot eyes flashing. 'These are serious sins and much is still needed for clarity.'

Then she grabbed one of Ulvhilde's arms, trying to drag her away from Cecilia Rosa, who kept the furious woman at bay with a strength she had not known she possessed. As a shield against the witch, she held up the red mantle between them and somehow the blood-red cloth baffled and stilled both the others. Then Cecilia Rosa quickly put the mantle over her friend's shoulders and pulled it tight as if it to provide an impenetrable armour against Mother Rikissa's wickedness. A new cold insight sustained her as she turned to her Abbess.

'You must control yourself. This young woman is no longer one of your enslaved creatures! Not a sad little maiden, without a coin or a relative to call her own, but Ulvhilde of Ulfshem. She's going home now. God willing, you two will never meet again!'

In the sudden silence that followed, Cecilia Rosa quickly led Ulvhilde away, through the cloisters and out through the great gate. For a moment they stood in sight of the carving showing Adam and Eve driven out of Paradise, panting as if they had been running.

'Ulvhilde, I warned you so often about the snake turning into a lamb.'

'I felt ... so very ... sorry for her.'

'So, maybe she truly is to be pitied, but it doesn't prevent her from being an evil witch. What did you say? You didn't confess ...?' Cecilia Rosa's voice was gentle but very worried.

'She made me forgive her and weep for her in her unhappiness.'

'And then you were meant to confess?'

'Yes, I was just about to begin but you arrived in time, sent by Our Lady. Please forgive me, dear Cecilia, I was just about to do something so very stupid,' Ulvhilde said, lowering her eyes with shame.

'I think you're right, it must have been Our Lady who took pity on us all and sent me in time. If you'd told her the truth about Sister Leonore, the mantle you're wearing would've been torn off your shoulders at once and you would have been forced to stay in there forever, drying up until you died. Let us pray to the Holy Virgin and thank her!'

They kneeled at the gate that Ulvhilde now had walked through for the last time.

They prayed for a long time with the most deeply felt reverence, asking the Holy Virgin to forgive their sins and thanking Her for the merciful rescue of them both and of the Queen, who could have been dragged down with them. They would always believe that but for Her wonderful intervention all would have been lost, because the witch had enticed Ulvhilde and she had been ready to put the noose round her own neck.

Afterwards, Ulvhilde recovered enough to ask about her precious red mantle. She kept caressing the red cloth, looking at her friend and entreating her wordlessly to explain its significance. The time had come for Ulvhilde to go home, Cecilia Rosa said. The mantle was a gift from the Earl, or maybe the Queen, but only one small part of what she owned, because now she was sole owner of Ulfshem.

Still silent, Ulvhilde walked at Cecilia Rosa's side to the *hospitium*. She was trying to understand with her heart and mind what all this would mean, before she met her benefactors. Just a short while ago she had owned nothing but the clothes on her back or – strictly speaking – not the clothes either, for the little dress she had worn when she arrived was a child's and long gone. There was nothing for her to go back and collect now that she was leaving.

The huge step to the red mantle and the position as mistress of Ulfshem was something impossible to understand without more time to think. When the two young women entered the *hospitium* they looked grimmer and paler than the Queen and her Earl had expected. The servants bringing beer and tending the roasting spits had started their work and the Earl, in a good mood, had been preparing to leap from his seat to greet the new mistress of Ulfshem with a deep chivalrous bow. He held back, noticing that all was not well.

Their feast got off to an unexpected start when Cecilia Rosa and Ulvhilde took turns to tell the story about Mother Rikissa's last ferocious attempt to bring about their downfall. Birger Brosa learnt for the first time of their conspiracy to help a monk and a nun and their love child. At first he looked unhappy, for it did not take much knowledge of Church affairs to realise that all their futures had been put at risk. Then he said firmly that the danger was past. When all was said and done, in all of the Nordic lands, only the four of them knew the true story. The two Cecilias would doubtlessly keep quiet and so would Ulvhilde, especially if she married into the Folkunga kin – the Cecilias looked cross at that point – especially if she cared for the peace and happiness of her friends, he quickly added. For his own part, he concluded with a broad smile, he had no intention of starting some religious war on account of a run-away monk.

This had presumably been Mother Rikissa's intention, he went on more seriously. Much more was at stake for her than just taking revenge on two disobedient maidens. It was worth remembering that she had been instrumental in getting Arn Magnusson sent into exile, which caused the pretender to the throne, Knut Eriksson, a lot of difficulties. Maybe her aim had been to get the Queen banned for complicity and so exclude her sons from the line of succession to the throne. Then war would have been close. Had Rikissa succeeded, she would have felt justified the rest of her life, even though it would end in hell, no doubt about that.

One way or the other, they had many reasons to enjoy a festive evening together, he said, politely drinking a toast to them all and apparently in the best of moods. And it was true that they had a good time together, with many jokes about how the meagre cloister rations had kept Cecilia Rosa and Ulvhilde in good health but the rich foods of freedom might not grant them such a long life. Meanwhile endless dishes of lamb and veal were put in front of them, with plenty of wine to drink and even more beer.

The women gave up long before Birger Brosa had stopped eating. His grandfather, the powerful Folke the Fat, was said to have been the greatest of earls – at least in waist measurement. But that evening Birger Brosa probably gave up on the delicacies, such as sweetened turnips and beans, earlier than he would have done in the company of men. He found it rather strange to sit eating alone while the other three watched him with growing impatience. He knew well that this interval before the serious drinking was the best for talking about important subjects. Birger Brosa had many such in readiness, as it happened.

When he realised that the women were chatting in their sign language and giggling a great deal, he pushed his platter to the side, poured another beer, stuck his knife in his belt and wiped his mouth. Balancing his tankard on the knee of his crossed leg, he said solemnly that there were more weighty matters to talk about.

'Take the fact the Sverker kin controls most of the cloisters, in fact all the nunneries,' he pronounced. 'This divide can have serious consequences and for some, like you two Folkunga ladies, that's something you've felt on your own skins.'

The Earl went on to describe the new cloister he had founded at Riseberga, to the north-east of Arnäs and beyond the Northern Forest. That meant it was located in Sviarland – but no need to look so doubtful, even the Sviars were on their way to joining the Goths under the rule of King Knut, he added when he saw the distaste on the three women's faces. It was much better to unite in reasonable projects than being at war all the time, he argued.

Soon Riseberga would be consecrated and ready to open its gates. They needed to find an Abbess and the headhunt was under way for a suitable, preferably experienced Folkunga or Erik nun. A good *yconomus* was also essential and, according to Birger Brosa, a survey of nunneries had shown that Godshome was the best run with regard to business.

'And imagine,' he said full of mock surprise, 'Godshome isn't managed by a man!'

'I told you that ages ago,' Cecilia Blanca reminded him crossly.

'Godshome did have a male *yconomus*, but he was an idiot,' Cecilia Rosa added.

'Just amusing myself with a little joke. Of course I know the real situation at Godshome,' the Earl said, pretending be so scared he had to hide behind his tankard. 'But I'm serious when I ask you, Cecilia Rosa, to take on the work as *yconomus* at Riseberga.'

'*Yconoma*', Cecilia Rosa corrected him, in her turn pretending hurt feelings.

'The most serious thing is that you have to stay here for some time yet. Before I can have you taken to Riseberga, the Archbishop must write and sign a document confirming this, that and the other. You'll be alone with Rikissa in Godshome, without friend or witnesses.'

'It's indeed serious,' Cecilia Rosa agreed. 'Once she realises that she'll be back to managing business on her own, goodness knows what she'll do. I don't think there's a limit to that woman's wickedness. But in the meantime, she might decide that getting Godshome's affairs into good order is more useful than trying any apish foolery with horsehair shirts and tearful confessions. She must be grinding her teeth with hatred and anger just now.'

At this point Ulvhilde said earnestly and at some length that she was sure Mother Rikissa knew magic arts, which for one thing could drain away one's strength of mind and make one do anything and admit anything against one's will, as if God had demanded it and not the Devil. She herself had been ensnared by magic, because despite her best intentions, she'd almost given way to Mother Rikissa's evil persuasion.

Cecilia Blanca interrupted all this with some crisp instructions. In her view, the best thing Cecilia Rosa could do was to talk to Rikissa some time soon, pretend to have forgiven her and then pray with her to thank God for having mercy on His sinful Abbess. So it was hypocritical, but God would understand and see the point, and besides there'd be plenty of time to beg His forgiveness at Riseberga. Birger Brosa had better keep his plans quiet, she advised, and perhaps even spread some false rumours about the position as *yconomus*. Anything was allowed when you were fighting the Devil. Then, one day, a cart would turn up outside, and Cecilia Rosa would step through that gate for the last time without saying any goodbyes – wouldn't *that* be one in the eye for that nasty witch!

They all agreed that the plan should work. God had to be on Cecilia Rosa's side, after all, not the treacherous Abbess's. Though Someone Else, not God, must be helping Mother Rikissa, Cecilia Rosa mused, adding that she would pray to Our Lady for protection every night. All these years She had held her hand over both herself and her beloved Arn.

When the young Mistress of Ulfshem rode out to her new life in freedom, it was just before harvest time, when the barns are empty but the haymaking has started. She was riding next to the Queen, just behind the Earl and his guards, who carried the banners with the golden lion and the three crowns. Behind them rode a group of some thirty men, most of whom wore blue mantles, though Ulvhilde was not quite alone in wearing red.

Along their route, men and women left their work in the fields to kneel at the roadside and pray that God should protect the peace, the Earl and Queen Cecilia Blanca. Ulvhilde's delight at being free overwhelmed her, and the gentle summer air seemed especially fragrant. She inhaled deeply, holding her breath so as not to lose the sense of liberation somehow.

Not that riding came easily to her. Ulvhilde was out of habit and although everyone believed that God wanted man to ride horses, just as all other animals were at mankind's service, she now felt that there must be better ways of travelling. As a child she had learnt to ride astride the horse, but now she had to manage in a side-saddle, like other high-ranking women. It was much more difficult, and she shifted about constantly to prevent a leg from going stiff or a knee from rubbing against the edge of the saddle.

The land around her took her mind off riding, for they passed ripening fields, sun-dappled meadows in oak woods, and rode alongside many glittering streams and rivers. When they reached Billingen, the forest grew thicker and half the men rode forward to protect the front. Cecilia Blanca said soothingly that it was because men love behaving as if it were only a matter of time before they had to draw their swords, but the land was peaceful and mostly orderly.

It looked unthreatening, with warm sunlight piercing the canopies of tall oaks and beeches. Sometimes they saw deer retreating cautiously but mostly the forest was still. Ulvhilde could not imagine a world looking more beautiful and welcoming. At twenty-two, she might have been a woman with children and a house to mind, but this was something she had not even dared to dream about in the cloister. She thought that this happiness of hers could not last and that liberty would soon enough show its harsher aspects, but for now, with Godshome behind her, she allowed herself to become intoxicated by joy and freedom.

They had quarters for the night waiting in the royal castle in Skara. While the Earl went off to deal with the affairs of groups of hard-faced men, Cecilia Blanca arranged for women to attend on Ulvhilde and bring her new clothes. They helped her take a bath, comb her hair and put on a soft green dress with a silver belt. Left on the floor was a small pile of un-dyed, woollen things, of the kind she had been wearing for almost as long as she could remember. One of the women picked up these rags and took them away to be burnt.

This was a moment that became etched into Ulvhilde's mind – the moment when her cloister clothes were carried off as something unclean and distasteful, fit only for the fire. Maybe that was when she truly realised that she was not inside a dream world, but had become the woman she could see in the polished glass held by two of her smiling attendants, while a third artfully arranged the red mantle around her shoulders. She watched her reflection do everything she did – stroke the rich red mantle, raise an arm to push a silver hair-clip into place – but she found herself looking askance at the woman in the mirror. Like Cecilia Rosa she had been marked for life by years in Godshome and the austerity of cloister life.

Then the first shadow fell over her great happiness. It was so unfair that Cecilia Rosa should still be in Godshome with that horrible witch in charge. During the fine evening meal that night, Ulvhilde was torn between enjoyment and sadness. One moment she was laughing out loud at the buffoons and the men's coarse jokes, the next Cecilia Blanca had to comfort her when tears came to her eyes.

What Ulvhilde remembered best afterwards was Cecilia Blanca saying that the two of them had reached the end of the hard journey they had set out on together, but that all three had always been true to each other and endured everything thanks to their friendship. She went on to say that now was the time to be happy, rather than grieving for Cecilia Rosa, who would soon be free too. Their love for her would never wane and for the rest of their lives they would be together outside in the free world.

Cecilia Blanca had wisely decided not to distract Ulvhilde by praising her beauty, not yet at least. It would probably mean nothing to her, still steeped as she was in piety. The time would come when she would realise how she had turned from a maiden no one cared for into one of the most desirable unmarried women in the land, beautiful, rich, and a dear friend of the Queen's. Ulfshem was a fine estate and soon she would be free to manage it as she pleased, with no nagging father or argumentative kinsmen insisting that she rush into this or that suitable man's wedded bed. Ulvhilde did not understand yet just how free she was.

The next day they arrived at the shores of Lake Vättern, where a small black-painted ship was waiting for them in the royal harbour. Its name was odd – The Short Snake – and its crew of tall blonde men turned out to be Norwegians belonging to the King's personal guard. It was well known that almost all his guardsmen at Castle Näs came from Norway. Some of them were childhood friends and others had joined after many of the Norwegian friends and relatives of the Folkunga and Erik kin had had to go into exile. In Norway, factions had been fighting for the royal crown for almost as long as the families in the lands of the Goths and the Sviars.

The evening of the party's arrival was unusually hot and still. Their mounted escort turned and rode back to Skara, and the three well-born travellers stepped into the small ship to be rowed across the shining surface of the water to Castle Näs, still out of sight. The Earl sat alone in the stern, to get peace to think, as he put it. The two women settled aft, next to the man at the rudder, who seemed to be the leader of the oarsmen.

Ulvhilde's heart was beating hard, because she could not remember ever having gone anywhere by boat. Enchanted, she watched the water swirl around the blades of the oars and inhaled the smells of tar, leather and men's sweat. The song of a nightingale followed them for a long while, mingling with the sound of oars creaking in their leather loops and water rushing round the stern at every powerful but apparently effortless stroke by the eight oarsmen.

The young woman felt a little frightened and took Cecilia Blanca's hand. They got out on open sea so quickly, and the ship seemed no more than a tiny nutshell floating over black, unimaginably great depths. After a while she dared ask about something that worried her. Was it true that people could disappear at sea because they lost the way? She was answered by a roar of laughter from the oarsmen. Two of them laughed so hard that they fell over.

'We're Norwegians and used to sailing greater seas than this puddle,' the man at the rudder explained. 'Dear lady, let me assure you that we wouldn't even consider setting sail on Lake Vättern, it would be below us.'

Wrapped tightly in their mantles, because the evening air was chilly now, they finally approached the castle on the southern tip of Visingsö. At the point, steep rock faces rose out of the water and continued up to become the two menacing towers and tall wall of the castle. A huge banner hung slackly from one of the towers. Ulvhilde thought the gold glinting in its folds must be the three crowns of the Erik kin. She was frightened, not only by the menacing fortress, but by the thought of soon having to face King Knut, the man who murdered her father. As if she had read Ulvhilde's mind, Cecilia Blanca squeezed the younger woman's hand and whispered that she mustn't feel bad about meeting Knut – it would be easy, she'd see.

The King had come down to the beach to receive them. Once he had greeted his Earl and his Queen he turned to Ulvhilde, looking at her gravely as she bowed her head. What he saw pleased him, as his wife alone had known it would. He put his hand under Ulvhilde's chin and gently lifted up her face. His eyes were kind and held none of the hatred she had imagined. Then he spoke, and his words surprised even Cecilia Blanca.

'Ulvhilde Emundsdotter, we bid you welcome to our castle. It's a joy that you've come, for what was once between us and your father has been buried by time. It was wartime then, now peace is with us all. We want you to know that we are happy to greet you as the mistress of Ulfshem and that as our guest here, you're safe among friends.' He looked at her for a little longer, then took her arm and his Queen's. The three of them led the way towards the castle.

Ulvhilde spent only a short time at Näs, but to her it seemed long because each day was crowded with things to learn; little things that she'd had no idea about. Eating was just as regulated as in Godshome, but the other way round like all the new rules. Ulvhilde had been told never to speak without being spoken to, except for greetings. Here she could speak to everyone and must only greet the King, the Queen and the Earl first. She had been causing confusion by politely greeting stable grooms and spit-turners and maids before they had greeted her. The worst thing was having to speak first, because it had been ingrained into her to wait with bowed head until addressed. Liberty clearly had to be learned.

Cecilia Blanca, watching her friend, was more than once reminded of a swallow she had found on the ground in her father's courtyard when she was a child. She had picked up the helplessly piping bird, which fell silent when it felt the warmth of her hands, and had found it a little box where she bedded it down with the softest tufts of lamb's wool. She kept the bird next to her bed for two nights. On the second morning, she took it out in the yard and slung the creature straight up into the air. It had saluted freedom with a cry and disappeared in the sky. No one had told her how to get the swallow to fly again, but she had instinctively known the right thing to do.

Ulvhilde, who had been a little girl of eleven when she arrived in Godshome, was as helpless as that swallow had been. The harsh strictures of the cloister were still hampering her every move. She didn't even know that she was beautiful, with her black hair and dark, slightly slanting eyes, characteristic features of her side of the Sverker kin, once headed by the two dark men Kol and Boleslav.

Although the King grumbled, Cecilia Blanca was determined to accompany Ulvhilde to Ulfshem. So far she had said nothing about the situation there, but she wouldn't stand for sending Ulvhilde alone to face a Folkunga man about to be thrown out and his two lustful sons. She knew the two young men slightly. The elder was called Folke and was a hothead of the kind whose sharp tongue can be the bane of his own existence. The younger, Jon, had been trained by his relation Torgny Lawman. His quiet manner probably reflected the fact that being Folke's younger brother had not been always easy. Folke was already renowned for his fighting skills, presumably first honed on little Jon back home.

What would the world do to a woman like Ulvhilde, a catch in so many ways but still as innocent as the cloistered maiden she had been for so long. During the riding practice she insisted on every day, Cecilia Blanca had tried to explain gently but precisely what was in the offing. However much Ulvhilde moaned about her tender buttocks, she simply had to learn to get about on horseback, and while she struggled Cecilia Blanca tried to steer their talk round to the topics the three friends had discussed so intensely in Godshome: Cecilia Rosa's love for Arn, for example, or the whole affair of Sister Leonore and Brother Lucien. Ulvhilde shied away each time, pretending to be more interested in the type of saddle and the horse's training than in men and love.

She seemed more open to such things during the time they spent playing with the two little princes, five and three years old. The love between mother and child seemed to fascinate her more than the love between man and woman, but she preferred to ignore the essential connection between the two.

Soon after the Feast of Laurence, when the haymaking was almost finished, Cecilia Blanca, Ulvhilde, and their guards started the journey to Ulfshem. The ship took them north to Alvastra, from where they rode along the large road to Bjälbo and on towards Linköping. Ulfshem was situated somewhere halfway between the two. Ulvhilde had become a better rider and complained hardly at all, in spite of spending two whole days in the saddle. But the closer they came to Ulfshem, the more silent and anxious she seemed.

When they rode into the yard, the buildings were somehow familiar to her because they were built on the old foundations and still shaded by the large ash trees she remembered. Apart from looking smaller, Ulfshem fitted with her childhood memories.

They were expected because a queen cannot go travelling without sending messages ahead. When their following rode into sight, Ulfshem came alive as the householders, their guards and thralls all lined up in the yard to receive the guests and offer them the first piece of bread to break before they stepped in under the roof.

Cecilia Blanca was a sharp-eyed woman but she reckoned that most people, except those who were as innocent as her friend, would have noticed the marked change that came over the posture and manner of the three male householders. At a distance they had been looking truculent, almost hostile, but the moment they saw Ulvhilde step off her horse and flick back her costly red mantle, their faces softened with surprise.

Master Sigurd and his first-born son, Folke, hurried forward to greet them and offer them bread. They had indeed not been looking forward to this encounter. Even if they would be able to buy an even more handsome place with the silver Birger Brosa had been robbing from the heathens, it looked bad for the Folkunga honour to hand over the estate to a little nobody of the enemy kin. But this Ulvhilde was another matter. They had not expected such a beauty.

Sigurd Folkesson had planned a few simple words in greeting but, as it was, he mumbled and stammered, while his two sons could hardly take their eyes off the new mistress of Ulfshem. When the confused little speech of welcome came to an end, Cecilia Blanca felt that she might have to move and save everyone's dignity. But Ulvhilde got in first.

'I greet you Folkunga men, Sigurd, Folke and Jon,' she began in a calm, clear voice. 'What was once between your kin and mine has been buried by time. It was wartime then, now peace is with us all. I want you to know that I'm happy to greet you now as the mistress of Ulfshem and that I feel safe with you as my friends and guests.'

Her words made such an impression that no one could think of a reply. Ulvhilde held out her arm for Sigurd to take and lead her into the main building. Folke finally pulled himself together and offered his arm to the Queen.

As they walked through the large double oak doors, Cecilia Blanca smiled with relief and amusement. Ulvhilde had simply lifted her self-assured words of greeting from the King's speech to herself at Näs, almost word for word.

She had been painfully trained in a cloister and knew how to learn, the Queen thought to herself. But learning by heart is no good unless you're able to work out how best to use what you know. Ulvhilde had just shown herself to have a full measure of that ability.

The swallow was flying, reaching into the sky on its small, determined wings.

IX

If it was truly the will of God that the Christian forces should lose their grip on the Holy Land, He showed it by leading them along such a long, tortuous road that, at any one turn, His intentions were far from clear.

The first, large step towards the final catastrophe might have been Saladin's victory over the Christian army at Marj Ayyoun in the Year of Our Lord 1179. What Count Raymond had said during that endless night in Beaufort, when he and Arn had been drowning their sorrows, was true: Marj Ayyoun was just one more in a historic chain of defeats. Over a hundred years of fighting, no one could count on winning every time, what with the vagaries of wind and weather, good luck and bad, reinforcements that did or didn't arrive in time, wise or foolish decisions on either side, and so on. And then, as many argued, there was the decisive factor of God's inscrutable will. However craftily you might try to explain why this or that happened, or however fervently you prayed to your God, some battles were won and others were lost.

Some of the most prominent knights serving in King Baldwin's army had been taken prisoner at Marj Ayyoun, among them the leading baron in Outremer, Balduin d'Ibelin. The entire history of the Christian presence in Outremer could have turned out to be utterly different if just this man had escaped imprisonment. The Christians might have remained for another few hundred years and, if they had resisted the onslaught of the Mongolian hordes, perhaps continued their occupation for a thousand years. Or forever. This was not how it looked just after Marj Ayyoun, of course. Then, if a man of Balduin's status ended up in prison, it was distracting and very expensive but in no way crucial.

Of all the contemporary commanders, Saladin took the greatest care to get to know his enemies. Saladin's spies were everywhere and nothing vital concerning the balance of power in Antioch, Tripoli or Jerusalem ever escaped him. He knew Balduin d'Ibelin's price and coolly demanded a totally outrageous one hundred and fifty thousand gold besants in ransom, the largest amount ever asked by either side in a war of almost one hundred years' duration.

What Saladin knew, and based his ransom demand on, was that Balduin d'Ibelin was the main contender for the throne of Jerusalem. The present King Baldwin IV was not only a leper in an advanced stage of that fatal disease, but had already failed once to secure the family hold on the throne by marrying his sister Sibyl to an Englishman called William Longwood, who promptly died. The story was put about that Longwood suffered from a lung condition, but everyone believed it was probably a shameful illness.

Be that as it may, Sibyl had given birth to a son after her husband's death and named him after her brother Baldwin. But she was in love with Balduin d'Ibelin and the King did not at all mind the alliance with one of the most highly respected families in Outremer. Besides, a marriage would improve the Court's standing and make it less controversial among these landed baronial families who held the traditional view that the Court in Jerusalem was a haven for adventurers and debauched favourites. Unfortunately, Saladin was well informed of these plans, so holding a would-be king among his prisoners, he demanded a king's ransom for Balduin d'Ibelin.

The d'Ibelin family could not provide such a huge amount in gold. In fact, in Outremer, only the Order of the Temple could have lent it, but the Knights adhered to strict business rules and, since the transaction offered no real opportunity of gain for the Order, they refused. But there was one man in that part of the world who could lay his hands on one hundred and fifty thousand gold besants and that was the Emperor Manuel of Constantinople.

Balduin d'Ibelin asked Saladin to free him against the promise, on d'Ibelin's honour, that he would either borrow the money or return to imprisonment. Saladin had no reason to doubt the word of such a respected knight and agreed to let him go to Constantinople. It was a successful mission, because the Emperor decided that his gold would give him an excellent, life-long hold over the future King of Jerusalem. He lent Balduin d'Ibelin the full amount, which was transported to Saladin in good order. Afterwards, Balduin travelled to Jerusalem with the good news that he was free and ready to continue his love affair with Sibyl.

But the men had failed to reckon with the women at the Court and, in particular, with their views on men burdened by huge debts. Agnes de Courtenay, mother of Sibyl and the King, was a born intriguer and had managed to persuade her daughter – seemingly without too much trouble – that no love was worth a debt of one hundred and fifty thousand gold besants.

Amaury de Lusignan was one of Agnes's many lovers, a crusader knight who had never once crossed swords with an enemy, but made many pleasing conquests in bed. Although no warrior, he was not slow to see the possibilities for manoeuvre in the many power games at Court. He told Agnes of his younger brother Guy, a handsome man with a reputation as a highly satisfactory lover. While Balduin was raising the money for his liberation in Constantinople, Guy de Lusignan was brought from France to Jerusalem.

So it was that when Balduin arrived in Jerusalem, after much hard travelling and negotiation, Sibyl seemed cool and distant. She had been spending her nights with young Guy, and the difference between the two men was like that between dark and light, or between fire and water. Without anyone, including himself, realising it, Saladin's correct treatment of d'Ibelin had shortened the road to a decisive Muslim victory.

The defeat at Marj Ayyoun deeply affected the Knights Templar, particularly because Odo de Saint Amand, their Grand Master, had been taken prisoner. The 'No ransom' rule, which also held for the Knights of St John, usually meant death for such unprofitable prisoners. Killing them off, rather than exchanging them for Saracen soldiers, was good tactics anyway, because they were the Christians' best trained fighting men by far. But a Grand Master in one of the warrior orders was a different proposition. As Saladin well knew, the holder of this office is the commander-in-chief, whose orders must be unquestioningly obeyed. It could be valuable to reach a working agreement with this eminent prisoner.

But Saladin got nowhere with Odo de Saint Amand, who kept quoting the 'No ransom' rule and let it be known that he regarded a prisoner exchange as a spineless attempt, as sinful as it was contemptible, to avoid the rule. After less than a year his imprisonment in Damascus ended with his death from unknown causes.

The new Grand Master was Arnoldo de Torroja, formerly Master of Jerusalem. His office was of major importance because of the tripartite division of power in the Holy Land between the two religious orders, the land-owning barons and the King of Jerusalem. The Grand Master's view on the ultimate aim of the war was of particular significance. Was it simply to kill all Saracens? Or did he agree with the argument that a policy of extermination was a folly that would spell an end to the Christian presence in the Holy Land?

Arnoldo de Torroja had worked for the Templar Order in Aragon and Provence before he was sent to the Holy Land. Unlike his warrior predecessor, he was above all a businessman and a power broker. As Saladin saw it, this was another promising development. First, the throne would probably go to an ignorant adventurer, likely to be a useless commander in the field, and now the powerful Order of the Temple was to be led by a negotiator, who preferred doing deals to making war.

Arn de Gothia, commander of Gaza, was directly affected by the elevation of Arnoldo de Torroja. He was called to take on, without delay, the office of Master of Jerusalem.

Father Louis and Brother Pietro, both Cistercian monks, had arrived in Jerusalem from Rome as special nuncios of the Holy Father. Their experiences in the centre of the world turned out to be a confusing mixture of appalling disappointment and delightful surprise. Hardly anything was the way they had expected.

Like all Franks, worldly and spiritual, the pair believed that the city of cities would be a wonderful place with streets of gold and white marble. What they found was an indescribable tangle of people, speaking every tongue known to man, crowding narrow streets deep in rubbish. Like all Cistercians, they had lived in the conviction that their military companion order had recruited ill-educated thugs, barely able to mumble the Pater Noster in Latin. In reality, the Master of Jerusalem spoke Latin with unselfconscious fluency and, while waiting with them for their audience with the Grand Master, quite intrigued them by his discourse on Aristotle.

The rooms of the Master of Jerusalem reminded them of a Cistercian monastery. Here was none of the worldly, rather ungodly fondness for ornamentation they had spotted here and there in the Templar part of the city. The long arcade with its view over the city had the familiarity of cloisters and the plain white walls were without sinful images. They had been served a very well cooked meal, free of any produce deriving from four-footed animals.

Father Louis, the long-standing representative of the Cistercian order in the Vatican, had a sharp intellect, schooled from his early youth by the best monastic teachers in Cîteaux. The holder of the office with the grossly overblown title Master of Jerusalem was very different from what he had assumed. He had been told that Arn de Gothia had a fine reputation as a soldier and had led a vastly outnumbered force of knights to a splendid victory over Saladin's army at Mont Gisard. This made him expect a modern version of someone like the Roman commander Belisarius, a rough diamond with no interests outside warfare.

Had it not been for the many pale scars on Arn de Gothia's face and hands, Father Louis now had to concede that this man, with his gentle eyes and pleasant conversation, could have been a brother from Cîteaux. Fishing a little, he learned that de Gothia *had* actually been educated in a Cistercian cloister. This was indeed an encounter with the incarnation of Saint Bernard's vision of the warrior in the holy war who is also a monk. Father Louis had not met one of these hybrids before.

It did not escape him that their host ate only bread and drank water, despite offering his guests such a fine table. It meant that this high-ranking Knight Templar was doing penitence for something and he was curious to find out what, though this was obviously not the right time to ask. As the nuncio of the Holy Father, Father Louis was bringing a papal edict that wasn't likely to be well received. He was also well aware of the Templar reputation for arrogance. Next, he would meet the Grand Master, who presumably regarded himself as second only to the Pope. If so, the Master of Jerusalem ranked somewhere close to an Archbishop. There were good grounds for suspecting that an ordinary *abbé* was of no particular consequence to them, not even when working closely with the Holy Father and acting as his special messenger.

After the meal had been cleared away, they became engrossed in a satisfying discussion about the divisions, according to the philosopher, between learning, knowledge and belief. Then there was the Master's interesting concept of a world of ideas that could not exist only in the higher spheres but had to be turned into tangible reality. It was just the kind of talk that Father Louis could not have imagined having with a Knight Templar, and he felt almost chagrined when they were interrupted by the arrival of the Grand Master.

Arnoldo de Torroja excused the delay in greeting his guests by explaining that he had been called to an audience with the King and had been asked to return soon, bringing the Master of Jerusalem with him. However, it would have been unthinkable to allow the whole evening to pass without meeting his Cistercian guests and hearing what they had to say. Father Louis' first impression was that this was the kind of man you would meet in the imperial embassy in Rome, a top-level diplomat and negotiator – again, far from a coarse Roman Belisarius.

He felt distinctly uneasy about having to give them his awkward message there and then, but his hosts didn't leave him much choice. He could hardly waste everybody's time sitting around chatting, only to present a hard-hitting edict the next day. He began by explaining the background to the papal bull as directly and factually as possible. The two knights listened attentively in silence, their faces bland and inexpressive.

Archbishop William of Tyrus had come back from the Holy Land, bringing serious complaints to the Third Lateran Council in Rome against both the Orders of the Templar and of St John's. According to the Archbishop William, the spiritual knights were, in some respects, consistently working counter to the interests of the Holy Roman Church.

For example, banned individuals who died in the Holy Land were given proper burials by the Knights Templar, who would even allow such persons to join the Order. A bishop may have placed an interdict over a whole village, withdrawing every provision of the Church from its sinning inhabitants, only to find that the Templar Order had moved in with its own priests. Such ill-judged behaviours undermined the power of the Church, indeed made it look almost laughably weak. The technical justification was that the spiritual orders did not answer to a bishop and therefore could not be banned or even punished by the Patriarch of Jerusalem. Worse still, the orders were not above charging for their services.

The Holy Father Alexander III had therefore decided, together with his Lateran Council, to make it clear that all such activity must cease forthwith. Archbishop William's suggestions of various punishments for the two self-seeking orders had however been turned down.

Father Louis put the papal bull with its seal on the table. It would confirm everything he had told them. What answer should he bring the Holy Father from the Order of the Temple?

'That the Order will undertake to carry out the instructions of the Holy Father, in spirit and in action, from the moment I, the Grand Master, receive this bull. I state our total submission to the will of the Church,' Arnoldo de Torroja replied in his conciliatory manner. 'We will act immediately, though bringing the changes to their conclusion may take some time. I trust that my brother Arn de Gothia holds the same view?'

'I don't differ from you in any way,' Arn replied as calmly. 'The

Knights Templar are good businessmen and need to be, in order to finance a long and expensive war. I'll be glad to tell you more about this tomorrow, Father Louis. Trading in religious services is another matter and strictly against our rules. Such traffic should be called simony, in my personal opinion, and I have every sympathy with the Archbishop's complaints and the Holy Father's decision.'

'I don't quite understand . . .' Father Louis began, surprised at their ready agreement with the criticism. 'If you both think these practices sinful, how come that they happen at all?'

'Our previous Grand Master, Odo de Saint Amand, was of quite a different mind. He is now rejoicing in Paradise,' Arnoldo de Torroja said.

'But surely two high-ranking brothers like yourselves could have made your objections known at the time?' Father Louis asked, still not understanding.

Both men merely responded with urbane smiles.

Arn called a knight and asked him to escort Father Louis and his companion, the so far entirely silent Brother Pietro, to their night quarters. After apologising for necessarily having to interrupt their evening together on account of the pressing call from the King, he promised to be a more attentive host the next day. Then the Grand Master rose and blessed the two monks, much to Father Louis's amazement and irritation.

After a slight mistake, when the Cistercian guests were taken to a worldly bedroom with sparkling fountains and beautifully decorated Saracen tiles, they found their own rooms. Small and plain, with white-limed walls, they were remarkably similar to their usual cells.

Meanwhile Arnoldo and Arn hurried along to their audience with the King. They hardly mentioned the bull, since their reactions to it were the same. It was actually a useful opportunity to rid the Order of a highly dubious line of business, made easier by having a papal edict to wave in front of any troublemakers.

The King's private rooms were small, and kept in semi-darkness because he was badly incapacitated with regard both to mobility and sight. He was just a shadow inside his muslin-curtained sedan chair and there were whispered rumours that both his hands were already gone. One personal servant was in the room, a heavily built Nubian who was a deaf-mute. He sat in a far corner, his eyes constantly fixed on the King's outline, ready to intervene at once in response to signs only he and his master understood. The two Knights Templar bowed silently to the unusual throne and sat down on two Egyptian leather cushions in front of it. The King was young, not yet twenty-five years old, and when he spoke his voice was light and clear.

'I'm pleased to see that two leaders of the Templar Order have agreed to visit me at this late hour,' he began and then stopped. He coughed and signed to the Nubian slave, who hurried forward and arranged something invisible behind the curtain.

'Although I believe I'm further away from my demise than many might think, or indeed hope, I'm much troubled,' the King explained. 'Now, the Templar Order serves as a strong backbone in our defences. That is why I wanted to speak to you face-to-face, using a language that's less elaborate than is usual. Does that suit you, Knights Templar?'

'Excellently well, Sire,' Arnoldo de Torroja replied.

'Good.' The King coughed again, but continued. 'First, the matter of a new Patriarch in Jerusalem. Second, the matter of our present military situation. As regards the Patriarch, Amaury de Nesle, the present incumbent, is dying. One might think that this would be the responsibility of the Church, but my mother, Agnes, seems to believe that it's hers – or at least mine. Two candidates have come to mind, Heraclius, Archbishop of Caesarea, and William, Archbishop of Tyrus. William is hostile to the Knights Templar, but no one doubts that he's an honourable man. Heraclius, on the other hand – and I'll be frank now – is a common scoundrel, a runaway choirboy or something like that, and is known to lead a thoroughly sinful existence. One of my mother's many lovers, it seems. However, he is far from an enemy of the Templar Order. So, how do you think the scales are weighted?'

Arnoldo de Torroja had to answer, but found it difficult to be direct. He launched into a long discourse about God's inscrutable will, obviously talking to fill the silence while he tried to work out what he really thought. Meanwhile, Arn was reflecting that the unhappy young King, disfigured and dying, spoke well and with strength and determination.

'To conclude,' said Arnoldo who by now had thought out something reasonably sensible to offer, 'it is of course bad for us if the Patriarch is our enemy and good if he is our friend. However, it's also important to have an honourable man as the highest protector of the True Cross and God's Tomb, and sinful to appoint a sinful man to that position. God's will is likely to be straightforward.'

'That's as maybe, but the question now is what my mother Agnes is going to do,' the King commented drily. 'Of course, I know that the formal decision depends on the vote of the Archbishops in the

Holy Land, but these pious priests can be easily bought. *De facto*, you and I decide – or my mother does. I need to know who you're definitely for or against.'

'Sire, as I suggested, for us there's no clear choice to be made between a sinner who is for us, and a true man of God, who's not,' Arnoldo sighed indecisively. Had he been able to see into the future he would have said something very different.

'Well, well. By standing back, you're leaving the decision to my mother and we'll no doubt get a most unusual character as Patriarch of Jerusalem. Maybe God will throw a bolt of lightning at him every time he chases a slave boy or a married woman or, I fear, an ass. Next, the war. Everybody is lying to me. It could take me years to find out the truth. I'm still not even sure what happened at the one major victory in my own war. Apparently, I was the great victor at Mont Gisard, where trustworthy witnesses saw St George hover over me in the sky. However, I've since learnt that you, Arn de Gothia, were leading the Templar force. Am I right?'

Arn had to answer a direct question from the King and spoke carefully

'It's true that in that battle a few hundred Templar knights defeated some three or four thousand of Saladin's best soldiers. It's also true that the worldly army of Jerusalem won a victory over an enemy contingent of five hundred men.'

'Is this the truth, Arn de Gothia?'

'Yes, Sire.'

'And who led the Knights Templar?'

'I did, Sire, with the help of God.'

'Good. You and your colleagues can be relied on for truthful answers. My final years would be easier if I could be like you, but I can't. So, tell me briefly about the military situation!'

'It's complicated ...' Arnoldo de Torroja began, but the King interrupted him quickly.

'You must forgive me Grand Master, but am I not right in saying that the Master of Jerusalem is the acting commander in your order?'

'Indeed, Sire. You're right.'

'Excellent. God, how great it would be to surround oneself with men who give straight answers to straight questions. I wanted to establish that it is proper for me to ask Arn de Gothia about military matters without offending against your rules in any way.'

'That is perfectly in order, Sire,' Arnoldo replied in a slightly strained tone.

'Then, if you please, de Gothia.'

'Sire, I believe the situation could be described . . . as follows,' Arn began hesitantly. 'We are facing perhaps the most dangerous opponent in all our time here. Saladin is a more formidable enemy than Zenki or Nur al-Din. He has united practically all the Saracens against us and is an outstanding commander in the field. He has lost once, against Your Majesty's forces at Mont Gisard, but won all other battles of any importance. Unless we can strengthen the Christian forces, we'll be on the run or locked into our fortresses for as long as we can last out.'

'And do you share this view, Grand Master?' the King asked sharply.

'Yes Sire, the situation is as the Master of Jerusalem describes it.'

'Very well. In that case, we need reinforcements from home. Messages will be sent to the Emperor of Germany and to the Kings of France and England. Grand Master, would you undertake to be our ambassador?'

'Of course, Sire.'

'Even if your colleague will be the Grand Master of the Hospitallers, Roger des Moulins?'

'Yes, Sire, des Moulins is an excellent man.'

'And the new Patriarch of Jerusalem, even though he'd be likely to go wandering at night?'

'Yes, indeed.'

'Good. You must go ahead as soon as possible. Another question now. Who's the best commander among the worldly knights here in Outremer, would you say?'

'Count Raymond of Tripoli and after him, Balduin d'Ibelin, Sire.'

'And the worst. Perhaps my sister's favourite choice, Guy de Lusignan?'

'To compare the men I named with de Lusignan, Sire, would be like comparing David with Goliath,' Arnoldo said with an ironic bow.

The King was quiet for a while after that reply.

'Grand Master, are you telling me that Lusignan could defeat Count Raymond with a slingshot?' he asked, sounding amused.

'Sire, I was quoting Holy Scriptures. It tells us that Goliath was the greatest warrior and David but an inexperienced lad. Without the help of God, David would be beaten by Goliath in a thousand of a thousand battles. If God chose to support Guy de Lusignan as He supported David, then de Lusignan would be an irresistible force.'

The King was heard to laugh, coughing at the same time.

'And if God ignores him?'

'Then any battle would be lost in the twinkling of an eye, Sire.'

'Grand Master, Master of Jerusalem – I could talk for hours with men like you, but my health will not allow me,' the King said, and beckoned his Nubian slave. 'I must bid you goodnight. May God be with you.'

The slave had hurried to his master's side. As the knights rose to take their leave, choking, snorting sounds emerged from behind the curtain. They exchanged anxious glances and tiptoed thoughtfully away from the King's private chambers.

To his great surprise, Father Louis was woken early by Arn de Gothia, who had personally come to escort him and Brother Pietro to lauds in the Templum Salomonis. The two monks were guided through a labyrinthine system of passages and tall rooms until, after descending a dark stairwell, they suddenly emerged into the large church with the silver dome. It was already crowded with Templar knights and sergeants, standing in total silence along the wall of the round central space under the dome. About one hundred knights were there, and twice as many black-clad sergeants. Nobody was late.

Father Louis thought the service beautiful. He was impressed by the seriousness shown by these men of war, and by their excellent singing. This, too, was unexpected. After lauds, Arn took his guests on the usual walking tour round Jerusalem, explaining that the best views were to be seen early, before the crowds filled the city.

They criss-crossed the whole Templar site, and passed the golden-domed Templum Domini, which was closed to pilgrims due to repairs and cleaning. They left by the Golden Gate and walked up to Golgotha. Among the merchants' stalls they prayed, deeply moved, at the place where our Lord had suffered and died. Then they walked back by the Gate of Stephen and the Via Dolorosa. Piously following Christ's road of pain through the waking city, they reached the Church of the Holy Sepulchre, still closed, and guarded by four Templar sergeants. When they saw the Master of Jerusalem and his visiting men of God, the sergeants opened the doors at once.

Inside, all three took pleasure in the familiar, pure beauty of the vaulted space, though the many different Christian factions that used the church had left a lot of clutter behind. In one corner Father Louis recognised gilt and coloured images of an unsuitable kind in the style of the Byzantine church, but there were many others that he could not identify. Arn struck him as barely conscious of the conflicting faiths wanting access to the Holy Sepulchre of God. Once they had descended into the dark, damp crypt of Saint Helen, they were all profoundly affected. This slab of stone was the core of their belief, for which so much blood had been spilt. They kneeled and prayed. No one wanted to be the first to leave the Holy Sepulchre.

Father Louis was so intensely absorbed that he could not tell afterwards for how long they had stayed there or what he had actually experienced. It must have been a considerable time, for when they stepped out into the blinding sunlight through the main gate, they faced an indignant crowd, kept back by the sergeants. The rumbling anger only stilled when they saw that the eminent visitors were the Master of Jerusalem and his guests.

On the way back, Arn led them through the Jaffa Gate and the worldly quarters. Powerful aromas filled the air from the hundreds of stalls and shops in the bazaar. There were the alien scents of spices, the odours of raw meat, caged poultry and burnt leather, smells from cloth dyeing and metal working and many other trades. Every language in the world seemed to be spoken. At first Father Louis thought that the majority of these strange peoples must be heathens, but Arn told him that many, such as Syrians, Copts, Armenians, Maronites and others, had been Christians since long before the Crusades. He added that, in the beginning, the first crusader knights had also been unable to tell the difference and indiscriminately killed everybody who looked native.

They ended their tour at the Templum Domini and prayed again at the Rock where Abraham would have sacrificed Isaac and where the child Jesus had been taken into the faith. Even Father Louis thought the church beautiful, splendidly ornamented though it was. The infidels' gilt lettering on the walls upset him, but Arn pointed out that for those who understood what the texts said and didn't see them as meaningless decoration, they were not so different from many passages in the Bible. This sounded like blasphemy to Father Louis, but he told himself that a long period in the Holy Land clearly changed people a great deal.

They hurried back to the Templum Salomonis to sing terce, after which Arn returned to his rooms, explaining that he had work to do. Outside his room were indeed many people of all kinds and persuasions waiting for him, but he asked his guests to return a few hours later.

When they came, he offered them a pleasing drink made from a fruit he called lemons, but drank only water himself. By now Father Louis felt that he could ask the question and Arn replied, cautiously at first, that he was indeed doing penance. Then he enlarged a little on his answer, saying that he would have liked to confess to his closest friend and most revered father confessor, Father Henri, the *abbé* in a distant cloister called Varnhem in West Gothland. Father Louis looked pleased and said he knew the Varnhem *abbé* well from Chapter meetings in Cîteaux, where Father Henri had had many interesting things to say about bringing Christianity to the wild Gothic tribes. So, they had a friend in common – what a small world!

For Arn this was like a greeting from his distant home and, for a moment, he wistfully recalled memories of his cloister years in Varnhem and at Vitae Schola in Denmark. He then referred to the sins he wanted to confess to Father Henri. Confusingly, he seemed to feel that one of his worst sins was his love for his betrothed, a fair lady called Cecilia. He was encouraged to talk more about his life: Father Louis was an experienced priest and easily sensed Arn's intense sadness. Arguing that he was as close to Father Henri as Arn would get here in the Holy Land, he offered to hear the knight's confession. After hesitating a little, Arn agreed, and Brother Pietro was sent to fetch the confessional bands.

When they were alone together in the cloisters, Father Louis blessed Arn and waited.

'Forgive me Father, for I have sinned,' Arn began, sounding strained. 'I have sinned by breaking our rules, which are as binding as yours. I have also kept my sin secret and thus made it graver. Worse still, I have been seeking and finding self-justification.'

'You must explain, if I am to advise you or forgive you.'

'I have killed a Christian in anger. For that crime I should have been deprived of the knight's white mantle and been ordered to do latrine duty for two years at best, or leave the Order at worst. But I did not admit my sin and so I rose through the ranks to one of the highest offices in the Order. I am unworthy.'

'Did you sin because you were driven by ambition and lust for power?' Father Louis asked. He was worried by what sounded like a very difficult case.

'No Father, I can deny that in all honesty,' Arn replied firmly. 'In our Order, men such as Arnoldo de Torroja, and even men such as I, exert great power by virtue of the offices we hold. We both do it well, but not because we're purer of spirit or better suited to lead men in worship or war than anybody else in the Order. The reason for our being well suited is that we both belong to the knights who seek peace, not war – endless war would spell disaster for us all.'

'Your defence for having sinned is that you protect the Holy Land?' Father Luis asked.

'Yes Father, that's what I feel, in all conscience,' Arn told him, completely unaware of the monk's discreet irony.

'My son, tell me . . . how many men have you killed during your time as a knight?'

'Impossible to say, Father. At a guess, not more than fifteen hundred and not less than five hundred. It's not always clear what happens when a lance goes in or an arrow hits a man. Take myself – I've been hit badly by arrows on eight occasions and gone down each time, so the Saracen archers must have thought they'd killed me.'

'And among the men you've killed, have there been any Christians?'

'There must have been. Some Saracens are fighting with us, so presumably there are Christians in the enemy forces. But that doesn't count, you see. The rules don't demand that we stop and ask enemy soldiers about their beliefs before we shoot them, or whatever.'

'What was it about that particular slain Christian that makes his death much more significant than the rest?' Father Louis was obviously baffled.

'One of our most important rules reads like this: "When you draw your sword, do not think of whom you must kill. Think of whom you must protect." I always remember that rule and it was in my mind when three foolish newcomers took into their heads that their task was to kill defenceless women, children and old people for the sake of the True Cross. This was when I was in command at Gaza and these people were under my protection.'

'I see. Surely you were right to defend them?'

'Yes, of course. And I did try to save two of the attackers and the third one too, until he betrayed me and killed my horse in front of my eyes. Then I cut him down without mercy.'

'Not so good,' Father Louis sighed, because now he saw the hope of an easy solution fade away. 'You've slain a Christian man for the sake of a horse?'

'Yes, Father. That's my sin.'

'Not so good,' Father Louis said again sadly. 'But explain this about a knight's horse – the animal is very important to you?'

'His horse often becomes a knight's closest friend, closer than friends among the fellow knights. To your ears this might sound more than a little mad and possibly blasphemous, but it's the truth. We depend on each other for our lives. I know that without that horse, I would have died many times over. We'd been friends since we were both very young and led long warriors' lives together.'

Father Louis was both amazed and touched by this declaration of true comradeship with an animal and reflected once more that things were indeed different in Outremer. What was sinful back home might be acceptable in the Holy Land and vice versa. He told Arn that he needed time to think until the next day and instructed him to seek God's forgiveness in prayer. Arn grimly wandered away to finish his day's work, but Louis stayed seated in the cloisters, staring out over Jerusalem and thinking.

It was a hard nut to crack and Father Louis enjoyed the mental exercise. The first point was that Arn had intended to protect women and children from attack from over-zealous newcomers. Arn had not mentioned that the would-be victims were Bedouins, simply because he did not think it important. Father Louis, himself a new arrival, might have taken a different view. Now he vaguely assumed that they might have been like the strange looking but right-thinking people they had seen in the bazaar.

Given that God couldn't want murderers to go unpunished and that He had sent a Knight Templar to intercept them, killing two of them was presumably righteous. But what about killing one man in anger for a horse's sake? He decided to follow the philosopher's method and see how the scales would tip.

On the objective side was the likelihood that the horse was agreeable to God, since it had helped to wipe out hundreds of God's enemies – at least if what Arn had said was true. Could a brave horse be worth as much in the eyes of God as a not altogether noble man, who had gone to fight in the Holy Lands for unknown and possibly dubious reasons? Theologically, the answer must be 'No', but in this case killing the horse could be seen as equivalent to killing the knight. And, of course, the man had proven sinful intentions in the first place.

Subjectively, things looked worse for Arn de Gothia. He was no ignorant sinner, because he knew the rules and the reasoning behind them, as well as speaking excellent Latin – with an amusing Burgundian accent that was, presumably, Father Henri's legacy to his pupil. There was no doubt that he'd sinned and simplicity of mind did not serve as an excuse.

But, and now Father Louis was thinking as a secret papal spy, the problem had a political dimension. The Holy Father was constantly troubled by bellicose churchmen in the Holy Land, who spent most of their time complaining about each other and demanding bulls and bans and other punishments of colleagues on largely spurious grounds. The place was frankly crawling with such priests, including bishops and archbishops. Sorting out their claims and counter-claims was near impossible, and Father Louis had been asked in the strictest confidence to serve as the Holy Father's eyes and ears in Jerusalem.

In that capacity, shouldn't he consider how Arn de Gothia was to be kept in his present position, rather than running the risk of getting a much less agreeable and well-intentioned man in his place? The answer was 'Yes', naturally. It would serve the Holy Father's purpose if Arn were forgiven his sins, could stop worrying, and continue to act as Father Louis' helpful host. Louis would grant that forgiveness tomorrow, but tonight he would start on his first letter from Jerusalem and include a discussion of this interesting conundrum. The Holy Father might send his papal blessing. That would get the problem out of the way, once and for all.

The following morning before lauds, Father Louis and Arn met in the cloisters and the knight was forgiven in the name of the Father, the Son and the Holy Virgin. Just as they were kneeling down to pray, Father Louis was shaken to hear a dreadful wailing coming from the dark silence. He had heard this noise before, but not got round to enquiring what it was. Arn explained that it was the infidels' muezzin calling out that Allah was great to his early morning congregation. Father Louis was dismayed to learn that the non-believers shouted their blasphemous incantations in the middle of the Templar sanctum, but kept this new problem for later.

Arn was grateful for God's mercy but not as astounded at being forgiven his grave sin as he might have expected. One week on bread and water was a very light penance, in any case, and once before his confessor had forgiven him as easily for killing a man. He had been very young, almost a child, but his sword-fighting skills had caused the deaths of two farmers when all Arn had intended was self-defence. The forgiveness then had been based on arguments he could hardly remember, but had had something to do with the dead men being at fault and Virgin Mary intervening to save a young woman from them and letting her go to her beloved.

The only sin in his life that had not been easily forgiven, so it must be his worst, was that he and his betrothed had lain together just before their wedding. The twenty years of penance for that act of love had still not passed. He couldn't understand this, any more than he understood God's intention in sending him to serve in the Holy Land. True, he had slain many men, but was that really all he was meant to do?

In the Holy Roman Church, the Patriarch of Jerusalem was second only to the Pope in authority. The new incumbent was worse than even the worst rumours had claimed, and the patriarchal palace soon became known as a place where night was turned into day. One of the Patriarch's most notorious mistresses became known as the Patriarchess, and when she ventured into the city people gathered to spit at her sedan chair. In the adjacent royal palace, the King's mother, Agnes de Courtenay, was close to her occasional lover, willing to overlook his other women because she slept with many other men.

The election of the new Patriarch had always been a muddy affair. Archbishop William of Tyrus, until then an obvious and excellent choice, not only lost his bid for the Patriarch's seat, but suffered the shame of being banned for a long list of alleged sins. That the allegations were entirely false was as certain as the fact that Patriarch Heraclius had comitted, indeed exceeded, every single one of those sins. William of Tyrus, whose name has gone down in history while that of Heraclius has tactfully been kept out of sight, had to abase himself, travel to Rome, and beg the Pope to rescind the ban. Informed opinion agreed that he would have succeeded in this and also that the great churchman would have been able to charge Heraclius with enough misbehaviours to make his appointment look very shaky. Curiously, and unhappily for the Holy Land, William was poisoned and died soon after arriving in Rome, without having had time to speak out. Documents he had carried with him disappeared without trace.

Not even Saladin realised how useful all this would be for him. Meanwhile the ceasefire that had been in place at the time of the murder of William of Tyrus was soon broken in a time-honoured manner. Reynald de Châtillon could not control his greed at the sight of the richly laden camel caravans travelling between Mecca and Damascus, which passed his castle Kerak in Oultrejourdain. He started his raids to plunder the trade routes again and the dying King in Jerusalem was unable to restrain his vassal. Saladin's declaration of war was inescapable.

As he had often done before, Saladin crossed the River Jordan near Lake Galilee and let his troops plunder the countryside, hoping to stir the Christian army into action. The curly-haired rake Guy de Lusignan was now married to the King's sister and effectively next in line to the throne. He was therefore also commander of the worldly army, and would have to lead it into the field to fight Saladin himself, a task that would have dismayed even Count

Raymond of Tripoli. Count Raymond had rather reluctantly placed himself and his knights under de Lusignan's command, together with the knights of the Orders of the Temple and St John's. The Grand Master of the Templars had given the command to Arn de Gothia, while the Hospitallers were led by its Grand Master, Roger des Moulins.

As the two armies came close to each other in Galilee, the bemused de Lusignan was assailed by different advice. Arn de Gothia, who had been permitted to use his Bedouin spies, claimed that the nearby enemy contingents were only a small fraction of the total force and that it would be very ill-advised to attack – in fact, it would be just what Saladin was hoping for. Defensive positions were easier to hold against the light Arabian cavalry, which could easily be crushed if the riders became impatient. The Christian army depended on foot soldiers with longbows, whose arrows could darken the sky like a storm cloud. A determined attack by these archers would eliminate the light enemy cavalry.

However, some of the worldly barons and Guy's brother Amalrik, who was second in command, argued in favour of an immediate attack because the enemy was obviously outnumbered. On the other hand, Roger des Moulins, who might have been expected to contradict his brother commander, agreed with Arn that an attack would be a mistake and that the trap of Marj Ayyoun was gaping wide again.

Listening to all this, the inexperienced courtier Guy de Lusignan was completely at a loss. In the end the contest petered out and neither side won. Saladin's plan to tempt the heavy Christian knights into another disastrous attack failed, but on the other hand no light riders ever attacked the well-entrenched Christian army because that was the last thing Saladin would try. As far as the Saracen leader was concerned, that the battle did not happen was no setback. There had been no threat to his position of power in Cairo or in Damascus and he had no angry prince to account to. He calmly regrouped, happy to wait for new openings.

Guy de Lusignan was feeling much less safe. For one thing, the retreating Muslim army was plundering Galilee once more. For another, back home at the Court he met criticism from those who felt he shouldn't have listened to these cowardly knights of whatever order, Hospitallers or Templars. The militarily inclined men insisted that they'd have known exactly how to defeat the enemy. Guy was getting fed up, and even his mother-in-law, Agnes, suddenly seemed unable to advise him how to manage the war against the Saracens.

By this time, King Baldwin could not move without help and was completely blind. He was incapable of dealing with the litanies of complaints. His main impression was that de Lusignan was a useless coward and that, from every point of view, to let such a man succeed to the throne would be an unmitigated disaster. Something had to be done, and soon, because death was stalking the leprous king. He named his nephew, Sibyl's six-year-old son Baldwin, the successor to his throne. Then he made Guy de Lusignan Count of Ashkelon and Jaffa, on condition that he actually went to live in Ashkelon and stopped plagueing Jerusalem with his presence. Guy, Sibyl and their sickly child moved to Ashkelon, after much grinding of teeth and many angry words. That the little prince was unwell was obvious for all to see. It was also clear that the King's appointment was a last desperate move to remove de Lusignan from the succession.

Now God's will alone ruled. Who would die first, the twenty-four year old King Baldwin or his six-year-old namesake?

Father Louis had had to wait a few months before he was again given the opportunity to meet the Grand Master of the Templars together with his Master of Jerusalem, both of whom travelled constantly on official duties. The Grand Master was the Order's judicial authority from Christian Armenia in the north to Gaza in the south, while the Master of Jerusalem, as the acting commander-in-chief, went on rounds of inspection at the Templar fortresses.

Father Louis wanted to meet them together at a moment when they were both relatively at peace. His business was so troublesome that he thought it best if the two men could support each other in dealing with it. He had no choice now but to reveal his secret. They had to know that he was no ordinary monk, a mere pilgrim and message-bearer, but a nuncio with a special relationship to the Holy Father. Arn de Gothia, he thought, might already have guessed as much. The hospitality he'd offered exceeded anything ordinary politeness demanded. For one thing, instead of housing Father Louis in the nearby Cistercian cloister at the Mount of Olives, he had been given rooms in the Templar complex, the centre of power in the Holy Land.

But analysing Arn's motives was not easy. This unlikely knight had become very fond of Father Louis and often sought him out for long conversations about both worldly and spiritual matters – presumably as he had once turned to Father Henri, long ago in that cloister in West Gothia.

By now, it was something of a habit for Arnoldo de Torroja, Arn de Gothia and Father Louis to meet in the cloisters after compline and sit talking in the fading light. On the evening of Father Louis' revelations, their talk had started out with joking references to the city and its mixture of sacred and unholy smells, and the tone was becoming rather unsuitably coarse. Father Louis waited quietly, ready to change the topic. He found it moving to watch the two men in front of him. Outwardly, they were very unlike each other. Arnoldo was tall, with dark eyes and black hair and beard, and an animated, sharp-witted and amusing conversationalist. He was a perfect diplomat with the manners of someone schooled at a great European court. Arn, so blonde his beard was nearly white, looked almost slight next to his heavily built companion. His talk moved more slowly and thoughtfully, often condensed into precise, carefully worded comments. Together, they presented a study in contrasts, the fiery South and the cold North, yet both were devoted to the same cause and had given up all worldly possessions and ambition for the sake of conducting a war in defence of Christianity and the Holy Sepulchre.

Father Louis imagined Saint Bernard smiling from his heavenly vantage point as he looked down upon these perfect embodiments of the Knights Spiritual of his dreams. In fact, it was intriguing to reflect that if these two men had been shaven and given the monkish cloaks, they were well enough versed in theology, philosophy and other scholarly subjects to be indistinguishable from men of the cloth in any of the great cloisters. This vision had only one flaw. Mild-mannered as they seemed, both belonged to a much feared, highly disciplined force of ferocious warriors.

The nuncio knew he had to break off the light-hearted conversation now, and bent his head in brief prayer. Arn and Arnoldo took the hint, fell silent, and sat back to listen. Father Louis steeled himself to speak.

First, he told them the truth about his mission, explaining that the quiet Cistercian monks who had come and gone in the wake of Brother Pietro de Sienna, had all been taking secret messages to and from the Holy Father. The serious faces opposite him did not reveal whether this was news to them or not, but they raised their eyebrows when Father Louis described some developments concerning a particularly unsatisfactory figure in the entourage of the Patriarch.

Exactly what Pleidion, a runaway servant from the heretical Church in Constantinople, was doing for Heraclius was unclear, though not unconnected with unspeakable nightly goings-on in the palace. His listeners didn't let on whether they had known about this man or not, nor whether they were shocked or merely surprised at how much Father Louis knew, so he went on with the most outrageous part of his story. Tragically, the death of William of Tyrus in Rome had by this stage been well established as due to murder by poison, on the basis of both the appearance of the dead man and of what had been found in his room. It was also known that he been visited less than an hour before he died by the self-same Pleidion, who must have removed the vital documents in the case against Heraclius. In short, the Vatican was already certain that Heraclius had sent his henchman to rid him of a dangerous enemy.

Investigations had shown that Heraclius had been born, around 1130, into a lowly family in Auvergne where he had been a church singer, but had never trained in the priesthood and was known to be unable to cope with Latin. He must have joined the adventurers crowding into the Holy Land and advanced by means of his skills as a liar rather than a fighter. Also, he had chosen his mistresses with care, including not only Agnes de Courtenay but also Pasque de Riveri, better known as 'Madame La Patriarchesse'.

In conclusion, the second highest office in the Church was now in the hands of a man who was no common sinner, but a cunning cheat, a liar, a degenerate and a murderer. Then Father Louis fell silent, because he was not prepared to discuss the decision of the Holy Father at this point.

'What you tell us, Father, is most distressing,' Arnoldo de Torroja said slowly. 'This man's capacity for evil is not unknown to us, but your shocking information about Archbishop William's murder is news to us, of course. Our first response must be to ask what you advise – indeed, what the Holy Father advises – that we should do now?'

'You must keep your knowledge confined to men of the ranks you hold. Should either of you leave your post, you're to tell your successor but no one else. To make it clear that this is the will of the Holy Father, I've brought you a bull.' Father Louis produced a parchment roll with the huge papal seals.

After they had studied the text, Arnoldo de Torroja rolled it up and placed it inside his mantle. After a few moments of heavy silence, he spoke.

'We will obey these instructions in every detail – that goes without saying. But may I ask one further question, on both our behalves?'

'In God's name, yes,' Father Louis said, and crossed himself.

'Something tells me that your question concerns the Holy Father's decision not to deal openly and firmly with this man.'

'Yes. It would seem that since Heraclius is known to have committed many mortal sins and since only a pope can deal with him, given the man's elevated position, that is indeed the question. Why not ban this treacherous murderer?'

'Because the Vatican Council has decided that a ban would harm the Holy Roman Church even more than allowing him stay where he is. Heraclius is sixty-seven years old, so the stretch of road to hell left to him in this world should be short. A ban would advertise throughout the Christian world that the Patriarch of Jerusalem is wallowing in every kind of noxious sin and the consequent damage might be impossible to repair. So you see . . .'

Instinctively, both the Knights Templar crossed themselves as they pondered this unwelcome decision. Then they nodded, as if having nothing further to say.

'Right, now. That's the poisoner dealt with.' Father Louis sounded remarkably brisk. 'The next problem – no, no need to look so alarmed, just a question. There's no papal bull to present to you. It's my duty to find things out, that's all.'

'We feel stronger for having been tested,' Arnoldo de Torroja said, with a little sweeping movement of his hand as if disposing of a small demon pestering him.

'I have noticed certain strange events taking place in this city,' Father Louis began, a little uncertainly because he wished to be polite as well as strict. 'Within your jurisdiction I've heard infidels announcing – exceedingly loudly, if I may say so – when their godless practices are to be carried out. Now you both seem to me like truly devoted men of faith and among the foremost defenders of Christianity. To say anything else would be a falsehood, and yet . . .?'

Arnoldo gestured to Arn to show that this issue was his to sort out.

'Father, you're right in your observations, though very generous to us. We do our best, fighting sword in hand for the faith and killing thousands of non-believers. So you find it paradoxical that at the same time we allow noisy Muslim praying in the very precincts of our Order?' Father Louis nodded and Arn continued.

'I've already spoken to you, Father, about the Golden Rule of our order, which demands that we fight to protect, not to kill. Yes, it reminds us to be merciful and never to commit one of the worst sins, which is to kill in anger; but it also has wider implications. Consider our determination to stay in the Holy Land for thousands of years to come, and also that we are, and probably always will be, vastly outnumbered by the Saracens. Even if we could kill them all, it would be a lethal folly to do so. We'd starve to death, for a start.'

'Very well,' Father Louis said, rather impatient at this lengthy discourse.

'Some Christians are actually fighting with the Saracens and many infidels support our side. The war here is not fought for Allah against God or vice versa, but for good against evil. Many Saracen beliefs are similar to ours and we have many friends among them – merchants, manufacturers, doctors, and so on. It would be useless to try to force them, or the thousands of peasants who grow our food, to be baptised. Take our trade with independent Mosul, which means that caravan-loads of the cloth called muslin arrive in Saint-Jean d'Acre for shipping all over the world. The traders travelling with the caravan find everything they want in Acre – a mosque and minaret, taverns serving their kind of food and so on. What would you want us to do? Forcibly shave them and drag them kicking and screaming to their baptism? The result would be the end of trade, as well as throwing the Turkish satrap into Saladin's arms. None of this would be good for the Holy Land.'

'But godless practices in the Sacred City are good, are they?'

'Yes, they are. We do know the pure faith, know that it is the truth, and are ready to die for it. Nine tenths of the people in Outremer don't know this, not yet. But maybe in a hundred years, or three, or eight hundred years . . .'

'You believe Truth will be victorious in the end?' There was a hint of amusement in Father Louis' voice, despite the seriousness of their discussion.

'Yes, I do. But we can rely on our swords for so long and no longer. We will have won only when we can put our weapons away for good. People everywhere have a profound dislike of being converted by violence. Trading, collaboration and good preaching gets you further.'

'So you argue that to win over the godless we must let them carry on as they were. Coming from some mad monk sitting on a pillar in Burgundy, this kind of talk would have sounded simple-minded, because he would've been ignorant of the power of the sword. But that's something you two know more about than most Christians, so . . . Grand Master, do you agree with what we've just heard?'

'I agree, and would've said the same, though I would no doubt have been wordier than my friend Arn.' Arnoldo de Torroja fell silent and Arn, after a swift glance to see if his superior was going to say anything else, began speaking again.

'Father, there's one related matter that you should know. About a week ago the Chief Rabbi from Baghdad came to see me. Baghdad has the largest Jewish congregation in Outremer, and the Rabbi wanted people of the Jewish faith to pray here. Apparently they believe that a section of the western wall was once part of David's temple or some sacred building anyway. Did you know that the Jews haven't prayed here for over eighty-seven years?'

'No, I didn't. Do many Jews live in the city?'

'Quite a few, most of them skilled metal workers. Father, you may not know what happened when our Christian brothers occupied the city.'

'No, but from your tone of voice I gather it was bad.'

'You're right, it was. Our "liberating" force was streaming into the city and the Jewish population sought refuge in the synagogue. We burnt it down, with the people still inside.'

'I don't believe that you can expunge such a crime by letting another erroneous faith practise next to the Holy Sepulchre. What did you tell the Chief Rabbi?'

'I gave him my word, for as long as I hold my present office, that the Jews could pray as they wished,' Arn replied quickly.

The Grand Master did not comment and Father Louis had to draw the conclusion that, yet again, he did not object to de Gothia's wilfully daring decision. It was consistent, of course, but God only knew what the Holy Father would think.

'If my Holy Master were to find your generosity towards the Jews ... out of order, what would you do?' he asked slowly and distinctly.

'As Knights Templar we obey the Holy Father and him alone, *in absolutum*,' Arnoldo de Torroja said emphatically.

'Our Very Reverend Patriarch had already let us know that he disapproves of the Saracens' prayers,' Arn said with a little smile. 'He says that the *muezzin* disturbs his sleep at night. Surely that can't be entirely true?'

This sly reference to the arch sinner's nighttime activities made Father Louis laugh, and lightened the serious atmosphere, presumably exactly as Arn had hoped.

'It's a relief to think that I answer to the Holy Father and not your Patriarch,' Father Louis chuckled contentedly. 'Still, my dear Arn, you're not saying that the Jews will be embracing the true faith in some hundred years' time?'

'The Jewish faith poses a very special challenge,' Arn replied in the new, light tone. 'But there's more to it. The Jews are powerful in Baghdad, the city of the Caliph. The Caliph, who has many Jewish advisors, is Saladin's master . . .'

'And so . . .?' Father Louis asked.

'So the Caliph is said to be the successor of the Prophet Muhammad, peace be . . . er . . ., their so called prophet. This means that he's above all other followers of Muhammad. He's not whole-heartedly in favour of Saladin, and what we definitely don't need is a staunch supporter of Jihad – the holy war – in Baghdad as well.'

'So by letting the Jews pray at the western wall, you're making a well-advised move to split the Saracens?' Father Louis asked, suddenly feeling in deep waters.

'There's that,' Arn replied. 'Also, our crusade – *our* holy war, if you like – began because pilgrims had no access to the Holy Sepulchre of God. What if we forbade the Jews to pray at their sacred sites while letting the Saracens have their way? A dangerous course! Recall what the great man we both venerate, Saint Bernard, said about the Jews. "Whoever strikes a Jew has struck the Son of God". My view is simple. Since we want to keep our hold on this city forever, what better way than to make our enemy's Jihad into an unholy war?'

'Arnoldo, is this the way you see it?'

'Yes, it is, but it requires much careful thought. Maybe one has to have been in Outremer for a long time – if you'll forgive me, Father – to really understand. I've fought here for thirteen years and Arn for longer still. The Saracen supply of fighting men is inexhaustible, certainly compared with what we can recruit, especially since Saladin united them all and stopped them from wasting time fighting each other. Father, it's a stark choice between having us all slain in endless wars, or reaching a *modus vivendi* so we can visit our sacred places at will.'

'Grand Master, what you say is practically blasphemy! Isn't God protecting the True Cross and therefore us? This is not a simple contest between local barons!'

'But Father, that's exactly what it is – as well. Look around and see how outnumbered we are, in every aspect of war, and now also in leadership, because Saladin is truly a great commander. Who have we got? The King's whoring mother? Her lover, the poison murderer Heraclius? Or the useless lapdog Guy de Lusignan? In the low world and in the high, the story is the same. The Christians are led by an assortment of sinners, traitors, whores and practitioners of foul acts.

God's will? I don't know, any more than you do, but it's impossible to think that He's not angered by his subjects. Our sins, for which we Christians will burn, will also mean that we lose the Holy Land. That's the truth.'

In Anno Domini 1184, three years before God finally passed angry judgement on the Christians in the Holy Land, the ambassadors for a new crusade were setting out – the Patriarch of Jerusalem, Arnoldo de Torroja of the Templars and his opposite number from the Hospitallers, Roger des Moulins. Their task was to persuade the Emperor of Germany and the Kings of England and France to provide leadership, men and equipment for new armies to defend the Holy Land against Saladin. No one knows if both Grand Masters were aware that their travelling companion Heraclius was a scorpion in human shape.

Their mission was successful in so far as they collected a fair amount of money. The King of England was particularly freehanded as atonement for the murder of Thomas á Becket. However, money was not the most important problem. For one thing, the Order of the Temple was richer than the Kings of England and France together. Their main task was to make the Christian rulers understand that the situation in the Holy Land had deteriorated because Saladin was a much more formidable enemy than his predecessors, and that Christian fighting men were badly needed.

But the western Christians had become used to controlling the Holy Land. Riding out in the name of the Cross to liberate an already liberated land no longer seemed such a priority. Also, it was common knowledge that the hordes of adventurers who had hoped for rich pickings in earlier crusades had got little to show for their efforts. Now the Holy Land was already carved up between local barons, and there was no sympathy for new arrivals wanting to enrich themselves.

Thus, apart from obtaining money, the ambassadors were unsuccessful. The Germans failed to produce another great army, and the Kings of England and France were far too concerned with keeping an eye on each other's European ventures to spare time and thought for Outremer.

It must be assumed that throughout the journey Arnoldo de Torroja kept a wary eye on the appalling Patriarch of Jerusalem. They both knew that their politics were crucially opposed. The Heraclius faction called de Torroja a coward on account of his preference for negotiations with Saladin rather than eternal war.

Heraclius believed that he held brave, highly principled views and surrounded himself by like-minded friends such as Agnes de Courtenay, her brother the Count Joscelyn de Courtenay, and also Guy de Lusignan and his ambitious wife Sibyl, who saw themselves as unfairly cut off from the succession to the throne.

Arnoldo de Torroja must have been vigilant, travelling far and wide in the company of a proven poisoner. Nonetheless, he was himself murdered by poisoning during the journey. He was buried in Rome.

At the time, only three men in the world had an idea of what must have happened. The newly elected Pope, Lucius III, was one, since he was aided by many helping hands rooting about in the papal archives. The Master of Jerusalem, now standing in for the dead Grand Master, was another, and the third was Father Louis.

It was clear to all three that Heraclius had added to his list of murders, following the killing of Archbishop William of Tyrus by getting rid of the Grand Master in God's Sacred Army. News, good as well as bad, normally travelled quite slowly, particularly in the autumn when much of the shipping was tied up. Father Louis heard when one of his Cistercian messengers arrived after a very difficult sailing and Father Louis told Arn de Gothia. Both men were crushed by grief and anger.

At first, Arn in desperation demanded loudly that this poisonous monster be banned. Father Louis pointed out, with the greatest regret, that a ban was even less likely now. Should Lucius III ban Heraclius, if would instantly become known how flawed his predecessor's decisions had been. The new Holy Father could hardly start his period in office by admitting papal fallibility.

How many murders does he need, Arn had asked bitterly, but without receiving an answer. Why should a whore-monger, a murderer, a cheat and a threat to peace and stability in the Holy Land increase his support in proportion to how many repulsive crimes he commits, Arn had called out, but there was no reply to that question either. The two men prayed together often, as they shared the dreadful secret.

Both had an excess of work to distract them from their sorrows. Father Louis had managed to get into court circles, using an opening provided by Arn. He wandered about looking trustworthy and pious, his mind sifting information with clockwork efficiency. Arn, with two high offices to fill, was finding that his many new administrative tasks claimed a lot of his time, even though they consisted mainly of signing and sealing endless letters.

During the winter of the following year, King Baldwin called his entire High Council to a session in which he intended to announce his last will. Every baron of any importance had to attend, not only those settled in the Holy Land but also the Count of Tripoli, the Prince of Antioch and the only Christian ruler in Oultrejourdain, Reynald de Châtillon. As the assembly slowly got underway, Arn added the role of innkeeper to his many duties. In all Jerusalem, the Order of the Temple had the greatest supply of rooms suitable for such high guests, as well as the biggest halls. Coronations always ended with a grand feast in the Templar precinct, because nothing in the royal palace was large enough.

The day before the Council meeting, Arn arranged for the traditional evening meal to take place in the Knights' Hall. It was located at the same high level as his own rooms, but was reached by a separate wide stone staircase from the western wall. This was meant to prevent worldly guests from disturbing the peace, an idea Arn appreciated when he heard the crowds of opinionated men, many already rather drunk, pouring into the hall.

The hall was plain, with white walls and black furnishings, but the banners of the Knights Templar families hung along the walls. Behind the King's seat, in the centre of a long table, swung Saladin's banners captured at Mont Gisard. The seating was according to rank, with the highest placed on either side of the King. Two small tables, at right angles to the High Table, were provided respectively for the men from Antioch, arrayed on either side of Prince Bohemund, and from Tripoli on either side of Count Raymond.

The knights spiritual were seated at the long table on the other side of the hall and there Arn had changed the usual order. Now the knights from the two main orders alternated, with himself and Roger des Moulins facing each other in the centre. It was a generous gesture and Arn had explained that it had its roots in the hospitality shown to himself and his wounded Templar men after the defeat at Marj Ayyoun. This innocent-sounding reason for his demonstrative friendliness towards the Order of St John was intended to diffuse his political aim. Arn wanted real collaboration between the best knights in the Christian ranks.

The two Grand Masters were apparently chatting pleasantly throughout the meal of cooked lamb and vegetables, and Roger des Moulins soon started a very serious discussion of their options, just as Arn had hoped he might. He began by gesturing vaguely towards the royal table, observing sourly that many of the men and practically all of the women were busy ruining Christian hopes in the Holy Land. As if on cue, Heraclius rose and staggered to the King's empty place, waving his overflowing wineglass as he progressed. He brazenly sat down next to his old mistress, Agnes de Courtenay, talking non-stop.

Arn and Roger exchanged glances, neither quite able to hide his disgust. Both found it easy to continue with the subject of collaboration. Given the situation in the Court, the sooner they could end any minor disputes between themselves the better. Roger des Moulin daringly suggested a large meeting of all their respective holders of high office and Arn heartily agreed.

Then he suddenly changed the subject and asked an opaquely formulated question about Roger's reaction to Arnoldo de Torroja's unexpected death in Verona. Roger looked searchingly at him, but his answer was straightforward. The two Grand Masters had so far agreed on most things, including the subject of a rapprochement between their Orders. Meanwhile, Heraclius had been disrupting any intelligent talk by harping on his obsession with slaying Saracens and his offensive declarations of personal bravery and everybody else's cowardliness. To cap it all, the godless old lecher had been accusing his colleagues of being obstacles to the enactment of God's will in the Holy Land. He had actually said more than once that the world would be better without them. Since Arnoldo's death, Roger had been most careful about any food and drink he took in Heraclius's company. He had had his suspicions and would be interested, he said, to know what Arn thought.

Arn, obliged to silence by the Holy Father, found a suitably equivocal answer.

'My lips are sealed.'

Roger des Moulins just nodded. That was enough.

The following morning the guests again arrived at the hall. Some were the worse for wear after a long night of drinking, but even red-eyed and stinking of vomit, all were driven by curiosity about the King's last will.

The King was carried in inside a covered box no bigger than a child's coffin. By now he was completely blind and had lost both his arms and legs. The bearers put the box on the throne, outsized by comparison, and placed the royal crown on a small table in front of it.

Although his voice was frail, the King gave a short speech, clearly intended to show that his ability to use language and to think were unimpaired. His relatives were already looking restive when a Court clerk arrived with the will, authorised by the King's large seal. The clerk proceeded to read out the document in a loud voice.

The Successor to the throne will be, for all time, my sister Sibyl's seven-year-old son, Baldwin.

Until my nephew's coming of age at ten, the Regent will be Count Raymond of Tripoli.

I have recorded as a special provision that Guy de Lusignan under no circumstances can hold office as Regent or as Successor to the throne.

Count Raymond will have the right, as a small sign of gratitude for his service to the Holy Land, to include the city of Beirut in the County of Tripoli.

The child, Prince Baldwin, shall be brought up until the day of his majority, by the King's uncle, Joscelyn de Courtenay.

Should Prince Baldwin die before reaching the age of ten, a Successor shall be appointed jointly by the Holy Father in Rome, The Emperor of Roman Germany, the King of France and the King of England.

Until the Successor has been appointed in this way, Count Raymond will continue to act as Regent.

Now the King demanded that everyone present should step forward and swear, in the name of God and by his or her own honour, to obey his last will in every detail as stated.

Many of the councillors stepped forward happily, among them Count Raymond himself, his friend Prince Bohemund of Antioch and the two Grand Masters, who took the oath on behalf of the men in their Orders. Others were less willing: Heraclius, Agnes de Courtenay, her brother Joscelyn and her lover Amaury de Lusignan. When they had all taken the oath, the small box containing the living parts of the King was carried out. The flickering flame of his gallant spirit was soon to be extinguished and many in the hall found it difficult to hold back their tears. They knew that they would not see his wrecked body again until the funeral service in the Church of the Holy Sepulchre.

The councillors were getting ready to leave when the growing roar of conversation was silenced by Count Raymond, pushing his way through the crowd with his familiar long strides. To everyone's amazement, Raymond sought out Arn, warmly took both his friend's hands in his own and asked for quarters for the night for himself and his guests. Arn replied, as warmly, that it would be a pleasure.

That night two very different groups were discussing the new situation. In the royal palace, the gathering was profoundly gloomy but an improvement on a day of rage. Agnes de Courtenay had been rendered speechless with fury, and Heraclius had wandered about the palace, roaring like a bull from – as he claimed – divine despair.

By contrast, the atmosphere was positively jovial in Arn de Gothia's private rooms, where Count Raymond's remarkable collection of friends were drinking good wine. Roger des Moulins was there, as was the Prince Bohemund and the two d'Ibelin brothers. They all agreed that this was a watershed in the politics of the Holy Land. It gave them a golden opportunity to rein in the wildest of the ruling beasts, notably Heraclius and his notorious companion Reynald de Châtillon. Agnes could be left to rot, but her brother Joscelyn was a worthless commander and must be forced to resign.

Raymond had a scheme, which must be acted on as soon as possible. The first step was to negotiate a cease-fire with Saladin on the reasonable basis that the poor winter rains would lead to bad harvests unless the land was looked after. This time de Châtillon's plundering ways would have to be effectively curbed.

Looking ahead, it was likely that not only the King but also his little nephew would soon die. The child was suffering from the effects of the sinful diseases carried by his parents and such inheritance usually resulted in death well before the age of ten. Between the Pope, the Emperor, and the two rival and constantly bickering kings, selecting a successor would be a long drawn-out process. Raymond would stay as Regent, unless he was chosen as king.

Maybe, as the last thing he did in life, their brave little King had managed to save the Holy Land from inside his box.

Or so they thought, for none of the experienced men gathered in Arn's rooms that night could see the storm clouds on the horizon. They believed the joint oath of the entire High Council had to constrain even the plotters in the royal castle. However carefully Count Raymond and his friends examined opportunities for sabotage, they could see no way out for Heraclius and his party.

As the wineglasses emptied again and again, the mood in the room became positively frivolous and everybody took their turn telling stories. There was many a tale to tell from the wonderful and dreadful history of Outremer.

Prince Bohemund began, drawing on his rich fund of stories about

Reynald de Châtillon. The arch disturber of the peace in Bohemund's opinion, Reynald carried destruction inside him like the spirit in the lamp. When the young Reynald had arrived in Antioch from somewhere in France, he served Bohemund's father and proved an excellent fighting man. As a reward he'd been allowed to marry Bohemund's sister Constance.

His wealth and security as Prince of Antioch would've satisfied a wiser man, but Reynald had an insatiable appetite for conquest and loot. Poor in his own right and unable to lay his hands on the wealth in the Antioch treasury, he solved the problem by torturing the Patriarch, Aimery de Limoges. Once Reynald had tied him naked to a pole, smeared him with honey and left him to the local bees, the old man quickly saw the point of handing over his money.

With his war chests filled, Reynald considered the best region to plunder and, of all possible places, decided on Cyprus, an imperial province of the Byzantine Emperor Manuel Komnenos. Imagine, the lethal fool had gone out of his way to anger his most powerful neighbour and, to make it worse, his raid on Cyprus was marked by wanton brutality. Reynald's men ran wild, cutting the noses off all Christian priests, raping nuns, robbing every church and destroying every crop. Reynald returned to Antioch without glory but laden with ill-gotten gains.

Emperor Manuel was furious, of course. The entire Byzantine army marched on Antioch, whose people quickly decided that going to war on Reynald's behalf was unthinkable. Instead he was given the relatively easy choice of being handed over as a prisoner or rolling in sackcloth and ashes at the Emperor's feet and handing over all the stolen goods. The Emperor accepted the deal, more fool he as it turned out.

Reynald hadn't learned his lesson; far from it. Two years later he was off again, this time invading the lands of Christian Armenians and Syrians, who of all things hadn't expected to be attacked by brothers in the true faith. Plenty of loot for Reynald, and plenty of death and destruction for his unhappy victims. His new-found wealth was taken off him on the return journey by Majd al-Din of Aleppo, who put him in an Aleppo prison dungeon, where he remained until he was released to Raymond by the commander who owed the Count a debt of gratitude!

You know the rest, Raymond went on. Although broke, and despised by all right-thinking people, Reynald travelled to Jerusalem, where things went remarkably well. King Amaury had just died and Agnes's child became Baldwin IV. Thus, Agnes, who had been banned from the Court with good reason, had to be allowed back and her brother Joscelyn and Reynald both benefited, with Agnes procuring the wealthy widow Stéphanie de Milly for Reynald. The scoundrel was back in business!

Someone then asked philosophically who gained most by life's games of chance, Saladin or the Devil. All agreed that they benefited equally, but that night, Raymond and his fellow conspirators thought themselves strong enough to control Reynald. Other tunes would be heard in Jerusalem, Raymond said happily, now that the ill King and the feeble de Lusignan were no longer among the players.

Then he raised another name, that of Gérard de Ridefort.

'Talking of useless blackguards,' Raymond boomed, 'does anyone know whatever happened to de Ridefort? Last I saw of him was when he left in a huff because I'd handed over his rich widow to someone else in return for her weight in gold. To take revenge he joined the Knights Templar, my former enemies.' Raymond paused, glancing merrily at Arn.

'Our former Grand Master, sadly departed, made Brother Gérard commander in Chastel-Blanc,' Arn told the company.

'That was a bit excessive, wasn't it? Surely de Ridefort can't have served long enough to merit such a high command?' Raymond asked, looking troubled.

'That was apparently the price Arnoldo de Torroja was prepared to pay to keep the man away from the Court and all his unsuitable friends there. Wisest so, I must say.'

The talk continued until the sky grew pale outside, even though the morning light came late during this dark time of the year. The men were happy, because it seemed as though, together, they could save the Holy Land from the misery caused by fools, weaklings, sinners and intriguers.

King Baldwin IV died not many months later, and under the new Regent came peace, and a flow of pilgrims who brought much-needed new income.

One day the new Grand Master of the Order of the Temple arrived by ship at Saint-Jean d'Acre. The Council of the Order had met in Rome, with many great office-bearers present, including the Masters of Rome and Paris. They had elected Gérard de Ridefort!

The Grand Master, ready to take over the leadership in the Holy Land, brought with him an entourage of brothers picked for high office and immediately rode towards Jerusalem.

The Master of Jerusalem only learnt of the high-ranking party a few hours before it was due to arrive. He spoke with Father Louis about this new disaster, then spent a long time praying in his innermost private room, a small, plain cell like those for monks in a Cistercian cloister. Then he began the preparations necessary for receiving a new Grand Master.

When Gérard de Ridefort and his companions arrived, almost all the side panels on their horses bore the black band. From the Damascus Gate to the Templar precinct, they rode between white-mantled knights lining the last part of their route. Large torches lit the staircase to the Knights' Hall where a festive meal was ready to be served. Arn de Gothia was kneeling at the bottom of the stairs, and greeted the new men with bowed head. Then he took the bridle of de Ridefort's horse to show that he was no better than a stable groom to the Grand Master. This was what the Rules prescribed.

Gérard de Ridefort was in an excellent mood. Seated in the King's place at the High Table in the Knights' Hall, he spoke loudly about what a merciful joy it was to be back in Jerusalem, and Arn had difficulty concealing how disturbed he felt. It was bad enough having to obey every whim of a man everyone described as vindictive, illiterate, unworthy and completely without qualifications for his post – particularly when compared with Arn himself. Worse still was the threat to the Order inherent in the new Grand Master being a sworn enemy of Count Raymond. Now the storm clouds were piling up for all to see.

After the meal the Grand Master ordered Arn to accompany him and two other men, both unknown to Arn, to confer in one of the private rooms. Gérard de Ridefort was still exuding good temper and seemed to take a special pleasure in certain changes he was about to announce. He settled contentedly in Arn's own old place, put his fingertips together, and gazed at his three companions in silence for while.

'Now Arn de Gothia – that's your name, isn't it? – I'm told that you and the late Arnoldo de Torroja were very close. Is that so?' he inquired in a voice that was excessively smooth but unmistakably tinged with hatred.

'Yes, Grand Master, that's true.'

'Ah, so maybe we've found the reason for your elevation to Master of Jerusalem?' The Grand Master raised his eyebrows, making a face of theatrical surprise.

'Indeed, Grand Master, that's of course perfectly possible. In our Order, the Grand Master nominates whom he pleases.'

'That's a good answer! Indeed it is,' the Grand Master said with great satisfaction. 'My predecessor did as he pleased and now I'll please myself. This man here, standing next to you, is an Englishman called James de Mailly, commander of the fortress in Cressing. You noticed his commander's mantle, I suppose?'

'Yes, Grand Master,' Arn replied flatly.

'Now, you're just about the same size, so why don't you simply exchange mantles!'

With a jovial expression, the Grand Master watched as the two men bowed to him submissively. Both had worn their mantles at the meal as was customary; now each turned to put on the other's sign of rank and status in the Order of the Temple.

'So now you're a commander again, de Gothia,' Gérard de Ridefort said, with evident satisfaction. 'Your old friend de Torroja chose to send me to Chastel-Blanc. How would you like my old post?'

'I will obey your orders, Grand Master. If I have a choice, however, I would prefer to return to my command in Gaza,' Arn said slowly and steadily.

'Gaza! Well, if you want to bury yourself in a provincial hole like that, rather than have Chastel-Blanc, you can go there. When can you leave Jerusalem?'

'Whenever you order me to go, Grand Master.'

'Off you go then. Leave after lauds tomorrow.'

'I shall, Grand Master.'

'Excellent. Now leave me to discuss important matters with the Master of Jerusalem. You have my blessing. Goodnight.'

Turning away, Gérard de Ridefort seemed to expect Arn to dissolve into thin air. He looked round with exaggerated surprise when Arn remained.

'It is my duty to give certain information to you, Grand Master and to you, Master of Jerusalem. It must not be divulged to any other brother.'

'If that's de Torroja's instruction, consider it cancelled – he's dead, after all. Now, tell us what's it about,' Gérard de Ridefort said sneeringly.

'It's not Arnoldo de Torroja's instruction, but the Holy Father's,' Arn replied, controlling his voice so that it would not become infected by the other man's arrogance.

The new Grand Master seemed uncertain for the first time. He looked about him and, realising Arn was serious, nodded to the third knight to leave the room.

Arn went to the archive and brought back the papal bull

containing the evidence that the Patriarch of Jerusalem was a poisoner, and detailing how it was to be kept secret. When he had silently unrolled the document, the Grand Master, who knew no Latin, realised that he had to humiliate himself and ask Arn to translate.

It did nothing for the tempers of either Gérard de Ridefort or James de Mailly to learn the truth about Heraclius, the man who had been most helpful in getting them both promoted to high office. Their joint debt of gratitude was owed to a proven murderer. The Grand Master waved irritably to Arn, indicating that he should leave at once.

As Arn walked to his private room, his main feeling was one of relief. It had struck him that he had served in the Holy Land for almost nineteen years, so his penance had little more than a year to run. The sensation, which felt strange more than anything else, had come to him when Gérard de Ridefort dismissed him. Over the years, he had never allowed himself to keep track of time, mainly because of the ever-present likelihood of a stray arrow sending him to Paradise. But with only a year to go and a cease-fire in place, he would survive. He would go home.

He hadn't experienced such an overwhelming longing for his homeland before. At first, twenty years had seemed an unimaginable time-span and, latterly, work had taken him over. It had been absorbing and even, sometimes, a source of happiness. He recalled the evening after Raymond had been appointed to Regent, when the future of the Holy Land had seemed bright and peaceful. Now all that was in ruins. It was as improbable that the Templar Order under Gérard de Ridefort would collaborate with the Hospitallers as with the Regent he hated.

When Arn got back to Gaza, he shook off his sense of foreboding. He was able to spend more time with his friend and kinsman Harald Øysteinsson. By now, Harald was utterly fed up with singing hymns and being fried alive by the Mediterranean sun. He had never been particularly impressed by the local style of warfare, but the dull existence of garrisoned soldiers in peacetime was worse.

They amused themselves by swimming and diving because Arn had realised that, as commander, he could oblige all those who had such skills to practise them. The military rationale was that it provided a means of sneaking through an enemy blockade of the harbour. They fact was that the two Nordic men were the only competent swimmers, and got a lot of private enjoyment out of the practice. The only snag was that they had to take turns because the rules forbade brothers seeing each other in the nude or bathing for pleasure.

A few years ago it would not have occurred to Arn to bend the rules in this light-hearted way, but much of his devoted strictness had given way to wanting simply to wait out his time and pass it as well as possible. He and Harald planned to travel together, because they both felt that a trusted friend would be a great support over such a long distance. As commander, Arn could at any time excuse his sergeant from further service. One big problem was finding the money for the journey. Arn was used to being without money and thought that, if the worst came to the worst, he and Harald would have to work for a couple of years to earn what they needed. Alternatively, he might try to borrow the money from one of the worldly knights.

Once they had started talking about the journeying northwards, the longing for their homelands grew on them both. They spoke together of places and people, trying to bring back the rhythms of speech in familiar voices. For Arn, one face lived in his mind stronger than any other. Every night he prayed for Cecilia and his unknown child.

But now and then travellers brought worrying news about events in the rest of the Holy Land and Arn was becoming convinced that Christian rule was slipping disastrously. All non-Christian praying had been forbidden in Jerusalem and neither Jews nor Saracens were allowed to work for the Templar Order, not even practitioners of medicine or law or trade. The old enmity with the Hospitallers had revived and become worse than ever, to the point where the two Grand Masters were refusing to talk to each other.

The Knights Templar, also, were systematically sabotaging the peace treaties that Count Raymond was struggling to maintain. Most alarmingly, the Templars seemed to have entered into an alliance at Kerak with the caravan plunderer Reynald de Châtillon. It would only be a matter of time before he was off on his highway robberies again, and that would finally bury the peace with Saladin. Perhaps this, too, was part of the plan.

Arn was now more concerned with planning his return home than worrying about politics, however dramatic the news. He told himself that his indifference didn't matter because he wouldn't be allowed to work for co-operation and peace in any capacity and, anyhow, what happened to him must be the will of God.

During this first, uneventful period in Gaza he rode his Arabian horses daily, spending many more hours with them than strictly necessary. The stallion was called Ibn Anaza and the mare Umm Anaza. The rules permitted him to own both of them and if he sold them they would fetch more than enough to pay for his and Harald's journey. Not that he had the slightest intention of doing so, because he thought them the best horses he'd ever ridden and was determined to bring them back to West Gothland.

West Gothland. To get used to the idea, he would say the name aloud now and then. But one morning when he had ten months left to serve, a messenger came from Jerusalem with an urgent order from the Grand Master. Gaza's commander should immediately get ready to provide an important escort and to ride with thirty knights to Ashkelon. Arn obeyed at once and made good time to Ashkelon, arriving in the afternoon the same day.

What had happened was what everyone had expected. The child King, Baldwin V, had died while in the care of his uncle Joscelyn. The knights were to escort the corpse to the funeral in Jerusalem. The dead child would be accompanied by his remarkably composed mother Sibyl and her spouse, Guy de Lusignan.

Well on the road, Arn gave himself time to think. It didn't take him long to conclude that all this was not set in motion just to bury and mourn a child, but was part of a larger power game. When only two days later Joscelyn de Courtenay proclaimed his niece Sibyl successor to the throne, the plan of the Court conspirators became clear. A morose Father Louis visited Arn in his bare room in a distant part of the Templar precinct and told him how the fight for the throne had been decided.

It had begun by Joscelyn de Courtenay suddenly demanding an immediate meeting with the Regent. He had told Count Raymond of the child's death and suggested that the High Council should meet in Raymond's Tiberias rather than in Jerusalem. This would allow their deliberations to proceed undisturbed by people such as the incurable chatterbox Heraclius and, worse, Gérard de Ridefort, who had declared himself free of any oaths sworn by the dismissed former Master of Jerusalem, including the oath to obey the previous King's last will.

Raymond allowed himself to be persuaded and left Jerusalem. Within the day, Reynald de Châtillon came thundering into the city at the head of a large force of knights from Kerak. Joscelyn promptly declared his niece the successor, effectively making her husband King of Jerusalem. Those who could have stopped these evil proceedings, including Raymond and the d'Ibelin brothers, were kept out of the city by Templar guards on the walls and at every gate. Later, Roger des Moulins was among those who refused to betray his oath to Baldwin IV.

The coronation took place in the Church of the Holy Sepulchre. First, the known robber and torturer Reynald de Châtillon made a strong speech emphasising Sibyl's paramount right to the throne, given that she was Amaury's daughter, as well as the sister of Baldwin IV and mother of Baldwin V. The Patriarch crowned Sibyl, who took the crown and placed it on the head of her husband. Then she put the sceptre in his hand and the transfer of power was done. As they processed to the coronation feast, Gérard de Ridefort could be heard shouting with relish at having taken his revenge on the absent Raymond in a most spectacular way.

Arn attended the coronation as the acting commander of the royal couple's guard, a task he found profoundly distasteful. He had been ordered to protect a band of perjurers who were pushing the Holy Land into final disaster. He kept reminding himself that he had only seven months of service left. A few days later he was angered even more by Gérard de Ridefort. The Grand Master came to see him, blandly stating that, as far as he was concerned, bygones should be bygones and that he had learned a number of new interesting things about Arn. People had told him of Arn's glowing reputation in the field, his archery skills and, especially, his victory at Mont Gisard.

To make up for any offence caused, he appointed Arn to the honorary position of commander of the Royal Guards. Arn felt slighted, but did not show it. Now he was counting the days to his release on 4 July, 1187, exactly twenty years to the day since he had sworn obedience, poverty and chastity for the duration of his service. Everything he saw during his time in the royal palace demonstrated the degradation that ensues when such ideals are utterly rejected. Earlier, he might have wept bitter tears to see the reins of power in the hands of these deplorable people. Now he was resigned to the only possible outcome, which was that God would punish them all and take the Holy Land out of their control

Reynald de Châtillon broke the cease-fire with Saladin by the end of the year and plundered the largest caravan that had ever set out between Mecca and Damascus. Saladin was more furious than he had ever been, and very understandably so, because his own sister was one of the prisoners put away in the dungeons of Kerak. Jerusalem was alive with rumours that Saladin had sworn to kill Reynald with his own hands.

The King had no conciliatory message for Saladin's ambassador, who presented himself to demand payment of damages for breaking the cease-fire and the immediate release of all prisoners. Unfortunately he had no power to control de Châtillon, the King admitted.

Now nothing could prevent the war. Jerusalem lost two potential allies when Count Raymond and Prince Bohemund immediately entered into separate peace accords with Saladin. That meant that Antioch, Tripoli and the land belonging to Raymond's wife Escheva, round Tiberias in Galilee were effectively on Saladin's side, and that the Saracen chief was made aware that the mad Court in Jerusalem was widely regarded as fair prey.

An internecine war was threatening to break out between Christian factions. Gérard de Ridefort won the King's support for sending the royal army, reinforced by Knights Templar, towards Tripoli, 'to teach Raymond a lesson he'll never forget'. Balian d'lbelin managed to stop this mad enterprise at the last moment, arguing that fighting between allies was the last thing they needed now that they had to form a united front against Saladin. Balian d'lbelin then offered to agree terms with Count Raymond and was asked to join a group of negotiators which also included the two Grand Masters and Bishop Josias of Tyrus, escorted by a handful of knights from the spiritual orders. Arn de Gothia was among them.

Meanwhile, Count Raymond was in a quandary. As if to test the strength of the peace treaty, Saladin had sent his son al-Afdal to Tripoli to announce that Saladin required safe passage through Galilee for a large contingent of advance units. Raymond agreed, provided that they would take no more than one day, from sunrise to sunset. He then dispatched a couple of messengers with a warning to the approaching group of negotiators to keep out of the enemy's way. They caught up with the group near Nazareth and were politely thanked by Gérard de Ridefort. The reason for his graciousness was not immediately obvious.

He had actually arrived at the conclusion that this provided an excellent opportunity to defeat a section of Saladin's army and sent an order to the Master of Jerusalem, who was visiting a fortress called La Fève at the time. James de Mailly had ninety Knights Templar at his disposal in La Fève, and in the city of Nazareth they managed to collect forty more assorted knights and a handful of foot soldiers. Before he left the city, Gérard de Ridefort urged the population to follow his troops on foot. This chance of looting must not be missed, he assured them. Then they all set out to find al-Afdal and his Syrian riders.

After some thought, Bishop Josias had decided to stay behind in

Nazareth, claiming that this kind of thing was outside his area of expertise. He was never to regret his decision.

Of course, the combined soldiery under de Ridefort's command was an impressive-looking small army, with about a hundred foot soldiers backing up one hundred and forty knights in full armour, all Knights Templar or Hospitallers to boot. But when they first encountered the enemy at Cresson, they could hardly believe their eyes. In front of them were not small advance units, but seven thousand Mameluke lancers and Syrian archers watering their horses at the Springs of Cresson.

The mathematics were straightforward. One hundred and forty well trained and armed knights might, on a good day, have a hope of success against seven hundred Mameluke and Syrian riders. Seven hundred – but not seven thousand. Roger des Moulins and James de Mailly immediately saw that their only course was a swift retreat.

Gérard de Ridefort did not agree, lost his temper, and accused everybody else of cowardice. He became very personal, telling Roger des Moulins that he wasn't worthy of his high office and offending James de Mailly by taunting him about being too careful with his pretty blonde head to risk it for the sake of God.

From his humble place at the rear of the leading group, Arn heard this and more. Sitting quietly on his Frankish stallion Ardent, he reflected that de Ridefort must be insane. It was nothing but a recipe for death to attack when outnumbered ten to one in broad daylight, and after the enemy had discovered the danger, mounted, and begun to get into formations.

In the end nothing could shift Gérard de Ridefort and the rules of honour left his companions no choice. They began regrouping into attack formation and, at that point, de Ridefort called on Arn to ride at his side as *confanonier*. It required a skilful and daring rider, because the role was a complex one. Apart from holding and protecting the banner of the order, he also had to serve as the Grand Master's shield, prepared at any moment to protect his high brother with his own life. The Grand Master's life and the banner must be the last to be lost in a battle.

As he rode forward to take up his position Arn was full of mixed feelings, among them fear. It did not dominate, for strongest of all was a feeling of deep disappointment. He had been so close to liberty and now he would die on the word of a madman and a fool. His death would be meaningless, as were those of so many others who had obeyed the orders of crazed or incompetent commanders.

The possibility of running away occurred to him for the first time, but his oath stopped him. His life was but temporal, his oath for all eternity.

The Grand Master gave the order to attack. Arn raised and lowered the banner three times and one hundred and forty knights went galloping down the slope towards death.

Because Gérard de Ridefort rode more slowly than the rest and Arn had to stay close to him, they ended up in the rear. At the moment the first knights were crashing into the Mameluke front line, the Grand Master swung sharply right. Arn followed, raising his shield against the rain of arrows that was falling over them. He felt himself hit many times, and a number of arrows pierced his chainmail. Next, Gérard swung again, setting off in the direction they had come from. Covered by Arn holding the banner, the Grand Master rode full speed away from the attack he himself had forced.

Not one single knight, including the Grand Master of the Hospitallers and the Templar Master of Jerusalem, survived the battle at the Springs of Cresson.

Some of the wordly knights who had joined up in Nazareth were taken prisoner on reasonable expectation of ransom payments. The people from Nazareth, tempted by promises of loot, were gathered up, shackled and taken off to the nearest slave market.

That evening, just before sunset, Count Raymond was watching from the wall of Tiberias as the Muslim forces under al-Afdal passed by, as agreed, on their way to the crossing of the River Jordan.

In the front line rode Mameluke lancers with over one hundred bearded heads speared on their upright lances. This sight brought about what the group of negotiators might have failed to do. Raymond decided that he could not betray his own kind and revoked the treaty with Saladin. However much it pained him, he must swear an oath of allegiance to King Guy. He had never felt more bitter about a decision in his life.

When Saladin attacked in earnest later that summer, he rode at the head of the largest army he had ever commanded. It consisted of thirty thousand men on horseback and his intention was to force a decisive end to the occupation.

Arn was in Gaza, being treated by his Saracen medics for the wounds from the Springs of Cresson, when he heard of the giant army on the move. By now King Guy had conscripted all men under military command to serve under the banners of the Holy Land. The Orders of the Temple and St John emptied their fortresses, leaving

258

only skeleton forces behind to maintain them and defend the walls. Arn left Harald Øysteinsson in Gaza, because an archer of his skill would be most useful leading the small group of defenders.

There was no notification of any plan, but the King's call-up meant that the knights spiritual alone would raise some two thousand men. The number of worldly knights was about four thousand and there were between ten and twenty thousand archers and foot soldiers to protect the flanks. In Arn's experience, this line-up would be invincible even against a much larger Saracen army. More worrying than the balance of forces was the possibility that one of Saladin's manoeuvres would tempt the large army off course and some of the cities would fall because their defences were so poorly manned.

He could not imagine that Gérard de Ridefort would repeat the idiocy of Cresson and, besides, he would be less influential in the disposition of the whole Christian army.

When Arn arrived in Saint-Jean d'Acre at the head of his sixty-four knights and barely one hundred sergeants, he had less than a week left to serve in the Templar order. He was less concerned with this now, because he clearly could not leave his post in the middle of a war. But towards the end of the summer, when they were about to drive Saladin back over the River Jordan, then the journey home would start.

West Gothland, he said to himself, tasting the unfamiliar sounds of the old language.

At Saint-Jean d'Acre, an immense army camp was forming under the hot summer sun while an almost continual council of war was sitting in the fortress. As usual, King Guy was incapable of making sense of the advice from his commanders, who all hated each other. The new Grand Master of the Order of St John argued against anything Gérard de Ridefort said, and Count Raymond thought them both fools. The Patriarch failed to agree with anyone.

Most of those present tended to support Count Raymond, who stressed the effects of the heat. Saladin was busy plundering Galilee with a larger army than ever before, but his supply lines – particularly the vital provision of water and hay for the horses and food for the troops – were very extended. If nothing much happened, the patience of his men would be worn down by waiting, discomfort and heat. This often happened with the Saracens. The conclusion was that the Christians could safely take their time, rely on their cities for supplies, and attack only when the Saracens were ready to give up and go home: True, they'd have put up with the plundering but this time it might be a price worth paying.

No one was surprised when Gérard de Ridefort contradicted all of this and called Count Raymond a traitor, a friend of Saracens and someone well inside Saladin's pocket, but even King Guy had ceased taking any notice of these bizarre outbursts.

However, the King listened attentively when the Patriarch argued that they should attack at once, for the tortuous reason that because Raymond's plan was the wisest they must do the unexpected – that is, something less wise would be even wiser.

Then Heraclius created a diversion because he had brought the True Cross. Could their forces ever be defeated when fighting under its protection? He answered the rhetorical question himself. Never, he cried. It would be sinful to doubt the outcome. The victory would purify all of their sins because God would be pleased. Therefore going to battle as soon as possible was the best possible course.

Unfortunately he was prevented from joining them, he added. His health would not allow it. The Bishop of Caesarea should carry the precious relic.

Heraclius carried the argument and on the last day of June in Anno Domini 1187, the hottest time of the year, the Christian army broke camp and moved toward Galilee to confront Saladin, travelling to the Springs of Sephoria where grass and water was plentiful. Then they learnt of Saladin's last move. He had occupied Tiberias and was laying siege to its fortress.

This was Raymond's city and his wife, Escheva, was in the fortress. Their three sons were with the army at Sephoria and they at once demanded that a force should be sent to Tiberias. The King was ready to agree when Count Raymond asked to be heard. He spoke calmly and clearly, while everyone listened in deepening silence.

'Sire, I have most to lose now and you must listen to me with the greatest seriousness. Do not attack Saladin at Tiberias. I know the area well. It is arid as a desert at this time of year. Stay here at Sephoria, where we have water and grass for the horses, and can easily defend ourselves. Saladin may take my fortress, but we'll not let him keep it. I'll rebuild it if he destroys it. I'll pay what it takes, should he imprison my wife. We can bear these things and must not lose the Holy Land because of them.'

This settled the matter for that day, but Gérard de Ridefort sought out the King late in the evening and insisted that Raymond was a traitor. Raymond, he alleged, had joined in a secret pact with Saladin and was trying to divert the royal army from a chance of winning a decisive victory. His motive was mainly envy, because King Guy had displaced him from his post as Regent, but he also wanted to steal the honour of defeating Saladin. As likely as not, he was after the crown for himself and wanted to be seen as a great commander.

King Guy gave in. If he had ordered a night-time march to surprise the enemy, they might have stood a chance, but the King said he needed a night's sleep. Instead they broke camp at dawn.

The Knights of St John rode in front of the worldly knights, with the Knights Templar bringing up the rear where the pressure was usually the worst. For obscure reasons, the Grand Master had declared that light Turkish horses were godless abominations and so all the brothers rode stolid Frankish beasts. There were too few foot soldiers for effective cover, so the knights and their horses had to wear full armour from the outset.

The Saracens had a long established method of harassing these heavy Christian armies. Light cavalry arrived in wave after wave, showering the enemy with arrows before riding off out of reach again.

The Knights Templar had been ordered by their great leader to stay in formation, come what may. Because they had no defence against the archers, most of them were hit by stray arrows that pierced their armour. The injuries were minor but added to the torment of the heat. In other ranks men were killed.

The day was hot indeed. The desert wind came whining in from the south and Raymond's warnings about the aridity of the land proved to be true. From dawn to dusk they were subjected to the deadly shower of arrows, and by evening they gave up trying to carry their dead with them. They were left where they fell.

By the evening they had come close enough to Tiberias to see the lake glinting in the sunshine. Count Raymond was trying to persuade the King that they must attack at once and fight their way to water before darkness fell. They would be defeated by lack of water alone if they spent the night without it after this dreadful day. This was all Gérard de Ridefort needed to argue that a night's sleep was much more strengthening and the King, who was exhausted, agreed and ordered his men to set up camp there and then.

The place where the army settled down was on a slope, close to a village called Hattin and between two small peaks known as the Horns of Hattin. Everyone was longing for the cool and quiet of the night.

The Saracen army was within sight of the exhausted Christians, and could be seen praying in the late evening. Saladin, on the shores of the lake, was thanking his God for the priceless asset he had been given. Up there on the bare, low slope, the Christians were in an indefensible position. Here was the final victory presented on a golden platter. Now they all had to thank God and do what they had to.

One of their first duties was to set fire to the sun-parched grass south of the Horns of Hattin. The stinging smoke ruined any hope of a good night's sleep for the Christian enemy.

The Saracens' next task was to move quietly under the cover of darkness. When dawn came, the Christians found themselves totally surrounded by a passive ring of armed men. Saladin was in no hurry to attack, time was on his side. While King Guy dithered, the sun was rising inexorably.

Raymond was among the first to mount his horse. He rode through the camp until he found the Knights Templar and a little later, Arn de Gothia.

'Arn, it's time to get some good men together and try to break out.'

'Can't be done, my oath binds me for one more day, until this evening,' Arn told him amiably.

They said goodbye and Arn wished Raymond well.

Then he prayed for his friend.

Raymond roused his tired knights, explaining that they might as well die attempting to break-out because if they stayed where they were they'd die anyway. Then he instructed them to form a narrow wedge rather than the usual wide attacking formation and ordered a full gallop at the enemy lines.

The rows of waiting Saracens had their backs towards the Lake of Galilee, as if they were guarding the water. When Raymond and his knights came storming at them, the lines opened to let them through. Then they closed again.

It was much later that the lookouts at the top of Hattin's Horns discovered Raymond and his men riding off into the distance with nobody in pursuit. Saladin had let them go unharmed. This was all de Ridefort needed to start raging about traitors again and ordering his knights to mount.

The sight of the seven hundred-strong line of Templar knights caused the Saracens to start milling about and shouting anxiously. It was a larger force than they had ever seen and everybody realised that this was the moment of truth. Were these white demons truly impossible to defeat? Or were they human beings, exhausted by a night and a day without water or much sleep?

Then the Hospitallers, too, prepared for attack and finally King Guy ordered the worldly knights to mount. But Gérard de Ridefort would not wait for anyone.

When the Templar force came thundering down the hill, the enemy lines opened for them and their attack lost its momentum. Heavily laden as they were, it took them time to turn round and this was made harder by the horses having come so close to the water. The thirsty animals did not much care for being forced back up the hill again. As the Templar knights rode back they met the Hospitallers galloping down the hill, and for some gruesome moments there was a mass of allied knights becoming entangled with each other.

That was when the Mameluke lancers attacked from behind and with full force. Retreating lost de Ridefort half his men and the Hospitallers' losses were even greater.

The next time the Christian army moved as one, but by then many foot soldiers were half mad with thirst and began running towards the lake, helmets in their hands and arms outstretched. Others joined them and all became easy prey for the Egyptian lancers.

The second attack by the knights almost reached the water's edge before they had to retreat. Only about a third of the Christian army now remained to close ranks around the King. Now Saladin ordered a full attack.

Arn had lost his horse from an arrow through its neck. He was beyond thinking clearly and his very last memory was of standing back to back with a group of brothers, fighting off Syrian foot soldiers who were surrounding them on all sides. He knew he hit many of them with his sword and the club he wielded with his shield-arm; the shield had long gone.

He never found out how he ended up on the ground.

Those knights spiritual who had been taken prisoner during the last hour of the battle at the Horns of Hattin were lined up by the lakeside and given water to drink. This was not charity, but to enable them to talk. The beheadings began at the far end of the line and the executioners worked their way up towards Saladin's victory pavilion. The surviving brothers numbered two hundred and forty-six Knights Templar and about as many Knights of St John. Both orders were virtually eliminated from the Holy Land.

Saladin was weeping for joy and thanking God as he watched the heads fall. This was a most wonderful gift of his God, to make him the instrument through which the presence of these dreadful Orders would be ended. Their half-empty fortresses could now be picked like ripe fruit. His road to Jerusalem was clear at last.

The worldly prisoners were, as was usual, treated quite differently. When Saladin had spent some time rejoicing at the good work of his executioners, he went inside his pavilion to meet his most distinguished prisoners, who included the unhappy King Guy and Saladin's most hated enemy, Reynald de Châtillon. Next to Reynald sat the Grand Master of the Templar Order, but Saladin didn't feel that de Ridefort would be a very valuable prisoner. Might be worth testing though, he said to himself. Facing death can do strange things to men who're usually brave and honourable.

One of his high-ranking prisoners could expect no mercy. Saladin had sworn in the name of God to kill Reynald de Châtillon with his own hands and he carried out his promise immediately, using his own sword. Then he spoke soothingly to the others, assuring them that he would let them live and politely serving them water.

Meanwhile the beheadings continued in front of an appreciative audience of Saracen soldiers. A group of Sufi scholars from Cairo also attended. They had been following Saladin's army on the understanding that Christians could be converted to the true faith. Some of the amirs had taken a cruel pleasure in inviting the learned men to try their skills on the captured knights spiritual.

The bemused scholars found themselves walking from one knight to the next, asking each if he was willing to embrace the Muslim faith. Everyone said no and each one was then beheaded by the questing scholar. This added to the general amusement, because only rarely was the unbeliever's head cut off in one blow. The learned executioners made a frankly terrible job of it, while their audience shouted jokes and helpful advice at them, and cheered every time a head finally came off.

Arn had revived enough from the water to understand what was going on, but found it hard to follow. His face was covered in blood and the sight of one eye seemed to have gone. Not that he was very interested because now he had to think only of making peace with his God. With all his strength he prayed for enlightenment. Why just this very day, 4 July 1187? Twenty years ago to the day he'd joined the Knights Templar. From sunset this day he would have been free. What was God's intention in letting him die on the same day that the Christians lost their hold of the Holy Land?

Then he accused himself of selfishness. He was very far from the only one to die for his God on this day and should refrain from demanding explanations in his own case. He started praying for Cecilia and for his child.

When the sweating, blood-spattered group of Sufi scholars reached Arn and repeated their babble about forswearing Christianity and embracing the true faith in order to live, they sounded

incoherent and desperate, past trying to make the prisoners understand the proposition in the first place.

A burst of pride made Arn raise his head, already bowed in
readiness for the sword, and speak in the language of the Prophet,
may peace be with him.

'In the name of the all Merciful and all Charitable, listen to the
word from your own Sacred Quran, the third sura and fifty-fifth
verse,' he began. He stopped to draw breath and all around him the
talking and shouting died down. He addressed the crowd with a
shaking voice.

'And God said to Jesus, I shall call you and you will come to Me
and I shall cleanse you from the accusations that those who deny the
truth have thrown at you. Until the day of the Resurrection I shall
place those who follow you high above those who deny you. And on
that Day you shall all return to Me and I shall judge between you in
every matter that you have quarrelled about.'

Then Arn closed his eyes and bowed his head, waiting for the
blow. But hearing the words of God from the mouth of one their
worst enemies had paralysed the Sufis. Then a high-ranking amir
pushed his way through the crowd and shouted that Al Ghouti had
been found. Arn's face was so badly cut that no one could have
recognised him, but everyone knew that only one among their
enemies could speak the sacred words so clearly and well.

Saladin had given the strictest orders that if Al Ghouti was
identified among the survivors, he must on no account be treated
badly but instead given all the respect due to an honoured guest.

When the sun set on the last day of Cecilia Rosa's twenty year-long penance, she was sitting alone by one of the fishponds in Riseberga cloister. The weather was hot and windless as usual around the Feast of Peter, when the summer had just passed its peak. The hay-making would be starting down in West Gothland, though not yet up here, north of the Northern Forest.

She had been to Mass twice that day and taken Communion, profoundly aware that on this day she had completed, with the help of Our Lady, the whole span of time that had once seemed without end. Tomorrow she would be free.

Or not free, for nothing seemed likely to change on the stroke of the hour of liberty. There had been no signs or omens on this perfectly ordinary summer's day.

Of course, she had long ago realised how childish it would be to think that Arn would come riding out of nowhere to take her away on that very day. The journey ahead of him would not be easy and would perhaps take as long as a year.

She now thought it wise to have firmly refused to imagine a celebration of any kind, and now anticipated how ordinary a day it would be. Here she was, thirty-seven years old and poor as a churchmouse, owning nothing except a few clothes. As far as she knew, her father was ailing after a stroke, alone and impoverished in Husaby Farm and entirely dependent on the Folkunga kin for managing its finances. It would not please him to have her back in the house. She would mean little more to him now than another mouth to feed.

There would be a cold welcome for her at Arnäs too, for her sister Katarina was the mistress of the house there. Katarina had been the cause of Cecilia and Arn's twenty-year penance and neither sister would enjoy coming face-to-face with the other.

True, she could ask Cecilia Blanca to invite her to stay at Näs on Visingsö and Ulvhilde would surely welcome her to Ulfshem for a while. But visiting friends as someone with a home herself was one thing; staying as a homeless dependant quite another.

Impulsively, Cecilia Rosa tore off her veil. Its weight on her head and neck was so habitual that she felt bald without it. She tossed her head to free her hair and combed the matted strands with her fingers. She had let it grow longer by creeping away from the last two of the six annual hair-cutting sessions prescribed by the rules.

Leaning over the edge of the pond, she tried to see something of her face in the surface of the water, but dusk had fallen and she glimpsed only a pale oval under the red hair. She felt that what she saw was a remembered image from her youth and nothing to do with her present self. There were of course no mirrors in Riseberga, as in any other cloister.

Awkwardly, she slid her hands over her body, as a free woman is allowed to do, and cautiously tried feeling her breasts and hips. Even touching such secret places wasn't forbidden any more, but what she felt told her very little. All she knew of herself was that she was thirty-seven years old and free – but not truly free.

Walls and moats constricted her freedom in every way. Birger Brosa had told her that should she fancy continuing as *yconoma* at Riseberga, the job was hers. He had sounded amiable but not very interested. As the first hour of freedom struck, his careless promise seemed less friendly and more threatening. Was she just to go on living as she had been for the last twenty years?

Not entirely, she promised herself, come what may. She'd no longer cover her hair with the veil. She'd stop singing lauds and matins and attending compline. It would leave a lot of valuable time for work. The biggest change would be going round the markets herself and selecting the goods to purchase on her own. She would become an ordinary human being with a right to speak to whom she wished and go where she liked, without the constant reminders of her sin and her punishment.

Above all, she could travel to Bjälbo to see her son Magnus for the first time since his birth. The thought of this meeting stirred her mind into producing images both fearsome and joyous. Many people, but above all the Church, pronounced Magnus the illegitimate offspring of a shameful coupling. Birger Brosa had made the boy his own by taking him away as a new-born babe and letting him be brought up at Bjälbo by his own wife Brigida. The Earl had taken him to the Folkunga kin's council at the time of the boy's majority. As a child, Magnus had believed himself to be a son of the house until wagging tongues let him know different.

After a lot of angry yelling at the gossips, Magnus went to see Birger Brosa and demanded to be told the truth. On learning that he was indeed not the Earl's son, Magnus had become something of a loner, glumly keeping himself to himself for a long time. He had been left to his own devices, for his stepfather had a shrewd idea that sooner or later the boy's curiosity would conquer his bitterness.

Birger Brosa was right. Magnus began asking questions about his father and mother. Who was Arn Magnusson? Birger Brosa described the conversation to Cecilia Rosa and had quite possibly laid on the praise for Arn especially thick. Arn, he claimed to have said, was the best swordsman in West Gothland and a better archer than any man he knew anywhere. The Earl explained apologetically that what he said was not strictly untrue and the proof was in stories like the one from Axevalla Thing. It still lived in common memory how Arn, barely out of childhood, had challenged and defeated the huge fighting man, Emund Ulfsbane, at the Thing of all Goths in Axevalla. It had brought to everyone's mind the battle of David and Goliath in the Holy Scripture, although Arn had spared Emund's life after cutting off his hand.

Magnus decided to try out the story on other relatives and heard it retold with remarkable embroideries by many, who all claimed to have been present at the Thing. Once some basic truths about Arn's unusual prowess had been confirmed, Magnus decided to start improving his own fighting skills. He had been an excellent archer since childhood and now he practised much harder than anyone would have demanded of him, and rather neglecting other parts of his education.

Next, Magnus went to see Birger Brosa to tell him that unless his father returned from the Holy Land, he didn't want to be known either as Magnus Birgersson or Arnsson. Instead he preferred the name Moonshield and had already taken the trouble to paint a small crescent moon above the Folkunga lion on his shield.

As for seeing his mother, Birger Brosa had advised both mother and son that it was better if they didn't meet until Cecilia was a free woman and not some creature beholden to a lot of nuns. Both had agreed at the time, but now Cecilia felt deeply anxious about meeting her son. What would he make of her? Would he be disappointed, especially after all the wonderful tales he had heard about his father? Did she look old and ugly? Too poorly dressed? Such questions hadn't occurred to her for many years.

That night the other women in Riseberga – six nuns, three novices and eight *conversae* – went to compline as usual, but Cecilia Rosa worked in her counting chambers. Such were her first hours of freedom.

As autumn drew closer, Cecilia Rosa ordered a couple of carts to be brought out and equipped for a buying trip. They needed to stock up on useful and beautiful plants for autumn, and many items were needed for a long season of sewing, cloth-making and dyeing. All these things had flowed smoothly into Godshome, but Riseberga was just starting up these enterprises. Birger Brosa had ordered some of his own armed men to accompany Cecilia, because she would be carrying quite a quantity of silver. Norwegian oarsmen took her across Vättern and a new troop of Folkunga men rode with her towards Godshome.

On this trip she was riding a horse for the first time since her youth and, because she had been a good horsewoman then, it didn't take her long to feel secure in the saddle. She told her guards that she would ride in front as they came close to Godshome. After many years as *yconoma* she was used to having her orders obeyed.

She surprised herself by feeling a surge of reluctant affection when Godshome came into view. It looked so appealing at a distance, with the wooded slopes rising behind it and late-flowering roses tumbling over the walls, just as she hoped to have happen at Riseberga. Although there was no place on Earth where she'd suffered as much as in Godshome, or any human being she detested as much as Mother Rikissa, she was a free woman now, Mother Rikissa couldn't harm her, and this made a difference to how she felt about the place.

Cecilia Rosa told herself that she was travelling on business and would meet Mother Rikissa as an equal. She spun a little fantasy about how the Abbess of Godshome and the *yconoma* of Riseberga would conduct a reasonable discussion about trade, and smiled as she recalled how little head Mother Rikissa had for business.

None of her expectations were met, however, for Mother Rikissa was dying. A Bishop Örjan from Växjö was in attendance, ready to hear her confession and administer the last rites. On hearing this news, Cecilia Rosa felt like leaving, but the journey was long and difficult. She told herself that life must go on and took rooms in the *hospitium*, where she was received like any other traveller.

That evening Bishop Örjan came to see her. Mother Rikissa had requested a last visit from Cecilia Rosa, who felt she could not refuse a dying wish. Reluctantly following Bishop Örjan, Cecilia Rosa knew that it was not the presence of death that worried her – during her cloister years she'd seen many old ladies pass on to a better world – but the fear of what she might discover in her own heart. It was hard to imagine anything but unholy triumph at seeing someone so wicked die.

With the muttering, praying Bishop at her side, she stepped into Mother Rikissa's room. Candles were lit on either side of the bed where she lay, deathly pale as though the Grim Reaper were already squeezing her heart with his cold, bony hands. With the Bishop, she kneeled by the bed and prayed, as she had to. Then Mother Rikissa's eyes opened slightly and her claw-like fingers clutched the back of Cecilia's neck with unexpected strength.

'Cecilia Rosa, God has called you to my bedside so that you'll have time to forgive me in this life,' she hissed. Then her grip relaxed a little.

For a brief moment Cecilia Rosa experienced the icy fear she'd always felt in the presence of this evil woman, but she controlled herself and gently removed the hand from her neck.

'Mother, what do you want me to forgive?' she asked, as neutrally as she could.

'My sins. Above all, my sins towards you.' Mother Rikissa was whispering now, as her sudden moment of strength deserted her.

'Forgive you for the many times you had me whipped for sins you knew I hadn't committed? Have you confessed these cruelties?' Cecilia asked coldly.

'I've confessed them all to Bishop Örjan.'

'And you confessed the times you tried to kill me by ordering me to spend several winter days and nights in *carcer* with only one blanket?'

'Yes ... yes, I've confessed that too.'

But by now Cecilia Rosa noticed that Bishop Örjan, who was kneeling next to her, was twitching a little oddly. She looked up quickly and saw surprise on his face.

'Mother Rikissa, are you lying to me on your deathbed? After confessing and receiving the last rites?' Cecilia spoke softly but inside she'd gone as hard as iron. She was sure that once more she could see the goat's slit-like pupils in the old woman's glowing, blood-shot eyes.

'No, no. I've confessed all that you ask me about. Now I need your promise to pray for me during my long journey, for my sins are great.'

'You've confessed also that you tried to kill Cecilia Blanca by throwing her in *carcer* during the coldest months of the year?' Cecilia Rosa asked relentlessly.

'You're tormenting me . . . show me some mercy on my deathbed,' Mother Rikissa panted, her tone of voice so ingratiating that Cecilia Rosa again felt that she was watching a performance.

'You must swear that you've confessed to trying to kill two young women in your charge. I'm but a humble sinner and cannot forgive such grave sins unless your confessor has heard and spoken to you. You do see that, don't you?' Cecilia Rosa had no intention of relenting.

'Yes, indeed. Now I've confessed all of it,' Mother Rikissa replied in a voice no longer so weak and broken but almost impatient.

'This is difficult for me. Either you're lying and I cannot forgive you, or you've confessed to the mortal sin of deliberately wanting to take Christian lives. That's a worse sin still for someone in the service of the Mother of God. Even the Bishop here cannot forgive mortal sins, for God will not allow it, so I can do nothing.' Cecilia Rosa had finally trapped her quarry.

She rose abruptly, as if she had an inkling of what would happen next. Mother Rikissa turned quickly and reached out her hands as if to grab Cecilia Rosa around the neck. When the tightly stretched blanket was pulled back an appalling stench spread into the room.

'Cecilia Rosa, I curse you!' Mother Rikissa cried loudly, her strength temporarily regained. Her red eyes were wide-open, the pupils again looking like vertical slits.

'My curses too on your wanton, lying friend. I curse you both to burn in hell forever and to suffer all the torments of war for your sins. May your families die with you in the fire that will devastate the land!'

The evil woman fell back into the bed as if stricken. Her veil had slipped and some of her dark, greying hair was showing. A small ooze of black blood trickled down her chin.

The Bishop quietly took Cecilia Rosa by the shoulders and led her out of the room. Then he went back and closed the door, as if he had decided that there was still work to do at the dying woman's bedside.

Mother Rikissa died that night. She was buried under the stone flags in the cloisters, together with the broken seal of an Abbess. After much hesitation, Cecilia Rosa decided she had no choice and went to the funeral service. She found it unreasonable and hypocritical to stand there, looking mournful and praying for wickedness itself. She couldn't think of anything you could plead for on behalf of someone capable of lies on her own deathbed.

But on the other side of the scales were weighed some worldly considerations. She had never heard of Bishop Örjan and hadn't even known that there was a bishop in Växjö. Of course it made sense to ask a minor bishop to officiate, presumably a Sverker and therefore Mother Rikissa's kinsman, but now he had information of a kind that no one else had access to. The dead woman's last words had been about the fires of war that she herself would start. If Bishop Örjan had any ideas concerning what she had in mind, he was worth cultivating. This, together with the practical need to settle the business deals which she had travelled so far to make, made her decide to stay at Godshome.

Bishop Örjan was a tall, thin man with a neck like a crane and a prominent Adam's apple. He spoke with a slight stutter and seemed none too bright. This was something Cecilia Rosa had felt immediately, and then reproached herself for making such hasty judgements.

But it seemed she was right after all. When she suggested she and the Bishop, together with some of their companions, should share funeral drinks in the *hospitium* before leaving, he agreed at once and apparently happily. As the only woman present, she sat next to the bishop and listened more than she spoke, as was only proper. The more the Bishop drank, the more garrulous he became.

He started by regretting the way clergy of the Sverker kin were given such poor openings in the Church nowadays, while the Folkunga and Erik families seemed to get promotion easily enough.

Cecilia Rosa had been handed her first piece of crucial information.

It didn't take him long to get round to asking if she might know exactly when Queen Cecilia Blanca had taken her vows. They had been so close at the time, he believed.

This question made Cecilia Rosa's blood run cold, but she tried not to show her agitation, sweetly telling him – which was the truth – that she was certain Cecilia Blanca had not taken any vows. On the contrary, they'd promised each other not to and had spent many years as close friends together in Godshome.

This made Bishop Örjan very thoughtful. He sat in silence for a while before saying that he could naturally not break the seal of the confession but might mention what was in the last letter from Mother Rikissa to the Holy Father in Rome. It stated that Queen Cecilia Blanca had taken her vows in Godshome.

Cecilia Rosa served some more beer, but her alarm combined with her lack of practice caused her to pour rather more than she had planned. Bishop Örjan drained the tankard greedily, while she considered this vital information.

'Shouldn't such a last will and testament be sent off to the Archbishop as soon as possible?' she asked, trying hard to sound innocent.

'No, no, there is no archbishop; not since the wild natives from east of the Baltic Sea raided Sigtuna and killed the last incumbent, Jon, as you might remember. Besides, if Mother Rikissa intended her missive for the Holy Father, it would hardly seem necessary to send to Rome via East Aros. It would just get stuck in some clerk's document-box until the new appointment is made. Some Folkunga favourite, presumably.' Bishop Örjan muttered the last comment under his breath and drank another mouthful.

'There you are, then,' he said, clearly unable to stop talking. 'I'll honour my oath taken on Mother Rikissa's deathbed and travel southwards to hand over her last words to my dear Danish friend, Bishop Absalon, in Lund. He'll take it to Rome.'

He drank some more, and began stroking Cecilia Rosa's thigh. She thought him utterly nauseating but controlled herself, giggled, and filled his tankard to the brim once more. After all, now she had another piece of crucial information.

Realising that she had all she needed, it seemed worth at least trying the probably hopeless task of making this Episcopal fool see some sense. She began by pointing out again that she and Cecilia Blanca had spent more than six years together as the closest of friends. That one of them should have taken her vows without telling the other was unthinkable.

Bishop Örjan made an effort to sound stern and told her the vows given to God would be forever beyond human knowledge.

Cecilia Rosa suggested that maybe His Most Reverend didn't have a very good idea of what happened in nunneries? If someone took her vows, she must go into her novice year. This meant testing her ability to live like a nun, almost completely separated from *conversae* and *familiares*. If Cecilia Blanca had taken her vows, this would instantly have made it known.

The Bishop had reached the incoherent stage by now and only

mumbled something about how God, and He alone, can see into the soul of human beings.

'But you must have heard Mother Rikissa admit that she was lying in her last confession and hiding her mortal sins. Surely that doesn't make her a very trustworthy witness? Especially not about serious matters such as the Queen having taken vows and then gone on to have four children. They would all have been born in sin. This is what it's all about, isn't it?'

'Well, that's not so easy to . . .' rambled the bishop, then pulled himself together. 'Yes, that's mostly what it's all about. The sinning must be the main thing. Regardless. Would you like to accompany me on the trip to Denmark?'

'I hardly think . . .'

'Of course I must remain celibate, officially that is, but there are ways and means. Speaking of means, I'm not so badly off now, actually.'

By now Cecilia Rosa felt dirty, as if the bishop had thrown muck at her. Still, she was well enough informed.

She rose, mumbled that for unmentionable female reasons she had to withdraw, slid out off his fumbling grip, and left. She was not very drunk at all, but outside in the fresh air she vomited. She prayed all that night. Awareness of her sins took away her sleep. She had tricked a bishop and almost seduced him, letting him touch her with sinful intent in order to betray him into admitting things he didn't want to tell her.

All this was shameful, but worst of all was that his touch had fired her longing in a way she had constantly tried to suppress. Helplessly, she was imagining how Arn Magnusson would look when he came riding in to get her. That such a vile man should have lit the flame of her pure love was – or so she felt then – an almost unforgivable sin.

The following day she concluded her business at Godshome, and had soon bought all the plants and handicraft items she needed from a disoriented Prioress, who could easily have been defrauded had Cecilia Rosa not helped her with benign advice. It seemed that the Holy Virgin was going to rule Godshome again, which should make everyone feel joy and respect.

As she got ready to leave, she thought that those who stayed in Godshome needed to step carefully on the flagged floors of the cloisters. Mother Rikissa was certainly not in Paradise; she might well be lurking just under the stones, her red eyes glowing evilly, ready to rise like a wolf and swallow someone she hated. After all, her entire life had been governed by hate.

Cecilia Rosa had arranged to stay with Cecilia Blanca at Näs on her way back to Riseberga. When she arrived in the royal harbour she had to wait while her rather irritable retinue of men unloaded and stacked her purchases. They obviously couldn't see the point of this stuff at all. She left them to it and walked down towards the rather threatening black ship that was waiting for her. Then she looked out over Vättern and turned very pale. The huge lake was covered with foaming waves, driven by the fierce gusts of the first autumn storm.

She asked for the leader of the ship. His name was Styrbjørn Haraldsson, and he greeted her politely, adding that it would be a pleasure to sail the friend of their Queen to Näs.

'Is it really advisable to sail in a storm like this?' she asked anxiously.

'That's the kind of question that makes me long to be back home in Norway,' he replied with a smile. 'Still, I can't go because I've sworn to serve King Knut.'

Then he silently led her by the hand across a stout plank onto the boat. His men were already preparing to haul in the moorings. They carried her goods on board with strong arms, stacking everything neatly. Then the square sail was set.

The wind filled it at once and made the ship fly forward with such a jerk that Cecilia Rosa, who was still standing, was thrown back into Styrbjørn's arms. He placed her next to the rudder and wrapped her up to the tip of her nose in coarse blankets and sheepskins.

The storm was roaring around them in the gathering darkness and the waves were foaming white against the ship's sides. The vessel leaned over so sharply that Cecilia Rosa felt she was looking up into the sky with its torn clouds on one side, while on the other the dark depths threatened. She was stiff with fear for a long while, before forcing herself to be sensible.

She told herself that none of these strange, big men seemed the slightest bit perturbed. Mostly they just sat there, now and then even joking with each other. Styrbjørn Haraldsson was standing upright with his hand on the rudder, the wind tearing at his long hair and a pleased grin on his face. He must be enjoying the whole thing.

Cecilia could not hold back asking whether the sailors felt someone divine was protecting them, but she had to shout it several times before Styrbjørn grasped what she was saying. At first he just laughed hugely, his face partly hidden by his windswept hair. Then he shouted back that she should have been there when they rowed out against the wind. Sailing with the wind was like a dance and they'd arrive within the half-hour.

He was as good as his word. Suddenly they were speeding across the waves towards Näs castle. Then the men leapt at the oars while Styrbjørn quickly hauled down the sail. On the left side, the men plunged the oars in the water first and began dragging them backwards. The men on the right meanwhile rowed forward powerfully. The effect was of a giant hand pushing the ship round against the wind, and they reached land after only ten-odd strokes. Even Cecilia Rosa realised the skill of the manoeuvre and felt ashamed of her early fears.

When Styrbjørn took her hand to escort her up the path from the mooring quay, she apologised, a little shyly, for having been so bothered – she realised now that she'd had no reason to worry at all. He smiled, and told her that many a lady from West Gothland didn't have the faintest idea of the sea or seagoing ships. Why, he recalled, once they'd taken a lady across who'd asked them if they didn't get lost out there on the water. This made him burst out in his huge laugh again, while Cecilia smiled vaguely. She couldn't think what was wrong with the lady's question.

Then she and Cecilia Blanca fell into each other's arms. The Queen kept repeating for everyone to hear that this was her dearest, dearest friend. Her speech flowed as eagerly and unstoppably as the lark's singing in spring. She called servants to deal with Cecilia Rosa's strange luggage, all bristling plants and rolls of cloth, and hurried her friend through many gloomy halls until they reached a room with a roaring fire, and hot wine standing ready in a jug. The very best thing to revive you after a chilly journey, she insisted.

Cecilia Rosa was warmed and delighted by her friend's loving reception, but the knowledge of what she had to tell her was like an ache inside her. She knew she must broach the subject soon, but it wasn't easy to interrupt Cecilia Blanca's flow of words.

'The King and Birger Brosa are away in East Aros to sort out this tiresome business about the Archbishop,' she said. 'Did you hear, some beastly plunderers from across the Baltic killed the old one when they sacked Sigtuna. The Estonians set fire to the whole place, you know, so it's time for another crusade. All the men are frightfully busy, what with needing ships and army recruits and so on. The good thing is, I'm in charge here at Näs when my menfolk are away so we can do what we like, you and I. Let's sit up all night and talk and drink too much wine!'

For a while Cecilia Rosa was pulled along by her friend's irresistible happiness. After all, it was a real celebration. Now they were all free, the three friends from Godshome. Then she was struck by the memory of her last visit to Godshome, but still could say nothing because Cecilia Blanca wanted to tell her about little Ulvhilde.

'Not so little, any more,' Cecilia Blanca said. 'Ulvhilde is expecting her first baby! Of course, not with the eldest son. The moment I saw Folke I just knew he wasn't right for Ulvhilde. Too pushy by far. Instead Ulvhilde took a fancy to the younger brother, Jon, who's interested in the law. Instead of trying to impress her with the rattling of armour, he kept talking about founding the realm on law and things like that. Sings like an angel too, so it wasn't hard to guess how things would work out. They have to get married really quickly, now that most people have worked out that she's expecting.'

'But isn't that very bad? I for one know how much that can cost young people!'

'No, no. Times have changed, you know. Besides, whoever they choose as the new Archbishop is not going to be too keen to ban somebody who's under the protection of the King and I. Ulvhilde's little sin will soon be blessed by God and forgotten. She's so happy, the little one! Freedom suits her.'

Relieved that Ulvhilde would not be exposed to the horrors that had befallen Arn and herself, Cecilia Rosa finally managed to hold up her hands to stop her friend's happy chatter and tell her the truth – she had bad news from Godshome. That made Cecilia Blanca fall silent at once.

But it began badly. When Cecilia Rosa drew a deep breath and broke the news that Mother Rikissa was dead and buried, Cecilia Blanca immediately clapped her hands with delight and burst out laughing. She quickly pulled herself together, crossed herself and, lifting her eyes towards the ceiling, said a small prayer to the effect that she was sorry to have sinned by taking pleasure in a Christian woman's death.

Then she smiled again and said that it wasn't such bad news after all.

Cecilia Rosa started all over again. She had not got very far with her story of the false confession and the last letter to Rome before Cecilia Blanca became very serious. When the story was done, they sat together in silence for a while. What could be said about the central lie? It was preposterous to think that any girl who had

278

endured the harsh life in Godshome, let alone the regular beatings, would make the crazed decision to take the veil in just that cloister. The mere thought that Cecilia Blanca, longing for her betrothed and for her royal crown, would do such a thing was like saying that birds flew in the water or fish swam in the sky.

Then Cecilia Blanca took her friend to meet the children before they settled down to spend what they knew would be a long night together.

Her oldest, Erik, had gone with his father to East Aros to learn about the royal duties. The two younger boys and the little girl, Brigida, were fighting about a wooden horse and the woman who looked after them could not stop the row before Cecilia Blanca came in. The children quietened down at once, but looked askance at Cecilia Rosa's strange clothes. Cecilia Blanca told them to say their evening prayers and then the two women amazed them by singing a hymn more beautifully than anything heard in Näs before. The children went to bed at once afterwards, still chattering excitedly about what their mother could do.

Back in their quiet room, where a fresh jug of hot wine was waiting for them, Cecilia Blanca explained that once she had become free, she somehow hadn't felt like singing again. Now she was embarrassed at having dropped it and said that it was different when they were singing together. It reminded her of how their precious friendship had sustained them on the many dark mornings when they had stumbled over icy floors to sing at the miserable lauds.

Then they settled by the fire, drank some wine, and tried to understand what to do for the best. Rikissa's intention had obviously been to provide evidence for a declaration by the Holy Father that the King of West and East Gothland and Sviarland was living in sin with a whore. That would mean that neither the little earl, Erik, nor either of his brothers, could ever succeed to the crown. It was logical that Rikissa should have wanted her lying message to go directly to Rome and that she'd decide to use a Dane as a mediator. The Sverkers had many friends in Denmark and there had been much inter-marriage. The arrival of Danish and Sverker armies to force the end of the Erik grip on the crown was the firestorm that Rikissa had threatened on her deathbed. She had calculated it all.

But the entire calculation was based on a lie, Cecilia Blanca said. What her last letter and testament said was simply not true. Maybe this would not be clear to Rome, but their own Archbishop would surely read between the lines. Could the lie succeed? Rikissa had sacrificed her own soul, like a suicide. It was frightening to think that there were people so wicked that they could contemplate their own soul burning in the eternal fires in exchange for revenge on Earth.

Maybe she saw it as the ultimate sacrifice for the sake of her kin, Cecilia Rosa suggested, much as a father or mother would sacrifice all for a child. This was still chilling but believable, especially for those who had suffered Rikissa's presence here on Earth. Suddenly they felt cold in the warm room. Cecilia Blanca went over to her friend, kissed her, wrapped her in sheepskins and called for more wine.

Then they tried to exorcise Rikissa's spirit and comfort themselves with the fact that at least they had enough information in good time to construct a defence. They would tell Birger Brosa; perhaps he could suggest how best to deal with this.

'Tell me more about Ulvhilde,' Cecilia Rosa asked. 'I can't believe that she became ready to wed the moment she stuck her nose outside the walls. Bride is all very well, but leaping into bed with the man is something else. Do you think it's really a good idea? What if she was just a lamb to the slaughter? I mean, here she meets the first two young men in her entire life and promptly marries one of them!'

'It seems a good idea to me,' Cecilia Blanca said happily. 'I know Jon now and think he's just right for her, as I said before. Besides, it's a union between the Sverker and Folkunga kin, which is a really good thing. There are people who're made for each other, like you and Arn. Maybe that's true about Jon and Ulvhilde too. Judge for yourself this Christmas,' she added. 'The Christmas Feast here at Näs will be really big and we'll all be here.'

This made Cecilia Rosa lose herself in thought for a moment. How easy it was now that she was free. Her dear friend the Queen had invited her to a Christmas feast. It was up to herself, Cecilia Rosa, to say yes or no. She would say yes, of course, but the option of saying no seemed a vital part of her new liberty.

Then she fell asleep, her glass still in her hand. She was unused to freedom, which also allowed her to drink as much hot wine as she liked. Cecilia Blanca called her maids and together they carried the sleeping lady to bed.

The next day Cecilia Rosa's transformation began. The Queen's maids washed and bathed her and spent hours on her hair, their careful brushing and cutting slowly removing the signs of the ugly cloister cut.

Cecilia Blanca had carefully planned the new clothes she would give her friend. Certainly not the finest, because the contrast would be too great between the crude, undyed cloister clothes and the precious robes of the mistress of a castle. Obviously Cecilia Rosa would be far too proud to move into Näs as the Queen's friend and so she would have to stay on at Riseberga for a while.

She understood perfectly that Cecilia Rosa longed for Arn Magnusson to come home. He might or he might not; it was impossible to know, and it was no good talking about Arn now, because only time would bring the answer, for better or for worse.

Cecilia Blanca thought that Cecilia Rosa might like to continue her travels still wearing a brown mantle, but a light and warm garment made from finest lambswool. A mantle in family colours would entail a delicate decision that was impossible to make at this stage. Cecilia Rosa had the right to the green mantle of the Pal kin, or the option of wearing the Folkunga mantle, but however warmly they agreed that Arn and Cecilia were betrothed in the face of God, the fact was that the Church recognised nothing of the sort.

When it came to dresses, the choice was much less troublesome, because an *yconoma* in a cloister could surely wear what she pleased. She had instructed her dressmaker to make a green dress in a shade that should suit Cecilia Rosa's red hair. Instead of the boring black veil, her friend would get a blue one in the Folkunga shade they had learnt to mix so exactly during their mantle-making years.

Getting Cecilia Rosa to wear all this took a little persuasion and practice. Then Cecilia Blanca demanded that her friend walk about for a whole day without a veil, getting used to exposing her hair. It had to work, because that evening they had guests at the table and there was yet another dress to try and definitely no veil this time. Cecilia Blanca produced a very handsome green dress, to be worn with a silver belt, and a silver clasp for her friend's hair. When Cecilia Rosa was dressed, the Queen marched her into her own rooms and made her look at herself in the long, standing mirror.

At first Cecilia Rosa was struck dumb at her own image. Her face remained impassive, almost vacant. Then she burst into uncontrollable tears, and it took a long time and many soothing words before Cecilia Blanca could persuade her to express what was troubling her.

'I'm so old and ugly,' she sobbed. 'This isn't me as I believed I was, it's someone else. I don't know her, she's an old woman.'

Cecilia Blanca looked at her sympathetically, kissed her and then smiled. Taking her friend by the hand, she led her back to the mirror and stood next to her.

'Look at us both now,' she said, pretending to be very strict. 'I've seen you for many years as you've seen me, but I've not looked hard at myself. Now I will, and I see a big belly and floppy breasts and chubby cheeks. Next to me stands another woman of my age to whom the years have been much kinder. The mirror doesn't lie. You're thirty-seven, still beautiful and young-looking for your age. I'm forty and look it. Please don't feel time has treated you ill, dearest Cecilia Rosa.'

Cecilia Rosa stood still and silent for a little longer, then she turned away from the mirror and hugged Cecilia Blanca.

'Please forgive me. Not having been able to see myself as I am for all these years has made me so silly,' she said, and soon seemed to recover her happy mood.

But Cecilia Blanca was worried about her friend's state of mind – there was no telling now how she'd react to the guests that evening – or at least, to one of them in particular. She realised that she'd been holding on to her secret for long enough. Among the guests at the feast, riding in from the northern end of Visingsö and travelling from Bjälbo, would be Magnus Moonshield. He had wanted to be there so that he could meet his mother. Should she keep silent and let the two of them find out about each other in their own time? Or was it better to let Cecilia Rosa know, even though it would cause her anxiety? She made up her mind to tell the truth while there was still time.

She asked Cecilia Rosa to come and have her hair brushed in front of the mirror to calm her, and chatted about this and that.

'Magnus Moonshield is coming tonight you know,' she said casually. 'Would you like us to ride out to meet him?'

Cecilia Rosa became very still. Her eyes, fixed on her mirror image, slowly filled with tears. Cecilia Blanca began to worry, but kept brushing the beautiful if still too short hair.

'Yes, let's,' Cecilia Rose finally said in a toneless voice.

The storm had died down by the time the two women rode out alone from Näs and turned northwards. They said little other than remarking how well Cecilia Rosa rode or how beautiful the evening was.

Then three men in wide Folkunga mantles came riding out from a small wood of large oaks. The first rider was the youngest and the setting sun glowed in his red hair. When they saw the Queen and her female companion they reined in their horses. The young man dismounted and walked forward, leading his horse.

Proper behaviour would have required Cecilia Rosa to stay calmly seated on her horse until the man had reached her, bowed and offered his hand to help her dismount for an exchange of polite greetings. Cecilia Rosa might have remembered all this at the age of seventeen, but it was possible that she had forgotten the rules of conduct during her many years locked away from the world.

Whatever the case, she jumped off her horse, as agile as if she *were* seventeen, at once hurrying off to meet the young man with strides too long for her sweeping green skirts.

When Magnus Moonshield saw her, he ran towards her. They met in the woodland meadow, and embraced without saying a word.

After a long moment of holding each other close, mother and son stepped back, hands on each other's shoulders, and looked into each other's faces. What they saw were their mirror images. Alone in Birger Brosa's family, Magnus had brown eyes and red hair.

Speechless, they kept gazing at each other. Then the young man kneeled, took Cecilia's right hand in his, and kissed it tenderly. This was the sign that he recognised her as his lawful mother.

When he rose, he offered her his hand. She placed her own hand on his, and he escorted her courteously back to her horse and kneeling again after handing her the reins, bent forward so that she could step into the saddle from his back. Only when he had completed the formalities, did he trust himself to speak.

'I've thought and dreamt much of you ... mother,' he said, sounding a little uncertain. 'I felt I might recognise you, though not at all as well as I have. And I did not dare believe, despite everything Birger Brosa told me, that you should seem to me more like a sister than a mother. Mother, would you graciously permit me to escort you at the feast this evening?'

'I think I just might, my dear son,' Cecilia Rosa said, smiling broadly at her young son's stiff, shy manner.

Magnus Moonshield was very young, with fluff rather than beard on his cheeks, but he had grown up in the castles of power. His manners were perfectly schooled, without any boyish awkwardness, and he wore his Folkunga mantle with the assurance of someone who well understood its value. That he knew its significance well enough was shown by his insisting, as they came closer to Näs, that Cecilia Rosa should wear his mantle for protection against the chill of the evening. He did not say that this was how he wanted her to enter the royal castle for the first time in his company, but his mother understood perfectly well.

At the feast he drank his beer like a man, while the two Cecilias preferred wine. Most of the talk between them was about the

Godshome imprisonment, because he had no concept of what it might have been like. This was how he learnt that he had actually been born in Godshome and something of how it had been.

But the Cecilias, using the secret cloister sign language, had already exchanged thoughts about how soon Magnus would start asking about his father. The first cautious questions about Arn Magnusson and his skills with sword and longbow came soon enough and Cecilia Rosa spoke warmly and easily, because by now her earlier fears had been swept away by her happiness. She said that although she had seen little of Arn's exploits herself, there were many stories, and of course she had seen him shoot brilliantly well once at a Husaby feast.

Cecilia Blanca immediately predicted in sign language behind his back, *He'll ask how good his father had been exactly.*

'What did my father do then, exactly?' Magnus asked.

'He hit a silver coin with first one and then a second arrow from twenty-five paces away,' Cecilia Rosa promptly explained. 'Well, it might've been twenty paces. Anyway, definitely a silver coin.'

Young Magnus sat stunned for a moment. Then he gave his mother a long hug. Behind his back Cecilia Blanca signed, *Was it really a silver coin?*

Well, maybe an unusually large silver coin, Cecilia Rosa signed back, and then gave herself over to the joy of being in her son's arms. In the smell of his body she detected a message reminding her of love and youth.

Just before the Feast of Catherine, in weather so cold it warned of a hard winter ahead, Birger Brosa arrived at Riseberga on an urgent visit. He had no more time for the Prioress Beata than minimal politeness demanded, given that the cloister belonged to the Virgin Mary. Mostly, Birger Brosa anyway saw it as his own property.

His main errand concerned the *yconoma*, and because it was too cold to speak in comfort outside, she invited him into her counting chambers, built according to the same idea as in Godshome. He asked some questions about business at first, but his thoughts were obviously elsewhere, and he constantly referred to his crusade in the east, planned to start in the spring.

Then he got round to his real errand. Because there was still no Abbess at Riseberga and because Cecilia Rosa had such long experience of the world inside the walls, she could have the post if she took the vows now. He had spoken about this with the new

Archbishop, who apparently did not see any problems and seemed impatient for an answer as soon as possible.

Cecilia Rosa felt as exhausted as if they had been fighting. She could not fathom why the Earl, who knew Cecilia Blanca so well, should ever imagine that she, Cecilia Rosa, would be prepared to take the vows. She pulled herself together and asked, keeping her eyes locked with his, what the true intention was behind his suggestion. She was not stupid and no one was wiser than the Earl of the Realm. What was all this about, in clear language?

Birger Brosa smiled his familiar wide smile, pulled one leg up and sat back, looking at Cecilia Rosa. Then he spoke out, but not without circumspection.

'You would be an ornament among our Folkunga wives, Cecilia. You are already, in many ways and that's why I come to make this heavy demand on you.'

'Demand?' Cecilia Rosa was frightened enough to interrupt him.

'Well – let's call it a question. Only Eskil in our family can match your skills with counting and managing business. You know that Eskil, Arn's brother, is actually managing the business side of our realm. I can see that you're not easily persuaded by pretty phrases, so I'll be blunt. We need an Abbess who can counter the falsehood of another Abbess. That's my reason for asking you.'

'You might have told me that at once, my dear Earl,' Cecilia Rosa said with a snort. 'So that old liar's fakery has reached Rome?'

'Yes, her letter was taken there by bearers who were only too willing,' Birger Brosa said bitterly. 'As if we didn't have enough to deal with in these rebellious easterners, who need to be curbed once and for all. Now there could be a big war on the horizon, unless we act quickly.'

'A big war against the Sverker kin and the Danes?'

'Yes, that's it.'

'Because were Rikissa's lies to be believed, then Knut's son Erik would be a bastard?'

'I'm afraid so.'

'And if I take my vows and become an Abbess, it'll be my word against that of another Abbess?'

'Yes. And then you'd have saved the realm from war.'

This silenced Cecilia Rosa. Of all the sharp minds in the realm, the Earl's was the sharpest, and she must not let the discussion rush ahead out of her control. She must have time to think.

'God's ways of steering the fate of men and women are very strange,' she resumed, sounding more pompous than she felt.

'Strange indeed,' Birger Brosa replied.

'Now, Rikissa sold her soul to cause war in the land, isn't that strange?'

'Yes, yes. Couldn't be stranger.' Birger Brosa was clearly getting impatient.

'And now you want me to hand my soul over to the Virgin Mary, while I'm still alive on Earth to – shall we say – cancel out Rikissa's deal with the Devil,' Cecilia Rosa said, looking innocent.

'In a nutshell, yes, my dear Cecilia. Very crisply put.'

'Do you know what they'll say? They'll say that this brand-new Abbess was once a maiden with every reason to hate Rikissa and refused to forgive her, even as she lay dying, and that's why her word is worth nought.' Cecilia Rosa's voice sounded so harsh, she surprised herself more than the Earl.

'Your mind is clear and ruthless,' Birger Brosa answered after a moment's silence. 'Consider the opportunity for yourself as well as the immense good you'll do by helping to avoid a war. You'll be the highest and Riseberga will be your domain where you rule like a queen. This has nothing to do with bread and water and the scourge under Rikissa's hard regime. Could you think of anything to do with your life that would better serve your kin, your King and Queen and your land?'

'You're ruthless now, Birger Brosa. Don't you know what I've spent the last twenty years hoping and praying for? Can't your warrior's soul grasp what spending twenty years in a steel cage has been like? I speak so frankly not only because what you ask me makes me despair, but also because I know you care for me and won't mind my openness.'

'My dear Cecilia Rosa, what you say is true. Of course it's true . . .'

Now that the Earl seemed to have weakened, Cecilia Rosa left him for a moment without a word of explanation. When she returned she held a particularly splendid Folkunga mantle in her hands. She let it fall open this way and that, so that the light from the wax candles glittered on the golden threads forming the lion on the back. She exposed the fur lining so that he could touch the soft skins of winter martens. He nodded admiringly but said nothing.

'It's taken me two years to make,' Cecilia Rosa explained quietly. 'It's been my dream to fashion it better than anything we can yet produce here at Riseberga.'

'It's a remarkable piece of work. The blue is unusually beautiful and the lion is drawn with real vigour and strength.' Birger Brosa sounded thoughtful, because he felt he knew what she would say next.

'My dear kinsman, can you guess for whom I've made this mantle?'

'Yes, and I wish to God that you'll one day place it over Arn Magnusson's shoulders, Cecilia Rosa. And don't underrate me, I have more insight than you think into what your twenty years of waiting has been like and what you dreamt while you were stitching this mantle. But you shall have to listen to me, nonetheless. If Arn does not return, I'll buy this mantle from you for the day Magnus Moonshield is wed, or Erik Knutsson is crowned, or whatever occasion suits my fancy. You cannot demand from your kin the right to wait forever, Cecilia.'

'Then let us pray for Arn's return,' she replied with lowered eyelids.

Not even an earl can refuse such a request, and especially not in his own cloister. He nodded, and they kneeled together among the account books and the abacuses and prayed for Arn's salvation and safe return to his homeland.

Cecilia Rosa prayed with the fervency of a love that still burnt as brightly as ever after twenty years; a love that she would rather die than betray.

The Earl prayed for several reasons, but sincerely. His main concern was that if he could not produce a trustworthy Abbess, then good fighters would be badly needed in the Folkunga forces. From what he had gathered over the years from the now late Father Henri at Varnhem, Arn Magnusson was God's own warrior in more than one way. It could well be that his skill would be put to much use in his homeland.

XI

Arn was cared for in the Hamidiyeh Hospital in Damascus. It was the best, but it still took his doctors two weeks to finally control his fever. They agreed this was providential, because no one could live for much longer in that state. He had already had countless scars on his body – more than a hundred, he thought – but had never been as badly injured as at the Horns of Hattin.

He remembered little of what had happened. They had got the chain-mail off him and stitched the worst of his gaping wounds before taking him, and their own wounded, up a hillside for coolness and milder winds. The transport had caused terrible suffering and most of them started bleeding again. The doctors still insisted that this was preferable to staying in the heat and the foul stench of corpses near Tiberias. He could not remember how he got to Damascus at all, because by then his fever was raging.

The hospital doctors had re-opened many of his wounds, tried to clean them, and stitched them up again with more care than in the field surgery. His worst injuries had been caused by a deep sword which had entered his calf through his armour, and by a powerful blow with an axe, which had cracked his helmet just above the left eye, tearing the left side of his forehead and eyebrow.

At first, he could not keep any food down and his headaches had been so murderously painful that the mists of feverishness were merciful. He didn't remember feeling much pain, not even when they cauterised his leg wound with red-hot irons.

When he came to and could think clearly for the first time, he realised that his sight had not been affected, although one of his last distinct memories was of being unable to see with his left eye. He looked around and found himself in a beautifully proportioned, blue-tiled room. Outside the widows tall palm-trees gave shade.

They rustled peacefully in the wind, and he could hear fountains playing in the courtyard below.

The enemy doctors, who were coldly polite, had treated him with every professional skill. There was a small black disc with golden Arab lettering above his bed, saying that this man was worth more to Saladin alive than dead. They acted accordingly, even though rumour had it that this was one of the white demons with red crosses.

When Arn became well enough, his doctors were delighted to find that their patient could speak properly and gathered round his bed to listen, astonished that a Knight Templar was expressing himself so well in the language of God. Doctors in Damascus were ignorant of what every amir in the army knew about the man whom they called Al Ghouti.

The leading doctor was called Abu Amran Musa and had travelled north from Cairo where he had been Saladin's personal medical advisor for many years. His Arabic accent sounded strange to Arn's ears, and the reason was that Abu Amran Musa had been born far away in the state of Andalusia. Life there had become hard for Jews, he explained to Arn in their first talk together. Arn had not been surprised to hear that Saladin's doctor was a Jew, because he was already aware that the Caliph in Baghdad employed many Jews.

Since Arn knew that Saracen doctors were usually well versed in both theology and philosophy, he asked about Jerusalem's importance to Jews. Abu Amran Musa raised an eyebrow at this, wondering why a Christian warrior should bother to ask. Arn told him of his meeting with the Chief Rabbi from Baghdad during his time as Master of Jerusalem and the decision he'd made about giving the Jews access to the sacred place.

'The Christians venerate the Holy Sepulchre of their God and the Muslims the Rock from which the Prophet, peace be with him, rose to Paradise. Both are understandable goals for pilgrims,' said Arn, then asked, 'but this temple of David, a man-made building, why is it important?'

'Jerusalem is our most sacred place and the prophets foresaw the day when we would return to our land and rebuild the Temple,' replied the doctor.

Arn sighed deeply and sorrowfully and the doctor looked at him with concern.

'Thank you for the explanation. It's obviously not the Jewish aspirations that worry me,' Arn assured his new-found friend, 'but the fate of Jerusalem affects me greatly. If it's not in Muslim occupation already, it soon will be, and then the Christians will stop at nothing to take it back. The last thing Jerusalem needs is yet another faction going to war about it. If the Jews enter into the fray the warfare will go on for a thousand years or more.'

Abu Amran Musa went to find himself a small stool to sit on by Arn's bed; he had decided that this discussion was the most important thing happening in the hospital just then.

'On two separate occasions I've discussed the fate of Jerusalem with serious men, enemies on the battlefield but who seem to think remarkably alike,' Arn continued. 'One is a Christian, Count Raymond of Tripoli, and the other a Muslim, none other than Saladin himself. Both argued that the only way to stop this never-ending conflict is to give all pilgrims the same rights, regardless of whether the place is called Jerusalem or Al Quds.'

'Or Yerushalyaim,' Abu Amran Musa said with a smile.

'Yes, indeed. This was what I had in mind when I advised the Chief Rabbi that praying by the West Wall was perfectly in order, even though I couldn't quite see why it was so important. Let's discuss this with Saladin once we hear that he's controlling the city.'

After entering into this pact, their friendship grew. After a few weeks the doctor insisted that Arn must get out of bed and start using his injured leg. The timing was crucial. Too late and it would weaken, too soon and the wound would heal badly or even open up again.

They began by taking little promenades among the ponds, fountains and palm-trees in the atrium courtyard. It was easy walking because of the smooth mosaic tiling that went right up to the trunks of the palms. After a while Arn was lent some clothes and they took their first walks together in the city, picking the great Damascus mosque as their first goal. They could not enter it, both being unbelievers, but were allowed into the huge central courtyard with its gold-tiled Christian cloisters, and floors from the Umayyad era in intricate patterns created from black, red and white marble. Arn was amazed to see the Byzantine Christian imagery left undisturbed, since the Muslims would view its humans and saints as offensive to God. The mosque must have been a church before the huge minaret devoted it to another faith.

His friend pointed out that it was the other way round in the case of the two large Jerusalem mosques, which were used as churches. It seems rational, he argued, that at least these sacred buildings are kept in one piece. Whoever takes over only needs to remove the crescent or the cross to get on with worshipping in these great spaces. After all, he remarked, imagine if you actually had to rebuild after each occupation.

They talked intensively about the Jewish faith, because Arn was eager to learn. Abu Amran Musa suggested that he should start by reading a little book he'd written himself called 'Guide for the Perplexed'. When Arn had got into the book, their discussions became endless because the learned doctor's goal was to find a religion that would link rationalism and faith, the teachings of Aristotle and the revealed truths. To fuse such concepts must be the finest task of philosophy, he insisted passionately.

Arn followed all this with some difficulty, for – as he said more than once – so much scholarship seemed to have been drained out of his head since his youth, when Aristotle's works had been part of his everyday learning. He agreed that no goal could be worthier than to make men see reason. Blind, unreasonable faith led to disasters worse than any earthquake, as the wars in the Holy Land demonstrated with awesome clarity. In his view, it was a kind of Devil's own miracle that men can walk across a land heaving with mindless suffering, and still see, hear and feel nothing.

As time passed, the scabs on Arn's wounds dried and fell off, leaving red but healing scars. At the same time, the warm, mutual friendship with Abu Amran Musa healed and stimulated him. Their unending talk loosened constraints on his thought after twenty years of obedience to unalterable rules.

He realised that by grappling with abstractions every day he could push to the back of his mind the awareness of what was happening in the here and now, but it grew impossible to keep knowledge at bay once he started speaking more to fellow patients in the Hamidiyeh hospital. They were jubilant as news came in about the fall of Acre and Nablus and then of Beirut and Jebail. This, and the many happily reported stories of sacked fortresses, made it hard for Arn to be the only Christian stranded in a flow of Christian misfortunes. Quite how bad the situation was did not become clear until Fahkr came to visit him, although in the beginning they spoke of quite different matters.

Both were delighted to meet again and hugged like brothers, which caused quite a stir in the hospital. Everyone knew that the visitor was Saladin's own brother.

Fahkr reminded Arn, who had already reflected on this more than once, of their joking together when Fahkr had been Arn's prisoner in Gaza; how, as he left for Alexandria, Fahkr had said he hoped it would one day be as agreeable for Arn to be his prisoner. God must have approved of the joke, he said. Then Fahkr grew serious.

'Al Ghouti, do any of your rules oblige you to attack Muslims while you're here? If so let, me know. We may just have to keep you more securely, now that you're getting mobile again.'

'My dear Fahkr, nothing of the sort. You have my word that I'll be as peaceful as is proper for a guest. I would say that Knights Templar always keep their word, but as it happens my oath of service in the Order came to an end on the evening of the battle at Hattin's Horns.'

'It must be a sign from God who is merciful that your life was saved at that very moment!'

'I think it's more Saladin who's been merciful this time, though I must say I can't remember much about it.'

Fahkr did not reply but hung a great medallion with Saladin's sign round Arn's neck, took his arm and nodded meaningfully toward the street. Arn, who still felt oddly naked in his borrowed clothes of light cotton, so different from the weight of his chain-mail, walked with him along the street. This time is was not just his blonde head that attracted attention, but the fact that he was walking with a Muslim and, to crown it all, a Muslim who was the Sultan's brother. Seeing a Christian taking a daily stroll in the company of a Jew had been much less startling.

Fahkr, a little irritated by the excitement they were causing, dragged Arn with him into the souk next to the mosque and bought some lengths of cloth. He twisted them together into a turban to cover the offending blonde hair, and then picked out a couple of Syrian mantles for Arn to choose between. Arn thought he recognised the blue Folkunga shade and decided that it was his lucky colour.

Now the two men were indistinguishable from the crowds in the winding streets of the souk. After a while they arrived in a small square piled high with Christian weaponry, including swords and helmets. Fahkr explained the reason for going there: he had promised Saladin that he would buy Arn a sword because, as Saladin had put it, Arn was owed a sword and a very fine one, in return for a gift he had sent him.

The merchant had pulled out the more costly items from the big pile and sorted them into two lots. The smallest lot contained what he regarded as the most splendid pieces, presumably once owned by Christian kings and high noblemen and inlaid and ornamented with gold and precious stones. The bigger pile consisted of perfectly decent and reasonably unscathed pieces of merchandise. Arn went straight to the mountain of cheap weapons and raked about until he had found three swords of the Knights Templar type with the right size numbers. He compared them, made up his mind and handed one to Fahkr.

'What? This is a mean-looking thing. You're losing a fortune by not taking one of those over there. Don't be stubborn – Saladin wanted the best for you!'

'I don't agree. These jewel-encrusted things suit men who never use their swords except for show. I've chosen the only sword I'd ever have at my side, a Templar weapon of the right weight and length.'

'Come on, come on. Tell you what, take an expensive one, this one, say. Then sell it, buy your cheap sword and keep the difference.'

'That's not right! I'd hardly honour Saladin's gift by that kind of horse-trading,' Arn told him crossly.

But still Fahkr wouldn't let him have his plain sword there and then. He went over to the merchant and negotiated something in whispers that Arn couldn't hear. Then they wandered away, still swordless, towards Saladin's palace where they were to spend the evening and night. Saladin might get back to Damascus in time to meet them. He wanted to see Al Ghouti as one of his first priorities, Fahkr said.

Saladin's palace was near the great mosque but was not one of the bigger buildings. It was simply decorated and constructed with just two floors. If it had not been for the two hard-faced Mameluke guards at the door, it could have been the home of any ordinary citizen. Inside, the rooms were sparingly furnished with carpets and cushions, but the walls were beautifully decorated with quotations from the Quran, which Arn amused himself by trying to translate.

Finally they reached an inner room with an arcade balcony. Fahkr ordered cold water and passion fruit to be served, settling back with an expression that clearly said this was a time for serious talk.

First, the state of the Holy Land. All that remained of the Christian territory in Palestine was Tyrus, Gaza, Ashkelon, Jerusalem, and a handful of fortresses, he said in a tone of barely disguised triumph. Saladin's plan was to take Ashkelon and Gaza next and he wanted Arn to accompany him. Afterwards, they would march on Jerusalem, and then Saladin felt he particularly needed Arn's advice. He would explain his ideas to Arn as soon as he arrived, but had wished Fahkr to prepare the ground.

Arn said sadly that he'd known for a long time that this was the only possible outcome of the wars, and that the Christians had only themselves and, above all, their own sins to blame for this immense misfortune. It was the truth, and so was what he had said about no longer being bound by his oath to the Order of the Temple. But even so, they couldn't expect him to simply side with the enemies of the Christians.

Fahkr listened, pulled at his thin beard, and said that Arn had misunderstood and that the Sultan would not wish him to act against his own people. On the contrary, there was a feeling around that too many Christians had been killed or driven from their homes by now. Soon, enough would be enough. No, more important things were afoot, but it was probably better that Saladin himself should explain what he had in mind.

By the way, he added, technically Arn was of course a prisoner, but Fahkr felt sure that when the time was ripe he'd be freed. Clearly, Saladin wouldn't have spared his life at Hattin's Horns only to have him killed later on, and he wasn't the kind of prisoner who could earn any ransom worth having, Knight Templar or not. Be that as it may, one might ask oneself what Arn would do with his freedom.

Arn told him that, with his twenty years of service in the Holy Land now ended, he planned to go back to his own people. There was a snag, though. In order to be released formally, the Grand Master must sign the order to let him go. Not a straightforward proposition these days, but unless it was done he would end up a deserter.

His weary reflections had an unexpected effect. Fahkr beamed at him and told him to rub the little oil lamp on the table twice with his thumb. His wish would be fulfilled at once. Arn looked doubtfully at his Kurdish friend and tried to work out what the joke might be. When Fahkr kept smiling and nodding towards the lamp, Arn gave up and did as he was told.

'There Aladdin – your wish will be fulfilled,' Fahkr cried happily. 'I promise you any document you like, signed with your Grand Master's own hand and sealed with his seal. You see, he's our guest here in Damascus, though perhaps a little less cordially treated than you are, and quite rightly too. So just draft your document and have no fears!'

Arn could well imagine Gérard de Ridefort ending up a prisoner. The idea of him fighting to his last drop of blood simply wasn't credible, but would he sign documents on demand? Fahkr smiled slyly and assured Arn that all would be in order. He could watch himself when the Grand Master signed his release. Better sooner than later, Fahkr added, and ordered a servant to obtain the necessary writing materials in the souk. Then Arn was left alone to compose his document while Fahkr went off to pray and plan the evening meal.

Staring at the blank page of parchment in front of him, Arn sensed rather than thought about the strangeness of the situation. He was writing his own order of release, sitting cross-legged and turbaned on soft cushions in front of a Syrian writing desk in the Sultan's Damascus palace. During the last few years, he'd many times tried to imagine what the end of his service would be like, but his imagination had never come anywhere near this.

Then he concentrated on writing down the familiar phrases he had often written on behalf of others. There was an occasional extra paragraph, which he decided to add. It gave permission to knights leaving the order with honour to wear all the Templar insignia of their last rank. He read through what he'd written, recalled that de Ridefort of course knew no Latin and translated the text into Frankish. Since there was still some space left, he amused himself by writing it once more in Arabic to annoy the not very literate Grand Master.

Waving the parchment to dry, he cast a glance through the window at the level of the sun and reckoned that it was at least two hours before the Muslim and Christian evening prayers. At that point Fahkr returned and curiously read the Arab version. He approved, but was unable to resist improving on some of the diacritical marks. He seemed very pleased with the whole thing and said His Holiness the Grand Master would surely enjoy their little surprise too.

'An evening walk?' he said, offering Arn his arm. 'The better class of Christian prisoner is housed just a few blocks away. The house is actually costlier in every way than this one.'

It was a bigger, more elegant house but more heavily guarded, even though it was hard to imagine what an escapee Grand Master might find in the streets of Damascus. The whole thing was a charade, Fahkr said. It was set up when the Grand Master and King Guy snootily declared that word of honour given to infidels had no validity.

The two high-ranking prisoners were locked into two fine, handsomely decorated rooms with Christian-style furnishings.

When their visitors entered, the door behind them being demonstratively locked, the two men were playing chess at a delicately carved Arabic table.

'I notice that you're indulging in a game forbidden in the Templar rules,' Arn said, no longer bothering with politeness. 'I won't distract you for long, I hope. Grand Master, I've got a document for you to sign.'

Arn handed over the parchment with a slightly too deep bow. Strangely, Gérard de Ridefort seemed more submissive than angry. After trying to look as if he had been reading the text, he turned to Arn.

'And the general drift of your document is what, de Gothia?'

Arn took the sheet of parchment back, read out the Frankish text and pointed out that he'd after all only sworn his oath for a fixed period, which was not unusual.

Now Gérard de Ridefort lost his temper.

'I'm not signing this! If you, the former Master of Jerusalem, have a mind to desert, that's your affair! It's between you and your conscience, de Gothia. Off you go!'

He stared hard at the chessboard as if only interested in the next move. King Guy had said nothing throughout, just staring in complete bafflement at the sight of Arn's Saracen clothes. Fahkr had taken in the situation and decided it was time to intervene. He knocked lightly on the door and when it opened, whispered a few words through the crack before it closed again.

Then he went over to Arn, told him quietly that this would soon be arranged but maybe he'd better use another translator. With Fahkr's hand resting lightly on his shoulder, Arn was conducted out through the door, just as a man entered. The newcomer's appearance suggested a Syrian merchant rather than a soldier. Not very long afterwards, Fahkr emerged with the now properly signed and sealed document, handing it over with a deep bow.

'What did you say to make him change his mind so quickly?' Arn asked curiously, as they pushed their way back to the Sultan's palace through the heavy traffic in the streets, packed with people going to their evening prayers.

'Ah, nothing too serious,' Fahkr said lightly. 'Just that Saladin would much appreciate a favour to a Knight Templar whom he admired. And also that Saladin would be very upset if this little favour wasn't done.'

Arn had a sneaking feeling that maybe Fahkr had expressed himself a little less amiably at the time.

That evening before the prayer time Saladin arrived back in Damascus at the head of one of his armies. The people came out to celebrate his arrival, lining the streets all the way to the great mosque. Now more than ever he deserved his honorary title al-Malik al-Nasir – the Victorious King. Ten thousand men and women prayed with him when the sun set, the crowds filling not only the huge mosque but also most of its courtyard.

After praying he rode slowly and quite alone through the throng towards his palace. He had told all his amirs, and the hordes of men who sought his decision on a thousand matters, that he wanted to spend the evening with friends and family, especially his brother and his son. He had been in the field for two months without a moment to himself.

As he walked from friend to relative, hugging everyone and beaming with joy, it really seemed as if he intended to abandon all affairs of state for the evening. Then he suddenly stood face to face with Arn de Gothia. At first he looked astonished and rather disturbed.

'The defeated honour you, Victorious King,' Arn greeted him seriously, and the happy talk in the room died down.

Saladin hesitated for a moment, then stepped forward, put his arms around Arn and kissed him on both cheeks. Murmured exchanges started up among the guests at this.

'Greetings, Knight Templar – you, who perhaps more than any other man, granted me my victories,' Saladin said, and offered Arn his arm to show that he wanted to have him at his side during the meal.

At the table al-Afdal, Saladin's son, sat next to them. He was a slightly built young man with an intense look in his eyes and a straggling beard. It didn't take him long to bend towards Arn with a question.

'At the Springs of Cresson last year, when our seven thousand men did battle with your small force, one of my amirs told me that Al Ghouti rode with the Templar banner. Is that true?'

Arn remembered Gérard de Ridefort's mad attack, forced on his one hundred and forty knights. Then, with a shudder, he recalled the shameful flight he'd had to join.

'Yes, I was there and yes, I held the Templar banner.'

'I see. I ordered all my amirs that you must be kept alive. What I couldn't understand, then or later, is this: what makes Christian knights ride into death like that, in full knowledge that it's meaningless?'

The room fell silent. Arn blushed. At first he couldn't think of an answer.

'I agree,' he said slowly. 'It *was* meaningless, just as mad as it must have looked to you and your men. On such occasions logic and faith part company, but I don't think it happens only in Christian armies. Muslims can be recklessly brave too, but maybe not as crazily.'

'Gérard de Ridefort forced the attack on his knights,' he went on after a pause, with such uncontrollable distaste that no one failed to hear it. 'Then he decided he'd better get away fast, once he realised that everyone under his command was doomed. As for me – well, I had the banner and my duty was clear. I had to follow the Grand Master,'

He felt ashamed and the silence around him was uncomfortable. Saladin broke it.

'God steered everything for the best,' he said soothingly. 'The best both for Arn and for me was that he was taken prisoner at Hattin's Horns, not earlier.'

Arn couldn't work out what Saladin meant by this comment, but he didn't feel like continuing the conversation by asking questions.

Later Saladin indicated that he wanted to be left alone with his brother and Arn. When everyone had left, they went to another room and settled down on soft cushions. Beakers filled with ice-cold water were served and Arn wondered inwardly at this wonderful chill. How was it achieved? Still, he couldn't really ask about trivia like that when the conversation ahead was doubtlessly going be about very serious things.

'Once a man called Ibrahim ibn Anaza came to see me,' Saladin said thoughtfully. 'He brought me a wonderful gift. It was the sword we call the Sword of Islam and it had been lost for a long time. Do you understand what your gift meant, Arn?'

'I know Ibrahim well and regard him as a friend,' Arn replied carefully. 'He took it into his head that I deserved this sword, but I was convinced that I was unworthy and that's why I sent it to you, Yussuf. Why I cannot quite say; the moment was difficult and I was grief-stricken, but something told me what I had to do. I'm very glad that old Ibrahim did as I asked him.'

'But you do not understand what you did?'

Saladin's voice was quiet but the silence after his question was tense.

'I felt I did the right thing. The sword was sacred to Muslims but not to me. That's what I thought at the time. God must have led me. I cannot think of any other explanation.'

'I'm absolutely certain that you were led by God,' Saladin said, and smiled. 'It was as if I'd sent you the True Cross – by the way it's safe and actually kept here, in this house. You see, it was written that whoever received the Sword of Islam would unite all believers and defeat the unbelievers.'

'If that is so, you must not thank me,' Arn said, completely shaken. 'Thank God, who made me his instrument.'

'I've thanked God, believe you me. But I do owe you a sword, my friend. Isn't it strange how I always seem to end up indebted to you?'

'I've got a sword now, Yussuf. You owe me nothing.'

'Come on. If I had sent you the True Cross, I'm sure you wouldn't have thought your debt settled by handing me a piece of wood, however prettily carved. But we'll talk about this later. Now I want to ask you a favour,'

'If my conscience allows I'll do anything for you. You know that, Yussuf. And after all, I'm your prisoner and one for whom you'll never get a ransom.'

'We'll go to Ashkelon together and take it, then Gaza and then Jerusalem. I want you to be my advisor throughout. Then I'll give you your freedom and you will not leave unrewarded. This is what I ask of you.'

'And what you ask me is truly dreadful . . . Yussuf, you ask me to be a traitor,' Arn wailed and everyone could see his agony.

'It's not what you think,' Saladin said calmly. 'I don't need your help to kill Christians, I have innumerable helping hands to do just that. But I have always remembered something from our first talk that night, the first time I got into debt to you. You quoted one of your rules: "When you draw your sword think not of whom you will kill. Think of whom you will protect." Do you understand me now?'

'It's a good rule, but I'm only partly relived and no, I still don't understand what you want from me.'

'I have Jerusalem here in my hand,' Saladin said, holding his fist in front of Arn's face. 'That city will fall when I want it to fall. The time I've decided on is when we've taken Ashkelon and Gaza. But winning victories is one thing and winning gloriously is another. I need to know what are good decisions and which are evil, and so I must listen to someone other than my amirs. They're all convinced there's only one decision and that's to do what the Christians did to us.'

'Kill anybody human, kill all the animals as well and leave the city to the flies,' Arn said sadly.

'Consider the reverse situation,' Fahkr said, joining their talk without his brother even frowning at him. 'What if we had taken Jerusalem from you, just one and a half man's age ago, and treated the city the way you did then? You would remember that, sitting in your tent outside its walls, and you'd be howling for revenge.'

'We would be just such fools – men like your two most elevated prisoners, de Ridefort and de Lusignan, would for once have been in total agreement. They'd have stamped on all opposition to subjecting the enemy to even worse slaughter.'

'Most men would think like that, but not my brother Yussuf. What can you say to convince us that he's right in condemning revenge?'

Arn looked at him almost hopelessly.

'Wanting revenge can amount to a passion in everyone – Christians, Muslims and Jews too, I'm sure. Behaving with dignity is not an argument that goes down well with the vengeful. True, I've heard both Yussuf and Raymond of Tripoli argue that all pilgrims must have access to whatever they believe is holy in Jerusalem, or the war will never end. But those who thirst for revenge want to watch the blood running in the gutters there and then.'

'All these are points we've discussed,' Saladin said. 'Any other thoughts?'

'One, maybe. All cities can be taken, including Jerusalem, and you'll do that. Keeping them is another problem, so maybe your first question should be directed to that. What do we do with our victory? Can we hold on to the Holy City?'

'No one will doubt that at present we'll easily hold it. The Christians are practically wiped out. Anything else?'

'Yes. Add "For how long?" Longer than a year? Ask how you'll feel when Frankish knights begin pouring in again. The more you behave like murderers, the more Christians will come back to take their revenge. The mathematics are simple. Killing every Christian you find and sacking their part of the city equals about one hundred thousand knights. Letting everybody who wishes to leave go in peace and protecting the Holy Sepulchre after taking back all your own places of worship equals maybe ten thousand knights. What would you prefer?'

The three of them contemplated the future in silence. Finally Saladin rose, turned to Arn and, pulling him up from his seat, hugged him. Then the Sultan wept, as he was known to whenever something moving, cruel or beautiful happened. His tears were famous and either scorned or admired by the faithful.

'You've saved me with your reason, you'll have spared many lives in Jerusalem next month and maybe given us the city itself to hold for all time,' the great commander sobbed.

His brother and son might have been moved to tears, too, but seemed able to control themselves.

A month later Arn had joined Saladin's army, now encamped outside the walls of Ashkelon. His old clothes and armour had been mended and spruced up. He looked like a Templar knight again but was not alone in this, because the Grand Master and King Guy were also following the army as human luggage. Saladin had decided that they had better not be entrusted with animals they could ride and should be stuck on top of camels. There they sat, clinging to their saddles and providing lasting amusement for the Saracen soldiery by their attempts to cope with the agony and look dignified at the same time. This was far from easy, since they were part of the camel train padding along behind the army.

Saladin had ordered ships from Alexandria to meet the army at Ashkelon and they were already there, at anchor just outside the harbour. The blockade looked more threatening than it was, because these were merchant ships with empty holds.

Once they had made camp, Saladin told King Guy to walk up to the barred city gates and shout that the inhabitants must surrender in order that their King should be set free. What did the fate of one city matter against the life of the King himself?

The inhabitants, some of whom turned up on the walls, had other ideas and began shouting insults at him as coarse any king might ever have heard from his subjects. The fate of their city mattered a great deal, it seemed. Soon more people joined in, bombarding their King with rotten fruit and other foul objects. Saladin seemed to enjoy the spectacle without bothering too much about the rejection of his attempt at negotiations. When he had had enough, part of his army was left to go about taking Ashkelon by force, while the rest marched on towards Gaza.

Gaza's walls were manned by many sergeants but there were only a few knights visible in their white mantles. The defenders seemed calm as they watched the rather small army arriving, realising that there was no siege equipment being pulled up. They remained just as unmoved when their Grand Master was led up to the city gates to plead with them. The message was that unless they gave in he would be executed in front of the gates.

The rules were actually quite clear about these situations and no one had any doubt about the correct way to behave. The life of a Knight Templar could not be traded, be it for money or prisoners or threats against others. The duty of the Grand Master was to die as it behoved a member of the Order, without wailing or showing fear. Few of the Gaza men felt any particular regret at the thought of seeing Gérard de Ridefort's head rolling in the sand. All you could hope for was that the next one would be less of a dangerous idiot.

Then something quite different happened, to their astonishment and indescribable shame. The Grand Master stepped forward and ordered his men to leave the city immediately. Each man was allowed to take his own weapons and a horse, but apart from that everything had to be left behind, including the well-filled treasury chests.

The rule left no room for anything except obedience to the Grand Master.

An hour later the Templar men of Gaza left their city. Arn watched, tears of shame in his eyes at Gérard de Ridefort's betrayal. Saladin was observing the retreating enemy too and gave de Ridefort a Frankish horse to ride, told him he was free, and bid him a cheerful, ironic farewell. The Grand Master did not answer, but turned his horse and caught up to his men, who were riding with their heads bent in grief. Without speaking to anyone, he took up position at the head of the line.

Saladin was pleased at his double victory. First, by deploying this spineless man he had gained Gaza, including its wealth, without firing a single arrow. Second, he had restored Gérard de Ridefort to the command of the Knights Templar. This alone should deliver more useful gains in the future.

Saladin's men stormed into the city but it did not take long for some of them to come back excitedly with the information that they'd found two horses that were said to be of the Anaza breed. Such horses were not to be found in the stables of Saladin or even the Caliph in Baghdad.

Saladin said that such a gift would please him more than all the gold in the city but he found the information incredible and asked the people around him. Could these horses really be Anazas? What were they doing in the Templar fortress? Arn told him that they were indeed of the Anaza breed and that they were once given to him by Ibrahim ibn Anaza, at the same time as he was given the sacred sword.

Saladin immediately and without hesitation offered the horses to his friend.

Ashkelon fell three days later. Saladin spared the inhabitants even though they had not given in and had them taken away by the Alexandrian fleet in the harbour. The trading contacts of Alexandria were such that sooner or later all these foreigners would surely be able to get back home.

Now only Tyrus and Jerusalem remained.

On the Friday, the twenty-seventh of the month of Rajab, the Prophet, may peace be with him, rose to heaven from the Rock of Abraham after his miraculous journey from Mecca the night before. On the same day, Saladin marched into Jerusalem at the head of his army. According to the Christian calendar this was Friday, the eleventh of October in Anno Domini 1187.

It had been impossible to defend the city. Other than the severely diminished ranks of spiritual orders, Balian d'Ibelin was the only knight inside its walls of any standing. Having dubbed every possible man over sixteen years of age, he tried to mount a defence. It was meaningless and only prolonged the agony. During the week when Saladin's army was marching on the city, ten thousand refugees had streamed out through the gates, making it impossible to sustain a siege for any length of time.

The city was not looted and no one was killed by the Saracen soldiers.

Ten thousand inhabitants paid for their freedom – ten dinars for each man, five for a woman and one dinar for a child – and were allowed to keep their possessions.

Twenty thousand inhabitants could not pay and remained in the city. No one was prepared to lend them the money that would have saved them from slavery, not even their Christian protectors and spiritual leaders. Heraclius, Patriarch of Jerusalem, and the Knights Spiritual all saved their wealth by sending heavily laden carts out of the city. Many of Saladin's amirs were in tears of fury and desperation as they watched Heraclius pay his ten dinars with a jolly smile, only to leave at the head of a gold-laden transport that would have rescued most of the twenty thousand Christian citizens.

Saladin's officers found their commander's generosity as childish as the Patriarch's greed was outrageous.

Once all the Christians who could pay had left, most of them to take refuge in Tyrus, Saladin freed the remaining citizens, showing them the mercy that neither their church leaders nor their knights could find in their hearts.

With the Christians out of the way, Muslims and Jews returned to the city. The sacred buildings that had been known for some time as Templum Domini and Templum Salomonis were purified with rosewater for several days and the crosses on their domes were torn down and dragged in triumph through the city's cleansed streets. After eighty-eight years, the crescent replaced the cross on Al Aqsa and the Dome of the Rock.

The Church of the Holy Sepulchre was kept closed and under constant guard while they discussed what to do with it. Saladin's amirs, to a man, thought it should be razed to the ground, but the great leader pointed out that the sacred part of the church was the grave in the crypt and it was pointless tearing down the building above. The heated arguments lasted for three days but, in the end, Saladin got his way – again. Still guarded against desecration by heavily armed Mamelukes, the Church of the Holy Sepulchre was handed over to Syrian and Byzantine priests.

It took a week to complete the purification of Al Aqsa, the most distant of the sacred places in Jerusalem and the third holiest place in all Islam. Then Saladin prayed there, in tears as usual. This time nobody wondered at this, because he had fulfilled his promise to God and liberated the sacred city of Al Quds.

In commercial terms, Saladin's capture of Jerusalem was the most unprofitable of all the long Palestine wars. He paid for this by being laughed and sneered at by his contemporaries, but he entered history forever as a unique leader, his name immortal for all time, and the only Saracen whom the Franks regarded with real respect.

Saladin had given Arn leave during the siege of Jerusalem, even though the conquest was as gently handled as the knight had pleaded for. Arn wanted to go home, but Saladin had insisted that he remain a little longer, which left him in a strange position. At the same time as he had Saladin's assurance that he was free to go when he pleased, the pressure applied to make him stay was relentless.

Predictably, a new crusade was on its way. The German Emperor, Frederick Barbarossa, was marching through Asia Minor with a huge army; King Philip Augustus of France and King Richard – known as the Lionheart – of England were bringing their armies by ship.

Saladin's idea was that the next war would be fought at the

negotiating table rather than on the battlefield, mainly because his experience told him that newly arrived Franks found war in Palestine hard and would be anxious to keep talking. Arn agreed and found the proposition that he was an ideal negotiator impossible to contradict. After all, he spoke God's language, was fluent in Frankish, and was a figure of trust both as a friend of Saladin and as a Knight Templar with twenty years experience in the Holy Land.

Arn was longing for his homeland so much that his most recent wounds, though perfectly healed, started aching. He also found it painful to participate in a war that did not involve him as a fighting man. At the same time, he had to admit to his immense debt of gratitude to Saladin for saving his life many times. Without Saladin's mercy he would never have gone home at all.

God stayed generous to the Muslims in more than one way. Emperor Barbarossa drowned in a river before even reaching the Holy Land. His body was brought along in a barrel of vinegar but rotted hopelessly nonetheless and had to be buried in Antioch. The German crusade faded away without him.

Arn's prediction came true. Ten thousand Franks arrived after the gentle occupation of Jerusalem, not one hundred thousand.

Saladin had let King Guy go without even demanding a ransom. He reckoned that his purpose would be better served by leaving Guy de Lusignan free to infiltrate the new Frankish crusade than by keeping him locked up. He was proved right, because King Guy's return among his own people immediately led to endless quarrels about the succession and much internecine treachery.

But Saladin did make one mistake that he would come to regret for a long time. When King Guy set out with an army raised in Tyrus to recapture Acre, the most important Christian city after Jerusalem, the Saracen commander was unable to take the enterprise seriously. When the siege of Acre started, he sent a force that ended up trapping the Christians between the Muslim defenders of the city and the advancing troops. Saladin calculated that time, camp disease and lack of food would be enough to win the war against a commander as useless as Guy. He could have sacrificed enough men to hit King Guy hard but thought the price too high to pay.

The delay meant that both shiploads of new crusaders landed, first the Franks under King Philip Augustus and then the English under Richard Lionheart. They promptly went to the aid of the Christian army at Acre and Saladin had to face the kind of warfare he had tried to avoid. Arn was called in, because now there were many issues on the negotiating table.

When Saladin had reassembled a large enough army of the men he had sent home in return for their service in long, victorious wars, he attacked with the arrogance of someone certain of his invincibility. He was mistaken on several counts. True, the new arrivals were just as unused to the burning summer heat as Saladin had expected, but waves of fast cavalry were not new to them, in particular not to the English, who were remarkably competent.

When the first wave of Saracen cavalry came galloping against the besieging units across the flat land outside Acre, the sky above them darkened mysteriously. Then thousands of arrows fell like a hailstorm, practically eliminating everybody within range. Only the first row of riders, not realising that the lines behind them were emptying, rode on and were picked off by the crossbows. Everything was over in less time than it takes for a horse to gallop the length of four arrow shots. A sea of dead and dying covered the Acre plains. Horses lay kicking in pain or running up and down in panic and knocking over wounded, confused and terrified men.

Then Richard Lionheart attacked with his knights. It was his fastest victory ever.

Arn watched what longbows and crossbows could do with a mixture of horror and the detached interest of a professional officer. The memory of this battle would never fade from his mind.

Now it was truly time for negotiations. In the first instance, they needed a cease-fire to bring back the wounded and bury the dead. This would serve both sides well, especially in the summer heat. Arn was asked to manage this agreement on his own, because he was dressed as a Knight Templar and could ride in safety all the way to the English lines. He was surrounded by jubilant English soldiers, whose language he found incomprehensible, and demanded to be taken to King Richard at once. To Arn's relief the King turned out to be a Frank from Normandy, judging by his accent.

King Richard Lionheart was a tall man with broad shoulders and reddish blonde hair. Unlike Guy, he looked like a King, and the size of the battleaxe dangling from his saddle showed that he must be exceptionally strong.

Their first talk was brief. All they needed to agree on was the straightforward matter of tidying up on the battlefield. Arn was asked to let Saladin know that the King would like to meet him in person and Arn promised to deliver his message.

The next day he returned with Saladin's answer, which was that he would not contemplate any royal meetings before the peace treaty was agreed, but that his son al-Afdal would be pleased to talk to the

King. Richard Lionheart became furious with Saladin and his negotiator, whom he called a traitor and lover of Saracens.

Arn replied that he was Saladin's prisoner and that he had given his word to be as much Saladin's tongue at King Richard's table, as Richard's tongue in the councils of the Sultan. The King's rage subsided a little, but he let it be known that he didn't think much of keeping your word of honour to an infidel.

Arn returned with this message and Saladin laughed for the first time in many weeks, saying that a word of honour presumed there was honour to swear by. As simple as that and as hard. When he had let King Guy go free, he had asked him to promise to leave the Holy Land and never take arms against the true believers again. The King had sworn on his Bible and his God and all his Saints, naturally. And naturally, as Saladin had expected and indeed hoped, de Lusignan broke his solemn oath and helpfully started splitting the Frankish side into factions.

The fact that the English could cut Acre off from the sea meant that supplying the city became problematic and Saladin's attempts to deal with the besieging army ran into trouble. The starvation which he had hoped would decimate his enemy affected them less than it did the defenders of the city. Any new attacks across the open plain against the English longbows were unthinkable. Saladin lost his race against time. Despairing, he had to stand by as the city opened its gates to King Richard and his men.

Riding back at Saladin's side was dismal, because his people in Acre had agreed to harsh conditions. King Richard intended to keep the city and all that was in it, but in addition demanded one hundred thousand gold besants, one thousand Christian prisoners freed and another one hundred named knights in captivity. And he wanted the True Cross.

Saladin wept, of course, when he heard these conditions. It was a high price for the two thousand seven hundred souls now at King Richard's mercy, but they had agreed to save their lives. Saladin's honour demanded that he protect his own.

Arn and al-Afdal returned to the city Arn called Saint-Jean d'Acre and al-Afdal called Akko. Once, the Romans knew it as Akkon. The negotiations ahead were likely to be lengthy and complicated, because many practical issues had to be resolved. They ranged from times and places to how payments could be divided and at what point the imprisoned Muslim population would be allowed to leave.

It was always time-consuming to sort out questions of this kind, and King Richard delayed further by celebrating his victory with games in front of the walls of the occupied city. When he finally agreed to meet Saladin's two negotiators, he was contemptuous and began by telling them that it was poor manners to interrupt a tournament. Then he turned to al-Afdal and casually asked if he dared meet one of the English knights in combat, lance against lance – or was he too much of a coward? Arn translated, and advised al-Afdal to reply that his preference would be to ride with his bow against two of the knights at the same time. The King ignored this, pretending not to have understood Arn's translation.

'What about you, Templar prisoner? Are you a coward too?' King Richard asked sneeringly.

'No, Sire. I've served here as a Knight Templar for twenty years.'

'So if I offer your new master a better deal, would you ride against one of my best knights? Say, the first fifty thousand besants and these prisoners we discussed, against my promise to let his Saracens go before I get the rest of the gold and the True Cross?'

'Yes, Sire, I would. Though I fear I might hurt your man badly.'

'You'll regret saying that, Knight Turncoat. You'll meet Sir Wilfred.'

'I need a lance, a shield and a helmet, Sire.'

'I'll see to that. You can probably borrow from your Templar friends – or former friends, I suppose – in the city.'

Arn turned to al-Afdal, explaining wearily that the childish English King had invented some kind of game with lances and insisted on Arn joining in. The young man drew himself up and pointed out that it was against the rules to use weapons against negotiators, or for negotiators to use weapons against others. Arn sighed, replying that rules didn't interest the King much, unless of course they benefited himself.

Friendly Brothers in Acre lent Arn the arms he needed and before long he was trotting out on the field in front of the city walls to greet his opponent, carrying his helmet in the same hand as his Templar shield. He felt quite taken aback by how young this Wilfred looked. He could not be much over twenty years old, his face still innocent and unscarred.

They circled the arena twice at a slow trot in opposite directions before stopping and meeting face to face. Arn was watchful, because he didn't know the tournament rules. When the young man spoke in his odd tongue, Arn asked him to use the language of his king.

'I'm Sir Wilfred, a knight who has won my spurs on the battlefield. I greet you, an honourable opponent,' he said bravely but in clumsy Frankish.

'I'm Arn de Gothia, and I have worn my spurs on the battlefield for twenty years. I greet you, young man. Now what do we do?'

'Now? We ride against each other until one man lies on the ground defenceless or dead. Or until he gives up. May the best man win!'

'Come on, I don't want to hurt you. Is it enough if I just push you out of the saddle a couple of times?'

'You'll not rattle me! Offensive talk will just cause you greater suffering, Sir Arn,' Wilfred said with what looked like a carefully practised cruel smile.

'Just one thing young man – you're a novice riding against an experienced Knight Templar for the first time. We never lose these games.'

That ended their exchange abruptly. Sir Wilfred swung his horse round and galloped back across the field. At the far end he turned again, reined in his horse and put on his helmet. It was the new kind that covered the whole face and made looking sideways difficult. Arn rode off rather more deliberately to get into position.

Then they sat there. Arn noticed that Sir Wilfred kept glancing at King Richard's pavilion, so Arn followed his example. Once the audience had become quiet, the King rose and stepped forward, holding a big red shawl in one hand. Suddenly he let it fall and the young knight immediately set off to attack.

Arn was riding Ibn Anaza, which gave him such an extraordinary advantage over his young adversary on his sluggish Frankish horse that it was probably beyond Wilfred's grasp. This alone tipped the scales in Arn's favour. His only problem was how not to harm his opponent more than by inflicting a few bad bruises.

Watching young Wilfred approach, Arn realised that the game entailed hitting the other man's head or shield hard enough knock him out of the saddle. It seemed a dangerous sport, with death as a possible outcome. He decided what to do and nudged Ibn Anaza into full speed ahead only to turn him very sharply left a moment before they would have crashed into the other rider. Now on the wrong side of his opponent, it was easy to sweep him out of the saddle by the broad side of his lance.

Then Arn turned back and trotted up to the fallen knight, who lay swearing and kicking in the sand.

'I hope I didn't hurt you too much,' Arn said kindly. 'Now, are we done?'

'I shall not give in,' the youngster said and grabbed the reins of his horse to pull himself up. 'I've got a right to three attacks!'

Arn sighed and rode back, thinking that he might as well not try the same simple trick again. Instead, he moved the lance to his left hand, pushing the shield high on his upper arm so that the manoeuvre should not show before they got close. Then it would be too late.

The King dropped the red shawl again and the young knight spurred his horse into its highest speed. Clearly there was nothing wrong with his courage.

This time Arn did not change sides. Instead, he angled his shield up against the approaching lance and held on firmly to the thick end of his own lance with his right hand. The effect on the young Wilfred was a tremendous blow across the chest, as if from an oar, and he was knocked even further into the air.

He still refused to give in. For the third encounter, Arn decided to leave his shield and grabbed the thin end of the lance in his hand so he could use it as a club. He rode ahead with this unusual club lowered until the last moment when he raised it high with both hands, lifting his opponent's lance. He followed this by ramming the blunt end of the lance straight into the other's helmeted face. Sir Wilfred flew off his horse for the third time. The helmet saved his life but not his self-esteem.

When Arn had examined his exhausted opponent for any serious injuries, he took off his own round, open helmet and rode forward to bow to the King.

'Sire, young Wilfred is worthy of great respect for his courage. Not all young men would ride so bravely against a Knight Templar.'

'You know some very amusing tricks, but I'm not sure they're according to our rules,' the King said irritably.

'My rules come from the battlefield and not the playground, Sire. Besides, as I told you, I have no wish to injure one of your knights. His skill and his courage will serve you well.'

There were two main consequences to what Arn thought of as a childish waste of time. The first, most immediately important, was that Saladin's conditions were made less harsh. The second was that the young Sir Wilfred, later known as Ivanhoe, would go to war many more times and deal with all his opponents easily, in the arena or on the battlefield – all, except Knights Templar. For the rest of his life the white-mantled knights would figure in his nightmares.

After his first tournament, Arn was invited to share a meal with the Master of Acre. They had known each other since many years back, when they met at the La Fève fortress. His stories about King Richard were interesting. Generally, it seemed that the tempestuous

King managed to make enemies of all his allies. The French King had been thrown out of the Templar quarters, where he had moved in after deciding that they were the second best rooms in the city. King Richard had, of course, got the best by taking over the royal palace. This incident generated such a row that Philip Augustus decided to go home and take all his men with him. Then there was the Austrian Count, to whose fury King Richard had insulted the Austrian banner. It had hung on the city wall with the French and English banners until Richard saw it, tore it to pieces and threw it in the moat. Austrian and English soldiers got into endless fights afterwards, and next the Austrian contingent was leaving too. All nonsense, but it had led to half the Christian force melting away. King Richard seemed convinced that his men and the Knights Templar were all that he needed to recapture Jerusalem.

This was as frivolous as it was dangerous, they both agreed. Marching the longbow men to Jerusalem under constant cavalry harassment and under a relentless sun would cause problems great enough to daunt anyone.

But the worst omen was not that Richard was moody and belligerent. The worst was that he could not be relied on to keep his word.

Saladin honoured their agreement. After ten days he was able to deliver the fifty thousand besants and the thousand freed Christian prisoners. It took a little longer to find the hundred named knights, who were scattered in the dungeons of many Syrian and Egyptian fortresses.

Richard immediately declared that this delay had broken the agreement.

His next action was to surround a hill just outside Acre, called Ayyadieh, with his crossbow and longbow men. Then the two thousand seven hundred Muslim inhabitants of Acre were led out. The men were in chains and the women and children herded along next to their husbands and fathers.

Watching Muslims could not believe the sight of the massacre that followed. Their tears blinded them as they saw the prisoners, due to be freed on that day, killed with arrows or clubbed to death with axes.

The Saracen riders were driven out of their minds with grief and attacked wildly. They were met with a rain of arrows that killed all of them. The slaughter went on for many hours, until the last of the small children had been found and clubbed to death. English looters rounded off the day on Ayyadieh by slitting open the stomachs of the dead in the hope of finding swallowed gold coins. At that stage, Saladin had long since left the nearby hill from which he had watched the beginning of the massacre.

He went away and sat by himself outside his tent. His own men left him alone, but Arn slowly walked over to join him.

'This is a difficult moment, Yussuf,' he said quietly. 'But this is the moment I choose to ask you to set me free.'

'Why do you want to leave me now, on this day of sorrows that will never be forgotten or forgiven?'

'Because today you've won a victory over Richard Lionheart, though the price is high.'

'Victory! A victory, when I've paid fifty thousand gold besants to buy the freedom of these corpses. In truth, a strange victory.'

'That's a most terrible loss. But you will not lose Jerusalem to this crazed murderer. He will be remembered for the massacre on Ayyadieh and as the butcher who lost the True Cross out of greed. Our children and our children's children will know him as a traitor. His cause is infinitely more damaged than yours. His allies have already left him in a flurry of childish quarrels, so your enemies are far fewer than ten thousand now. Besides, he too might have to leave soon, because I hear his brother is after his lands. This was what I meant, Yussuf.'

'Still, why leave me, when grief still overshadows hopes of revenge?'

'I cannot negotiate for you now. Negotiation with King Butcher is useless. I want to go home to my own people and my own lands.'

'What will you do there, back in your homeland?'

'No more war for me, that's all I know. I swore an oath of true love once and hope to find my beloved. And I shall try to think. I want to find a meaning in all that I've done and seen. Find out God's will, when after twenty years of fighting my side justly lost the war.'

'Justly. You're thinking of people like Agnes de Courtenay, Guy de Lusignan – people like that?' Saladin whispered and now a hint irony had crept into his grief.

'Yes, people like that. I fought on their behalf and I need to understand why.'

'I can tell you, and I will in moment,' Saladin said. 'First and foremost, you're now a free man. You only asked for fifty thousand gold besants when my brother was your prisoner, though you could have pushed the price to double that and more. Now, I think it's God's will that this is exactly the amount I've got left after paying the

Richard Butcher. Take the gold. If you like, think of it as a gift in return for the sword you gave me. By the way, a sword is waiting for you in Damascus, which I hope will suit you. Leave me to mourn now. Ride in peace with God, Al Ghouti, my friend. I'll never forget you.'

'Wait, you know the meaning, you said. God's meaning,' Arn insisted. He stayed where he was, oblivious of the fact that Saladin had just promised him a fortune.

'God's meaning?' Saladin said. 'As a Muslim I can tell you that God wanted you, a Knight Templar, to give me back the Sword of Islam and bring me victory. As a Christian, you can tell yourself something different. When you gave me the reason why we shouldn't do to the population of Jerusalem what Richard just did to the people of Acre, I took your advice to heart and followed it. Your word saved fifty thousand Christian lives. This was God's task for you in Palestine. He who sees all and He who hears all brought us together.'

Arn rose and stood hesitant and silent for a moment. Saladin rose too.

They fell in each other's arms and embraced for a last time. Then Arn turned and walked away,

His long journey home had begun, home to a land where he promised himself he would never again wield a weapon.